Also by John Drake

The Fletcher Series
Fletcher's Fortune (Book 1)
Fletcher's Glorious 1st of June (Book 2)
Fletcher and the Mutineers (Book 3)
Fletcher and the Great Raid (Book 4)

Fletcher
and the Blue Star

JOHN DRAKE

LUME BOOKS

First published in 2021 by Lume Books
30 Great Guildford Street,
Borough, SE1 0HS

Copyright © John Drake 2021

The right of John Drake to be identified as the author of this work has been asserted by them in accordance with the Copyright, Design and Patents Act, 1988.

All rights reserved. No part of this publication may be reproduced, stored in a retrieval system, or transmitted in photocopying, recording or otherwise, without the prior permission of the copyright owner.

ISBN 978-1-83901-269-3

Typeset using Atomik ePublisher from Easypress Technologies

www.lumebooks.co.uk

In fond memory of
David Burkhill Howarth

----------- DBH -----------

1946 – 2009

PATRIFAMILIAS AMATISSIMO
MAGISTRO DOCTISSIMO
INGENIOSISSIMO TECHNITAE
OPTIMO AMICO

Introduction

This sixth 'Fletcher', covering the period January 1800 to May 1803, describes the further adventures of Admiral Sir Jacob who was unique among seafaring heroes in declaring that he never wanted to go to sea, but wanted a career in trade. This, despite the fact that he was a huge man of tremendous physical strength, and a magnificent seaman and gunner, who was instantly recognisable to his contemporaries by a thin white streak in his black hair.

Since this book is one of a series, please note its style. Thus, I am merely the editor of the twenty-five volumes of Fletcher's memoirs, as dictated to his clerk the Rev. Dr Samuel Pettit in the 1870s. But I have extemporised chapters between Fletcher's narrative, drawing upon my archive of documents concerning events touching upon his life, prominently including 'the Saga of Inyathi' an epic Zulu poem intended for choral singing in rhyming couplets.

I stress that these inserted chapters are guesswork but they are as accurate as I can make them. In addition, I have inserted transcripts of letters where these speak for themselves, and also one newspaper cutting.

Returning to Pettit, he always claimed to be embarrassed by Fletcher's lurid dictation and to be afraid of him since, although Fletcher lived a long life (1775 to 1875), he retained great strength to his dying day. Note Pettit's words in a letter of August 1870 to his elder brother the Very Rev. Archdeacon Ignatius Pettit.

> *"Yesterday morning there arrived at our door three men whose business is the collection of debt: big, rough fellows all three. They were totally in error having mistaken our house for another, thus – on hearing them force entry and demand payment – the Admiral arose, and old as he is, he knocked down the three of them, then seized them up, threw them from the house, and pursued them*

down the drive with kicks and curses, for such a primal force is he when angered.

"Furthermore, even when not in anger and dictating to myself, he sits in his chair like the demon Grendel: enormous in bulk, prodigious in strength, mighty in voice and fearful in address. Many times has he threatened to 'gut and fillet' me – his favourite threat – should I hesitate in the work of transcription."

But Pettit also says, in the same letter:

"Yet Fletcher is adored by the ladies. Young or old, housemaid or duchess, all are charmed by him, and equally he is worshipped by the little children whom he permits to clamber upon him like some monstrous gorilla, laughing all the while at their pranks and at their tugging of his hair."

However, I now believe that Pettit's embarrassment was pretended, because the journals are dog-eared from much reading, and I suspect that it was Pettit who turned the pages. I imagine the Reverend Doctor – at the dead of night with a candle – gaping at Fletcher's adventures, especially the erotica. Also, I note Pettit's lyrical descriptions of Fletcher: *"enormous in bulk, prodigious in strength, mighty in voice etc."* These words suggest admiration not contempt, and readers must judge for themselves.

Meanwhile, it is certain that after the Admiral's death, Pettit added footnotes to the journals, often expressing indignation, and these I represent:

[in this different font, inside square brackets, signed by his initials: S.P.] I must also comment on the remarkable similarity of Fletcher's adventures among the Zulus, to those described in Sir H. Rider Haggard's novel *King Solomon's Mines* first published in 1885. Since Fletcher's memoirs were then unpublished, I am unable to explain this truly amazing coincidence.

Finally, I thank the many scholars whose translations from Arabic, French, Latin and Zulu have enabled me to write my inserted chapters.

John Drake, Cheshire, England, July 6th 2021.

Prologue

Lixus,
Atlantic coast of Roman North Africa.
The Ides of June in the 2nd year of the Civil War.
(June 15th 42 BC)

"The colossal treasure of the Carthaginians was held by the 41st Legion, still loyal to the foully-murdered Caesar the Great."

(From Vol II, Chapter VI of 'Civilis belli Mauritanium')

The Great Hall of the Basilica – largest chamber in the city of Lixus – was lavish in decoration, with statues, lamps, wall paintings, and sandal wood furniture. There was also an enormous floor mosaic of chariot racing, and a magnificent shrine to the Capitoline Trinity at the innermost end where magistrates sat.

Normally the Basilica was busy with citizens, but not today. Today the Basilica and the city were empty. The Basilica was empty because the people – all of them – had taken to the boats and gone north to the Mediterranean in ocean-going ships.

The Basilica was empty except for the officers of the 41st legion, who stood in groups with their conversations echoing in the emptiness. They shone in polished armour; they wore plumed helmets; they were draped in ceremonial red cloaks; and then, at a word of command, their right arms shot out in salute and their nailed boots crashed down on the mosaic floor sending further echoes bouncing off the walls.

"Hail Quintus Aniensis Alba!" they cried, as the commander of the legion marched into the Basilica with his retinue. "Hail to *The Greek*!"

they cried. This nickname had once been a slur on Alba's Greek freedman father. But that was before Alba had won battles and proved himself a lifetime career soldier. Alba came in at the march, followed by the legion's chief centurions, a train of clerks and a dozen men in civilian robes.

He stamped to a halt, looked round, and shouted at the clerks. "Put 'em there!" he said, and the clerks swiftly set up a row of easels bearing coloured charts, and stood to attention beside them. "Right!" said Alba. "Gather round and pay attention!"

They gathered round: six Tribunes, the Camp Prefect, the Engineer-in-Chief, the Artillery Commander, the Master Builder, the Chief Medic, the Chief Veterinarian, and all junior centurions not on vital duties. There were over seventy of them: men of every age and shape from pink-faced Tribune to the First Javelin himself, the senior centurion with forty years' service who was old and scarred and stooped.

"So," said Alba, "can everyone see?"

"Yes, noble sir," they said.

"Chart one!" said Alba, taking the pointer handed to him by a clerk. "See here! Lixus is on a hill on the right bank of the Loukkos river."

"Yes, noble sir," they said.

"The city is eighty feet up on dry ground, with marshes all round, and just two roads." Alba tapped the chart. "The road to the port *here*, and another road *here*." He tapped again. "This runs north to the coast road, up to the city of Tingi at the mouth of the Med. Right?"

"Yes, noble sir."

"Next chart!" Alba pointed with his stick. "This is the coast road and they're coming down it. Three, full-strength legions plus cavalry and auxiliaries, and every man" – he put a sneer into the word – "a liberator! That's what they call themselves: the men who stabbed Caesar from behind!" There was a growl of anger and another shuffling of feet. "Our scouts are watching them," said Alba, "and they've got forty-five miles to cover, but it'll take four days because it's an old road that won't take wagons or heavy equipment. Their engineers are in front making good, while their cavalry is ahead and already in sight." He looked round. "Is that understood?" he said.

"Yes, noble sir."

"Right." He looked round again. "We can't hold the city! They're coming with artillery and siege engines and we're under strength. Our duty is to

2

save the treasure for our side." He paused. "For Rome and the Gods of Rome!" He glared at them all. "Did you not hear me?" he cried. "Who are we? What do we fight for?"

"Rome and the Gods of Rome!" A great shout filled the Basilica.

"So!" said Alba, "we've got four days to load everything into the big ships in the port, and these men are Veneti ship-masters in Roman service. He pointed to the civilians. "The Veneti are the finest seamen in the world and will carry the treasure, and some of us – *some of us* – into the Med to a friendly port." This time there was whispering, not growling and the officers looked at one another.

"Next chart!" said Alba. "See here! Cohorts one to eight will fortify the coast road here." He tapped the map. "There they will hold the enemy, while cohorts nine and ten will shift the treasure into the ships." There was more whispering. "Ah," said Alba, "I see that even the dimmest light among you has realised that we can't all get away in the ships. Am I correct?" There was silence. "So this is how it shall be," said Alba. "I personally, will take command of the force holding the road, and I shall not give up that position." He paused. "Not ever. There will be no retreat. Is that understood?"

"Yes, noble sir."

"Good!" said Alba. "Then I will now give detailed instruction for our deployment on the coast road, while his honour, the First Javelin, leaves us to address cohorts nine and ten. Is that understood?"

"Yes, noble sir!"

Alba turned to the First Javelin. The two men clasped arms. They spoke quietly.

"Goodbye old comrade," said Alba.

"Gods be with you, noble sir," said the First Javelin.

"You know they're wobbling?" said Alba. "Cohorts nine and ten?"

"Stupid bastards."

"You talk to them. You can do it."

Later, on the broad paved area of the Forum, lined with columns and bright with sunshine, the First Javelin stood on half an old wine barrel, up-ended to make a speaking platform. The men of cohorts nine and ten were closed up round him in a dense-packed mass of helmets, shields and arms, rattling and clanking against each other. They stood in a semi-circle, facing him with a good flat wall behind him to throw out the sound of his voice: the usual drill for speeches.

They looked up at the First Javelin, who also had a nickname. He was 'the Monkey', for his old, lined face. So the Monkey looked down at the two cohorts. There weren't many of them. Maybe three hundred? There should have been four times that but the 41st had been campaigning for years with no replacements.

The First Javelin drew breath and delivered a Roman speech in Roman style, in a voice trained by a lifetime of speeches, because no man could be a Roman officer and not exhort the men to their duties. The Monkey was old but he could still do it, and he boomed and bellowed in rhythmic phrases. He projected his voice like an announcer at the Games, and he had all the tricks. First he had to surprise them, to take the surly looks off their faces. He had to say something they weren't expecting.

"Soldiers of Rome!" he cried. "What is the worst enemy that a Roman legion can face?" They puzzled over that. Then:

"The Germans!" said a voice.

"The Parthians!" said another.

"The Spartans!" said a third.

"No!" cried the Monkey. "The worst enemy that a Roman legion can face, *is another Roman legion*! So thank the gods that it's not you that's facing a Roman legion – three of them – because you are going to be…" He chose words carefully. "…stevedores and marines." He paused and saw frowns and fear. Looking at their stupid faces, he could hardly *believe* their stupidity. They were going to escape! They weren't going to be slaughtered! But they were too proud to load goods, and they were afraid to go out onto the Atlantic because they were Saphentine Mihtraists who believed a man lost his soul if he drowned. They would mutiny rather than go willingly aboard a ship. So he had to surprise them again.

He drew his sword. He raised it over his head. Cohorts nine and ten gasped.

"Up swords!" he cried. They blinked and looked at one another; then, one by one and finally in a ringing of steel they all drew. "Up!" said the Monkey. "Up over your heads!" They raised swords. They stared. He had their uttermost attention.

"We shall make sacrifice!" he cried, "because Rome and the Gods of Rome need the treasure. You must load it into the ships, and go with the ships to guard it. So you will make blood sacrifice before the gods!" They gasped. They looked on with round eyes. "You will follow my lead!" he cried. "*This* for Mithras!" He raised his left arm, and sliced sword into skin to draw blood which ran down his arm. "Do it!" he cried. "For Mithras and Rome!"

"Mithras and Rome!" they cried and three hundred men drew blood.

"And this for the sea gods!" cried the Monkey, and sliced his arm a second time.

It worked. The blood sacrifice followed by promises of mighty rewards persuaded cohorts nine and ten to do their duty: albeit with bandaged arms. Then, after only two days of hard work, the big ships sailed, bearing two cohorts and the treasure.

The Monkey saw them go. He didn't like ships because they made him sick. He rode with a cavalry escort to see the fleet rise to the Atlantic waves. He noted with surprise that the fleet was blown south by strong winds, which was not the way to reach the Mediterranean. The plan was to go north. He shrugged. What did he know about the sea? Then he went to join Alba on the coast road, planning to die in battle as he had always hoped.

But that plan did not work either because the 41st were tremendous engineers, and they dug in so hard and fought so well that their enemies finally gave up and marched back the way they had come. So the Greek and the Monkey both survived to write their memoirs in later years, and the memoirs were eagerly read because of the great public interest in the disappearance of the Veneti ships, which were never seen again: not a plank, splinter, or man ... and not one jewel of the greatest treasure ever assembled in all of Roman history.

Chapter 1

There have been many times in these memoirs when I have given you youngsters the benefit of my advice, and another such time has come. And so, my jolly boys, we must now discuss the matter of *being caught out*, by which I mean being caught out so utterly and completely that your enemies chuckle in the happy belief that they've got you at last, and there's nothing you can do about it.

But there is. There is indeed and you'll need to know it because if you youngsters grow into the bold creatures that I hope you may, then there will be times in your careers when you are obliged to act in a manner that is not listed in the Articles of War, nor preached by the Parson, nor governed by Queensbury Rules, and when you do it, you may do this for many reasons. It may be for the good of the Service! It may be for the defence of Old England! It may be for the overthrowing of tyrants! But above all, it will be for the salvation of your own infinitely precious and beloved arse.

For whatever reason you do it, you will inevitably do it. Trust your Uncle Jacob. You will do it, and then there will come a time when you are *caught out doing it*, and they will bring chains and lawyers and a great body of evidence to prove that really, truly, and undeniably, you did it.

Then when it happens, even though you know that you are guilty: YOU MUST NEVER ADMIT IT! Never, never, never! Instead, you must act as if filled with righteous indignation. You must stand like a true-born Briton and swear your innocence by God and by Jesus, and declare that the evidence is false and was put together by a secret alliance of persons acting for political motives. Note well – that before all else – you should always blame the politicians, because everyone else *thinks* they are lying, devious rogues, and politicians *know* that they are.

So if you do this, however much your accusers believe that you are guilty, then to some degree — to some small but irritant degree — you will rattle their confidence and create a gap through which you might later escape. Conversely, if you are mad, brainless, or blockhead stupid enough to admit guilt, then the game's over there and then, and all you'll need — and serve you right besides — is a pair of heavy boots to haul you down to a quick finish when they hang you.

[Note that the foregoing sentiments were attended throughout by the Admiral's fist pounding the table in emphasis, until — when coming to his description of politicians — he fell into a rage and was obliged to leave the house and pace the gardens in recovery, attended only by his bulldog, Rufus. S.P.]

But where — you may ask — is this leading? Be patient and your Uncle Jacob will tell you. First you should know how things stood with me at the tail of '99 and early in 1800. Thus, in November '99, I returned from the Far East aboard *Euphonides* frigate: a magnificent ship, but worn out after so long a voyage. She was therefore decommissioned for a refit, and her people were paid off including myself.

I had by then acquired an unwanted, but substantial fame with the newspapers, who presented me as a cross between Lord Nelson and Barnacle Bill the Pirate. On the other hand, I was also a very wealthy man, what with prize money from other adventures and the vast cargo of exotic eastern wares we brought back from the East. This latter wealth was — by the traditions of the Service — shared out with my ship's people. Consequently, on the paying off of *Euphonides,* there was a deal of celebration dinners among us, and at one of these I was presented the most magnificent gift I ever received in all my life: a so-called *portable chronometer,* plus gold chain, by Weatherby & Grove of Bond Street, the King's own clock maker.

It was a licensed copy of Watch H8 as designed by the genius, John Harrison, and was as accurate as a sea-going chronometer, but it was neat enough for a gentleman's vest pocket. Mr Pyne, who was First Lieutenant aboard *Euphonides,* gave me this technical wonder, which surely cost a fortune, at the biggest of our celebration dinners when all hands were crammed into Portsmouth's Guildhall on long lines of tables. Every face was red and beaming, and some of the tars had already fallen off their benches with grog, but were still grinning merrily. Then, eventually, Pyne called for silence, stood up in the crammed, steaming hall, bright with candles, and tried to speak.

"Captain, sir," says he, and was drowned out with cheering.

"Silence on the lower deck!" says I, in a mighty roar, but even I was drowned out by the thundering of feet on floor and chanted cries.

"Jacky Flash! Jacky Flash! Jacky Flash!" For that was me, my jolly boys. *Jacky* for Jacob, and *Flash* because seafaring men being mainly from the West Country said my name more like *Flash*-er than *Fletch*-er. But finally Pyne got them something like quiet and spoke:

"This is by free donation of us all, Captain, sir," says he.

"Aye aye!" thunders the entire company.

"And if you click open the outer case like this," which he did by pressing a neat little stud, "and look here, Captain, here are the words which all have agreed." He read aloud what I now quote from memory:

Given with respect,
affection and gratitude,
to
Captain Jacob Fletcher
from all hands, as brothers united,
of the good ship Euphonides.
December 15th 1799

As you should know, I never wanted the Navy and fought hard to leave it, except that the damned Navy wanted me even harder, and was forever determined to deny me my true vocation of a career in trade. But none the less, my lads, when the ship's people give such a gift as that, and give it freely with such words as that, then even I was deeply grateful, and pleased and proud and happy. But I still resigned my commission as soon as I was free of the formalities at Portsmouth. I sent in my papers to their damned Lordships, and told them precisely what to do with any future offers of employment.

I was, therefore, detached for a while from Britannia's wars with Napoleon. I had no part in smashing his fleet at the battle of the Nile, nor the kicking of his tiny backside out of Egypt, which he'd lately invaded with his armies. But the little bugger's actions eventually dragged me into Africa, as you shall see.

But enough of that for now because, meanwhile, I got myself to Canterbury in Kent where my family lived: my sister Mary; her husband Josiah Hyde, the noted coach builder, and their children. I was made welcome and they were a merry crew, even if they laboured under Mr Josiah's insistence on prayers before bedtime and not a bottle of drink allowed. God only knows how I bore up under that. What was even worse was strict attendance at the local Wesleyan chapel, twice on Sundays, and the opportunities which these attendances dangled before me, but which were forever out of reach.

Thus, chapel attendance was the social highlight of the week. Everyone turned out in their best with much chatter and small-talk after the service, and I was a celebrity because everyone had read about me in the newspapers. Also, I was a big, bold fellow, known to be rich, and I always turned out in full dress uniform because my sister liked to show me off. The result was that I was given the glad eye by all the women. Some of them were very tasty and, by George, I'd have had the drawers off 'em given half a chance! But you didn't get half a chance among Wesleyans down in Kent. So I had a hunger building up on me like a man six months at sea, and dreaming of the pushing-schools ashore.

As a considerable comfort, I discovered that my sister had exactly the same talent for business as myself, so she and I were soon putting investment into some profitable ventures, and I enjoyed the longest and most profitable time in my life to indulge in trade. It was a most happy time and one that I remember with the deepest of fondness.

But then it was March of 1801 and three things happened that pulled me out of trade yet again. The first was meeting His Majesty King George III, and the second was meeting a magnificent ship. But these events were nothing compared with the third, which was being obliged to run from Dominic Gardens to Drummond Street, at three in the morning – stark, bollock naked.

This is how it happened. I was hauled away from Kent to London for the ceremony whereby I was to be rewarded with the Knighthood of the Bath, for past efforts on Britannia's behalf. But note the politics that lay behind this: politics involving not only Earl Spencer, the First Sea Lord, but Billy Pitt, the Prime Minister, because even before resigning my commission, I had refused to act as a secret agent any more for this pair of beauties: something I had done in past adventures and was firmly resolved never to do again.

Spencer and Pitt didn't like my refusal and could have threatened me with the events in my past to put a rope around my neck. But all the newspapers were begging for more juicy tales from Jacob Fletcher, the big, bad sailor *who knew all the dark political secrets*. The papers would have printed anything I gave them, and Spencer and Pitt were wary. Instead of threats, I was given a sweetener to keep my mouth shut. Hence the knighthood, but in all truth they needn't have bothered. I didn't like the newspapers any more than Spencer and Pitt did, and all I wanted was a quiet life out of the Navy. But Mary and Josiah were delighted with the honour, and all was laughter and smiles and the buying of new clothes. Up to London we went in a travelling chaise and horses fit for a duke. That was Josiah's business, after all.

We stayed in the Metropole Hotel, Drummond Street, which was extremely expensive, extremely well fitted out, and was new, fresh and clean. It had a top-class restaurant too, and even Josiah didn't object to my taking wine with my dinner.

"I suppose that in London, we should expect London ways," says he, as we sat to table on our first night.

"You are most understanding, sir," says I.

"Well," says he, smiling, "on such an occasion, we may compromise a little." Mary nodded agreement, all beaming and happy in her new clothes, plump and pretty and gazing round the room at the white cloths, fine furniture, bright candles, lavish decorations and fashionable folk all around us. So I summoned the wine waiter.

"Captain Fletcher?" says he with a grovelling bow, working hard for his tip.

"A bottle of the '87 Margaux, if you please," says I, "and another when that's done!"

That was the Monday night, and the ceremony was on Friday, giving Josiah and Mary time to see the shops, St Paul's, the Tower, the theatres, and whatever else they wanted. Meanwhile I excused myself.

"I'm away to my club this morning," says I, at breakfast on the Tuesday. "I have some business ideas to discuss."

"Of course, Jacky," says Mary. "You do as you must." She paused and raised her voice a little. "But don't be too busy," says she. "Not when you are to be knighted on Friday!" She looked round to make sure that everyone heard, which they did. So she smiled. As I've said, she was proud of me, and fond of me besides. Mind you, she was the sharpest accountant I ever met in all my life. It's in the blood.

So I forgave myself for deceiving Mary and Josiah because they wouldn't have wanted to know where I was really going, and because my need to go there was so great that I was near bursting with it. In fact, merely on impulse and for the Navy gossip, I first went to Saint's of George Street, a club patronised by sea officers.

[Note once more Fletcher's interest in the Navy's affairs, which all his life he pretended to disdain. In truth he was fascinated by all matters appertaining to the Sea Service and its officers, and would discourse on them at length given any chance to do so. S.P.]

As I say, it was on impulse, but I met Sir James Sumarez, who got his knighthood for commanding HMS *Orion* at the battle of the Nile, under Nelson. He was in a circle of admirers, retelling his exploits.

"You see, gentlemen," says he, "the French were anchored in Aboukir Bay, chained together fore and aft, so's we couldn't get between their ships, but must face them as a floating battery, dense-packed and impregnable!"

"Just one long line, sir?" says someone, because there was a crowd of us listening, all sat round in Navy blue. In fact, everyone knew how the French had anchored because the battle was famous. But Sir James was popular and everyone likes a good story.

"One long line, sir!" says Sir James. "And themselves confident that we couldn't get round the lee side of them for the massive sandbanks on that side. But Nelson was bold, and ordered half of us to run down the lee side, risking the sandbanks, and so we took them on two sides at once and won."

"Hear hear!" says everyone, and we all nodded to one another. But then Sir James said something I'd not heard before.

"The odd thing was," says he, "that the French thought we did it by superior navigation – and I heard this myself from French prisoners – they were convinced that we are so obsessed with map-making and soundings that we always know the rocks and sandbanks better than them." Everyone sighed at that piece of nonsense, wishing only that it were true.

"I know," says Sir James. "It was just Nelson taking a risk, but the French think it was because of our maps!"

Later, on more pressing business, I went on to my bank, Child's of Temple Bar. I thereby established that Mr Nathanial Ordroyd, owner of half the cotton mills in Yorkshire, and whose influence had put five MPs into parliament, was out of London until Thursday. I also discovered that, having poured gold into the Tory party for years, Mr Ordroyd was to receive a baronetcy at the very same ceremony as that which would make me a knight! And finally, I learned that his son – my old shipmate Mr Midshipman Phaeton Ordroyd – was promoted lieutenant and was at sea.

Thus, the decks were cleared for action and I proceeded under all plain sail to number 55 Dominic Gardens, which was Mr Ordroyd's house, where I had stayed on a past visit to London by invitation of young Phaeton. I had stayed there under such circumstances of delight as are beyond belief, and I was hoping for more, as delivered up by Miss Persephone Ordroyd – whose name was Ordroyd only for show. She was Mr Ordroyd's most gorgeous and delectable little mistress, with brown eyes, creamy skin, round limbs and a repertoire of tricks that leave even a sailor amazed.

I rang the bell, adjusted my cravat and waited.

The butler answered. He was tall, fat, in livery, and he looked me up and down in calculation of my standing in society. I passed the test and he nodded.

"Ahem," says he. "How might I be of service, sir?"

"Mr Jacob Fletcher to see Mr Ordroyd on business," says I, just to be careful, and I did have business to discuss if need be. I'd made sure of that.

"Mr Ordroyd is out of town, sir," says he, "but, if you wish, I might inquire if Miss Persephone is at home so that …"

Which is as far as he got because there was the most delightful scampering of female feet. Miss Persephone – Perse – came running down the corridor to the front door, with a cluster of little maid servants who were damn near as lovely as her, because it always was fairyland in that house, and everyone – Butler and Cook excepted – were lovely little fairies. By Jove and by George, it did a sailor man's heart good to see them. Their eyes were so bright and their faces so fine.

"Captain Fletcher!" says Perse, stopping with the grace of a ballerina. "My husband is in Yorkshire, and not expected until Thursday, but will you not step inside, sir," says she, "for tea and rout cakes?" As she spoke, she extended an arm – all smooth and round – and smiled wonderfully, inclining her head in a tiny bow. By God Almighty, I could have eaten her up and had the pretty serving girls for dessert.

"Ma'am!" says I, "I had wished to speak to Mr Ordroyd, but perhaps I might stay a brief while … if you please?" She smiled so artfully as to raise joy within me, because there was always the chance I might have been forgotten, or someone else taken my place. But no.

After that we had a correct and proper conversation in the morning room, where tea and rout cakes were delivered up by the serving girls, and where everything in this cotton millionaire's house was silver, and linen, and bone china and Colza oil lamps, and all the furniture was Parisian. But I didn't look at that. I looked at Perse, and we chatted about what she'd done and I'd done since last we met.

And here I turn again to you youngsters, in warning against the immoderate gratification of the pleasures, since a lady is a lady even if she's a rich man's mistress, and ladies have different feelings than men: especially sailormen. It's decent at least to *pretend* you're only here to discuss the weather. In any case, the anticipation is a damn fine thing. So when you've been apart a while, you don't charge in like a bull among the heifers, just in case your attentions are no longer wanted. Indeed you don't. You take a bit of time.

In practise, and since we had much to talk about, I suppose that it was over an hour before Perse wondered if I'd like to go upstairs:

"… to see the fine collection of illustrated travel books that my husband keeps in his study. Since you are something of an explorer yourself, Captain Fletcher?"

"Indeed, ma'am," says I, "that would be most enlightening."

So up we went, but by some mistake we took the wrong turning and ended up in Perse's bedroom with all the servants seeing nothing, and hearing nothing because they knew what was good for them. Or so I thought.

And so to sweeping Perse off her feet, and her laughing and throwing her arms around my neck which, by God and the Devil and all things in between, felt so wonderful that I haven't the words to describe it, except that it was like Mr Faraday's electricity in my spine, making every nerve tingle and shout for joy. Then off with the clothes, and out with the laces, and all thrown aside – except my money and my beloved watch which went on a side table – and so to business. Once more, I haven't the words, because merely feeling her arms around me was glorious. But to see Perse: nude, gleaming, shining, and laughing and posing like a dancer, beckoning me on, I just haven't the words – I wish I did.

But another word of caution! If any of you youngsters grow anywhere near as big as me, and you've got so sweet a creature as Perse in your arms, you must not make a beast of yourself. It should always be you that lies back to receive the charge, so that she can climb aboard as best suits, and in a manner pleasing to herself. She must not get squashed and smothered, but rise to the trot as if on horseback, to the mutual delight of all concerned. It's selfishness that kills with the ladies, so don't you ever be selfish because I may be a monster in a fight, and I'm proud to be a master gunner, but God help him that harms a lady in my presence. Or any woman.

Eventually, and hours later, I staggered away deeply happy and with an invitation to dinner on the Wednesday night. So I'm afraid another falsehood was needed opposite Mary and Josiah.

"I'm invited to dinner, tomorrow," says I, as we sat in the Metropole's Grand Salon, taking tea. "It's a club dinner, so I shall have to go alone." I smiled. "Terrible bore, actually, since I'll have to stay overnight."

"Really?" says Mary. "What a shame! Josiah and I have booked tickets for us all at the Theatre Royal."

"What a pity," says I, "but it's a club rule to stay the night at least once a year, and I've not done so for some while." That made me feel guilty because they believed me: why should they not? It made me guilty, and it may be that what followed was the punishment of providence which despises the wicked liar.

So I took a few things, called a cab, arrived at number 55, and was surprised to find that there was indeed a dinner arranged: one for Perse's set of elves and fairies. Her friends were all so sweet and pretty – boys as well as girls – that they made me feel like the monster in the play by that damned gabbler Shake Spear that's so dense in words and foggy in meaning: the Kaliban.

[Caliban, in 'The Tempest'. Fletcher disliked Shakespeare and all his works – note his insistence on a misspelling of the Bard's name. He especially detested 'Othello the Moor of Venice'. The details are too well known to be repeated here, of his attack on the actor

Edmund Keen at the Theatre Royal, where Fletcher stopped the pretended strangulation of Desdemona. But note that in his reply to the Bow Street magistrate's questioning, Fletcher did not blaspheme, but spoke as follows:

Magistrate: *When you climbed upon the stage, did you not know that Mr Keen was an actor performing a role?*

Fletcher: *Of course I did, but it was a disgusting role, and he deserved a thrashing for it.*

Also, the prison sentence of six months was given not because Fletcher refused to pay the fine – which he did – but because he refused the magistrate's instruction to apologise to Mr Keen, and it was only Mr Keen's pleading that caused the sentence to be suspended. Mr Keen famously declared: *"I can only be honoured that any man should so seriously be moved by my art."* S.P.]

Mind you, Perse and her chums took me as hero of the hour, and listened most flatteringly to my sea tales, some of which were even true. Then they got me up singing shanties, and songs such as 'Big Fat Molly' which they loved even when I gave the verses you don't normally sing in decent company. But Perse got rid of them soon enough, and upstairs we went for another few rounds of utter delight. By God but that woman was lovely. I used to bite her bum on both sides, then turn her over and kiss the bits in front.

After that, it may be that I'd had a drop to drink, because eventually we fell asleep in each other's arms and I slept so sound that I heard nothing until one of the housemaids came scratching on the door, hissing frantic words because she didn't dare shout.

"It's the master! It's the master! Wake up!"

"Oh God save us!" says Perse and she leapt out of bed faster than me. We had a night light burning and she stood like a white marble nymph with hands to her mouth. Then came the sound of voices downstairs: respectful servant voices followed by a man's voice, loud and confident.

"Persephone?" says he. "Where are you, my dear?"

It was Ordroyd: returned a day early.

Chapter 2

(Transcripts of Letters translated from the Arabic.)

January 21st 1801

To the exalted Abdel Boutros, Famous Merchant of Cairo,
  At the House of Abdel Boutros, By the Perfume Market of Muizz Street.
Honoured Abdel Boutros, I send a thousand thanks for your order of fifty Zulu girls, each to be pure virgin, with excellent teeth, perfect skin, firm breasts, slender form, small in the waist but with rounded hips and exquisite limbs. Each to be less than a year into puberty and of sound mind.

  I believe that it may be within my power to fulfil this esteemed order, despite the ferocious savagery of the Zulu warriors, and the need to enter into North Zulu Land first by ship, down the Nile and other rivers, and then by prolonged march. I have therefore appointed the celebrated Mert Yasin the Turk, to go forth with fifty Bedouin horse and one hundred Sudanese spears, to act in your service.

  Thus, all is agreed and there remains to be decided only the trifling matter of price per girl to be paid unto myself by yourself.

  Thus, with temerity I must ask that for each Zulu girl, I should be paid ten times the price which – doubtless by mistake – you currently offer.

  I will also need five cases of English-made muskets, together with three dozen fit young camels and five horses, stout and strong.

In anticipation of your Worship's reply, all persons in my House send heart-felt greeting and pray that God may prolong your well-being and prosperity.

Your loving and sincere servant,

Mustapha El Malmuk Amir, The House of El Malmuk, By the Baths of Ibn Oban, The Street of the Artisans, Cairo.

*

January 22nd 1801

To Mustapha El Malmuk the Slaver, The House of El Malmuk, By the Baths of Ibn Oban,

The Street of the Artisans, Cairo.

Esteemed and worthy Mustapha El Malmuk, I rejoice that God keeps you in good health, and assure you of my deep awareness of the difficulties and dangers of your profession.

I am therefore reassured that you feel able to send an expedition south on the business that I have in mind. But I likewise note that there are others in the city who might do the same and whose services are to be had at a lower cost than yours.

I am therefore prepared to offer you twice the original price per girl. But I regret that I cannot supply muskets, camels or horses.

Hoping that by God's grace this finds you well, I remain your dear friend,

Abdel Boutros, At the House of Abdel Boutros, By the Perfume Market of Muizz Street, Cairo.

*

January 22nd 1801 Afternoon.

To Abdel Boutros, At the House of Abdel Boutros.

Esteemed friend, God's grace be upon you.

I remind your Worship, that three previous expeditions into Zulu Land have returned in ruins with the survivors declaring that they will never face Zulu spears again.

Therefore, despite my limitless admiration for yourself, I cannot accept less than six times your original offer, together with the muskets, camels and horses.

Ever your dearest friend.

El Malmuk, The House of El Malmuk.

*

January 22nd Evening

To El Malmuk, The House of Malmuk.

Dearest Malmuk,

In God's name I cannot offer more than four times the original price, together with the muskets. Any further expense must surely bring ruin upon my house and starvation upon my children.

Ever your friend,

Abdel Boutros.

*

January 22nd Midnight.

To Abdel Boutros.

Your Worship,

Five times together with muskets, camels and horses. Nothing less.

Malmuk.

*

January 23rd

To Malmuk.

Plague and leprosy upon you but yes. Now go forth and come back only with beauties.

As an afterthought, the French stole from me a cut stone of no great value, but the blue colour pleased me, and I know of others

who have interest in such trinkets. It is known that the elite of Zulu wives wear headdresses bearing such stones. So, while it is no great matter, please command Mert Yasin the Turk to bring back some of these headdresses should he come across them.
Abdel.

Chapter 3

By now Mr Nathanial Ordroyd was halfway up the stairs, and calling out loudly to his beloved Persephone who was stood naked beside the bed, pointing at the window and whispering fiercely to me.

"Out!" says she. "You'll have to get out that way. There's a balcony at the back, and a drainpipe. You can climb down that. Quick! Quick! Quick!"

I leave it to you youngsters to guess how it was that the lovely Perse was so swift to summon up what seemed like a practised drill. But summon it she did. So there was indeed a balcony outside, and beside the balcony there was a heavy drainpipe, bound to the wall by cleats which made a ladder going down. Likewise, she was quick to haul open the French windows, and heave my clothes over the balcony rail. It was almost as if she'd done it before. I wondered about that later, but at the time I was simply anxious to escape for fear of what my sister and brother-in-law might learn.

Besides, there was the nasty fact that husbands – which Ordroyd damn near was – can turn vicious on such occasions and if Ordroyd had just got out of a travelling chaise, fresh down from Yorkshire, then there'd be pistols and carbines aboard. There would have to be because nobody travelled unarmed in those days: not if you'd come down the Great North Road where the highwaymen played. So out of the window I went, bare arsed and urgent, with just time to grab at my watch, which I fumbled and dropped, so I seized a handful of coins instead.

Then the window slammed behind me, with my poor fingers hanging on to the drainpipe – left hand only as the right hand was full of money – and down I slipped. I hardly even felt the icy draft up my beam ends. I fell the last ten feet and into a rose bed with bloody damn thorns but soft earth, which broke my fall. By luck alone, I missed going down into the railed-off area, which was another fifteen feet deep and designed to let the daylight into the windows of the kitchens below. But damn, damn, damn, all my bloody clothes went in, and even my bloody shoes.

So there was your Uncle Jacob, my jolly boys, without a stitch in the freezing March dark, and looking up at the cosy bedroom I'd just left, and even faintly hearing dear little Perse greeting her beloved Mr Ordroyd, as lights were lit for the staff to welcome the master. So it was time to cut and run which I did at once, knowing the garden well, and I was out by the gate at the end, by the servant's privy, which led into Dominic Mews.

And then, and here's another piece of advice. Sometimes, my jolly boys, there just ain't no clever plan, and no easy way out of the shite. Sometimes you just have to put your head down, grit your teeth, and take the plain hard road, because it's the only one that's open. So that is what I did. Which means that I had to run, because that would at least minimise the time that I was exposed – and I really do mean exposed – as an object of ridicule through the streets of the most populous city in the world. So if ever you're placed as I was, then good luck to you if you have the confidence to saunter through the streets, bidding polite greeting to those you meet. Perhaps you have the panache to do that, but your Uncle Jacob did not.

So I ran like the Devil. I ran hard even though I'm not built for running and even though it was wicked cold with frost on the ground and my feet were aching. I ran hard even though it's nasty for a man to run with no drawers because he instantly finds out why they call it 'bollock naked'. They call it that because your tackles swing side to side and bounce off your thighs most painful and awkward, such that you're grateful if it's as cold as it was then, because everything shrinks tight and don't bounce quite so much, which helps a bit.

Fortunately, from Dominic Gardens to the Metropole wasn't very far, not when you're running. I suppose it took ten to fifteen minutes, during which I was grateful that the street lamps threw only miserable little glows in those days, with plenty of shadows to hide me. And I was grateful that it was so late that near nobody was on the streets. I did pass a couple of night watchmen, poor old souls who I scared witless, especially one I came upon who thought he was alone, and was piddling against a wall with his staff and lantern beside him. I still remember his wide-gaping mouth and his little white dicky, held between his ancient fingers. What was worse was a hackney carriage full of young bucks, blind drunk, yelling mockery out of the windows, and calling on the cabby to turn and follow me. But lucky for me, the cabby shook his head and continued on his way, which was lucky for them too, considering what I'd have done with them if I'd got hold of them.

The worst moment was arriving at the Metropole – half dead with effort and damn near spitting blood – and hammering on the door for the night staff, the sweat freezing on my back. I got no answer for what seemed an hour. But they came at last: a pair of footmen, one with a blunderbuss, and they gasped and gaped. But they recognised me and let me in. One or two little maids appeared at the back of the foyer, caught site of me, and received an education. But the footmen did well, once I gave them a guinea each. They quickly found a greatcoat to cover me, and I didn't even have to speak. The guineas spoke for me.

"Not a word of this to anyone!" says the senior to his mate.

"Not a word, Captain Fletcher!" says the other, and they didn't speak a word, either. They just took me into their night parlour where there was a lovely fire to warm my bones, and they got me an exceedingly welcome brandy, and a big piece of fruit cake. Later, they let me into my room and, by Jove, I gave them the rest of my handful of coin and they damn well earned it.

Meanwhile, and at this stage of the story you youngsters must think that what you've just read was the fearful example of *being caught out* that your Uncle Jacob was talking about. Well it wasn't. So read on.

The next day was Thursday, when even I thought it best to have a normal breakfast with Mary and Josiah and to spend a normal day with them, doing what normal people do. So that's what we did, viewing the Chelsea hospital, and then Covent Garden Market: which was great fun. There were drovers with cattle and sheep and the stallholders bellowing, and every imaginable variety of food on sale, and fights between some of the women fruit vendors who went at it with boots and nails, and hair flying. Later, we ended up in some sort of Quaker meeting house which interested Josiah what with his dissenting religion. It bored me solid but he and Mary loved it.

But Friday was the big day. We were summoned to St James's Palace, and everyone had to wear court-levee clothes except officers of the Land and Sea Services who wore full dress uniform. I was allowed two guests, which meant that Josiah had to have his hair dressed and powdered, and wear a fancy outfit with knee-britches, silk stockings and little black shoes, which all cost a fortune. In fact, being a countryman with a tanned face, he looked good against the white hair, though he was fearfully embarrassed. Mary on the other hand was in her glory. She had the obligatory ostrich feathers in her hair, and a vastly heavy, complex gown with antique-looking panniers beneath that made everything stick out at the sides. It was all made out of brocades and embroidered silk, hitched up and pulled in at a time when the ladies of fashion were wearing plain, white muslin that floated around as if it barely existed. But what do I know about fashion? I'm a sailor.

So we climbed out of our carriage and my invitation was checked against a list by a clutch of mighty minions. These noble servants manned the doors wearing court livery, while grenadiers of the foot guards stood in lines, all up the steps with gleaming firelocks, pipe-clayed slings, and saluting anybody with the King's Commission. That included me, even though I'd resigned mine. But they didn't know that. So in we went, with all the others likewise in fancy dress, the ladies' feathers waving, and the gentlemen tripping over the small-swords they had to wear, and which they weren't used to. It was comical to see some of them, fat and rich as they were, stumbling and trying not to fall over.

Once inside, we all paraded up and down in a great chamber with huge windows, red-velvet drapes, lines of royal portraits on the walls, and massive gilt chandeliers hanging from the ceiling. Since this was St James's and a day when honours were handed out, I was not surprised to recognise some of the great and powerful of the land in attendance. That's only what you'd expect. But Josiah and Mary were awestruck when two of the greatest of all, not only recognised *myself*, but approached me and spoke to me!

One of them was Lord Spencer, First Lord of the Admiralty and absolute ruler of the Royal Navy. In his early forties, he had a long straight nose, a big chin, heavy brows and a God-damn-you expression. He wore the Star of the Garter, and folk got out of his way like the waves before a line-of-battle ship. I wasn't pleased to see him as I thought I'd long since got out of his grip. With him came a man I recognised only by his pictures in the satirical prints: late thirties, fat-faced, slightly pop-eyed and with small lips. He wore Field Marshal's scarlet draped all over with stars and orders. He was Frederick Augustus, Duke of York, the King's second son, and commander of the British Army. At least he knew how to wear a sword without tripping.

"Commodore Fletcher!" says Spencer, beaming a smile as we bowed, and inclining his head politely towards Mary. "I take this opportunity to present you to His Royal Highness, and ask that he and I be introduced to this gentleman, and this charming lady." Well, that was nicely spoken and no mistake, and we chatted about nothing a while, until Spencer and the Duke bowed and moved on, working their way around the room.

"Oh how wonderful!" says Mary, totally overwhelmed. "Wait till we tell the children and everyone in chapel."

"Indeed, indeed," says Josiah. "We're in your debt, Jacob, for climbing us so high up the tree. And wasn't the Duke of York so charming? What a decent fellow he must be!"

That gave me a fright. I realised I'd not listened to a word the Duke had said, because my entire mind had been attending Spencer, to see if the blighter was trying to pull me back into the bloody Navy. And I still didn't know if he was or not. I didn't trust the way he looked at me with a smile, as if he knew something that I did not.

Soon, some other mighty minions entered the room, dressed in fantastical robes I won't attempt to describe. Their leader – The Lord High Pauncefoote of the Bed-Pan most likely –thumped a white staff three times on the floorboards for silence, and since he looked about one hundred and thirty years old, I wasn't surprised that his voice was so weak that we barely heard it. But there were footmen to deal with that. They went round collecting the herd of us who were to receive our Orders of Chivalry, and led us into a side chamber where The Lord Pauncefoote read us the rule book concerning how we were to behave in front of the King. We could hear him better in this small room with only a few of us there: a couple of dozen being honoured and some dignitaries at the back including Spencer and the Duke of York. We had just been issued with the special robes that went with being knighted when I really did come up against this business of BEING CAUGHT OUT that I have laboured so heavily.

Just as Lord Pauncefoote was turning to the second page of his notes, a man standing behind me pushed forward and raised his voice. He was small and thin, with a hard face shaved close. He was a man who'd made his own way in the world and stood no nonsense. I had no idea who he was then, but he knew me.

"Your Grace, my lords, and gentlemen," says he. "There's a creature here among us, as shouldn't be here." He had the tones of the North Country, and in that instant I guessed what was coming, which promptly it did. "Him there," says he, jabbing a thumb at me, "this here Captain Fletcher is a well-known villain that has spent his evenings in beastly fornication, inflicted on the lady of my house, and is not worth being made into a knight!"

"What?" says everyone.

"What do you mean?" says they, and Lord Pauncefoote dropped his notes. But Nathanial Ordroyd – for it was he – pressed on.

"Not only do I have the sworn testimony of my butler," says he, "that this Fletcher was coupling with my lady, but I have this!" And he pulled out my presentation watch – my portable chronometer – and flicked it open. "See here!" says he, shoving it into the hand of the man next to him. "Look at it! Read the inscription! This watch was found at my lady's bedside, and this villain's clothes," he jabbed his thumb again, "were found in the area outside my lady's bedroom when he escaped into the night!" He looked at me with hideous venom. "I've got you, you damned rogue!" says he. "I've got you with proof that I've got you, and I'll be damned if you'll be made into a knight or any decent thing, because I've got you to rights!"

So they all turned and looked at me, and there was a very long silence. You could hear the chatter in other rooms; you could hear the carriage wheels grinding and the horses clip-clopping outside. You could even hear a sergeant somewhere yelling at the grenadiers. There was a very long silence while Ordroyd snapped his fingers in triumph and everyone stared at me. So there we were, my jolly boys, we've come to it at last, because this was the moment.

But now your Uncle Jacob must be allowed some pride in himself, because there's nothing praiseworthy in being big and strong, or in having a mind for figures, or in being a seaman or a gunner. There's nothing praiseworthy in these talents because they are bred into us, and are not earned by hard work and diligence. On the other hand, note the manner of my reaction on being dropped so utterly down the bog-hole. It took a few seconds to get it straight in my mind, but this was it:

"Rubbish!" says I, in a great roar, drawing myself up in dignity, and glaring down upon Ordroyd, who blinked and stood back. "Sir," says I, "you must be part of some plot, cooked up for political reasons to discredit me! My watch was stolen yesterday by pickpockets in Covent Garden, and I demand to know how it came into your possession! As for the rest, the clothes you mention could be anybody's, while your butler is an insolent fellow who took against me when I called at your house with a proposal of business. I assume that he has therefore fabricated this insult to myself and to your lady, Miss Persephone, who is both modest and virtuous!" I looked round and saw some odd looks but a few nods, which was a good start. "So!" says I, to Ordroyd, "I defy you, sir! And I warn you, sir, that should you persist in these defamatory lies, then I shall see you in court seeking substantial damages!"

"Hear, hear!" says someone.

"Hmmmm," says others, not quite sure. So on I went.

"In fact," says I, as if dawn had arisen to illuminate the truth, "I perceive that this is some French-republican ruse to attack the means whereby our King rewards his faithful subjects!" I glared at Ordroyd. "I see that it is your plan to deprive these gentlemen ..." I waved a hand at the company. "It is your plan to deprive these gentlemen ..." I paused before thundering out the conclusion. "... to deprive them of the honours they have so justly won!"

"Uhhhhhhh!" came a gasp of horror, and all present clutched their robes like children in fear of the bogeyman. They clutched good and hard because some had got there merely by facing shot and shell, but most had invested a lifetime of hard grind. They'd granted favours, swallowed insults and kissed bum-holes. They'd given employment to idle sons of powerful men; they'd voted correctly; they'd done charity through clenched teeth and always smiled; and – before all else – they'd poured treasuries of money into the right pockets. So? Were they going to see all this wasted just because Jacob Fletcher had bounced a juicy tart?

"Nooooooo!" says they, as if guessing my thoughts. Meanwhile, Earl Spencer and the Duke of York came forward. Spencer was fighting to keep a straight face, but the Duke took my hand and shook it.

"Well spoken, Captain Fletcher!" says he.

"Ahhhhh!" says everyone as they saw who the Duke supported, and they nodded at me. So Spencer moved fast.

"Your Grace?" says he to the Duke. "Is it your wish that the ceremonies should proceed?"

"Indeed it is!" says the Duke, shaking my hand again, and looking me manfully in the eye.

"Huzzah!" says the entire room, and that was it, my jolly boys. I later learned that Spencer had a private word with Ordroyd afterwards, and contracts were awarded to soothe his feelings. So thank you, Lord Spencer, because Ordroyd made no further trouble. I suppose he wanted his baronetcy after all. He kept Perse in his house too and I've often wondered what she told him, though I suppose it might be more what she *did* than what she said.

[Fletcher did not come away entirely free from his connection with Miss Persephone, because his escape from her bedroom and his naked run through the dark streets of London became widely known, heaping further scandal upon his name. S.P.]

A while later, I duly knelt before King George, who was a pop-eyed, older version of his son, the Duke. He was also something remarkable sharp for a man supposed to be mad, and he was extremely well informed on matters of mechanism.

"What-what!" says he, as I entered, "Jacky Flash I do believe!"

"Oh," says I, surprised, while all the courtiers beamed.

"Jacky Flash of the submarine boats and the steam ships?" says he. "I'll have you back, sir, for further conversation! I've a hunger for such matters as high-pressure steam and would like to discuss the regulators and governors needed for safety."

"God bless Your Majesty," says I, because that's what you say to a King, and you youngsters should never neglect to say it. But I never was asked back. The poor old devil went clear round the bend soon after, and stayed there for years. Meanwhile, I was happy in the knowledge that I'd saved my knighthood and got myself out of trouble, and was now free to get back to business with my sister. But on the debit side, I never got my watch back because that bastard Ordroyd kept it, and I thought it wise to let matters lie. That was bad enough but there was worse to come, because Spencer grabbed my arm as I walked out of the throne room with my sash and star.

"Congratulations, Sir Jacob," says he, and he laughed. "You infinitely cunning rogue! I damn near believed that tale you told Ordroyd!" He laughed again. "Now come with me because I have something to show you."

Chapter 4

The hill of the White Cow's Flank,
North Zulu Land,
In the summer of the 12th Year of the reign of
King Ndaba KunJama,
(1801)

"The men of the Turk were as children. The deception was complete."

(From the Saga of Inyathi: Translated from the Zulu)

The slave-catcher, Mert Yasin the Turk, was careful. He was very careful because a slaver's business was exceedingly dangerous. He'd been a soldier once – under Sultan Selim III. He'd been a Yamak, one of the elite corps that fought pirates on the Bosphorus, and that had been dangerous enough. But it wasn't as dangerous as fighting Zulus, who were cunning and organised. Above all they were organised.

"Take my place!" he said to one of his attendants, who rode close behind.

"Yes, Effendi," said the man and touched brow in salute. Yasin took up the fore-guard, riding ahead of the column and trying to look every way at once, and especially into the long bush grass that grew nearly the height of a man. Meanwhile, he reined in his horse, which snorted and whimpered. He leaned forward and patted her neck.

"Softly, softly," he said to comfort her, because she too knew that there was danger about. Yasin looked up and down the column. There were fifty mounted musket men. They were Bedouin and fine horsemen. Every man rode with his gun in hand, and wore a pair of pistols in his belt and a Persian scimitar besides. On foot there were twice that number of

Sudanese spearmen, with wild hair, and long, broad-bladed spears. The Bedouin were reliable because they stuck together for fear of being caught alone, because they knew what *they* did to prisoners and assumed that any enemy would do the same to them. But the Sudanese were different. They stood firm if the enemy was weak, but they were amazing runners and would be gone like the wind if the Zulus came in force.

Then, in the middle of the column there were fifteen Zulu girls, taken from the small kraals raided so far. It had to be done by raids because Zulus would never sell their daughters, not even for guns and powder. Yasin shook his head. That's why the work was so dangerous and the Zulus so angry. But he rode down the line and looked at the girls. They were good. They were carefully chosen for beauty, and everyone else in their kraals had been left to the Sudanese.

Of course, the girls had to ride. They rode on camels with Egyptian camel drivers to lead them. They had to ride to keep them fresh. Also it was good that it would take so long to get them back to Cairo, on the lesser rivers and the Nile. It was good because most of them had gone barefoot all their lives, and the journey gave plenty of time to soften and prettify their feet. Meanwhile, they rode camels. They rode, and sneered at Yasin in hatred. But that was normal. A slaver hardly noticed that.

There were fifteen of them so far, which was only a break-even number. On a good day, if sold in the famous Cairo market, fifteen girls would cover the expenses of the expedition. But that was nowhere near enough for a profit. Thirty or forty girls would be a safe number. Yasin smiled to himself. "Safe?" he thought. "In this trade?" But then he frowned. He saw one of the girls shout out and kick at a camel driver. She drew Yasin's attention instantly because she was the best of them all. She was special, exceedingly lovely, and she would sell for a fortune. Her name was Ulwazi. Yasin knew all their names because it was his business to do so. He knew some of the Zulu speech besides.

"Don't touch me!" she said. "Let go of my leg!" She kicked again and the camel driver staggered back, but he was grinning. Yasin rode forward, slashed with his whip and the camel driver screamed. He screamed in pain and then in terror as he looked up at Yasin.

"Do that again, and you know what you'll get!" said Yasin, and the camel driver fell to his knees, raised hands to Yasin, and whimpered in fear.

"No, no, no, Effendi!" he cried. "Please-please-please-please! I make mistake. Big mistake. I never-never-never do it again." He begged and gabbled until Yasin gave him another swipe to shut him up, then stared at him, wondering if it was time for the usual punishment. The camel driver saw the look on his face, and wrung his hands in agony. "No-no-no-no-no!" he said. "Oh, no-no-no-no-no!"

"Bah!" said Yasin. "Just behave, you son of a pig-fucked whore."

"Yes-yes-yes, Effendi. Thank you, Effendi! I be good, Effendi. Very good." Yasin shook his head and rode off. The camel drivers never learned. Then he forgot the camel drivers and rode up and down the column warning the Bedouin, because they were approaching a dangerous place where the track rose over high ground, and the bush grass was thick.

"Keep good watch!" he said. "Left and right! Check your priming!"

"Yes, Effendi!" said the Bedouin. They checked their guns, and made sure the flints were secure. Then Yasin spoke to the Sudanese head boys. He had enough of their speech for that.

"Keep good watch!" he said. "Keep your men close around the girls!"

"Yes, Baas!" they said, raising spears. "Yes, Baas!" Yasin rode ahead of the column, and stared and stared into the hot, bright light. The trouble was that there was no better way. The thorn-scrub was so dense around the hill as to tear open even a camel's hide. It had to be over this great hill. Up and over he went, leading the column with heart pounding, because the real danger might be over the crest which you couldn't see. Soon Yasin was on the summit, looking round and round, and there was nothing but bush grass and a few old, wizened trees, and …

"Ah!" said Yasin. Just ahead, and coming up the slope towards him there were some small boys. They were a few hundred paces off, and they were driving cattle: about a dozen of them. The boys waved long sticks, and drove them forward. The cattle moaned and cried. Yasin stared carefully. He stared hard. There was nothing else there. He looked and looked, and there was nothing there but boys and cattle. Not all the way to the horizon. "Good!" thought Yasin. Meat would be welcome, and the Sudanese drank blood and milk. Better still, there was a side-market for Zulu boys if small and well-formed.

"With me!" cried Yasin to the Bedouin, and drew his scimitar.

"Hi! Hi! Hi!" cried the Bedouin and there was a pounding of hoofs as they followed Yasin. Good skirmishers that they were, they needed no word of command to spread wide on either side of the track, to enclose the boys and their cattle, with the aim of coming round behind them to prevent escape. "Hi! Hi! Hi!" they cried, and they laughed with the excitement of the charge. They raised a great dust; they sped forward; they completed a most excellent manoeuvre and reined in, with prancing horses and merry faces and raised swords in triumph. Even Yasin laughed for a brief moment.

Then there was a sound more terrifying than thunder. It rolled and pounded and beat upon the ears as an entire Zulu regiment rose from hiding. They threw off the scrub and bushes that had covered them in the ambush trenches cunningly dug on either side of the track. Then they beat iron spears on leather shields in synchronised pounding:

Boom-boom-boom! Boom-boom-boom! Boom-boom-boom!

They beat shields and formed ranks that could have been drawn with a ruler. There were a least a thousand of them, and even the furthest was no more than a hundred paces from the track. They were tall men with long shields, under fierce discipline. There were leaders with plumed headdresses, and one – with a shield of black buffalo hide – was the commander. He yelled an order, and the closest ranks ran forward and launched a volley of throwing spears that curved up and down, and even in that first instant of the fight, nearly a third of the Bedouin were either falling from the saddle, or had horses killed under them.

Now the Zulu commander raised his spear in a high, exaggerated gesture, bringing it down to point at Yasin and his men. He yelled a war cry and the regiment answered in deep bass voices. The sound was enough to strike terror into a block of stone, as the regiment closed in at a steady trot, dressing their lines all the way until the final twenty paces when they leapt forward at the run so that the shield-line struck the surviving Bedouin in a hammer blow.

No more than a handful of muskets were fired, some shots wasted in the air, and all the rest missed their targets. The Bedouin and their horses went down under mass stabbing with short *Iklwa* spears, so named for the sound of the blade being pulled out of an enemy.

Most of the Sudanese never even saw the attack because they were on the other side of the hill. But those that saw it ran, and the rest ran at the doomful sound of beaten shields. They ran and escaped, being able to cover ground even faster than a Zulu regiment.

The camel drivers also tried to run but were easily caught and easily speared and not one of them survived.

The fifteen beautiful girls were saved and were soon promised in marriage to men of high status such that each girl – on marriage – would wear a jewel in her headdress.

The little boys who had tricked the slavers were given the cattle to keep for their own and they were granted the rank of full-grown men.

Mert Yasin the Turk, being an old soldier, was wise enough to flee in the instant that the Zulus rose out of the ground. He might well have escaped if his horse had not stumbled and thrown him.

Chapter 5

Spencer led me from room to room of St James's Palace with flunkies and pages genuflecting as he passed, and why should they not? He held a powerful office, had an inherited peerage, and George II had been his godfather. None of which is surprising because how else, but by such connections, did a man rule the Navy in those days? So on we went until Spencer found the room he wanted, and inside there was something amazing for me to look at.

The room was modest in size but lavish in fittings. Long windows faced south for the light with the usual red-velvet drapes and the usual framed paintings, though this time of ships, together with fine mahogany furniture and an oriental carpet. But that was nothing because two things took all my attention. First, there was quite a crowd in there – mostly in Sea Service uniform – and they burst into applause as I entered. I was surprised to recognise some of the lieutenants from my old ship *Euphonides* led by Pyne, my old Number One. Also, Dr Goodsby the Chaplain was there and Mr Unwin the Gunner, and there were others besides. They instantly began to cheer, which was all very jolly but for some reason I was uneasy. What was going on? Why were they here?

But that thought was pushed out of my mind by something wonderful that was sitting on a table in the middle of the room, with a good light from the window, and everyone looking from it to me, and from me to it and smiling. The *something* was a ship model, built exquisitely to scale, and complete with every fitting from anchor to capstan. Oak shone, brass gleamed and guns sat sullen black. Such a thing was made by only the finest craftsmen from the finest dockyards, and it was about six feet long from bow to stern, not counting the bowsprit. As was usual with warship models, her masts were token stumps, and no yards or rigging were added, because these were standard fittings regarded as replaceable, and therefore not worth showing. It was the hull that mattered. That's what you had to look at.

I should explain to you youngsters that there was a long tradition of accurate ship-modelling, especially for the King's ships because the blockhead politicians who control the King's purse cannot imagine from a paper plan what a ship might look like when built. In fact, it's hard enough even for a seaman to decide what's good and what's bad in a new ship just from the plans, especially if some novelty is under consideration, or the ship is fearfully big and expensive, which a man o' war generally is. And this one, my lovely lads – the one that sat on the table beaming at me – was a whopper: a belter. She was a thundering great ship, thunderingly well armed and lovely to see from any angle.

I started to count her guns, but Spencer laughed. They all laughed.

"She's a 90-gun ship, Sir Jacob," says he, "a second-rate, and supposedly inferior to a first rate of 100 guns, except that she is *superior*!"

"Aye!" says the all the seamen present.

"Yes!" says all the landmen, and I could see why. Her lines were wonderful to behold. She was a work of genius in her underwater form and she looked fast. She was a very big ship but she looked fast. So I walked round the model, loving all her beauty, and everyone chuckled and muttered all the while. Finally I had to speak. I turned to Spencer.

"Well, my Lord?" says I. "She's very pretty. Very pretty indeed. But what's she to me? Why am I here?"

"You are here, because you have resigned your commission, sir," says he, and he walked over to the model. "This is *Tromenderon* of 90 guns, named for the mythical wrestler of Ancient Greece who was so strong that he could not be thrown by men and therefore wrestled with bulls!" He looked round the room. "Perhaps we know of such a man?"

"Ho! Ho! Ho!" they all said but my heart sank because I could see where this was leading.

"*Tromenderon* is launched, and is fitting out at Chatham," says Spencer. "She will carry 32-pounders not only on the lower gun deck, but the upper too, and she will therefore be capable of battering any normal first rate, while being as fast as a frigate." There was now silence in the room as everyone pondered on these remarkable claims, and I must admit that I was curious.

"So who built her?" says I. "She looks French!" This brought roars of laughter, and a cheerful paying out of bets from one man to another.

"I knew he'd say that!" says Pyne, taking a guinea from Mr Unwin.

"So did I," said Dr Goodsby, taking money from a glum lieutenant, while two well-dressed, civilian gentlemen frowned and clenched fists.

"French, sir?" says one. "Never, sir!"

"British from main-truck to keelson!" says the other.

"Ah," says Spencer, smiling upon the two civilians and turning to me. "Sir Jacob, may I introduce Sir Robert Lee and Mr Charles Kennedy? They are Senior Naval Architects of the Chatham Royal Dockyard, and are *entirely* responsible for the design of *Tromenderon:* the finest ship in the fleet!" There were sniggers at *entirely* because you can't miss French styling, and this ship looked French from end to end. More than that, although nobody dislikes the Frogs more than me, I have to admit that they had a genius for ships, and that's a fact. So *Tromenderon* wouldn't be the first 'finest ship in the Fleet' that was really a copy of something French.

Meanwhile, I stuck out my hand to greet the pair of them, who sniffed a bit before taking it, and everybody sighed and smiled, and once again I had to admit plain truth.

"If this ship sails as well as she looks," says I, "she'll be a wonder on the seas, and a peril to England's enemies!"

"Ahhhh!" says everyone.

"Thank you, Sir Jacob," says Lee.

"Thank you indeed," says Kennedy. Then everyone looked at Spencer, and there was a bit of a silence. They looked in expectation and shuffled their feet, and they grinned as if he was about to announce that it was Christmas, Easter, and the cat's birthday all come at once.

"*Tromenderon* will be all that you say, Sir Jacob," says Spencer, "and she will be yours! She will be yours if you will have her, and a very goodly number of those who were with you aboard *Euphonides* have volunteered to go into her with you."

"Aye aye!" says all the seamen in the room. But I said nothing. I said nothing because I didn't know what to say. There was a silence and everyone looked at Spencer. They weren't grinning any more, but they weren't disheartened either, and I could guess from their dear little faces what was in their dear little minds. You see, my jolly boys, they all knew rather a lot about me. I was bloody famous by then, wasn't I? So they knew that I was out of the Navy and into trade. But they were willing to forgive me this extreme peculiarity if Earl Spencer could turn me round and show me the right course to steer! Spencer looked at them, and looked at me.

"Sir Jacob!" says he. "Will you please stand fast," he turned to the rest, "while I ask these gentlemen to leave us?"

"Aye aye, my Lord," says they, as Spencer beckoned to a main in civilian clothes – none too smart – who was standing at the back of the room.

"Captain Barker?" says he. "Will you also stand by me?"

"Aye aye," says he, touching his brow like a common seaman. Then, as others left the room, he came towards Spencer. His hair was pulled back in a greasy queue, and he walked like a seaman. Spencer had addressed him as 'Captain' but he didn't have the swagger of a King's officer. He was a straightforward tar, who'd come up the hard way. He was in his twenties, but sea-tanned and sea-wrinkled as seaman are, and was obviously nervous in the presence of so mighty a panjandrum as Spencer.

"I'm come aboard, M'Lord!" says Barker as if he'd come over the side of a ship, and he saluted again.

"So I see," said Spencer, with little warmth.

"Sir Jacob," says Spencer, "I present Captain Samuel Barker of the Nova Scotian Canadian whaling fleet, who is a true loyalist to our King. His father was a New England loyalist before him, until he and his family were driven out by the war of the American colonies, and obliged to seek refuge in Canada."

"Were they indeed?" says I and frowned. I did not offer Barker my hand. You see I'd met American loyalists before, and a damned dangerous meeting it had been, involving just the sort of espionage work that I was resolved never to touch again.

So I thought I'd get in first.

"My Lord," says I to Spencer, "I've made myself clear in the matter of secret agents and the like. Also, I'm no longer in the King's service, having resigned my commission to follow a life of my own, a life which is ready and waiting with my family."

"Sir Jacob," says Spencer, "I know all that! But I want you back, and I therefore assure you that – should you take command of *Tromenderon* – you would not be a secret agent, but would act with the full and open recognition of His Majesty's Government, bearing such documentation as befits a formal enterprise of diplomacy. You would become a roving ambassador to the Americas, acting in concert with such other of His Majesty's diplomats that you might meet." That shut me up. I wondered what this meant, but it definitely wasn't espionage. Then Spencer shot off on a new tack, going I knew not where: "Captain Barker," says he, "please explain to Sir Jacob, the extent and importance of the New England whaling trade."

"Enormous!" says he. "Enormous hundreds of ships and enormous fortunes of money. Thousands of seamen and ports depending on it all up the coast." He had one hell of a Yankee accent for a loyalist, but I suppose he got it from his father.

"And whence comes the profit of the whaling trade?" says Spencer. "What is the substance of its great wealth?"

"'Tis the whale oil, my Lord," says Barker, "or *train oil* as we calls it, which we melts down from the blubber, and puts in barrels."

"How many barrels?" says Spencer.

"Thousands and thousands," says Barker, "Enormous thousands in vast profusion."

"And to what purpose," says Spencer.

"For the lamps of all the world, my Lord," says Barker, "and for the lubrication of fine instruments, and for the fattening of every kind of food."

"And is the whaling trade very much an American trade?" says Spencer.

"It is, my Lord," says he. "We have some share of it in Nova Scotia, and would like more, but mainly 'tis American."

"And what harm would come to the Americans if they were to lose the whaling trade?"

"Enormous vast, my lord," says Barker, "catastrophic vast."

"Thank you, Captain Barker," says Spencer. "You may leave us. Do close the door as you go out."

"Aye aye, my Lord," says he, and he touched his brow and off he went, leaving me with Spencer beside the wonderful model ship, which I couldn't help looking at.

"Oh for God's sake, Fletcher," says Spencer, "take your eyes off the damn thing. It's not a naked woman!" He laughed. "By heaven but you're a bloody rogue. I don't doubt you've had your leg across Ordroyd's lady, because I hear she's a beauty." He thought about that and couldn't help adding, "*Is she?*" But I said nothing. "Huh!" says he, "now listen to me and listen well." He pointed to the model. "You're being offered a command that every officer in the Service would sell his soul to get. And his mother's soul besides, and his grandmother's too! You know that, don't you?"

"I suppose so," says I, "and what about Captain Barker. What does he have to do with all this?" Spencer nodded.

"He was fortuitously in England," says he, "and I summoned him here so that you might learn, at first hand, the extent of the North Atlantic whale fisheries, and their great importance to the Americans." Spencer stared close at me. "Captain Barker is a son of the lower deck, as you have seen." I nodded. "But he was bred up in the whaling trade, and he knows every coast and port of the Canadian coast, and should you – in your infinite condescension – choose to accept what I offer, then Barker would be your guide and pilot along that coast and among the people there. You may trust him and act on his advice. Do you understand?"

"Yes, my Lord," says I.

"Good!" says he, "because Barker is a straight and honest man, who speaks whereof he knows, and he did not exaggerate one jot concerning the vital importance of whale oil. Think of the Americans angered by our taking away the whale oil trade. Think of that, then think of America becoming our deadly enemy at a time when we are fighting to contain the French. Think of the vast resources of the American continent, and their proven capacity to build warships. Think of their ability to man them and fight them just as well as we do, for the Yankees are fine seamen and come of the same blood stock as our own selves!"

"Beg pardon, my Lord," says I, "but where is this leading?"

"This is leading to the fact that the French have surprised us with a most cunning stroke of diplomacy. They have sent ambassadors to Boston, Washington and Philadelphia, who have delivered cunningly forged papers – diplomatic papers – that have convinced the Americans that the Royal Navy is about to attack and seize their whaling fleet to give the whaling trade to our loyal subjects in Nova Scotia." He blinked a bit as he said that.

"And are we?" says I. He paused a while.

"No," says he, "not quite. Nearly, but not quite, because we truly would like to give the trade to Nova Scotia. But we're not at war with America. Not yet! Though if they *did* take sides with the French – and they might, because America hates King George – then we would attack *all* their shipping, including the whalers."

"So what am I to do about this?" says I.

"Oh?" says he, "then do you admit that you *might* do something?" I said nothing.

"Look at her, Fletcher," says he, gazing at the model. "Have you ever seen anything more splendid? Do you really not want her?" Again, I said nothing. "Because somebody," says he, "will take this ship to America, and will – in turn – visit all the major seaports to show them that we can build ships capable of smashing anything that they can build." He leaned close, getting into his argument. "Meanwhile," says he, "the chosen captain of *Tromenderon* must be a cunning user of words and a masterful, clever-devil in a sudden emergency, who wriggles out of disaster. He must be well-connected in America, and be himself an American citizen! That man will use every trick that God gave him to convince the Americans that we are not after their whaling fleet, and he will deal efficiently with all such perils as may arise." He looked at me. "So who is this man? Who am I talking about?"

He made me smile. I couldn't help it. I did know people in Boston from previous adventures, and I was proud of the American citizenship that I had won on that occasion. If I couldn't be British, then I'd wish to be American because we two nations are put on Earth as an example to lesser folk. Anyway, Spencer was saying that I was quick-thinking, and I liked that.

"Hmm," says I.

"In addition," says he, "this captain might have to deal with three ships of the line. They are 80-gun ships of novel design which are believed to be heading for America, and they recently broke out of our Blockade of Le Havre."

"Broke out?" says I. "I didn't know the Frogs have broken out."

"Nobody knows," says he, "because we have kept the matter secret. And it wasn't all of them. Just three. We caught the rest and they turned back, but the leading three escaped."

"Three ships?" says I. "And you're sending just one after them?"

"But such a one!" says he, "and we don't know for sure that the three are truly heading for America." He turned again to the model. "Look at her, Fletcher! Such a ship deserves the best that we have in command of her!" He shrugged. "She is of course copied from the French. The original was their *Immense*, driven aground off Lamb's Head in Ireland in '98. Sir

Robert and Mr Lee were commanded to build the same but better, which they did, putting 32-pounders on the upper deck where *Immense* had 24s." He smiled. "But don't tell them she looks French, because it upsets them." I gazed at the model. I couldn't help it. What a ship! What power! What beauty! "So here is what I propose," says Spencer. "*Tromenderon* will not be ready for some months. So go down into Kent and do whatever it is that you wish to do in ... *trade*." He made it sound like a vicar fumbling choir boys. "Do it for a while," says he, then give me your answer." I nodded. He nodded. "I await your decision," says he.

40

Chapter 6

(Letters translated from the Arabic)

March 15th 1801

To the most exalted Abdel Boutros,
  At the House of Abdel Boutros, By the Perfume Market of Muizz Street, Cairo.
It is with deep regret that I approach your worship with sorrowful news of our expedition into Zulu Land under the command of Mert Yasin the Turk.
  Thus, I have received testimony from three of the Sudanese head boys on the expedition who declare that the Turk and all his Bedouin are slain.
  May God's peace be upon them.
  I turn, therefore, to your worship's enquiries concerning the delay in the setting forth of the second expedition which we had planned in pursuit of Zulu maidens. In this, we must thank God for His warning that the Zulu are even more dangerous than we feared.
  I must therefore – with tearstained eyes and rent garments – advise your worship that if such a soldier as the Turk was overcome by the Zulu, then I am unable to set forth without one hundred Bedouin horsemen and five hundred Janissary foot soldiers, all supplied and armed at your worship's expense, together with two 12-pounder field pieces of French design, complete with trained gunners, and all horses, carriages, tackles and ammunition. Also, camels and drivers to carry one hundred girls. Also, supply wagons provided with all necessaries.

I must also point out that the slaughter of the Turk's expedition, rather than extinguishing the market for Zulu girls, has inflamed it like fat upon a fire, such that each girl is now sold for the price of a fine house with servants. And so, I must seek renegotiation of the price to be paid by your worship to myself, on safe delivery of each Zulu virgin.

Your loving and sincere Servant,
Mustapha El Malmuk the Slaver, The House of El Malmuk, By the Baths of Ibn Oban,
The Street of the Artisans, Cairo.

*

March 16th 1801

To Mustapha El Malmuk the Slaver, The House of El Malmuk, By the Baths of Ibn Oban,
The Street of the Artisans, Cairo.
Esteemed Mustapha El Malmuk, I believe that the heat of the day has touched your unfortunate brain, if you can imagine that my small purse will fund the huge army that you propose, not to mention foreign artillery.
As for renegotiation of the generous price already agreed between ourselves, I beg you to think again, and to utter prayers to God that he might guide your ways.
In concern for your health, your dear friend,
Abdel Boutros, Leader among Merchants of Cairo,
At the House of Abdel Boutros, By the Perfume Market of Muizz Street, Cairo.

*

March 17th 1801

To Abdel Boutros,
Beloved friend, I know that you do not act alone, but as the mouthpiece of many others including some who are very powerful. Thus money is plentiful and so:

Twenty times the original price.
One hundred Bedouin.
Five hundred Janissaries.
Two 12-pounders.
Camels and drivers for one hundred girls.
Or I do not step beyond the walls of Cairo.
Malmuk.

*

March 19th 1801

To Malmuk,
  May the fleas of a thousand camels infest your bed, but yes. And do not forget the jewel stones. They are of very little importance but do not forget them. Ask after them and seek their origin, not that it matters greatly. But do not forget to ask.
Abdel.

Chapter 7

I wrote a letter. I wrote a letter that any other officer in the Sea Service would have considered a nonsense. I – Jacob Fletcher – wrote personally to the First Lord of the Admiralty, agreeing to take command of *Tromenderon* and to take her on an independent cruise. The nonsense of this was that I did so with utmost reluctance! So just in case any of you youngsters don't understand how mad this was, then let me explain.

In the first place, even in wartime there were always far more Sea Service officers than there were ships to command. So all those officers without commands were not real officers at all, since in those days you held rank only when commissioned into a specific ship for a specific purpose. Thus, you were a lieutenant, a commander, a captain, a commodore or an admiral *only* when the Admiralty sent you a formal document – your commission – requesting and requiring in the King's name that you enter into His Majesty's Ship *Whatever*, to take command of her and God help those aboard who didn't obey your orders.

That's how it worked, and even then you weren't actually in command until you went aboard and had read out your document of commission before all hands and the ship's pig.

Until that moment, you were a lost soul on half pay, waiting for the summons of a commission. So, one of the sad sights of London was the crowd of would-be officers, all shabby and decayed, who forever hung about the Admiralty's offices as they begged for employment. They were so desperate that they'd take command of a ruptured fishing smack; they'd take an Amsterdam shit-barge; they'd take a raft. So what would they have thought of myself – having dithered for weeks – only grudgingly taking *Tromenderon*?

That's point one. Now for point two. Note well that the most beloved dream of any Sea Officer, and the reason why families – especially impoverished families – sent young gentlemen to sea ... was PRIZE. By prize I mean the wonderful custom, established by law, whereby any ship of the enemy captured by HMS *Whatever* could be taken into harbour, declared a lawful prize by the Court of Admiralty, and sold – together with her cargo – and the proceeds shared out among the crew of *Whatever* with very much of that going to the Captain. So think on that, my jolly boys. Think on that and the fabulous examples of the taking of Spanish treasure ships, or of French East Indiamen laden with silks, spices and all the wealth of the Orient.

But here's the nasty part, because *Whatever* could not take prizes if she were part of a fleet. In a fleet, all she'd get was the chance to face the enemy's shot, and if, by rare chance, *Whatever* did manage to take a prize, then the riches had to be shared out among the rest of the fleet, with most of it going to the Admiral.

Thus, all sea officers dreamed of an independent, roving commission that put his ship out of sight of anything else British, such that any ship they took was entirely theirs, and by George and by Jove, there were captains who'd become vastly wealthy by such commissions. Everyone in the Service knew all the famous lucky ones, such as Anson who took the Manilla galleon in '43, and wallowed in riches for the rest of his life. Therefore, and once again, I ask you: what would any captain think – who was doomed and damned into a plodding ship of the line – what would any captain think of Jacob Fletcher given the chance to take *Tromenderon* out on a roving commission, and *Tromenderon* as fast as a nimble frigate?

So damn it all, I wrote the letter, and in due course of weeks, my commission was sent to me at Hyde House. My sister shed tears, and my brother-in-law looked noble. Three of the children clung to me and said they'd come with me, and the youngest, Sophia, bawled her eyes out just like her mother. They weren't the only ones who shed tears. They were my family and I knew I'd miss them. But the very next day I went to Chatham in one of my brother-in-law's fine posting chaises. It was a thirty-mile journey with four changes of horses, which took five hours including stops, and the weather was cold but bright.

Chatham was a major sea base, heavily fortified with walls, ramparts and guns, and the smoke of its chimneys rising in a grey cloud. There were dry-docks, marine barracks, rope-works, block-machines, an arsenal, and a huge gun wharf capable of arming any ship that ever sailed, and with any kind of shot. We went in through the main gates where we were stopped by the marines and challenged by a sergeant, while his men stood with sloped muskets. So the driver bawled out my name.

"Captain, Sir Jacob Fletcher!" says he, "come to take command of His Majesty's ship *Tromenderon*!"

"Ooooh!" says the sergeant, and he saluted and the marines presented arms with a stamp and a snap.

"I'm Fletcher!" says I. "Sergeant, please be so good as to direct me to the Port Admiral's office."

"Yessir! Yessir! It be that way, Cap'n! It be round there past the rope-works and the victualling yard, and straight on. Union flag's flying over it, Cap'n sir, and Admiral's Pennant. You can't miss it, Cap'n sir!"

So in through the walls we went, with the sound of hoofs and wheels bouncing back off the masonry, and into a sea world where the masts and yards of big ships rose on every side; ships were being built, and others were being broken; the harbour was constantly busy with boat traffic; everything stank of seaweed, and everything that floats was working there. There were sheer-hulks for the lifting-in of masts, rakish cutters setting forth with despatches, long boats bearing ships' stores, and wherries taking the town whores out to the anchored ships.

I got down from the chaise outside the Port Admiral's office, where two old Spanish 48-pounders – massive pieces – stood outside the doors with more marines besides. Inside I found many servants, and Admiral Lord Penholme-Forbes behind a big desk on the first floor, with a sweeping view out over the harbour. He was one of those who didn't like me because they'd never forgiven me for sinking a ship by navigating beneath it in a submarine boat with a gunpowder mine towed astern. I did that in Boston Harbour in 1795 and if you youngsters want to know more, read earlier volumes of these memoirs. But for the present, take note that the likes of Penholme-Forbes thought submarine boats to be damned unfair, damned un-British and likely to cause the dastardly French to turn them on us.

"Ah!" says Penholme-Forbes with a scowl, as I was shown in. "Made your bloody mind up at last, have you, Fletcher?" He was very old and yellow in the face, and looked ill. He'd lost a leg in the Seven Years war, and by repute had undergone later operations when the stump turned septic and the surgeons had to trim it. So I forgave him his rudeness because the *trimming* was a very nasty business in those days before chloroform. "There's your bloody ship," says he, pointing with a walking stick, "so why don't you take a bloody look at her?" He had a couple of clerks or the like, who nodded approval of everything he said and stared at me over their spectacles. But I paid no attention because I was looking at *Tromenderon* anchored in the harbour, and clearly visible through his Lordship's window.

The model had been splendid, but the reality was awesome: such a combination of wonderful beauty and wonderful power, and now fully rigged and armed and showing every appearance of being ready for sea. Penholme-Forbes was blathering again and very rude. So I was concentrating on the sheer joy of looking at the ship. But a few of his phrases stuck:

"You'll have to bloody well get yourself a crew ... bloody well put up posters ... you've got just three hundred from your old ship ... another two hundred who like your name ... but you need seven hundred at least ... and if you want extra powder and shot you can bloody well pay for it ... Fletcher! Fletcher! You're bloody well not listening!"

Nor was I. I was only there out of courtesy. I had the King's Commission in my hand. I waved it at the old blighter, and he knew he could deny me nothing in the way of ship's stores and the recruiting of seamen. Mind you, I did have to pay for extra powder and shot, which was an annoyance. I always insisted on that aboard any ship I ever commanded, since the only way to secure victory at sea is by live firing practice, and that takes extra powder and shot. The damned arsenals always made me pay for it since it was 'extra to establishment'. But I had plenty of money by then so I paid up. I always bargained though, because it's in my nature to do so.

Soon I was out of the office and getting a boat to take myself and my kit out to *Tromenderon* and I was astounded to see a crowd gather at the dockside. There were marines, officers, a few women, and plenty of craftsmen from the various dockyard departments. And damn me if they didn't cheer. They were all smiles, and chaps thumping me on the back and yelling my name: my sea name.

"Jacky Flash! Jacky Flash! Jacky Flash!"

I almost blushed. I'd not expected that. It was the newspapers, you see. That and the knighthood. That and something else.

"Who's our lovely Flashy-boy then?" yells one of the women. "Who's the night-time runner?" That brought the most enormous cheer from every one of them and a great clapping of hands in approval and I soon discovered that all hands aboard *Tromenderon* knew the story, as did the entire service. Perhaps that was another reason why Penholme-Forbes didn't like me, because he was an evangelical angel-maker, known as 'Preaching Penny' behind his back, and he had a particular dislike of fornication.

Then we were pulling out from the quay, and making our way round the anchor cables and boat traffic. *Tromenderon* grew bigger and bigger, and the coxswain lifted up his voice in a great shout.

"*Tromenderon!*" says he, the word which told the ship that her captain was coming alongside. We came round to the stern quarter, lee side of the ship and her massive sides rose over us. Men were goggling through the gun-ports, and I could see mouths uttering the words 'Jacky Flash', and calling to their mates.

Then came the moment I most hate, aboard ship, which is to say climbing aboard ship and which – in the absence of a rigged stairway – has to be done via stumpy bars nailed to the ship's side, to form the ghost of a ladder. These are fine for nimble topmen, but not for me with my size and weight. I heaved myself up, puffing and blowing, hauling myself over the rail to the screech of boatswain's calls, and marines presenting arms and ship's officers running forward, taken all unawares and led by Mr Pyne, the First Lieutenant.

"Sir! Sir!" says he, "welcome aboard, sir! We didn't know you were coming, sir! Look at us; we're a disgrace! And no stairway rigged, and every man in working dress!" He was right. Even the marines weren't in red. They wore canvas work-slops and forage caps, while some of the officers were in undress, and others were togged out like seamen. It seemed that all hands were coming up from below. There was more cheering, and there seemed to be hordes of ship's boys. But the ship herself was very much not a disgrace. It was all white decks, polished brass, coiled lines, and guns secured for sea. Well done, Mr Pyne. I'd not expected less. But now there were several pieces of theatre to be performed.

First I made sure that all hands were present and read aloud my commission to command the ship. That made me legally the master of every thing and person aboard. My word was now law and I could promote or dis-rate, reward or punish. I could stop grog, clap men in irons or flog them: not that I ever did. I have always disdained such brutal punishments preferring simply to knock down any man who gives offence, and to do so on the instant that he gives it. This is a kindly and gentle way with the ship's people and it has never failed me. Furthermore, I have it on good authority that those who served under me would even boast that this was how Jacky Flash kept discipline.

Having read the commission, I gave all hands the usual speech, which was formulaic, but the hands expect it and would not have been happy without it.

"Men!" says I. "It is my intention to take this ship to sea and inflict the utmost violence on the King-God-bless-him's enemies, and most especially upon the French!"

"Huzzah!" says they, very properly.

"It is further my intention to take prizes ..."

"HUZZAH!"

"And so," says I ... and so on, and so on. In fact it was a regurgitation of the first such speech I'd ever heard, as given aboard my first ship *Phiandra* by my first Captain, Sir Harry Bollington when he took command. But it was a damn fine speech and I've used it ever since, because even bloody Shake Spear couldn't do better.

[Another deliberate misspelling, at Fletcher's insistence. S.P]

Then, when I was done and the cheers had faded, I spoke to Pyne.

"Mr Pyne," says I, even as my things were hoist aboard. "I am glad to see all hands in working dress! So, have you got your stopwatch?"

"Ah," says he, and he smiled. "I'll send for it instantly." He looked at one of the ship's boys who ran off like lightning. "Might I presume, Sir Jacob," says he, "that you will follow your accustomed usages, on coming aboard?"

"I shall, Mr Pyne," says I, "in your own time and at best speed."

"Aye aye!" says Pyne, and credit to them, two marine drummer boys were already running for their drums and sticks, and as soon as Pyne's watch was brought up, they beat a rumbling, rolling drum call. They beat the rhythm and growl of *Heart of Oak* which, aboard any ship of mine, was the signal for all hands to go to 'general quarters'. It was a drum call never sounded for any other reason because it was the order to clear the decks, run out the guns and load for action. It was a powerful sound stirring powerful memories. It was a sound that stood up the hairs on the back of men's necks, because it was a tolling bell that said some of us were going to die.

It was also a sound which meant fearful labour for the ship's people and a labour performed by the clock, since if the enemy were bearing down, then whichever ship was ready to fire first would probably win the fight. It meant clearing away every obstruction to the working of the guns: thus collapsible bulkheads were struck down and run below, thereby removing all divisions between cabins and compartments to leave the gun decks open from end to end. Likewise, all furniture, crocks, clocks, books, boots, flutes, fiddles and candlesticks were run below and stowed in the holds – and, by George, I do mean *run!*

It meant that the surgeon and his mates must prepare for operations deep down below, out of reach of shot. There, they spread sailcloth on sea-trunks for an operating table; lit all the lights they could find; put on leather aprons; laid out lint, bandages, sponges, and buckets of water – *empty* buckets for 'wings and limbs' my jolly boys – and they lined up all the glittering tools of their trade.

It meant the Gunner giving keys to the Yeoman of the Powder room and his mates to unlock the powder magazines, of which there were three: main, fore, and aft. There, the cartridges were prepared for the guns, and water-soaked blankets hung at the magazine entrances, for the avoidance of sparks reaching the ship's fifty tons of gunpowder and annihilating every man of us in a vast explosion.

It meant the marine sharpshooters getting up into the fighting tops ready to pick off the enemy's officers, should the enemy come alongside, and also to stop the enemy's sharpshooters from killing my own officers: including myself! So God bless the marines and give them steady hands and sure eyes.

It meant the ship's boys spreading handfuls of sand out of buckets, all round the guns for sure footing, and it meant the gun crews casting off the sea-going lashings that kept the ninety, 32-pounders secure when the ship pitched and rolled. Then, united in strength and drill, they must haul the guns inboard so that rammers could be heaved down the bores, even as the gun-captains stowed away the sheet-lead, put waterproof covers over the flintlock triggers and over the touch-holes, checking that the flints gave a good spark when the firing lanyards were pulled.

As well as this, the 68-pounder carronades on the quarterdeck were cleared for action. There were ten of these on their advanced swivel-carriages firing massive shot that took two men to feed into the gun-mouths. Each of the complex pieces had a different drill of its own, being a different breed entirely than ordinary ship's guns, and intended for short-range work and hitting power.

So that's what the ship's people did, and the only thing they did not do – could not do – in harbour was load cartridge and shot. But they knew their duties, because most of them were old shipmates from *Euphonides*. So I was pleased to see that, among all the complex heaving and straining and rush, there was no confusion and nobody tripped or got in anyone else's way.

But it was slow: dangerously slow.

"Nine minutes and forty-five seconds, sir!" said Pyne, when all was done and the men stood gasping and sweating by the guns.

"And so, Mr Pyne?" says I.

"It'll have to be quicker next time, sir," says he, and I was pleased that he made no excuses about being short-handed, or being aboard a new ship, because there are no excuses at sea: only success or failure, survival or death.

"Quicker indeed," says I, "and now, Mr Pyne, secure the guns, rig ship for harbour duties, and muster the entire ship's company assembled on the main deck where we have another matter to settle."

"Oh?" says he, having served with me before. "Would it be the usual matter, Sir Jacob? Such as you always resolve when first you join a new ship?"

"It would indeed, Mr Pyne," says I, "and I rely on your good judgement to find a suitable man for the purpose."

"Oh yes, Sir Jacob," says he, "we have been expecting you for some while. The men have been most competitive in this respect and are now waiting in expectation."

"Good!" says I. "Then I'll go below." I looked at my watch, which was new and not to be compared with the one I'd lost, but it told the time. "Give me ten minutes."

"Aye aye, sir!" says he. So I went below to prepare for the final piece of theatre.

Chapter 8

"A ship of war cannot be got into fighting condition in harbour. There must be drills at sea."

(Translation from the journal of Enseigne Antoine Leclerk, aboard *Triomphe du Peuple*, April 1st 1801)

Contre-Admiral Barzan snapped his fingers for joy. He laughed and darted round the quarterdeck, poking his officers in the ribs, knocking off their hats, and twisting their noses.

"*Mes enfants! Mes braves!*" he cried, and they called his name with joy and with admiration, from full hearts. They called his name and so did a red-haired man who was not properly one of the crew.

"Barzan! Barzan! Barzan!" they cried, because there was nobody like Papa Barzan in any navy of the world, including that of the English Rosbifs, and they loved Papa Barzan. Every man in the squadron loved him. They loved him even though he'd served in the Bourbon Navy before the enlightenment of the Revolution. He'd served in those days, because what else could he have done – Barzan who went to sea as a little boy, running away from his father's farm to do it? Who else could he have served in those times? They loved him and they loved the republican Navy that had raised Papa Barzan from the lower deck to high eminence. They loved his faith in the Revolution and his deep love of France.

More than that, there was nothing seamanly that any man of the squadron could do that Papa Barzan couldn't do better, whether it be bending a sail, splicing a rope or training a gun. He was a splendid seaman. He fought like a devil and, above all, he possessed the gift to inspire men to follow where he led. He had the gift of inspiration and the luck of a winner too, being one of the very few officers of the modern French Navy who'd beaten a Rosbif ship by gunnery and manoeuvre. And he'd done it off the American coast where the squadron was heading.

So what did any man of the squadron care for Barzan's flaws? What did the educated navigators care? What did the gunners of the Corps D'Artillerie care? Who cared that Barzan could not work a sextant, or calculate a ship's position? Who cared that he could barely read and write, that he got drunk, and did not bathe or wash? They only cared that he was no longer young and could not go aloft any more, and that they might lose him to old age.

Quickly, Barzan was down the companionway and onto the lower deck, into the smoke of the broadside the ship's people had just delivered. Down there, he ran to each gun in turn as the gun crews swabbed and rammed and ran out. He went to each gun and greeted every man by name.

"Henri! Marcel! Robert!" The men cheered and cheered, and once – by chance – Barzan passed the red-haired man in his plain civilian clothes. The red-haired man was looking at everything. He raised his hat politely to Barzan. It was a round hat, once fashionable but now shabby. In fact the whole man was slightly shabby. He was a man that nobody noticed: undersized, pale, and with front teeth that crossed one upon the other. He had no charisma of bearing whatsoever and yet he had the confidence to look Barzan straight in the eye. He raised the round hat and smiled.

"Monsieur Donovan!" said Barzan, in reply. But he did not smile. Instead he turned to his crew and waved his hands, palm down, for silence.

"And now, reload and fire again!" cried Barzan. "And?" He paused and grinned, awaiting their response.

"It's got to be quicker!" they roared. He said that every time, and they usually gave it to him every time. He'd had them at the guns every day since they broke free of the Rosbifs. He worked them like slaves, and nobody complained because he worked himself like a slave. He barely slept and was everywhere about the ship. He knew everything about everyone. So there was no need for punishment aboard any ship under Papa Barzan's command because all hands did their best for him, and would be ashamed to do less.

Of course, although there was no flogging in the French service – thanks to the Revolution – any seaman who *was* caught slacking and not doing his best for Papa would find himself beaten up at night by his own shipmates.

So the gunners gave another broadside. Barzan ran up to the quarterdeck and climbed up into the mizzen shrouds. Everyone gasped as he did so, for fear that his grip might fail. They tried to convince themselves that he was still as agile as ever he'd been, which of course he was not, his poor old hands tormented by arthritis. But he did not fall. Up he went because he needed a clear look over the side, and that was obscured by the rows of rolled-up hammocks stacked like a line of giant, white sausages in the racks over the quarterdeck rail. From that position, he took a good long look over the grey Atlantic. And grey it was, and heaving at this time of year when sensible men did not venture out upon it.

But good! *Bataille du Peuple* was a cable's length astern of Barzan's ship, *Triomphe du Peuple*, while *Ascendent du Peuple* was a cable's length behind *Triomphe*. Barzan hung on as his ship rolled under him, pitching on the massive waves. Especially she rolled because that was her only flaw. Then ... Ah! *Bataille* fired: successive spouts of fire from the guns, successive clouds of white, and then, seconds later ... Thud! Thud! Thud! As the sound of the guns came along behind. Barzan stared and stared, counting slowly in his mind, until there came another series of gun flashes and clouds of smoke and thud! Thud! Thud! He nodded. That wasn't bad. *Bataille* was getting quicker. Then *Ascendent* fired, in accordance with Barzan's drill, whereby each of the other two gave two broadsides in turn, so that he, Barzan, could judge their speed of fire.

Bah! *Ascendent* was slow. And this was her first fire, with cold guns. "Shit!" said Barzan, and shook his head, because it was Barzan's fixed belief – and Barzan was a tremendous gunner – that it was the first few broadsides that did the job in a ship-to-ship encounter. The first few broadsides, when every gun is carefully loaded, and nobody is yet wounded, nor guns dismounted by the enemy's fire. Barzan cursed a bit more and resolved to signal the squadron to heave to, so that *Triomphe* could lower a boat to take him to *Ascendent* to speak to the ship's gun crews himself. He got himself back on deck, waving aside the many hands reaching up to help, and he gathered his officers around him.

They stood in a semi-circle with hats in hand, and faced Barzan who stood on the windward side of the canted deck. The quarterdeck guns surrounded them; the ship's masts reared overhead; the sails bulged; the rigging whistled with wind; and the vast ocean heaved and wallowed, and threw salt spray over them. But they all stood firm, bracing themselves against the ship's roll without even noticing. They'd already been at sea long enough for that, and Barzan saw it and was pleased. Even Callum Donovan, the red-headed man, stood firm. So what did it matter that *Triomphe* rolled somewhat? Her crew would live with that. But then Barzan spoke.

"My lads!" he cried.

"Papa Barzan!" they said.

"These ships are special!" he said, and waved a hand to include all three: *Triomphe, Bataille* and *Ascendent*.

"Special!" they said.

"They're the *du Peuple* class line-of-battleships!" he cried. "They're not 74s, but 80-gun ships! And our main deck guns are 36 pounders! And while other French ships have been special, ours are the latest! The latest as planned by the Ecole Maritime Nationale de Paris. So they're not only more powerful than anything less than a 100 gun first rate, but faster. They've got the speed of a frigate and the force of God's hammer!" They cheered and cheered at that. "But take care, my boys, because it's the men that count, not the ships."

"The men! The men!" they said, because they'd heard all this before. They all knew Papa Barzan's views on this matter. But they listened, enwrapped, as he told them again. He could do that, could Papa Barzan; he could hold an audience in his hand. Which he did as he went on:

"That's why the God-damn Rosbifs – with worse ships than ours – keep God-damn beating us," he cried. "Because their seamanship and gunnery are better, and they're better because they practise at sea! So every man among us will do the same, all the way to America: practise, practise, practise!"

When he was done, everyone cheered and everyone was sent back to his duties, and Barzan stood alone. Donovan joined him, smiled a smile and spoke to Barzan in excellent French.

"You've done a fine job with the ship's guns, Captain. You work very hard."

"Of course," said Barzan. He didn't smile but was careful to be polite. He was polite because a man had to be careful with Donovan because Donovan was political: powerfully political. He was an Irish Fenian: a dedicated revolutionary against the British, and God bless him for that by Barzan's reckoning. But Donavan drank too much and had an unsavoury reputation concerning women. It was even rumoured that charges of rape had been supressed on Bonaparte's orders because he thought Donovan useful. Whether or not that was true, Barzan knew as fact that Donovan had come aboard with sealed orders from the Ministre de la Marine. Barzan knew that because his superiors had told him, and told him that he must obey whatever was in those orders. So Papa Barzan did not like Donovan: he didn't like him one little bit. But Barzan was careful to be polite.

"Thank you, Monsieur," he said. "You are too kind. I work hard at the guns and I make everyone else work hard because that way we shall win when we meet the English."

Chapter 9

If I'm a monster, I can't help it. That's the way I'm made. It's in the blood like my knack of making money and striking a deal. So I should not have been proud of myself when I came up on to the quarterdeck wearing only woollen britches, and a pair of dancer's pumps. But I *was* proud, because I've had sculptors come up and ask me to model Hercules, and I've got muscles where other men don't even have imagination. So every soul aboard *Tromenderon* roared out a cheer as they saw me. Men were in the rigging. They were climbed on the guns, and they were jammed in close on every side: hundreds and hundreds of them, down on the main deck where Mr Pyne had organised a proper ring, with ropes and posts, and stools in the corners.

You see, it was known throughout the Service that whenever Jacky Flash took command of a ship, he always picked out the chief masher of the lower deck, to batter him for the good of ship's discipline and for the education of the young gentlemen, bless their hearts. So there I was, with my officers in blue or scarlet behind me, the marines paraded grinning with muskets and bayonets, and the Boatswain ducking into the ring, hauling with him a man who made me frown. He was half my weight, and he was scrawny, darting about and pretty-faced. That amazed me. He had a face like a girl! But then I saw how he moved: springing and bouncing, and sparring with the air, and I saw that he was a skilled boxer. The pretty face was a badge of skill because nobody had managed to land a blow on it.

"Ah," says I to myself, "this might be interesting." Then the Boatswain was bellowing.

"Captain, Sir Jacob!" says he.

"Jacky Flash!" says the crew in a roar of voices. "Jacky Flash! Jacky Flash!" I scowled at such impertinence, but I grinned on the inside.

"Captain, gentlemen, and all hands aboard of us!" cries the Boatswain, clapping a hand on the pretty-face's shoulder. "This here is Mr Toby Carling: Toby Carling, the Hoxton Chippy, 'cos he was bred up as a carpenter, but found his way in pugilism!" The crew cheered him enormously. The Boatswain waved them silent. They chuckled and muttered and smiled. "Mr Toby Carling is come aboard – come aboard voluntarily – to serve under Captain Fletcher."

"Jacky Flash!" cries the crew.

"He's come aboard to serve under Captain Fletcher," says the Boatswain, "but he begs the chance ... *to knock down Captain Fletcher!*" At this, they must have heard the cheers in Hoxton, and afterwards I didn't hear much more of what the Boatswain said because on these occasions you don't. You're inside your own head and hardly hear the yelling of the crowd.

I just got myself down into the ring, and the Boatswain shouted a bit more. Then, there I was facing the Hoxton Chippy as he took up a boxing stance, raised fists and darted towards me. So I swung a blow to get the matter done with. But then ... where was he? He was gone as if invisible and my punch went into empty air. Then smack-bang-smack, he caught me in the ribs and it hurt, and he was gone again. It was bare fists in those days, my lads, so it really hurt. By Jove but he was fast. He was a little devil. I never met a man with reactions like him, and smack-bang-smack! He did it again: left-right-left!

He was an absolute marvel. He didn't punch anywhere near as hard as me because that would be comparing a 68-pounder to a 9-pounder. But he didn't need it. His method when fighting me was to keep out of harm's way with his dancing, prancing speed and just wear me down over time. The infuriating thing was that in a real fight, in a boarding action, Mr Chippy's method couldn't work, because there's never the space to jump out of the way, and you just go at it hammer and tongs. His method could only work in a boxing ring, but unfortunately that is precisely where we were and in front of the entire crew of *Tromenderon*.

Smack-bang-smack! The little tinker! He did it again and again, and I never landed a blow. Smack-bang-smack! Then the ship's bell sounded. The Boatswain was timing rounds with a sand glass and the Hoxton Chippy was sitting in his corner, grinning at me. So I sat down in mine with Mr Pyne offering me a mouthful of water from a bottle.

"Why don't you hit him, sir?" says he. "Hit the little tyke!" But I just shook my head. That wouldn't serve in this case: not yet. I could see that because, as I have tried to tell the world for most of my life, I'm not just a hulking bruiser but a thinker besides. So when the bell rang, up we got again, and it was more of the same. I swung a few, just in case he got too close, but he didn't. He just went smack-bang-smack over and over again, and if anything he got cocky and bounced around rather more than he should have, just for show, and the ship's people loved it.

"Hoxton Chippy!" they roared. "Hoxton Chippy!"

So he did well. He did very well indeed, facing myself in a boxing ring. But it could only end one way considering the size of me and the size of him. He shouldn't have shown off the way he did, because after some rounds, with me conserving strength and him bouncing like a robin on springs, he got a bit tired. Now, I'm not taking away his credit, not one bit, because in all my life no man ever stood up in front of me for as long as he did, and that includes professional boxers. But after a dozen rounds, he bounced a lot less, and though I missed several swings, I caught him at last. It took only one, which I gave him in the bread basket with nowhere near full strength, and I never even aimed at the pretty face since it would have been a shame to spoil it.

Finally, I heaved him to his feet, gasping and groaning, and faced the ship's people.

"Three cheers for the Hoxton Chippy!" says I. "For he's a true British bulldog and a true British tar!" They cheered, and you youngsters should note the manner of my speech, which reflected the mind of the lower deck regarding compliments, just as my next words reflected that mind concerning rewards. "Double grog for the Hoxton Chippy and his messmates!" says I and they cheered even louder. So that ended well, except for the fact that my ribs were soon black with bruises, such that the surgeon had to wrap me in vinegar and brown paper. I ached for weeks. I smelt of vinegar too.

After these pieces of theatre, it was down to the hard and tedious work of getting *Tromenderon* fully ready for sea. So, in order that you might understand how great a job that was, and what diversity of stores and tackle must be taken aboard, I must remind you that even short-handed, a 90-gun ship was a village afloat, containing an amazing diversity of talent. As well as hundreds of seamen, we had every trade aboard from cobbler to tailor and from surgeon to carpenter. I won't bore you with a full list, but to give you some idea, *Tromenderon's* people included:

Eight Sea Service Lieutenants,
One Captain of marines and three subalterns,
The Sailing Master who was senior navigator,
The Chaplain, Surgeon, Purser, and Schoolmaster.

All the above being gentlemen who messed in the wardroom. Then there were:

The Boatswain, Carpenter and Gunner: who were long-service veterans,
The Cook, who very much did not cook, but supervised those who did,
Dozens of skilled men: Sailmaker, Caulker, Cooper, Rope-maker, Armourer etc.
Twenty-five Midshipmen, plus a greater number of ship's boys,
A sergeant of marines, two corporals and ninety men.

And every one of these – apart from the marines – had come aboard freely: *voluntarily* as the Boatswain had said. Even the ship's boys came from charities ashore who swept up street urchins, scrubbed them clean, and sent them to sea for a better life than going down the mines or up the chimneys. So all were willing and in the case of the trade specialists and officers – though not the able seamen – the getting of them was not just easy, but an embarrassment of riches.

Thus, the first thing waiting for me when I went down to the great cabin, was my Chaplain, Dr Goodsby, with an arm full of letters from persons begging berths aboard for themselves or others. You wouldn't believe the number and variety of them, because the captain of so big a ship usually went aboard with a whole retinue such as I'd not bothered to accumulate, having thought that I was done with the Service. So the begging letters came in shoals. There were persons wanting – variously – to be captain's servant, his cook, his laundryman, his barber, his physician, or one of his cluster of young gentlemen volunteers. Also numerous musicians applied, wanting to be in my band of music, which indeed I wanted too, having seen the benefits of music aboard *Euphonides*. Neither was it just letters because an amazing number of persons later accosted me during my visits ashore on business, and some were quite blunt:

"Captain, Sir Jacob?" says a prosperous-looking gent with a fat wife on his arm as I was going into the Chatham branch of Child's Bank. He raised his hat and they stood in my way, forcing me to stop. I wasn't pleased because he wasn't the first to do this.

"Yes?" says I to him and, "Ma'am," to the lady, while folk walked past and traffic rumbled over the cobbles.

"I'll be short, Sir Jacob, and not waste time," says the gent. "There's my eldest boy, Ralph, recently made lieutenant and shamefully unemployed, and myself ready with a substantial sum for the Captain who takes my boy into his ship. May I count on you, sir?"

"No, sir, you may not!" says I, "and good day to you!"

[Note that what affronted Fletcher was the public nature of this attempt at bribery. After dinner and wine, he would joke about the hard bargains he struck following other, discreet approaches. S.P.]

The gent was wasting his time anyway, because better opportunities of finance were now presenting. That's why I was going to see Child's Bank because, when a King's ship was sent across the ocean, a captain might – for suitable payment – oblige a banker by giving safe passage to 'specie' as it was called: that's gold and silver coin. They did so because banks occasionally had to shift it overseas and what safer way could there be than aboard a warship? I never did find out if this was entirely legal, and sometimes it's best not to ask a question for fear of getting the wrong answer.

So a great sum in gold eventually went down into the hold of my ship, outbound for Cantor and Fine's Bank in Boston, with a percentage becoming mine – or rather credited to my account with Child's. In addition, I took aboard as private cargo, a careful selection of precision instruments which might just be worth more than gold. Ramsden theodolites, Maudsley screw-cutting lathes, and some Boulton & Watt engineers' flats: these were the ultimate in technical perfection and likely to be attractive to the machinists of America who were working hard to catch up – and overtake – their European equivalents.

[Carriage of private cargo aboard HM ships was outright illegal as Fletcher well knew. But HM Government recognised the need for international banking to function efficiently and therefore turned a blind eye to the carriage of specie. S.P.]

But I digress. We were dealing with the ship's people aboard *Tromenderon* and how few of them I'd got on the lower deck. Because once all the volunteers had come aboard, including some two thirds of the crew of my last ship *Euphonides,* I was still far short of the seven hundred at least which I would need to put to sea and man the guns. For that, I needed hundreds more: hundreds of strong arms for hauling on lines, and quick feet for going aloft. I needed that, and something else besides. I needed able seamen who – totally unlike a soldier – may have to make instant decisions on their own judgement. Thus, a seaman may be a hundred feet up the main mast in a vicious gale when a spar is carried away. Or he may be in the dark of the magazine when fire threatens. In either of these cases, he can see what his officers cannot, and must act accordingly, even if it is contrary to orders.

Consequently, on that first day aboard *Tromenderon* I had to deal at once with the matter of recruitment. That is, once I'd greeted my officers – commission and warrant – and once I'd gone round the ship to see what crew we did have, and for the joy of looking her over, relishing the delight of her splendid fittings.

Thus, I cannot help but digress still further to remark on one example, which was the astounding size of the cast-iron Brodie stove in the galley which cooked food for all hands. By Jove, I'd seen actual cottages that were smaller! And there it sat on its floor of bricks, four-square, black-leaded and burnished, with red heat glowing from two coal fires and all its tools hanging ready for use. What a marvel! It was enormous. The ship's main bower anchor was supposed to be the biggest piece of iron aboard, but that stove ran it a close second.

But enough. What of manning the ship with sufficient numbers of men? This was my great and immediate problem, but fortunately I was ably assisted in this by Mr Pyne, my Number One, and Dr Goodsby, my Chaplain. Pyne was a straightforward Sea Officer, and totally incapable of failing his duty because he was totally reliable, totally diligent and totally dull. Goodsby, on the other hand, was a prize oddity for a Chaplain and I'll explain how odd by quoting a conversation I'd had with him last time we were at sea.

"Why don't you preach to the men on Sundays," says I. "You never make up a sermon of your own. You just read bits from the Book of Common Prayer."

"That is because I have not quite the conviction to preach, sir," says he, embarrassed.

"What does that mean?" says I.

"Well, sir," says he, "consider the immaculate conception, transubstantiation and the Holy Trinity."

"Yes?" says I.

"Well, sir, while they may be noble concepts, who can believe them as fact?"

The astounding truth was that our Chaplain was an atheist, who was only in the church because he was third son of a family where the first son got the Army, the second got the Law, and the third got rammed into the Church. Mind you, with his warrant as ship's chaplain, Goodsby never complained because a chaplain was exceedingly well paid. Aboard *Tromenderon*, he was the second highest paid, coming equal to the First Lieutenant, and after only myself! That's the Navy for you, and don't ask your Uncle Jacob why, because I didn't set the rules. But never mind because Goodsby thoroughly deserved his wages: his real duties were not religious but financial, as my secretary, chief clerk, and manager of all things business-like and he was damn good at it.

So, on that first day aboard, when we got down to the discussion of recruitment, Pyne, Goodsby and I went down to my day cabin at the stern on the main deck. We found it ready rigged out and furnished as the ship's meeting room – courtesy of the First Lord in his gratitude as I later discovered. We sat at the big, shiny table with a decanter and glasses, and plenty of neat stacks of papers brought in by Dr Goodsby. Pyne looked depressed because he hated paperwork, but I smiled because I did not. There's nothing I love more than a book of accounts.

Then Goodsby surprised me.

"With your permission, Captain," says he, "may we first discuss this?"

"Ah!" says Pyne, cheering up, because Goodsby unrolled a large poster, fresh printed, and flattened it out with paperweights. He looked at me and explained.

"Mr Pyne and I took the liberty of having this trial copy run off for your approval," says he.

"That we did," says Pyne." I looked at it. It was three feet high by two feet wide; it was strikingly bold, and I represent it here:

Jolly Tars of Old England
Who among you would save Britannia's women from rape?
Who would DAMN the French and BLESS King George?
Who would wish *to become RICH?*
All such as these
Should instantly repair unto CHATHAM DOCKS
Where lies, fitting out for an
INDEPENDENT CRUISE
And resolved to take prizes
TROMENDERON of 90 guns, under Captain
———— *JACKY FLASH* ————
This lucky and magnificent ship still has a few berths vacant for
PRIME SEAMEN!
But *hurry* and *be warned* that
only those capable of carrying a *hundredweight* of Spanish Dollars
---for a whole mile---
should apply.
GOD SAVE THE KING!
Wilson Kepple and Betty, Printers. 116 Wilmot St, Chatham

"Ahem," says Goodsby, "I trust, Sir Jacob, that you will excuse the familiarity of using the name whereby you are universally known on the lower deck? And not just on this ship but throughout the fleet?"

"Hmmm," says I taking a good look, because I'd seen the like before, and what a load of Cod's wallop they always were. "A hundredweight of Spanish dollars?" says I. "Do seamen really fall for this bladder wash?"

"Oh yes, sir," says Goodsby. "It never fails!"

"There's always a few come in," says Pyne, "if we post these up around the sea towns."

"A few?" says I. "How many?" Pyne looked at Goodsby.

"Twenty? Thirty?" says Pyne.

"More!" says Goodsby. "Everyone knows that Jacky Flash ... beg pardon,

Captain ... that *you* came back from Japan with a ship laden with riches and all hands got their shares."

"So?" says I.

"So I would estimate fifty," says Goodsby.

"And what about the rest?" says I.

"Press gang, Captain," says Pyne, with apology in his tone. He and Goodsby exchanged glances, well-knowing my history. They sat quiet for a while as they thought about that, and so did I: me, Jacob Fletcher, who was press-ganged and forever denied my true vocation. Was I going to do the same to others?

Chapter 10

The Cave of the Widow's Mouth,
North Zulu Land,
In the summer of the 12th Year of the reign of
King Ndaba KunJama,
(1801)

"The magic was the magic of women. The first of the chosen ones was the lovely Ulwazi."

(From the Saga of Inyathi)

M'thunzi, the witch woman, was very ugly and very old. She was bent, and crooked, and wore ragged animal skins. A row of shrivelled, twisted things hung from the belt round her waist, and she stank with a foetid and stinking smell. She was a terrifying and powerful woman. Even the men were afraid of her. Even the King listened to her with respect.

She was attended by a dozen old women as ugly as herself who were chosen for their madness after been disowned by their families. They wore scraps and tatters; some were bald; some had ugly diseases; all were thin, and all carried sticks and rocks that they beat together in rhythm, chanting the name of M'thunzi, or muttering and bickering among themselves. They stank even worse than she did.

M'thunzi and her attendants stood outside the cave mouths in the mountainside: the mouths resembled M'thunzi's own, being toothless, wrinkled and gaping. M'thunzi looked around and saw that everything was good in this faraway place by the river, days from the nearest kraal. She looked at the folk she had led here, bringing food, water and cattle for the journey. She remembered the many times she had done this before, over many years. She relished the memories. She cherished them.

Then she shuffled away from the cave mouths. She shuffled in time to the clicking beat of her followers. She shuffled as if dancing, going forward in the bright sunlight to approach a line of the King's White-Shield guards, and even these elite men shuddered as she approached, and the plumes of their headdresses trembled. The White Shields were there to stand between the caves and fifteen sons of powerful families who had recently become high-ranked married men, but every one of them was pleased that the line of shields kept them from the direct sight of M'thunzi, the Witch.

One of the fifteen husbands stood alone. He was the General, Prince Inyathi, the Buffalo. He stood alone except for one servant who held a fan of ostrich feathers to shield him from the sun, plus another to wield a fly-whisk, and another with a gourd of beer in case the Prince should become thirsty. But even Prince Inyathi was kept away from the caves as if he was an ordinary man, and not tall, splendid and handsome, and enormously admired. He was kept from the caves by the White Shields and he, too, had no wish to catch the eye of M'thunzi.

But M'thunzi merely sneered at the men. She sneered at the White-Shield guardsmen and the married men. She even sneered at Prince Inyathi, because this was women's day. She danced close enough to the White Shields to frighten them, then spun round and headed for the women. As she did so, her followers began to chant an ancient song, established by custom for this ceremony.

M'thunzi approached the women. There were fifteen of them too. They were the girls – now married women – rescued from the Arabs. All were beauties, and one was to be honoured by M'thunzi. The girls stood in a line with their mothers behind them in support. Of course, these were not blood-mothers, since all the blood-mothers had been murdered by the Arabs. But each girl had been adopted by good families, and each adopting mother was a head wife of great honour and reputation. They were women of substance, well-dressed in formal regalia. As M'thunzi approached, each mother threw arms around her adopted daughter to comfort her terror of the most famous witch in the Kingdom, who could kill with a curse. M'thunzi could kill by sniffing out a woman as possessed by demons, and once sniffed out, the possessed woman could not be fed, sheltered, or even offered water, but must go into the bush to die alone.

M'thunzi danced up and down the line of women, stopping now and again to sniff, and each girl and mother shuddered with horror as she passed. But there was no smell of demons. Not this time, and instead, M'thunzi stopped in front of the girl she judged the most beautiful.

"What is your name, O married woman who has not yet lain with a husband?" The girl tried to turn her face away, but M'thunzi frowned and the adopted mother turned the girl's face towards the witch. She did so because she had to, just as the same thing had been done to herself by her own mother. "Your name?" said M'thunzi.

"Ulwazi," said the girl, "Ulwazi, daughter of Zenzeli, now wife of the General, Prince Inyathi, the Buffalo."

"Come!" said M'thunzi, and gripped the girl's hand with force as she turned and shuffled off in time to the beaten music, heading towards the cave mouth. Ulwazi let out a howl of fear and reached her free arm towards her adopted mother, but the mother folded her arms and shook her head, with tears in her eyes. It was tradition.

All the men sighed at the sight of so lovely a girl in the hands of such ugliness. They measured the grace of Ulwazi's body and the poetry of her movements, against the hideous age of the witch. They watched as M'thunzi led the girl to one of the cave mouths, where M'thunzi was given a flaming torch by one of her attendants, and turned to go into the cave. The men sighed with deep emotions, but they too knew that this was tradition. They watched in silence except for Prince Inyathi, who knew – as everyone knew – that some of the girls M'thunzi took into the cave were never seen again. He raised his voice in a great shout.

"Ulwazi!" he cried, "be brave and show no fear. Show no fear because I cry death upon any thing that harms you, be it beast, man … or even woman!"

All present gasped at this colossal affront to tradition, and M'thunzi glared at Prince Inyathi with the venom of a black mamba. But Inyathi wielded men's magic: the magic of a thousand spears, and for the moment he was too powerful. M'thunzi cleared her throat, spat with vigour, and dragged Ulwazi into the cave.

Inside, with the echoes, the flickering light and the moving shadows, M'thunzi moved fast. The cave branched into many directions of tunnels and more tunnels. Ulwazi soon lost track of where they were but she was intelligent enough to notice two things: some of the tunnels bore markings cut into the rock.

Then M'thunzi stopped. Bent as she was, she had to look up to face Ulwazi, and she was even more ugly in torchlight than daylight.

"Did you bring the leather pouch?" she said.

"Yes, O M'thunzi, the Witch," said Ulwazi. "Here it is. We were all told to bring one."

"Good," said M'thunzi. "Now stay here. It will be dark for a while, but I will return, and there is nothing to fear in darkness." She paused. "Nothing except the many traps and pitfalls of this place." She smiled. "Because in this place there are things which will bring down the roof if you touch them by mistake." She let Ulwazi contemplate this truth and then continued. "And worse," she said, "there are demons, and the spirits of the dead. So do not cry out in fear, and do not tremble, because that will bring them down upon you, especially the spirits of the dead."

Then she was gone, taking the light with her, and Ulwazi was left in such intensity of darkness that she found it hard to stay upright, but had to sit on the rock floor, hugging her knees, and thinking of demons and spirits. She kept silent and tried hard not to tremble, especially as the cave was not silent. There was a constant creaking and groaning as if the rock was uneasy with itself. Ulwazi began to dread the things which must not be touched for fear of bringing down the roof. At least that stopped her worrying about the undead.

Then the light came back. M'thunzi returned, moving fast and sure, and holding the torch.

"Here!" she said. "Open the pouch!" As Ulwazi opened it, M'thunzi dropped a great jewel into the pouch. Then she stopped and looked at Ulwazi with as near to a smile as her face could contort. It was not a pretty smile.

"Well done," she said. "Well done O Ulwazi, daughter of Zenzeli, wife of Prince Inyathi the Buffalo. Usually the girls scream so hard that even the rocks are afraid. Some go mad and run away and die." She smiled. "Their bones are all around us. I know them all. She reached out and shook Ulwazi's arm. "Fasten the pouch!" she said. "Hold it tight!"

"Yes, O M'thunzi, the Witch," said Ulwazi, and now M'thunzi took hold of Ulwazi's chin. She grunted at the smoothness and perfection of Ulwazi's face. "I was like you once," she said. "Men wanted me. They fought over me. I had the power of great beauty, and you have it now. That is why Prince Inyathi chose you of all the fifteen." M'thunzi squeezed Ulwazi's chin hard. "I shall need a successor one day, and you are very lovely and very brave. I have plans for you, and later I shall explain them. But as a beginning, I will share with you a sacred sign." She raised the torch, let go of Ulwazi and waved a hand to include all the mysterious darkness. "This sign is everywhere," she said. "It is the sign of the ancient folk who found this place, made it strong and stored the gemstones." She passed the torch to Ulwazi, then crouched on the cave floor and drew lines in the dust with her finger. "See!" she said. Ulwazi looked and saw:

L XL1

Chapter 11

You youngsters must understand that the world of the past was not the world of today. Thus, the Navy is now a career service taking only volunteers, and these come forward because they know they'll be paid on time, and given shore leave to spend their money. And that's how it should be, because what young man of spirit would want to give up his freedom, and female company, for a year or more on blockade off the French coast, as was common experience for the lower deck in my young day? Worse still, the government sometimes paid the men years in arrears, or tried to pay them with 'Notes of Payment' to be cashed with the shore-bound sharks that paid out only a fraction of the face value.

So that's why your Uncle Jacob had to bite the bullet and resort to pressing. Because, yes, we did get a few starry-eyed innocents – fifty-two in all – who read the Pyne and Goodsby poster, believed every line of it, and came aboard *Tromenderon* of their own free will. Furthermore, for reasons beyond my understanding, most of them were indeed prime seamen. So thanks be to every one of them, but I certainly don't know why they bothered.

[Fletcher is avoiding the truth. There is no doubt whatsoever that it was his name that brought in the volunteers. I have heard from old seamen - too many times for doubt - that he was enormously popular on the lower deck and superstitiously believed to be lucky. S.P.]

So if others wouldn't come in willingly, and if a ship had to be manned, then they had to be persuaded. But here's the second odd thing, and it has to do with the minds of common seamen, which are not like yours or mine. For one thing, you are reading this and most seamen of my days couldn't read or write. Instead, they were bred up to the sea from childhood, bred up to strange beliefs that could not be shaken or argued with, and a big part of these beliefs was fatalism. For instance, note well that most of them never learned to swim because they believed that if the ship went down, then you inevitably drowned, and that swimming only prolonged the agony.

This fatalism explains how they behaved when they were pressed. Yes indeed, they'd play every trick to avoid being pressed. Yes indeed, they could be violent in resisting the press. There were even cases of merchant ships exchanging broadsides with the Navy to avoid the press. But mostly, having fought their fight, when seamen were pressed aboard ship, they grinned and put up with it and obeyed orders. That's seamen for you. As I've said, they ain't like you or me.

So in the end I used the press. I used the press but not the press gang. By press gang I mean the Impress Service which was a branch of the Navy run by its horny-handed, horny-brained old brutes and failures. I was resolved never to inflict them upon others and if you want to know why you should read the early pages of my memoirs, because I was pressed by the gang, and it was nasty and filthy and cruel.

Instead, Mr Pyne and I went ashore in plain clothes and made a tour of the local inns and tart-shops: not partaking of the latter I strongly point out, considering the poxy-doxies on offer. There, we made friends and found things out, with the grease of a little money.

"Sailormen?" says an elderly trollop in the Crown and Anchor. It was a sleazy, greasy establishment, just outside the dockyard, pretending to be an alehouse. But it had a dozen shabby rooms at the back with shabby beds within. "Sailormen?" says she. "Where do sailormen go for their pleasures?" She laughed, in my face. "What's wrong with this house right here?" She jabbed me in the ribs. "You're a lovely big boy, so why don't you have a go?" She laughed, and the other trollops laughed with her. Pyne blinked and shrivelled at that. But I laughed louder than her and passed a coin into her hand. "Is that all?" says she. "A measly shilling?" So I gave her a Spanish dollar. "Ah," says she, "what a gentleman you are, Cap'n Fletcher, 'cos don't say it ain't you, what with the size of you!" She thought a bit and sniffed. "You want the Blackamoor's Arms up on Covey point. But you'll have to climb out of the bay, and watch for sentries." She leered at me with her head on one side. "And are you really sure you won't have a poke, now you're here? I'll do *you* for nothing, lovey. I'll do you myself!"

We had quite a tour did Pyne and I. We visited the likes of the Crown and Anchor many times over and then drew up a list of lonely inns where jolly tars fancied themselves safe from the press. I planned the venture as if it were a cutting out expedition into a French port. I had all my officers, and the Boatswain and his mates, sat down in *Tromenderon's* great cabin, with the middies there too, since they must take part with the rest. Copies of maps were handed out, all neatly drafted by Dr Goodsby and his mates. Every officer and the Boatswain got his copy, each marked out with the inn that was his target, and every man was allocated to one of five teams under a named lieutenant.

After the obligatory serving of drink, I stood up and rapped the table.

"Gentlemen!" says I.

"Sir!" says they.

"The business has to be done in one night," says I, "at one stroke, before every merchant seaman on the coast knows what we're at!"

"Aye, sir!" says those who'd done the like before, and they nodded to one another in agreement.

"We're after seamen, remember," says I, "and only seamen. We don't want pen-pushers or clergymen!" They laughed at that, but believe me, my jolly boys, the real press gang wasn't particular who – or what – it took. "So look at your plans," says I, "and note well where you're going, and mark well the shoreline, 'cos it will mostly be done by boat work." I gave them all the details; then I had the lieutenant commanding each team give me back his orders to make sure he'd got them right.

After that I had nothing to do with the actual catching of the men, other than stand on the quarterdeck as night fell, watching our boats lowered, and other boats – hired for the occasion – coming alongside. Such a task was below the dignity of *Tromenderon's* lord and master, and there were lieutenants and mids who needed the exercise. So I stood and watched, and saw the merriment among the men as they went into the boats, chuckling over what they were going to do to lubbers who thought they could keep out of the King's service.

They went armed with belaying pins for actual use, and cutlasses should things turn ugly. But only the officers had pistols, and there were no marines because this work needed creeping feet, not heavy boots. I stood with hands folded behind me and watched them go. After they'd left, I went down to my cabin to continue the task of going through the account books of the Purser, Cook, Boatswain and others, just to show them how unwise it was, and exceedingly unpleasant too, for them to attempt fraud on my ship. Here again I step aside to point out that such a task is pleasant relaxation for me, because I do love a book of accounts that balances nicely and shows a profit.

Of course I did have a bottle of something for company and I think I must have dozed, because the next thing I remember was the bump of boats coming alongside and the shouting of commands. I remember that, and a ship's boy sent down to fetch me. Up on deck, by lantern light and a bit of moon, I saw the parade of fresh victims come over the ship's rail and out of our longboat, with the marines paraded, and the Master at Arms and his mates flexing their muscles and swinging ropes' ends. A midshipman came over with them and he ran up to me and touched his hat.

"Beg to report twenty-five men taken from the Blackamoor's Arms, Captain," says he, "and all prime seamen!"

"Well done," says I. "Any heads broken, or blood shed?" He looked round and pointed among the fresh intake.

"Just those two, sir. They tried to fight, sir, being very drunk." I saw two bandaged heads and the rest of them gawping at *Tromenderon's* enormous masts and yards rising high above them in the dark. But gawping was all they did. As I've said, seamen accepted their fate, and we were at war. Soon, more boats came alongside, unloading more men, so I left them to it and finally Mr Pyne came down to my cabin to report.

"One hundred and fifty-five men, sir!" says he with a rare smile. "So now we have plenty, and enough to man the yards and fight the guns."

"Any casualties?" He smiled again.

"The usual sprains and bumps, Captain," says he, "and an idiot who stuck a cutlass into his own foot. But nothing worse."

"Good," says I, "then take a glass with me now and tomorrow morning, once the surgeon's looked them over and they're entered into the ship's books, muster all the new hands on the main deck for my inspection."

"Aye aye, sir!" says he. "At one bell of the forenoon watch? After breakfast?"

"Yes," says I, "don't want them fainting from hunger, do we?"

Next morning, I walked up and down the lines of them, all stood to seamanly attention, and all touching their brows as I passed. Since we were in harbour, most of the ship's company were on deck or in the rigging to watch the proceedings, hoping to see the fun if any of the new hands gave insolence. But one glance at the new hands told me I'd not need to knock down any one of them. So I wasn't looking for insolence. I was looking for something more serious, even though the surgeon had passed them as fit. Were any of them lousy? Were any of them ruptured? Missing fingers? Afflicted with rashes? Were there any with facial tics? Were any of them mad? I was looking hard because if a Captain took what the Impress Service delivered, then there'd be plenty such as these. But no. They were clean; they were young; they were seamen. So well done Mr Pyne, and the rest.

After that I gave the usual speech. I raised my voice, looked them in their eyes and read them the rule book of the good ship *Tromenderon*.

"All aboard this ship that does his duty," says I, "need fear only God ... blah, blah, blah ... if you work hard you will rise high ... blah, blah, blah ... be proud of what you do in England's name for Britons never shall be slaves!"

You who've read my memoirs this far will know what I think of such speeches, and you will equally know that it is unavoidably vital that they be given because the men expect it. Perhaps you will also know that, by now, I had become expert in giving these speeches, such that I could deliver them while thinking of three or four other things.

In the end, after a week or two, the ship was manned, provisioned and armed, and only two things prevented her from setting sail. The first was to take on board the menagerie of live beasts that any ship took with it on a cruise because that was the only way to provide fresh meat once at sea. That meant chickens, ducks, pigs, sheep and bullocks, all of which had to be accommodated in pens made by the carpenter and his mates. These pens cluttered up the decks in a manner you'd not believe unless you saw it. So I wasn't going to take livestock aboard until the latest possible date before we set sail. But something still prevented me from sailing.

That was the absence of the documents I'd been promised by the First Sea Lord: those that established me as a diplomat recognised by His Majesty's government, able to call on the support of His representatives overseas, and charged with the mission of persuading America that we British were not after its whaling fleet. Because, believe me, my jolly boys, having once been forced into acting as a secret agent who could be disowned at will by His Majesty, I was never going to be caught that way again.

But still no papers came and I began to fret. I filled in time by exploring the ship from end to end, and in exercises to keep the men sharp: striking and raising topmasts, lowering and recovering boats, sail-drill, fire-drill and gun-drill. It's just as well that I did, because there was an enemy waiting for me at sea that I'd never seen the like of before.

Chapter 12

"The enemy were three line-of-battle ships, thus being a single frigate, I attempted escape."

(From the Journal of Captain Leonard Weakes, HMS *Philonides*, dated June 24th 1801)

Philonides came round on to her new course, and did so most neatly and well, with her people united in a teamwork that was a joy to behold, because *Philonides* was a smart ship. Going as hard as she could, and with a good way on her, she turned into wind and the head-yards came aback, driving her to leeward. Then, the mid and after-yards were swung and braced up on the new tack, filling and swelling splendidly. Finally, round came the fore-yards, and away went *Philonides* with the wind on her quarter and Mr Gough, her First Lieutenant, standing by as the log was hove over the stern and the line ran out, timed by the sand glass to measure her speed.

Seconds later, Gough was on the quarterdeck, touching his hat to Captain Weakes.

"Ten knots, sir!" he said, "and the wind steady a point east of north."

"That should be sufficient," said Weakes. But then he noticed that some of the young gentlemen were muttering, with the hands nodding agreement as they stood by their guns on the main deck. The mids were muttering and peering through the gun-ports for sight of the French, and they were looking at their Captain and frowning.

"God shut your damn traps!" cried Weakes, and pointed back at the three ships that were now well up over the horizon. "There's three of the line in pursuit!" he cried, "and any one of them able to pulverise a frigate bearing 18-pounders such as ourselves!" The mids shrank and avoided his eye and stopped muttering. But now Weakes was annoyed and he yelled at everyone. "Or is there any other little maggot that thinks different?" There was not. "God damn my soul!" said Weakes, because he too felt the shame of running from the French. He felt it bad. "Mr Gough!" he said.

"Sir?"

"You've got damn good eyes, far better than mine. Just get yourself up into the main top with a good glass and tell me what sail the enemy are wearing. Be a damn good fellow now, and get up there pretty damn fast!"

So up went Gough, up where a first lieutenant had no business to be, but he did have the best eyes in the ship, and he did keep good watch over the next hour as the three Frenchmen manoeuvred into line abeam as if spreading arms for a capture, and then as they cracked on sail, including stun-sails to the t'gallants and topsail yards.

"Captain Weakes, sir?" he cried.

"Mr Gough?"

"Permission to set stun-sails?"

"As you please, Mr Gough!"

So it was a stern chase with *Philonides* running and the French chasing, and Captain Weakes setting every stitch of canvas he dared, and then fretting that if anything was ripped or blown away he'd be caught for sure, because the seas were heavy, the sky was grey, the wind blew hard, and *Philonides* was doing her best in weather that wasn't frigate weather. There was too much of a blow and the waves were too high for her to work up best speed.

Up aloft, Lieutenant Gough shivered as he clung to the shrouds rearing up from the main top, wishing he'd thought to bring up a greatcoat. But he couldn't send down for one when the lookouts were watching. That would be soft. Instead, Gough frowned because he could see how well the three French ships rode the seas. They shouldn't have been able to do that. They were heavy ships: ships of the line, designed to bear heavy artillery. So how could they come on quite so fast in this weather?

On the quarterdeck, Captain Weakes thought the same thing.

"Heave the damn log!" he said.

"Aye aye!" said the Second Lieutenant, then minutes later. "Eleven knots, sir!"

"Eleven!" said Weakes. That was damned good in these seas! He hailed Gough. "Are we losing them?" he cried. Gough put his glass on the three French ships. He took a good hard look, wanting to say 'yes'. But he couldn't.

"No, sir!" he cried. "They're closing on us."

"Closing? Damn well closing?" said Weakes. "How the hell can they close on us? We're a damn frigate and they're ships of the line?"

Nobody was daft enough to attempt an answer. They knew Weakes too well for that. As for Weakes himself, he saw that he was being overhauled, steadily and definitely, by a force of ships that had no right to be coming on at such a rate of knots, and which had such a battery of guns aboard, that his ship's 18-pounders were worse than useless. All they'd do would be to draw a return fire that would splinter her timbers and kill her people: those that didn't get their eyes blown out or their limbs blown off! Weakes knew it. He sighed. He'd always said he'd never surrender. Not ever. Not under any circumstances, because there were other measures to be tried first.

"Stern-chasers open fire!" he cried, "full charges and steady aim!" *Philonides* had a pair of long 9-pounders in the Captain's cabin, mounted to fire astern. The gun crews ran to their work and soon a steady *thud thud* came from the guns, and the wind took their smoke back over the ship to the cheers of the men. The gunners aimed at the middle ship of the three, but the range was far too great. They barely saw the splashes. Weakes sighed heavily and gave an order so dismal, aboard a fighting ship, that it was second only to surrender in its capacity to spread misery upon all hands.

"Heave the main deck guns over side!" he said, "larboard and starboard, and work from bow to stern! Smartly now!"

"Aye aye," said the ship's people, and set to with the ingenuity of seamen. They dismounted the guns with pulleys and levers, and heaved each eight foot, thirty-seven hundredweight iron deadweight out through its own port to tumble end-over-end to plosh heavy, and plunge deep into the ocean. It was an awful thing to do but Weakes kept them at it and even did his best to cheer them up. He walked along the main deck and spoke to them all.

"Come on, lads!" he said. "Just one more. Heave 'em over. Lighten the ship and she'll run all the faster and leave them Frogs behind!"

Soon, half the guns were gone, and Weakes had the carriages heaved over the side to go with them. Everyone worked hard and worked with a will, because nobody wanted years as a prisoner of war in France. They sweated and worked, and even got another knot out of her.

"Twelve knots, Captain sir!" cried the mid with the sand glass, and the men cheered. But Gough didn't cheer. Up in the main top, he could see better than anyone that it was no use. The three French ships were matching twelve knots and beating it. It was impossible. How could ships of the line sail that fast? Worse still, smoke and flashes came from the French bow-chasers: six of them. And while *Philonides's* pair of long 9s seemed to have scored no hits, the very first fire of the French sent a ball roaring *voom-voom-voom* over Weakes's very head: or so it seemed to Weakes. The shot hit nothing, but the French had got the range, and a few rounds later, they put a ball into *Philonides's* stern. It smashed the rudder head precisely at its junction with the tiller.

It was a lucky hit, but deadly serious.

"We'll jury rig, sir!" said the Second Lieutenant. "Pass a weighted spar astern and steer by heaving on it with tackles!" But Weakes said nothing. "Sir?" said the Second Lieutenant. "Sir?" Weakes still said nothing. He could see that the French had split into two divisions. Thus, two of them were overhauling *Philonides* to larboard, and the third to starboard. Weakes looked along his main deck. It was half empty, but even if the full battery had been there it would have made no difference. Also, the rudder was gone. But still Weakes said nothing. "Sir?" said the Second Lieutenant.

"Strike," said Weakes. Then he sobbed, tears running down his cheeks. "Haul down the colours."

The French were most gracious and kind. But that was hardly surprising. They'd taken a British frigate in near perfect condition, and not a man killed or wounded on either side. So all four ships wallowed in the Atlantic while boats passed from the French squadron, taking officers and men to board *Philonides* and insisting on no more than normal, civilised terms.

All British officers went into one or another of the French ships. All British lower deck hands were secured below, with French swivel guns aimed at the hatches, and a French crew took over the ship. Also, there were generous assurances from the French that an exchange of British for French prisoners of war was in everyone's interest and would soon follow. There was only one moment of unpleasantness.

Among the French officers, seamen and marines who came into *Philonides* there was a civilian with red hair. He looked at everything. He looked particularly at Captain Weakes and his officers under guard of French marines. The British stood in a glum, downcast clump, not even wearing their swords because they'd been taken away. The civilian walked past them taking care to keep out of the streams of busy Frenchmen. But someone bumped him accidentally. It was a British tar, being herded below by a French marine. The tar knocked the red-haired man stumbling and his hat fell off. Without thinking, the tar picked it up and handed it to the red-haired man.

"Here y'are, mossoo!" he said.

"Thank you," said the red-haired man. It was just two words, but the English ear is acute for accent and Captain Weakes was close by, with only a couple of French bayonets between him and the red-haired man. Weakes looked at the red-head and frowned heavily.

"Are you English?" he said.

"No!" said the red-head, "I am proud to be Irish."

"So what are you doing with these Frenchmen?" said Weakes.

"Aye!" said the other British officers.

"What I am doing is none of your English business," said the red-head.

"Are you *with* them?" asked Weakes, and the red-head merely smiled.

"You traitor!" said Weakes. "King George is King of Ireland too!"

"Not by consent of the Irish!"

"You filthy traitor!"

That was just the beginning. Much worse was said. Very much worse indeed, since both sides were arguing from a passion of opposite conviction: violently opposite conviction. So French officers had to hold back the red-head, and French musket-butts were needed to get Weakes and his men out of the ship.

Later, when the red-haired man – Callum Donovan – had calmed down and ceased to shake with anger, he went below. He found the Captain's cabin and searched, finding many useful things including a shot-weighted bag, ready for any secret papers which must be thrown over the side to prevent the enemy seizing them. Presumably Captain Weakes – in his despair – had either forgotten about this duty? Or perhaps he had nothing secret? No matter. The bag was an old leather satchel, much worn and used, and with the fouled anchor emblem stamped boldly into it. That was good because it was authentically English and would save the trouble of making something that looked English. Also, there was plenty of English letter paper with English watermarks, and there were plenty of English Admiralty documents to give example of style, phrases, signatures and the rest. Donovan smiled, then helped himself to the Captain's brandy. It was French after all.

Chapter 13

It seemed a long time before the papers came from Spencer, and it was an uneasy time, with all hands wondering what we were doing, and gossip going round Chatham harbour that *Tromenderon* was no more than a 'painted ship on a painted ocean' as described by the Ancient Mariner.

Finally, Lord Spencer made good his promise and my papers arrived by special courier. I've still got the papers and they were everything that I was promised. So now, I really was a proper diplomat, recognised by His Majesty's Government, and incapable of being disowned if the wind blew the wrong way. I therefore represent here, the following and remarkable letter since – just for once in my career – one of the Great and Good declared in writing that I had his full support, and apologised for the mess he was dropping me into. Mind you, he'd have apologised ten times over if he'd known how bad that mess was going to be.

Captain Sir Jacob Fletcher,
His Majesty's Ship Tromenderon,
Chatham.

Monday 31ˢᵗ May 1801

Sir,

Among the documents passed into your hand by the bearer of this letter, you will find all warrants and appointments to be as previously discussed between ourselves. Please advise at once if anything is lacking or unclear.

I wish God speed your enterprise in the Americas, which enterprise is of exceptional importance since an alliance between the United States and France might lose us this war.

82

I therefore take opportunity to advise that we now know that the three French Sail of the Line, which broke through our blockade of Brest are 'Triomphe du Peuple', 'Bataille du Peuple' and 'Ascendent du Peuple': all ships of a most novel and powerful kind, and which are, of certainty, bound for America.

Therefore, should you fall in with these three, you must make what shifts you can. I offer apology that I am unable to place reinforcements under your command, which I am totally prevented from doing by the overwhelming need to concentrate our heavy ships in the Channel, since if the French main force should likewise break through our blockade and win command of the approaches, then Bonaparte's enormous army would invade. This is a very great peril to our Nation itself and must be guarded against with every ship that can be spared.

I rely upon you and repeat that in all these matters you act in my name and may call upon my support.

Yours etc, etc,

Spencer.

The Admiralty, London.

Thus, at very long last, on Wednesday June 23rd I upped anchor and took *Tromenderon* to sea. But you can forget all your images of a man o' war going out in its glory, and all hands manning the yards in salute, because being so large a ship with so many mouths to feed of fresh meat, we went out with every square inch – both above and below decks – full of animals in pens. We were a floating farmyard: cackling, baa-baaing, and moo-mooing, and the piddle and shite sluiced out through the scuppers by a hose from the wash-deck pump. The very waters of Chatham dockyard turned up their noses as we passed.

But still, what with *Tromenderon* being so special, the people of Chatham dockyard turned out with boats alongside of us, so long as they could keep up, with the shore folk waving goodbye, and I had the ship's band playing as we went. They gave 'Heart of Oak', 'Rule Britannia', 'Britons Strike Home,' and the rest, with all hands and the beasts joining in.

After that, once we'd saluted the battery, coiled lines and run down the Medway past Sheerness and the Isle of Grain, we were at sea and into sea-going watches and routine. Such routine, in a great voyage across the Atlantic, is weeks in the living of it, but boring to tell, except that *Tromenderon* proved even lovelier at sea than she had in harbour. She was sweet on the helm, a steady gun platform, and even early on in the voyage before we'd learned the tricks of her, we had her running eleven knots in an easy blow on moderate seas, which is pretty damn fine for a 90-gun ship of such a size.

I was careful at first not to strain her, because it would have been a fearful shame to lose a spar, or snap a line of her beauty, and also a fearful disgrace for Jacky Flash before the ship's people. Fortunately, in all this learning of the ropes, I had the advice of my Sailing Master, Mr Tilling, who was a new shipmate I'd not sailed with before, and who was very young for such a rank on such a ship. He was just over thirty years old, when the rank normally went to a veteran in his fifties. But Tilling came from a family of shipowners in the merchant service, and they'd doubtless worked influence. He was a lanky creature, with prominent teeth and untidy hair. He had long hands and feet and walked awkwardly. But he had the respect of the men, being bred up to the sea, having spent his years afloat in a variety of different vessels.

Such experience was vital in the ship's Master, since I remind you youngsters that while he did not hold the King's Commission like myself and the lieutenants, and was merely a craft tradesman, he was responsible before all others for the safe navigation of the ship, and even the ship's captain was in peril of the Admiralty's wrath should he act contrary to the Master's advice and run the ship into danger. So here's a flavour of Mr Tilling from the description he gave of an incident aboard a Margate lugger in past times.

"The lubber of a mate put her in stays while coming about," says Tilling, "and she grounded on the sands a whole tide, where we was all hands unstowing spars and shoring her lest she should settle bulge-square. Then on the ebb, we carried the stream astern so as to wind her off on the flood."

Now ponder on his further words regarding a voyage aboard an East Indiaman bound for the Cape of Good hope.

"When we got into the south-east trade, we hauled out our outriggers, and set up our pendants – very strong – thereby fortifying our rigging and giving power to our lower mast. We could then proceed with a full press and a flown sheet, and the fore-tack ahead o' the cat: the sooner to make way."

That's how he spoke, because that was the commonplace speech of veteran seamen. But I seldom report it, because it might as well be arse-up in Chinese for all that it means to you landmen. But there was another matter involving Tilling that is worth reporting.

Two weeks into the voyage, north of the Canaries and on our way down to pick up the trade winds, we encountered a waterspout on the open ocean. This being a rare and dangerous phenomenon, I summoned all hands, and all hands looked on in dread, since a waterspout is a fearfully unlucky sight among the lower deck people. There were groans and sighs as they saw what was coming.

We were heading two points west of south, on a northerly wind. The sky was clear astern of us, and black ahead. The ocean was vast, as the ocean always is; the seas were slow and heavy, and the most hideous overcast was coming down upon our bow. From the centre of this overcast, the black clouds dipped horrible and formidable into an enormous funnel-shape that became a long, black tube, turning and bending upon itself, and reaching down to the surface of the sea, like the finger of God, or maybe the Devil, because it looked more like the Devil's work than God's. The tube was dark and ugly, and it bore down upon us at the speed of a galloping horse. It roared and hissed, and we could even see froth and solid things – fish perhaps – plucked up out of the sea, swallowed and hurled aloft within the waterspout.

Soon the noise was becoming painful. The seas were angry. The monster bore down at such a speed as no manoeuvre of ours could escape it. It was whirling a cable's length ahead, fifty yards wide and a thousand feet high, and we could actually see the fish swept up it. It was undoubtedly coming towards us and – believe me, my lads – it wasn't only the lower deck that was afraid. What if that ghastly thing came upon us? Would it drag us little humans out of our ship and into the clouds? Would it pluck out our masts like twigs? Would it pull the whole ship into the air? It was a very nasty moment, for myself too, since I'd never seen such a thing before. But Mr Tilling had.

"Captain, sir?" says he, shouting over the din. "We could run out and fire on the bloody thing. I was in a ship once that did that and it went away: the waterspout, sir."

"What?" says I, and I was about to ridicule the idea. I thought that you might as well fire at the wind! But I saw the hope in everyone's eyes who'd heard what Tilling said and, in any case, what did a few pounds of powder and shot matter?"

"Mr Pyne!" says I bellowing mightily to be heard.

"Sir?"

"General quarters, Mr Pyne! Put down the helm to bring our broadside into action, and fire as the guns bear upon the enemy!" I pointed to the waterspout just to make sure he knew what the enemy was, and when the drums rolled, there was a glad roar from the hands and all was set in motion, according to drill and in good time.

"BOOM-BOOM-BOOM!" said the guns in ripple broadsides, and boom, and boom again. Smoke clouds rose, the waterspout disappeared behind them, then re-appeared as the wind cleared the smoke. So we fired and fired again, and to my utter amazement, we did the job with three broadsides! Which is to say that the waterspout changed its direction and went somewhere else! The men cheered till the ship trembled and once we'd set all to rights aboard, I ordered a tot for all hands, and so back to the safe boredom of routine.

Now … I freely admit that I have not the slightest idea whether or not our fire had anything to do with the waterspout going away. But it did go away and so-called experts in the matter have given contradictory judgements to me ever since. But, by Jove, we all felt better for giving the Devil a round-shot up his fundament, because that's what it felt like when we did it.

After that, the sea was kind and nothing stood between us and the troubles awaiting in America.

Chapter 14

The Royal Kraal of King Ndaba KunJama,
North Zulu Land,
In the 12th Year of the King's reign.
(1801)

"Then the witch M'thunzi approached the slender and lovely Ulwazi, wife of Inyathi the Buffalo."

(From the Saga of Inyathi)

M'thunzi was wary because Ulwazi was now Head Wife of Prince Inyathi the Buffalo, and was attended by many women because all sought alliance with so powerful a wife.

M'thunzi moved slowly as she approached the round house of Ulwazi, which was surrounded with a cluster of lesser houses where maidens lived whose families had begged Ulwazi to adopt them so that they might find good husbands under her guidance and meanwhile act as her servants.

Thus, thirty women sat outside the house as M'thunzi approached, creeping like a spider. They were well-attired and sat in order of rank. The most senior – some with jewelled headdresses – sat close around the stool where Ulwazi sat, while the maidens sat beyond them. But all stared nervously at M'thunzi because no woman wished to be near the witch that pronounces death.

"Sing!" said Ulwazi, seeing their fear. "Sing formal greeting to one of high rank!" The women began to clap hands in rhythm, as they lifted their voices in the melodic chant which was the proper greeting for a respected person.

"Huh!" said M'thunzi, hearing this, and she stood a little straighter. She nodded her head in appreciation, and her feet followed the rhythm of the song. She approached until the song ended, then sat down a few paces from the ring of women around Ulwazi, waiting to be received. Ulwazi saw this and nodded to two of the youngest girls.

"We obey!" they said, and they ran to fetch a gourd of water and a bowl of grain. These they placed before M'thunzi before taking their places again.

"Huh!" said M'thunzi, and raised the gourd to her lips and took a grain. She put it into her toothless mouth and swallowed it. Having taken food and drink, she was now formally received.

"So!" said Ulwazi. "This house is honoured by your presence, O M'thunzi, the Witch."

"As I am honoured to be received by this house, O Ulwazi wife of the Buffalo," said M'thunzi. More formal words were spoken, but then M'thunzi spoke the first of the cunning words that she had brought for this meeting.

"I ask for a private audience with the wife of the Buffalo," she said. Noting the frowns from Ulwazi's women, she added, "Otherwise I would have to sniff for demons, to make sure that no woman hears my words who is unfit to hear them." This brought a gasp from all present. Ulwazi blinked and thought fast. What would be best? Her husband had said that he would put an end to demon-sniffing one day, but not yet. Meanwhile, what would be best when M'thunzi knew every whisper of politics in the entire land? What might she have to say?

Ulwazi made her decision.

"I will listen to your words," she said, "and all others may leave us."

Soon, M'thunzi the Witch stood beside Ulwazi whispering.

"Be warned, O Ulwazi wife of the Buffalo: you whom I may name as my successor. Be warned that your husband is threatened by Prince Zithulele, who is the true son of King Ndaba. He is jealous of your husband and will move against him." There was more: with detail and names, and all of it invented by M'thunzi out of spite for Inyathi whom she knew was determined to stop the practice of smelling out demons. This practice was the foundation of M'thunzi's power, second only to the knowledge of the jewel caves which was power above all else. It was the power of naming a king because of all men in Zulu Land, only the King and his firstborn wore a jewel on the brow.

Therefore, the next day M'thunzi approached the house of Prince Zithulele who wore the great gem of the heir apparent. The approach was difficult because there were plumed guardsmen outside the house and there was a ring of wise men and many others. All these men rose in dignity and frowned that any woman should approach without being led by a father, husband or brother. But M'thunzi persisted, creeping forward, and none dared to lay hands on her. When she came close to Prince Zithulele, and with his attendants looking on in horror, she spoke.

"I have private words to say to you, O Prince who would wear the jewel of a king. I have words for you and none other."

Prince Zithulele was sitting on a throne of black ironwood. He was splendidly dressed in royal attire and he was a huge and powerful man. Huge and powerful but not splendid as Inyathi the Buffalo was splendid, since Zithulele was ugly, with ungainly features and one eye looked in towards the other. But handsome or ugly, he was sharply intelligent and was affronted by this old woman daring to ask for private speech.

"Speak if you must M'thunzi, the Witch," he said, "but speak in front of these, my loyal followers."

"*Yebo!*" cried his followers in deep voices: Yes!

"Of course, O royal cub of the royal lion," said M'thunzi, "but first I must sniff for demons to make sure that no man hears my words who is unfit to hear them." This brought instant outrage. Venerable councillors cried out. Men stamped their feet and waved fly whisks, walking sticks and clubs.

"No sniffing!" they cried.

"Away with the witch!"

"Put her to the spears!"

But Zithulele was sharper than a spear. He was sharp enough to see that despite their outrage, most of those present were terrified and were trying to raise anger as a shield against fear, because when demons were sniffed in a man, he was not driven out as women were driven out, but instantly speared to death by his own comrades. Zithulele understood the fear in his advisors. In any case, M'thunzi knew all the politics of Zulu Land, and a King's son must follow the shifts of politics. Therefore, Zithulele made his decision.

"Come to my side, O M'thunzi, the Witch," he said, "and all others may depart."

Soon M'thunzi was whispering into Zithulele's ear.

"You are the true son of our King," she said, "but the Buffalo plans to take your place. He is not of the blood, but the regiments love him. So listen well, O Prince, because the Buffalo will come after your father, and he will take your headband and tear out the jewel!"

Chapter 15

"I never saw such a jewel and a hunger for it burst within me and consumed me entirely up."

(From a letter of July 18th 1801: Mr Ezekiah Cooper to his brother Ephraim.)

The jewel rolled out of the soft leather pouch and Ezekiah Cooper gasped. Even Callum Donovan gasped, and he'd seen it before.

The stone was lovely in the extreme. It was pure, and clear, and blue-white, and the precision of its cut was exquisite. It was a diamond of massive size. Donovan sat in front of the big desk, and Cooper sat behind it, and they stared and stared.

"Pick it up," said Donovan. But Cooper never heard him. Cooper was entranced. "Mr Cooper," said Donovan, "you may pick it up." Cooper blinked.

"May I?" he said.

"Of course."

So Cooper picked up the stone and gazed into it, and was consumed with the lust for diamonds which afflicts rich men who already own everything any man could want, and who therefore want something more. Donovan saw this in Cooper's face and sighed in satisfaction, because this was Mr Ezekiah Cooper, multi-millionaire merchant of the city of Boston. This was Ezekiah Cooper, whose stone-built office building stood five storeys high. Donovan and Cooper were seated in Cooper's office in that building.

"Do we have an understanding, Mr Cooper?" said Donovan. "Please take your time, because the squadron won't leave till I say so." Cooper came out of his trance and frowned.

"You?" said Cooper. "What about the French Admiral?"

"Barzan?" said Donovan, and smiled. "He's a splendid officer." He paused. "But I speak for Napoleon Bonaparte."

"Do you now?" said Cooper. "So what's Barzan doing? He's brought three ships into Boston that are the wonder of the age and shown them off to everyone. He's also come in with a British frigate took with hardly a scratch on her, and all her people prisoners!" Cooper rapped the table in emphasis. "Barzan's the hero of the hour."

"All true, Mr Cooper," said Donovan, "and more than that, Barzan has proved that the British frigate was under orders to attack your American whaling fleet, and that's close to a declaration of war by Britain upon America!" Cooper considered that.

"The French have been peddling that rumour for months," he said, "and the British have been denying it. I've personally heard it denied from their Consul General in Boston, and he's an honest man that I trust."

"What about the secret letter in Captain Weakes's possession?" said Donovan. "The letter ordering him to prey upon your American whalers?"

"Huh!" said Cooper. "One letter?" He stared hard at Donovan. "Letters can be forged! And why didn't Captain Weakes throw it over the side when he struck his colours? He'd have had plenty of time for that. D'you think we Americans are fools?" Donovan smiled and changed tack.

"Could we concentrate on the important matters?" he said. "What I am offering you is the chance to shift power on this continent, and shift it away from the British. You surely want that because you fought them at Bunker Hill."

"I did!" said Cooper, and he remembered his youth. He remembered standing behind the barricades as the British grenadiers and light companies came up Bunker Hill, with drums beating, colours flying, and the fifes playing 'Yankee Doodle'. It was the bloodiest battle of the Revolution, and he'd been there. "I gave them fire from my musket," he said.

"Well done, sir!" cried Donovan, "because I'm another patriot against the British for what they've done to Ireland. So look what I'm offering. You're a merchant with major shipping interests." Cooper nodded. Donovan continued. "And there's a need for ship's stores of every kind to be delivered to a certain location in massive quantities. You'll be paid in gold by the French government." He placed a finger on the diamond. "And this will be yours, when the supplies are delivered." He tapped the diamond.

"Look at it, sir!" he said. "It was part of Bonaparte's loot, brought back from Cairo, and when he showed it to the Paris jewellers they said they've never seen one like it! They're calling it the Blue Star."

"Blue Star," said Cooper. "How could you carry it through the streets? Are you armed?"

"No," said Donovan, "but there's half a dozen Frenchmen waiting for me outside, just in case anyone tries to take the stone away from me, Mr Ezekiah Cooper. And they're all armed."

"Huh!" said Cooper. "You're a careful man, Mr Donovan."

"That I am," said Donovan.

"Then carry it through the streets again tonight," said Cooper, "and come to my house at seven." He looked again at the diamond. "I'll have a jeweller of my own there, because I'm a careful man too and I'll need to know that your stone isn't glass." Donovan nodded. "Then, you and I will have dinner, and discuss details," said Cooper.

So they had dinner, and a most profitable agreement was reached. Callum Donovan was impressed with the quality of Mr Cooper's cuisine, and of his house and his servants – especially one of them. Donovan grew so happy that although he was a very clever man, and an excellent secret agent who had turned Cooper to Bonaparte's plan ... Donovan drank too much, and the old weakness rose within him.

Chapter 16

We sighted Boston eight weeks after leaving Chatham, which was a slow time for such a ship as ours, but in those days a ship sailed only as fast as the wind should blow, and you youngsters must remember that, who've grown up with steam ships. You must also remember that in those days, sailing ships crossed the Atlantic on the westward-blowing trade winds in latitudes well to the south of America. Having once crossed, and reached the Caribbean, a ship would make a northerly course up the American coast to the chosen destination.

So those of you with maps will doubtless note that, although I was ordered to Washington and New York, as well as Boston, I passed them by on my northerly course, and chose Boston instead as my first port of call. This I did because I was ordered by Spencer to use all my knowledge of America for this mission, and Boston was a city I knew well, having been there before, and having friendships and connections from past experience.

Heading for Boston also gave us the opportunity to pass plenty of coasting ships on the way, and deep-water ships too, and all of which we hailed for news for fear that Britain and America might already have declared war. This would be uncomfortable to say the least, since to reach Boston I had to take *Tromenderon* into Massachusetts Bay, past batteries of heavy guns on Deer Island, Governor's Island, Castle Island, and Noddle Island which would have had an excellent opportunity to pound us into splinters.

Even without batteries it was a slow and careful run into Boston, what with the shifting sandbanks of Dorchester flats to be avoided, and I was much relieved when a couple of neat little pilot boats came racing out towards *Tromenderon* just east of Governor's Island. So we heaved to, and took the winner aboard, who was a smart Yankee skipper with a smart

Yankee twang, and who was the first to declare what every other soul in Boston would pour into my ears.

"Good day to you, Cap'n, sir!" says he, raising his hat as he was brought on the quarterdeck, gaping at the enormous size of our ship. "I'm Cap'n Stanwick, sir," says he, "stood ready to con you in." He shook his head in regret. "But you missed 'em, sir. You missed 'em by days!"

"Oh?" says all the quarterdeck people.

"Good day to you, Captain Stanwick," says I. "But who did I miss?" He frowned.

"The French, sir," says he. "The French squadron. Those that came in with a British frigate taken captive."

"What?" said every man aboard who heard these words.

"*Philonides*, frigate of 18 guns," says Stanwick, "under Captain Weakes, who surrendered in the face of hopeless odds."

"WHAT? SURRENDERED?" says our entire ship.

"Ah," says I, with a very nasty feeling in my bowels and already guessing what he'd say next.

"That's right, Cap'n," says Stanwick. "The French brought her in to show us, then sent her back to France under a prize crew."

"So what was the strength of this French squadron?" says I, although I had already guessed.

"Three ships of the line, sir," says he, "such ships as was never seen before." But then he looked at *Tromenderon*. He looked hard. "Not that yours ain't *also* a fine ship, Cap'n, so what a pity it is that you missed them." He shook his head again in regret, as did most of Boston, as was made clear to me repeatedly in the coming days, because oh dear me, but what a bloody tragedy it was for the fine folk of Boston, and all the dear little children, that so splendid a British ship and such splendid French ships had not met in sight of Boston and proceeded to hammer the hell out of one another. And what a shame that the entire town could not turn out to see it. What fun it would have been for them all, and the boatmen would have made fortunes taking the good people out for the performance at a dollar a head with picnic lunch extra.

So yes, it was them all right. It was the three ships Spencer had told me of: the three new specials that together out-gunned even *Tromenderon*, because they were 80-gun ships, mounting 36-pounder guns against Tromenderon's 32-pounders. Stanwick told me all about them as he took us into Boston through the sandbanks. Being a seaman, he had a lot to say. He'd even been aboard the flagship, *Triomphe du Peuple*, since the French wanted to show off their ships, and all visitors were welcome. So I learned that the squadron was under command of an old salt from the days of the Bourbon Navy: Barzan, his name was, who was famous for never bathing and for knowing nothing of celestial navigation. But his men loved him, and he was fearfully keen on gunnery, and practised his men constantly.

Which, my jolly boys, put a fright right up your Uncle Jacob: gunnery practice indeed! That was as bad to hear as the horror of a British ship having to surrender. Britons surrendering to the French? It was hard to bear and aboard *Tromenderon* we were in the dismal blues. I kept coming back to the worry of the French ships practising their gunnery, because where would we be if they got as good as us?

After that, having passed on his bad news with a merry grin, Captain Stanwick took us in safely into Boston Harbour past the batteries, which stayed nice and friendly and we saluted one another with blank charges and dipped ensigns. Finally, when I paid him off, he went over the side still saying what a shame it was we'd missed the French. Then we anchored just east of the town, and clear of its dense mass of wharves and piers, since *Tromenderon* was far too big to moor at any one of them.

I should mention that in 1801, Boston was a rich and fast-growing city and was ideally placed for a sea-trading port. It was open to the Atlantic to the east, and to the west it was connected to the limitless American interior by a set of big rivers. The town itself was on a peninsula, with a skyline of spires, roofs, grand buildings and towers, and its streets weren't laid out on a grid, like New York's. Instead, they wound like those of London and were equally full of civilisation: everything from banks to barber shops, and from clock-makers to suppliers of coloured wig-powder to the carriage trade.

As soon as we anchored, boats came out with the customs and harbour officials that attend an uninvited guest, and since *Tromenderon* was the biggest and most powerful ship that had ever come to Boston, there were not only official visitors but shoals of others. Soon our ship was in the middle of a bumping, clanking mass of every kind of boat, all wallowing and thrashing their oars. Their occupants were grinning up and shouting, begging to come aboard, and the ship's people were shouting back from the shrouds and out of the gun-ports.

I left Pyne to the civilians, and took the customs and harbour men down to the great cabin for the paper formalities and the obligatory bottles of wine. In fact, there were soon more and more uniforms in the great cabin, since officers of the American Army and Navy came aboard and were goggling, anxious to look over the ship. They crowded aboard, came down the companionways with rumbling feet, and elbowed forward, grinning and staring at everything.

"I see you mount 32 pounders on the gun deck," says an artillery officer, with red-facings to his coat and a Tarleton helmet on his head. "That's a mighty weight of ordinance, so does your ship roll? They say the three Frenchmen roll heavy."

"God bless my soul!" says a Yankee Sea Service lieutenant, in a uniform just like ours except for the buttons. "Such a ship, sir! What's her best point of sailing? How many souls aboard? What a shame you missed the French!"

"Have you heard about your *Philonides* surrendering to the French?" said someone else, and I did my best not to groan. But then, since I was exactly like the French in being here to show off my ship, I left Goodsby to deal with the harbour formalities and took a crowd of Americans in their various uniforms on a tour of the ship, and even made a friend on the way.

"You must come to dinner, sir!" says a big, grey-wigged gent in expensive clothes, who was not in uniform, but had a couple of minions in tow who nodded at everything he said. Also, all the uniforms stood back to let him through.

"I'm Benson, sir," says he, "and you are Captain Fletcher I believe?"

"Benson," mouthed his minions, as if he were royalty.

"I'm Fletcher," says I, offering my hand.

"And I'm Jos Benson, Chairmen of the Committee of Selectmen."

"Chairman," mouthed the minions. Benson smiled and showed some humanity.

"Have you a wife, sir?" says he to me.

"No, sir," says I.

"Well, when you get one, Captain Fletcher," says he, "you'll know that life won't be worth living if so fine a ship as this drops anchor, and you don't invite the officers to dinner that very night!"

So that evening at seven o'clock, I presented myself with half a dozen of my officers and Goodsby at the eastern end of Franklin Place, where

Mr Jos Benson had a most charming and happy wife. She beamed in her middle-aged merriment and old-fashioned gown, and made us cordially welcome. The house was magnificent: in Grecian style, complete with pillars and huge, round-topped front windows. It was one end of a terrace built to best London standards in front of a neat oval of grass planted with ornamental trees. It faced right on to the slightly less grand terrace of Tontine Crescent, a most familiar place where I had myself stayed in '95 as a guest of the wealthy Cooper family. It was also a very fond place in my memory since, there, I made a very dear friend.

I'd asked about Jos Benson by then, and discovered that he was top man in Boston's city government, which meant that Jos Benson was vastly wealthy in trade, because trade was what made a man in Boston, not accident of birth or a title. I liked that. It's one big reason why I am so proud of my American citizenship, and it's why I had a word with Jos Benson, once the ladies had withdrawn and left the men to the port.

One man I did not have a word with, among a fine selection of Boston society gathered that night, was a man I already knew and knew well. He was one of the reasons for my going to Boston. He was Mr Ezekiah Cooper: another vastly rich man. He knew me of old and I knew him. You see, my jolly boys, in '95 before I was in His Majesty's Sea Service, I was first mate in a merchantman that got captured by a Yankee privateer during the little war of that year between us and America. The privateer captain was one Daniel Cooper, who entertained me as his tame prisoner of war, in his house in Tontine Crescent. His house was a fine one, but not to be compared with that of his Uncle Ezekiah, which was the mirror-image of Jos Benson's house, at the other – western – end of Franklin Place.

So Ezekiah Cooper was a man who moved mountains in Boston, and since much had gone on between us in '95, in the way of trade, I'd expected that he and I could do the same again. But no, because although Cooper smiled and made polite conversation, he was shifty and wouldn't meet my eye.

"My dear fellow, how are you?" says he, coming up to me. But after saying not much, he broke away.

"Do excuse me, Captain Fletcher," says he, looking over my shoulder. "I have an urgent matter to discuss with a gentleman over there." Off he went with a weak smile. I found out why eventually, and could almost forgive him. But, never mind, because I spoke to Jos Benson instead, and we did some very fine business regarding my precision engineering cargo, and he promised introductions to Cantor and Boston bankers who were awaiting the specie aboard *Tromenderon*.

"Well stap my liver," says he, when we reached agreement, "and there was me thinking you were only a sea captain. You bargain like a fish-wife, and I've seldom met a man with such grasp of figures!" He laughed. "If ever you want employment ashore, just come and see me!"

But so to the ladies because as I've said before in these memoirs, after a long voyage, when the ship's people get ashore, the first thing they think about is the ladies. For the officers, this often means scanning the horizon at dinner parties, because – just as Jos Benson said – the officers of a newly arrived ship, if she's a King's ship and a big 'un, will be invited to dinner by the leading society hostesses. On these occasions, as the officers sit round the table, supposedly admiring the silver and the marble fireplace, they are really studying the ladies. Meanwhile, the ladies are studying the officers, and each officer must judge which lady is more interested in himself than in her husband.

Once that's settled, it's a matter of a quiet word with the lady to see if some private place can be found, and then it's interesting to see which officer is not aboard the boat going back to the ship. On that night – would you believe it – the most notable absentee was the Rev. Dr Goodsby, who'd been in close conversation with a jolly little creature with big eyes and curly hair, who put a hand most playfully on his and laughed at all his jokes. Her husband was snoring over his wine all the while, so serve him right, and when the foremast hands heard of their Chaplain's exploits, they thought the world of him. So well done him. He never believed in God anyway.

After that, I had to put in the hard grind of diplomacy, which went on day after day. So there were more dinners, and I was received by the British Consul General, Sir Roger Blenheim – an elderly gent in full-bottom wig. He did his best to help, by leading me round the town to meet everyone of note. Also, he warned me that the French had been showing off a secret letter, found in Captain Weakes's cabin aboard *Philonides*, which was an order from the Admiralty instructing Weakes to begin warfare against the American whaling fleet.

"It is, of course, a forgery worked up by the French," says Sir Roger, though he was wobbling when he said it, and I soon became wary of him because he'd been in America so long that he had a Yankee accent and saw the Yankee point of view too much.

"See here, Captain Fletcher," says he, pointing with his stick when we were about to enter the New State House to meet the Governor of the Commonwealth of Massachusetts. "See what a noble edifice this is!" I looked and agreed. It was truly massive, in fine red brick, with a dozen or more columns in white stone, a smart pediment over the columns, and a huge, gold-leafed dome on top. "Look at it!" says he, "and look at Faneuil Hall and other Bostonian architecture. Is it any wonder that folk capable of such works should aspire to their liberty from the Crown?"

So he took me in, made the introductions, and I swore on my soul to everyone that the secret letter was an obvious forgery, since I'd heard directly from the First Sea Lord that Britain had no interest in the whaling trade. But they just smiled and after that I endured everyone's regret that *Tromenderon* had not met the French squadron.

"Isn't it a pity that nobody knows where they have gone," says the Governor, Mr Samuel Philips. We were in a huge library where cakes and wine were served, and it was crammed with State House Representatives. "Nobody knows," says he, "because they would not say."

"Yes," says everyone, nodding.

"And even if you knew their course," says Philips, "and while your ship is wonderful powerful, Captain, could she beat the French three?"

"Could she indeed?" says everyone, and they all stared at me.

"Beat them, sir?" says I, stoutly. "Never a doubt of it, for there's nothing to beat British gunnery!" I paused, and became a bit of a politician myself. "Except perhaps American gunnery," says I, and they loved that. They roared with laughter and drank my health. All you youngsters should take note of the nature of your Uncle Jacob's words, so as to be ready with the same if need be. Wasn't I a clever little diplomat? I just wish that I'd believed *Tromenderon* could beat the three Frogs, because I was getting very worried on that account, especially as Governor Philips spoke to me privately before I left the State House.

He drew me away, even from Sir Roger, and smiled.

"If you do fall in with the French squadron, then I wish you well," says he, "because not everyone here is on the side of the French, with their damned guillotine." He sniffed. "Do you know how many heads they've cut off in Paris?"

"No," says I.

"Seventeen thousand at least," says he, "and I'll be damned if that constitutes Liberty, Equality and Fraternity." I nodded. Nobody needed to tell me to hate the French Revolution.

"So mark my words, Captain Fletcher," says he. "Time will tell whether or not your government is after our whaling fleet, though I don't believe you are, and plenty of others agree with me. You British would be mad to attack our whalers, since that would drive us into the arms of the French!"

"Ah!" says I, much pleased. "Quite right, sir! I'm glad you see it that way." But he frowned.

"Don't misunderstand me," says he. "It's not all sweetness and light between us and the British, because everyone is waiting to see if your fine, new ship can beat three fine new ships of the French. Do you understand?"

"Not quite," says I.

"Well, it's like this," says Philips. "If the French can beat the best ship you British ever made, then maybe the French are as good as you and we should be on their side? Now do you understand?" I did understand. Indeed I did.

But at least all this diplomacy kept me from dwelling on my worries until I did find out where the French had gone. I also found out why they had gone there, and why Ezekiah Cooper couldn't face me. I learned all this at once from the very dear friend that I mentioned earlier.

Chapter 17

"You were kind, and you treated me with respect, and I remember that most of all."

(From a letter of July 20th 1801, from Mrs Lucinda Dobson to Captain Fletcher, *Tromenderon*.)

Dobson, the butler, opened the front door and stood back as the little shit of an Irish Frenchman grinned before stepping out into the night. The little shit paused on the doorstep and whispered to Dobson.

"There's a gold piece coming your way if you can talk her round, me boy," he said. "Push her in my direction and I'll pay you well. And there's a gold piece for her too if she shows sense!"

The little shit was talking about Dobson's wife: his own Lucinda, but Dobson said nothing and showed no emotion even though he was in a fury. He was used to men looking at his wife because she was lovely. But this was different. The little shit thought black folks could still be bought and sold, even here in Massachusetts. But Dobson kept his dignity.

"I'm afraid I can't help you, sir," he said, and stood back as Mr Callum Donovan left the house and got into his carriage, all full of himself, and still grinning and winking at Dobson. Dobson closed the door and took a deep breath. Then he resumed his normal calm, which he could do because Mr Peter Dobson had risen high for a black man born on a plantation. He'd bought his own freedom by thirty years of hard work as an indoor servant, steadily climbing the ladder of promotion, and then he'd moved from cotton-slave Georgia to free Massachusetts where there was no slavery at all, under law.

And now Dobson was sixty years old and was butler to Mr Ezekiah

Cooper of Boston, and had the manner and bearing to go with his well-paid, comfortable job and his well-tailored clothes. Since he took his duties seriously, he made sure that the maids and the footman cleared away and made everything right before locking up for the night. When they were done, they stood in a row for his approval. He looked at them. They were black and they were servants. So the master and his guest never even noticed them and thought they'd seen and heard nothing. But they'd seen and heard everything, just as all servants did in every house that ever had servants.

Then Dobson nodded.

"Goodnight," he said.

"Goodnight, Mr Dobson," said the footman, with a bow.

"Goodnight, Mr Dobson," said the maids, with a curtsey.

Finally, Dobson went to the suite of rooms that he shared with his wife: a privilege of his rank in the house. She was waiting for him as he closed the door. She wore the elaborate clothes of a senior waiting woman, and she was tall: very tall for a woman. She was six feet high, ebony black, long-limbed and splendid with a figure greatly admired by men. She had huge eyes, white teeth, and was trying to be angry. She stood with hands on hips, blinking and trembling. But then she gave up trying, and threw her arms around her husband in despair.

"That man!" she said.

"I know," he said, and patted her back and said soothing words, and tried to think how lucky he was to have such a wife: less than half his age and highly intelligent. She was Mr Cooper's housekeeper and manager of everything that was bought and sold, or hired and fired. She was also a woman that got noticed. She didn't fade into the background like the maids. So the little shit of an Irish Frenchman had noticed her.

"He wanted to buy me!" she said.

"But the master said no," he said.

"But he laughed," she said. "The master laughed."

"He still said no."

"We shouldn't have come into this house."

"Sweetheart, we tried farming and didn't like it, and the money here is real good."

"But he wanted to buy me! He thought he could buy me, and then ..."

"I know. Little bastard even offered *me* money! For my own wife!"

"You don't know everything."

"What d'you mean?"

"He said he went to the privy, yes?"

"Yes."

"But he didn't. He come looking for me, and tried to put a hand up my skirt."

"Bastard!"

"He said, if I tell Mr Cooper, he'll say I was offering myself like a common whore."

"Look, sweetheart, at least Mr Cooper said no."

"Only 'cos I'm too useful running his house."

"Sweetheart," he said, "Mr Cooper said no."

"But he laughed. So I want to pay him back. Him and that little bastard."

A few weeks later, Lucinda came running into the Cooper mansion, gasping and out of breath. She used the servants' entrance, charged into the kitchen and shouted at the cook and the maids.

"Where's Mr Dobson?" she cried. The cook and maids curtseyed.

"He's in the garden," said the cook. "He's talking to ..." but Lucinda was gone. She found her husband in the garden giving orders to the men building the new gazebo.

"Mr Dobson! Mr Dobson!" she said, and everyone looked.

"Mrs Dobson?" he said.

"Come here!" she said and drew him away from the rest and whispered, "That English ship, the special big one! The one everyone's talking about?"

"Yes," he said. "It's called *Tromenderon*."

"*Tromenderon*," she said, "and the captain's name's Fletcher and he's here chasing those French ships. At first I didn't think it could be the Fletcher that I knew. *But it is!* It's him. I heard people talking about him. He's a great, giant man and he's the one I know. It's him!" Dobson frowned.

"How d'you know the captain of an English ship?"

"Never mind. I just know him. So tell me again. What did that man Donovan say to the master? Tell me everything." Dobson looked round. He made sure that nobody in the garden could hear: not the builder and his men, not the servants. But still he led Lucinda further off, and still he whispered.

"Those French," he said, "they want a seaport. They want a base for their navy ships. They want it up in Canada where there's French-speaking people who don't like the British. Those three big French ships that were in Boston, they're going up to Canada to put forts and guns round the port, so the British can't take it from them. And Mr Cooper, he's being paid to send everything the port needs in his ships: all kinds of supplies, everything! He's being paid in gold, and he's gonna get that big diamond I told you about. He's mad for that. You should have seen his eyes." Lucinda clutched Dobson's arm.

"What about the whale-catching ships?" she said. "Weren't Donovan and Mr Cooper talking about them?"

"Yes. But the whale-ships don't count for anything," he said. "They ain't what the French want. Those French, what they *really* want is their seaport to make trouble against the British."

Later, when Mr and Mrs Cooper were both out, Dobson and Lucinda went into Mr Cooper's study. It was large, and furnished in mahogany, hung with paintings, and decorated with Chinese pottery and bronzes. It also had a huge, Louis XVI cylinder desk, which was tightly locked. But no matter: between them, Lucinda and Dobson had every key in the house.

Soon the desk was open and a secret compartment revealed.

"It's where he always puts anything special," said Dobson. "See how this whole panel slides out? There's rows of pigeon holes behind that you'd never even suspect."

"Where's the map?" said Lucinda. "You said Donovan gave Mr Cooper a map."

"Here!" said Dobson. He pulled out a roll of thick paper and flattened it on the desk. "See here," he said. "Look where they drew a ring round a place and put numbers next to it." He looked at Lucinda. "They're sailors' numbers, ain't they? Navigation numbers."

"Yes," she said, "it's how they find somewhere, with north and south an' all."

"And that's where they're going," he said. "That's where the French seaport is gonna be. That's what Donovan told Mr Cooper."

"So!" she said. "Now we tell Captain Fletcher everything you heard from Donovan and Cooper. We tell him where the three big ships have gone, and why, so Captain Fletcher can spoil it for them."

"Spoil it?" he said. "You mean fighting and men killed."

"Why not?" she said. "What do I care about the French and the English? But that little shit: he grabbed hold of me, and he was kneeling and grinning and putting his hand up my skirt. He's an ugly little runt of a white man, and he's got it coming."

Chapter 18

I looked at the letter from Lucinda. It brought back memories of a gorgeous and silky-black body wearing nothing but a set of red ribbons. I sighed and sighed. She was a wonderful fine figure of a woman. She had the grace of a ballerina and the manner of a duchess. So the memories were warm and cosy, but the letter was a whopper of a challenge to the reasons for my being in America, because it showed that we'd got everything wrong.

The Frogs never were trying to start a war between us and the Yankees over the whalers. Or at most it was a diversion. What they really wanted was a naval base up in the far north that might threaten our entire hold on Canada! Everything was deeper and more strategic than we'd dreamed. But that's the Frogs for you. They're logical blighters, and efficient besides. Nobody can deny it.

So here was myself with all due diplomatic papers, sent out with *Tromenderon* to persuade the Americans away from the French lies about the whalers: lies which were never the real threat. To do this I was supposed to use my American contacts – including Ezekiah Cooper – to talk the Americans round. But all the diplomacy was wasted, because Governor Philips and others didn't believe the French lies in the first place, and Cooper was part of the bloody plot!

Meanwhile, and contrariwise, all the secret truth of the French plans had been dropped in my lap, without any effort on my part, in just one letter from a lady who remembered me fondly, and didn't like some swab called Donovan who'd had too much to drink, and got her in a corner. By Jove, but she was angry about that. She was angry enough to give the details: nasty little swine that he was.

So now I knew the truth, my jolly boys. But what was your Uncle Jacob going to do about it? Because what with knowing the Americans didn't believe the tales about the whalers, and my profitable connection with Jos Benson, I was beginning to think that this voyage was going to end peacefully. Nobody knew where the three French battleships had gone, so I had planned to cruise the American coast for long enough to make a show of searching for them, before heading back home to England with a sigh of relief that I'd not had to risk my ship against superior odds.

[Nonsense! Once again Fletcher affects a disinterest in engaging the enemy, which utterly conflicts with the truth. It is all part of his lifelong refusal to admit his love of the Royal Navy and its fierce rivalry with the French equivalent. See below for his eventual decision in this matter. S.P.]

But now I knew everything. I knew what the French were doing, and why, and where the three *du Peuple* ships had gone: *Triomphe*, *Ascendent*, and *Bataille*. So all I had to do was set sail, and I must surely find them. Or ... I could burn Lucinda's letter and nobody would ever know! So there was still an open door through which I could pass and end up safe in England, with never a chance of a round-shot splattering my entrails all over the quarterdeck.

So I went up and paced that quarterdeck with hands clasped behind back, as a ship's captain should, and everyone made way as I went to the weather side which was the captain's privilege. I paced the deck and looked at the spires and domes and chimney smoke of Boston and I looked at the other ships anchored nearby. They were minnows and sprats compared with *Tromenderon*. Then I looked at the teeming busy wharves, the boats going to and fro, the twinkling waters, and all the young gentlemen with their sextants under the instruction of Mr Pyne and the Schoolmaster. Some of the other officers were likewise out with their sextants, and Barker the Nova Scotia whaler was there too, looking on, though he had no sextant: indeed he never did. Barker was the man that Spencer had sent along with me as my expert in whaling, not that whaling mattered any more.

"Cap'n, sir!" they all said, and touched hats.

I looked at the ship's longboat pulling out from one of the wharves, bringing back the latest cargo of lower deck tars that I'd given leave for a run ashore. They were well drunk, and merry as could be, bawling out some song or other at the tops of their voices, and still swigging from bottles. But the middy in charge of the boat had them shut up and heave the empties overside before they came aboard.

I looked at everything and I groaned. What the hell was I going to do? I thought and thought. It took a while but in the end I thought of Lucinda and what her opinion of me might be, depending on what I did next.

[True in some degree. Fletcher did indeed cherish fond memories of Lucinda Dobson, but his antagonism to the French was very great and in dictating this passage, he thumped the table repeatedly, and declared that he'd be d****d if he'd let them have Canada. S.P.]

Then, once decided, the thing had to be done completely and well, so you youngsters should note the manner of it, in case ever you are similarly placed.

"Mr Pyne!" says I, when he'd done with the middies.

"Sir?" says he.

"All commission officers and the Master to the great cabin, as soon as you may," says I. "Also Dr Goodsby and Captain Barker."

"Aye aye, sir!" says Pyne. Barker turned round at that and looked at me. He must have heard his name. He'd been an oddity aboard ship, because while he was a ship's captain, he was no gentleman and he neither wished to mess in the wardroom with the officers, nor would he have been welcome. So he'd messed with the Boatswain, Gunner and Carpenter, though he felt himself superior to them. But now we were going to need him after all, though not in the way we'd first thought.

So I had them all below and had a chart of eastern Canada laid out on the table, and told them everything that Lucinda had told me, except that I didn't say it was her that had told me.

"I have it on high and trustworthy authority," says I, "and from a source that can be relied upon, but which I am compelled to keep secret."

"Aye aye, Sir Jacob!" says Pyne and the rest nodded. It was better that way, because what would they have thought of the truth? A letter full of loving endearments? A letter from a lady of my past? And the lady not a lady but a servant woman? So I never told them that, but I told them everything else. Then I looked at Barker and put my finger on a cross I'd marked on the chart, according to the latitude and longitude given to me by Lucinda.

"Captain Barker," says I, "this is the bay where the French are heading. This is where they will attempt to fortify a stronghold."

"Aye aye, sir!" says he.

"You are a dedicated seaman of these waters," says I, "so please give me your best opinion of this location and the use to which the French propose to put it!"

"Aye aye, Cap'n," says he, and he looked at the map and thought a bit. Finally he spoke. "This here is what we call Queen Charlotte's Bay," says he. "Queen Charlotte's Bay on St Michel island. But the people on St Michel – the Michelois – are all Frenchies, and they still call it Marie Antoinette Bay, since that's what it was before we took Canada in the Seven Years War, and in which the Michelois fought against us."

"So they're hostile to British rule?" says I.

"Oh God bless you, sir!" says he, smiling at my innocence, "them Michelois? Why, they hate us worse than the French do."

"Go on, Captain Barker," says I. "Tell us all you know about Queen Charlotte's Bay."

"Well see here," says he pointing. "St Michel, and Queen Charlotte, they're right in the middle of the Gulf of St Lawrence! Here's Newfoundland twenty miles east, Prince Edward Island twenty miles south, and Anticosti island to the north-west, with the mouth of the St Lawrence seaway beyond that." He looked up at me. "And the St Lawrence seaway, sir, why that's the highroad into Canada and all its ports and towns and cities."

"So a naval base in Queen Charlotte's Bay would dominate shipping going into Canada," says I.

"It would, sir," says Barker, "and Queen Charlotte's Bay'd be precious easy to defend, 'cos there's narrows at the mouth of the bay, just ideal for forts. It's all rocks and cliffs, so it'd be heavy work to cut out the gun platforms, but it could be done. Then, whosoever has hold of Queen Charlotte's Bay, is master of the approaches to Canada."

"So why didn't we fortify it ourselves?" says I.

"Nobody thought there was need," says he, "not with the French fleet trapped by our blockade. Everyone thought the French couldn't come near Queen Charlotte's Bay." We all nodded at that, and then Goodsby spoke.

"Forgive my interruption as a mere landman," says he, and everyone smiled, "but even if the French did fortify this bay, could not a fleet be sent to batter in their fortifications, or land marines on the island to take them from the rear?"

"Captain Barker?" says I. "What do you say to that?"

"Well first of all, sir," says he, "'tis dreadful hard for ships to face shore batteries, especially when they'd have to do so at close range."

"Aye!" said everyone, including me, because wooden ships don't do well against stone forts and earthworks.

"And as for landing men," says Barker, "why, there ain't nowhere else to do that on St Michel, what with rocks and shoals and vicious currents. It's only in Charlotte's Bay that ships can come to anchor."

"There's even another problem," says I. "Such an assault would need a powerful squadron of ships of the line, and with the French wanting to invade, we have to *keep* their fleet under blockade, so we dare not send our heavy ships out of the Channel." I shook my head. "I know that's true because the First Sea Lord told me so himself!" I looked round. They were all seamen, including Dr Goodsby, and I could see they already knew what was coming next. But I told them anyway. "So gentlemen," says I. "It's up to ourselves aboard *Tromenderon* to sail north to St Michel Island, and batter the French flat before they have time to get their guns ashore and build their forts!" I got a cheer for that. As I said, they were all seamen, and unlike myself it was their entire chosen life. They were actually looking forward to exchanging broadsides with the French. It was the same with the rest of the ship's people when I had them mustered on deck to be given a speech by myself in which I told them where we were going, and why, and took care to tell them with all the proper words.

"It is my intention," says I in a great roar, and with near on eight hundred men listening, packed shoulder to shoulder. "It is my intention to wreck, smash, destroy and burn everything belonging to Britannia's enemies! It is my intention to save British Canada, and protect British wives and daughters from the beastly French! It is my intention ..." and so on, and so on. It's what you have to say. It was what any officer would have said in those days. Mind you, your Uncle Jacob does take credit for the creative thought of having the ship's band standing by, such that when I was done, I had them strike up 'Rule Britannia', for all hands to bellow and to shake the spires of Boston. Then we gave 'Heart of Oak', 'The British Grenadiers' and finally 'God Save Great George Our King!' and we gave them with full hearts and true.

[Once again, note the much-denied patriotism that pours out from between Fletcher's words. Note also that on such occasions, when giving mention of 'Rule Britannia' etc during dictation, Fletcher would summon all the house-folk and cause them to sing, led by himself in his deep bass voice. S.P.]

It was a good start. But we couldn't up-anchor and away that very minute. There were still stores to get aboard, to replace those used up on the Atlantic crossing, and two final boatloads of men were due their run ashore: which matter – deeply precious to the lower deck – I hold out to you youngsters as no mere trifle. Because if I was going to ask the lower deck to fight, when outnumbered three to one, then I wanted them happy and willing, and believing in Jacky Flash.

In any case, the French squadron was not that far ahead of us: a few weeks at most, and it would be the work of months to build a fort to defend Queen Charlotte's Bay. So provided we left within a few days, and provided the sea didn't turn nasty on the way north, then we must catch them well before their work was done and Charlotte's Bay made invincible. The only problem then would be fighting one ship against three, and the three commanded by a man – Barzan – who was just as much a gunnery enthusiast as I was myself.

So I drove the people hard to make ready, and I wrote letters to Sir Roger Blenheim, the Consul General, because it was my duty to tell him what I was going to do, and to Jos Benson and Governor Philips besides, since both seemed inclined to look well on the British interest ... provided only that *Tromenderon* really was capable of defeating the French three.

There was one other duty in which I could never fail, and that was to thank Lucinda for remembering me and for writing her letter. But sadly I could never do this in person, not now she was a married woman, and not now that she was a servant in Ezekiah Cooper's house. Because what would the world think if I went ashore, knocked on Cooper's door and asked for Lucinda? All Boston knew me by then. I'm too big to hide among you little folk, and there's the white streak in my hair. What would her husband think? What would Cooper think? Myself a British officer and herself a household servant? I didn't dare even to write a letter in case he saw it.

So I sent Dr Goodsby on my behalf, knowing he was clever enough to find some way to speak to Lucinda without damning her reputation. I sent him ashore in the ship's smallest boat, so as not to make a show, and the crew were ordered to wait for him and not get drunk or God help them.

To my great surprise, he was back within a few hours, and reported privately to me in my day cabin.

"I had planned to take station in a bookseller's near Cooper's house," says he.

"Go on," says I.

"My intention was then to find some street urchin," says he, "and pay him to deliver a message which I would contrive to bring her to the shop."

"And?"

"It proved unnecessary, sir! On walking past Cooper's house, I saw the very lady herself coming out."

"And you knew it was her? Were you sure?"

"Oh yes, sir! What a lady! Taller than me, and dark. And of such exotic beauty. She would most wonderfully play Titania in 'Midsummer Night's Dream' if she ..."

"Get on with it," says I. "Did you say what I told you?"

"Yes, sir, of course, sir. I followed her and stopped her, and raised my hat as if to ask directions."

"Go on!"

"And I said ... Madame, I am Chaplain aboard *Tromenderon* and I speak for Captain Jacob Fletcher, who is most immeasurably grateful for your letter, and who hopes that you will understand that you and he may not meet, but who thanks you, and shall always remember you with the utmost fondness and respect."

"And what did she do?" says I. "What did she say?"

"She seemed much moved, sir," says he. "She smiled and said to thank you, and to say God bless you and keep you, and that she remembers you equally well."

So well done Goodsby. That was my farewell to a very special lady, and a few days later, on August 31st, we finally brought in our anchors and left Boston behind, sailing for St Michel Island. If you look at a chart, you will see that our course had to be eastward, some two hundred and fifty miles into the Atlantic, curving around the south of Nova Scotia. Then we were to head north-west through the forty-mile passage where Cape Breton on Nova Scotia reaches out towards Cape Ray on Newfoundland, and so into the Gulf of St Lawrence to find St Michel. If you step it out with a pair of dividers, it's a voyage of about five hundred and fifty miles, which a fine-lined, well-found ship like *Tromenderon* would gobble up in a few days, given easy seas and a steady blow, though no man aboard was mad enough to say as much, because that would be unlucky.

Thus, I say again to you youngsters, bred up as you are into an age of iron ships and steam power, that you should always remember how things were under sail when nothing could be predicted, and every seaman cherished his luck and took care not to spoil it. And don't you ever think that luck isn't real and doesn't have power, because by God it does when you're at sea.

> [Note that the above passage on luck at sea, is a mere summary of a passionate rant by Fletcher, during which he railed against '*landmen who think they know the sea*' and repeatedly cried '*b****r 'em all for their ignorance*'. S.P.]

So perhaps some swab did speak out of turn because we didn't get easy seas and a steady blow. We got a gale that drove us far out to the east and blew spars away that had to be rebent, and made good. In the end it wasn't until September 5th that we were well inside the Gulf, making good way for St Michel, at which time Barker, the whaler, suddenly ceased to be the ship's oddity and became no end of a fine pilot. And this he did by the ancient craft that was practised by seaman for centuries before anyone dreamed of longitude or chronometers, all of which Barker was ignorant of.

Thus, just after noon observation on the 5th, when I was on deck with officers and men all around, Barker came to me, all deferential with his hat in his hands.

"Cap'n, sir!" says he. "Sir Jacob, sir! Can I beg a word?" I looked him over. He was none too clean, he had front teeth missing from the scurvy in past years, and he looked battered and worn out for a man of his age. But that's what old salts looked like in those days, and before all else he was a man that Lord Spencer had chosen. And he was polite.

"Yes, Captain Barker," says I, giving him his title, which made him stand up straighter.

"Sir," says he, touching his brow and stamping a foot like a common seaman, "we're coming hard up on the Iles de la Madelaine which is perilous hard to navigate, but I can show you the safe way through, as will give a quicker passage if God be willing." He touched his brow again, and concluded with the words, "And on that I akses to be judged." He said *akses*, not *asks*, because he spoke like a common seaman too. But he was a bold fellow to come up to me like that, when I'd hardly spoken a word to him since our first meeting, and myself so mighty a being aboard ship. I was intrigued, and I turned to Tilling and Pyne who were nearby.

"The Iles de la Madelaine, gentlemen? What do the charts say?" Tilling was first. As Sailing Master, it was indeed his duty to be first in such matters, because – on a ship of war – although the Captain commands where the ship must go, it's generally the Master who sets the course. Tilling had just come from his day cabin under the quarterdeck, where he'd been working with the charts.

"The Iles de la Madelaine, sir?" says he. "Those are an archipelago of small islands and rocks, sir. They're fifteen miles long; they're a day's sail ahead, and they lie between us and St Michel. They're roughly north-westerly across our course and I shall steer around them to the south, sir, to avoid hazarding the ship."

"Beggin' your pardon, Mr Tilling, for the learned man that you are," says Barker, "but it'd be quicker to go north, and through the archipelago, between Old Harry and Brion." That brought silence from Pyne and Tilling, neither of whom had ever heard of Old Harry or Brion, whatever they might be. Barker saw that and pressed advantage. He bowed to Tilling and spoke. "Now I ain't no scholar such as you are, Mr Tilling, 'cos I'm just *lead, log and latitude*. But I've sailed these waters since I was a nipper, and my Pa and Grandpa before me. So I knows every cove and rock, and if I'm to be of service, and hammer the French, why, I akses you to test me and judge me!"

Tilling thought about that and he looked at Pyne who shrugged, and then he looked at me. He was frowning was Mr Tilling, and he wasn't pleased because he was fearfully proud of his mathematical skills. But he could see that I was grinning at Barker's cheek in approaching me. So Tilling said nothing for the moment, and Barker's proposed test was left wobbling in my mind, because if I let Barker run the ship on the rocks it would be *me* that the Admiralty condemned ... which led me to a very naughty, wicked thought indeed. It came like a sky-rocket bursting in the night. Boom! I realised that if I let Barker run *Tromenderon* onto the rocks, then the Admiralty would throw me out of the Navy, just as I'd always wanted! Oh joy! Oh bloody rapture! So I impress upon you youngsters that sometimes a man can be entirely right for entirely wrong reasons.

[Poppycock and nonsense. Fletcher is posing once again. He

would never have allowed a ship to be run into hazard in such an unknown and uncertain manner. The truth is probably that he already esteemed Captain Barker as a fine seaman and wished to try him out. S.P.]

"Captain Barker?" says I.

"Sir!" says he.

"I shall do as you ask," says I. "You may con the ship through the Iles de Madelaine."

So he did. Indeed he did. When the Madelaine was in sight, he got himself up into the foretop, where he had the best possible view of the seas ahead of the ship. He had a chain of middies keeping observation on him and copying his signals – which he gave by pointing and by singing out – and thereby passing his orders to the helmsmen to bear away to larboard or starboard as he directed.

In the end it was nervous work and precious tight. It turned out that Old Harry was an island to the far north-west of the Madelaine, and Brion was the biggest of a deadly cluster of rocks to the north of Old Harry, as Mr Tilling pointed out, near dragging me into his day cabin to see.

"Look, sir!" says he, bending over the chart and hitting it with a forefinger. "It's all death and destruction between Old Harry and Brion. There's no safe way through! It's rocks and shoals and we'll lose the bloody ship, sir!"

That was a nasty moment: very nasty indeed. We were under topsails and fore course and we did at last have a steady blow. We were making ten knots under a clear sky with the sun shining and the seas almost blue. There were gulls in the air, with us being so near land, and we could see the dark bulk of the Madelaine islands with a bit of green on them. All hands were in the shrouds or at the rails to see the white water go sliding past, with the black rocks beneath, as the ship forged into the gap that Barker said was there and which Mr Tilling denied.

In practice and at worst, we shot past some of those rocks with only a few fathoms to spare and angry waves breaking all around. But the gap was there, and Barker was right. We came through, clear of danger and all hands cheered. Thus, Barker became ship's hero and if Mr Tilling never forgave him for it, then Mr Tilling had to bear that bravely, because we sighted the enemy soon and I was obliged to put Barker to another test – one far more severe – which would either save us, or sink the ship and drown us all.

Chapter 19

The Plain of the King,
North Zulu Land,
In the summer of the 12th Year of the reign of
King Ndaba KunJama,
(1801)

"The hostile arrays were of magnificent splendor. Many thousands of men were in arms."

(From the Saga of Inyathi.)

It was a mighty gathering of spears because Prince Inyathi the Buffalo, was contesting the throne with Prince Zithulele of the blood royal. A great debate had followed with some men following Inyathi as a proven general, and some following Zithulele as the King's true son. Thus, even within kraals there had been divisions, and even within families. But the tradition of North Zulu Land was that such matters were decided on the field of battle, and were not private business for individuals to fight over.

Men of the same kraal or family had made their way, in two divisions, singing and marching to the Plain of the King, to stand with their chosen leaders. Now, many thousands of men stood in ranks within two armies, each facing the other and waiting for the order to go forward. They stood under excellent discipline in the hot sun, on the chosen ground, with White-Shield guardsmen to the fore, backed by companies distinguished by shield colour and the shape of headdress plumes. Sharp spears gleamed by thousands, and men would soon die by thousands.

Meanwhile, the armies stood two hundred paces apart, such that nothing thrown or shot could fly from one to the other, while thousands of women waited upon the outcome of the battle in finest costume. They stood apart from the armies, but equally divided into hosts, and they sang and clapped and stamped in the rhythm of rival songs, and the jewel stones of the senior women flashed in the sunlight.

Fifty paces in front of each army, the two leaders – Inyathi and Zithulele – stood with their elite men around them, and they too awaited the sign to commence the battle. For this, they looked to the King himself, Ndaba KunJama, who sat on a mound raised for this purpose. He sat upon a throne, splendidly dressed in royal regalia, and wearing the greatest of all jewels. He sat surrounded by the wisest men in the land, and with the witch M'thunzi at his elbow. She was there because the King had listened to her all his life. He'd listened because – in the deep of his mind – he was afraid of her. Or rather, he'd been afraid so long as he'd had a mind. But his mind was gone, taken away by old age, along with his teeth and manhood.

The King sat silent, and the dribble ran from his mouth, and his eyes gazed at nothing. He trembled so badly that his spear was bound to his hand for fear that he might drop it, and beside him the witch M'thunzi glared at everything because everything had gone wrong. She had acted out of spite, to make trouble between Inyathi and Zithulele, and she had intended that Zithulele should win. She had intended that he would take private action against Inyathi. She had never intended the matter to be settled in open battle. Perhaps she should not have warned Inyathi? Her mad women were with her, and the boldest tugged her arm.

"Mother of mothers?" she said, grovelling hard. "Why has it come to this?" M'thunzi snarled and struck the hand away.

"It's not my fault," she said. "I told Zithulele it should be a spear in the night while Inyathi slept. But men are fools and he listened to other men with their foolish traditions of battle."

"So shall it be a battle, mother of mothers?" M'thunzi groaned and looked across the Plain of the King where all great matters were decided in blood. She looked, and even she was moved by the beauty of such fine regiments and such magnificent men. She looked this way and that, and saw no alternative to prodding the senile King into giving the signal for battle: a battle which might go the wrong way! She leant forward to whisper in the King's ear ... and in that moment, in the corner of her eye, she saw the tiny figure of a speeding man, running hard towards the Plain of the King. She stood up and shaded her eyes.

"What is it, mother of mothers?" said her followers, and a murmur grew among the thousands present. It grew and rose as all could soon see that the runner was a man who bore no spear or shield, but only a long white stick that marked him as a messenger. He ran hard and dashed between the two armies, throwing himself at the feet of the King. He spoke quickly and both armies and their women strained to hear. But they were too far off. Then the witch M'thunzi beckoned both Zithulele and Inyathi. The two ran forward and found the messenger gasping and panting, the old King babbling like an infant, and his wise men standing in agitation.

"What is it?" said Zithulele.

"There can be no battle," said M'thunzi.

"No!" said all the wise men.

"Why?" said Inyathi.

"An army of the Arabs is coming from the north," said M'thunzi. "They have many spears and hundreds of muskets, and they have also summoned two magic weapons which are made of gold, and are drawn on wheels. These are not yet arrived but will soon come." She paused and stared at Zithulele and Inyathi in turn. "Now listen to me, you men! This army comes for our virgins and for our sacred stones." Zithulele and Inyathi looked at one another. The hatred between them was so great that, even in this instant, each wanted to spear the other. But the threat to their women and sacred stones was unbearable. It was an outrage. It was an insult to the soul of their folk. So both men knew that – for the moment – they must be united. Then Inyathi frowned.

"We know the Arabs come for our virgins," he said, "but how do we know they want our jewels?" M'thunzi poked the messenger with her fly-whisk.

"Speak!" she said, and the messenger bowed low.

"O lion of lions!" he said to Inyathi. "O royal son!" he said to Zithulele. "They are undoubtedly coming for the sacred diamonds. They ask constantly about them. They ask who has them, and they ask where they can be found. They ask if there is some mine from which the jewels are taken."

Chapter 20

"A diamond, a colossal diamond. Donovan said that that it would buy the American."

(From the journal of Enseigne Antoine Leclerk, aboard *Triomphe du Peuple*, August 20th 1801)

The jewel sat in the middle of the documents that Donovan had laid out on the table. There were plans, maps and instructions but everyone stared at the diamond. They stared in such silence that the ship sounds of *Triomphe du Peuple* came creaking and moaning into the great cabin where Barzan sat with his officers around him, and Callum Donovan beside him.

"This will buy the American," said Donovan.

"It had better!" said Barzan, "because your secret plan and your secret orders have a shitty great hole in them!" Donovan tried hard not to lose his temper.

"I've told you, Admiral, it's not my plan, it's Bonaparte's." He seized a letter and pushed it at Barzan. Barzan looked at it. It was elaborately drafted on the finest notepaper. The signature was the single word, *Napoleon*, and in case any idiot didn't understand the meaning of that mighty name, the calligrapher had added beneath it:

Napoleon Bonaparte,
First Consul and Father of the Nation.
Protector of the French Republic.

"See?" said Donovan. "It's from the man himself! And it says here." He read aloud from the letter. "Every officer and citizen will render utmost cooperation to citizen Donovan, who in this matter speaks for me." But Papa Barzan still frowned.

"I don't care whose plan it is. I want to know why you kept it secret until we were in the God-damned shitty Gulf of St Lawrence. And the God-damned shitty great plan still has a shitty great hole in it!" Donovan breathed hard. The officers around the table glanced at each other, wondering who to believe.

"Admiral," said Donovan, "it was kept secret for fear that it might swing the Americans the wrong way. They might not want the French up north of them, any more than the British."

"Bollocks!" said Barzan. "The whole shitty great plan *depends* on an American: this shitty great bastard Cooper! The one who's going to send supplies up to St Michel, and without those supplies, the base can't survive!"

"Yes!" said the officers, nodding.

"Admiral," said Donovan, and he reached out and picked up the great blue-white stone. "Can you even dream what *this* shitty great bastard is worth?" Barzan sniffed.

"Pah!" he said. But that was all.

"Now listen well, Admiral," said Donovan. "In the first place, I'm telling you direct from Napoleon that you must follow his plan: yes? You must follow it whether you like it or not: yes?" He looked round the table. "Or is there anyone here who wants to go against Napoleon?" There was not. There was silence. "Right," said Donovan. "So I'm telling you that Cooper is after the huge profits he'll get from supplying St Michel, and I'm telling you he's damned-well bewitched and enchanted by this thing." He held up the stone so that it glittered and shone. "He's that kind of man, and it's that kind of stone."

Barzan looked at the stone, looked at Donovan, and looked at Napoleon's signature. He sighed. Everyone knew what happened to people who crossed Napoleon.

"All right, Mr Irish citizen Donovan," he said, "show me the plans. How many guns must we put ashore? How many men to serve them and build the earthworks? And what support – if any – can we expect from the local people?" Donovan smiled.

"You must trust me in this," he said, "because the word from our agents is that the Michelois think Bonaparte is the second coming of Jesus."

Three days later, Admiral Barzan's squadron was anchored in Queen Charlotte's Bay in St Michel Island, and French military and naval engineering was on display at its finest. Aboard each of the three big ships, main deck 36-pounders were being hoist from their carriages by triple-blocks made fast to the main stay, and the hands were hauling on lines. Longboats were alongside, ready to receive the guns and take them ashore, while on the beach, tripods and lifting tackles were rigged to hoist the guns out of the boats and into carts skilfully contrived by the squadron's carpenters, so that the guns might be hauled up to the battery sites. Meanwhile, officers of the fleet were busy all around the bay, surveying, measuring and recording to find the best possible location for the three batteries that were planned, and four of them if possible. And all this was done with a will. Field kitchens were set up, tents rigged, and every man of the fleet happy in knowing that they were striking a blow for France, and that – just for once – the Rosbif Navy had not got in the way!

Best of all, the Michelois people gave such a welcome as Barzan's men could hardly believe. On sight of the squadron and its *Bleu-Blanc-Rouge* banners, they'd come out to greet the ships in every kind of boat. They'd provided pilots, guides, hospitality for the officers, and they even sang La Marseillaise as they came. Thus, when Barzan went ashore to see the works – with Donovan always beside him – he was approached by a delegation from the local fishermen, who pressed through the busy seamen, carpenters and engineers, waving hats in the air, and calling out.

"Monsieur? Monsieur? Monsieur the Admiral?" Barzan's marine guards stopped them, but they smiled as they did so for there was not a drop of harm in any of these French-speaking, wildly friendly men: five of them, all seamen born and bred from the look of them, and Papa Barzan liked the look of them. They were men like him.

"Let 'em through!" he said, and the marines stood back.

"Monsieur the Admiral!" said the delegation leader. "Vive la France! Vive La Republique! God bless you for coming! God bless Napoleon and God damn King George!"

"Aye!" said the other fishermen.

"Aye!" said Barzan, and as the intuitive leader that he was, he threw his arms around the Michelois fisherman, kissing him on both cheeks, and the Michelois folk were his to command from that instant.

Later, Barzan sat at dinner on the beach in the biggest tent. He sat with some of his officers and with Donovan beside him. The food was good; the wine was good; the mood was merry. Barzan even smiled at Donovan.

"Well, Monsieur," he said, "looks like you were right about the Michelois."

"You are most gracious, Monsieur the Admiral!" said Donovan and raised a glass.

"And here's to your blue stone!" said Barzan. "And just for curiosity, where did it come from?"

"Egypt," said Donovan. "Napoleon took it off an Arab merchant: well, one of his men did, and gave it to Napoleon. The Arabs get them from somewhere in Africa. There's a tribe there called Zulus that live by a river." He shrugged. "They have these stones."

"And where do they get them?" said Barzan. "These natives?"

"I don't know," said Donovan. "I suppose they have a diamond mine."

"Well if such a mine exists," said Barzan, "why didn't Napoleon go after it? He's a tiger when he gets an idea in his head, and such a mine would finance armies! It would finance battle fleets!"

"Ah," said Donovan, "it's the damned British. They kicked his army out of Egypt and broke your fleet at the Nile. Don't you remember?"

Barzan nodded.

"I remember!" he said. "Who doesn't? But what about the Arabs? If they know there's a diamond mine, why don't they go after it?"

"I don't know," said Donovan. "Perhaps they will?" He clutched at the leather pouch that hung round his neck. He thought about the diamond mine. He'd heard so much about the stones and the Zulus, and the river by the diamond caves that he thought he could probably find it, given a ship, and some men. He thought hard about that.

Chapter 21

When we finally sighted the enemy, it wasn't really the enemy at all. It was the Michelois, as Barker called them.

We'd been blown well off course by black skies, foul weather and vicious white waves, such that I'd been obliged to shorten sail, and bring us bow-on to the blow. Otherwise we'd have been shipping the ocean, green and solid, all over the stern rails. Landmen often can't believe this when they see a big ship like *Tromenderon* all sleepy quiet and anchored in port. They look at the massive oaken stern, and can't believe that the sea could climb so high as to wash over it. But the reality is that the ocean waves are so enormously high, and the troughs between them are so low, that even the biggest of ships is at one moment raised high up above the ocean, with a view over the heaving grey-green world, and the next plunged so deep and dark, that the slimy waves tower over the topmasts, such that the fishes can look down and count the hairs on your head.

So that's how it was for days after we came through the Madelaine archipelago, and then the weather changed its mind and we got clear skies and a bit of weak sunshine and a steady blow from the west. By my reckoning and Mr Tilling's, we were fifty miles west of St Michel, with New Brunswick just in sight to our west. Then, just after six bells of the morning watch, and the dawn coming up in the east, the foremast lookout sang out:

"Sail ho!"

"Where away?" cries the officer of the watch.

"Fine on the larboard bow!" cries the lookout and out came all the glasses. The quarterdeck people, including myself, got up into vantage points and searched the seas.

"Enemy in sight!" cries the lookout, and every man's heart thumped and we all looked twice as hard.

"There, there, Cap'n!" cries Barker, because I'd kept him close ever since he'd conned us through the Madelaine, and now he was standing with Tilling and Pyne, beside me. He pointed. I looked, and I focussed my glass, and there it was: heaving and moving on the blasted ocean, as every ship does when you try to get a look at it, because it's an art is using a four-draw glass when you're stood on a heaving ship and trying to hold steady the field of view.

"It's a *Marie*, Cap'n!" says Barker. "Fast and nimble they are: gaff-rigged on the main and foremast, with tops'ls, and a couple of stays'ls to the jib. She's a *Marie*." I scanned where he pointed and I got her! I had her in my glass. She was small, perhaps fifty or sixty tons, and rake-masted with white water boiling under her bow, and very obviously fast. But that was nothing compared with the fact that the ship – the *Marie* if that's what it was – had the French tricolour flying from its mainmast.

"What's a *Marie*?" says Pyne. "And why's she flying French colours?"

"She's a fisher-ship" says Barker, "a Michelois 'cos that's a real Michelois rig. So that's a Marie and they're built for speed to get the catch down to Quebec while it's fresh."

"Very nice," says I, "but why's she under French colours?"

"Ah!" says he and so did everyone else, because the Marie had most neatly come through the wind, swung her booms, and was bearing away on a new course.

"She's seen us!" says Pyne.

"Aye!" says a dozen other voices; then, "Oooo!" as a bright streak shot up from the Marie, bursting into stars.

"Captain Barker!" says I. "That's a rocket! It's a bloody signal isn't it? And why the bloody French colours?"

"I dunno Cap'n," says he. "But we're too far from France for her to be French when she's so small. So she's a Michelois what chooses to wear a French jack. A rocket's a distress call in these waters, but she ain't in distress so she's telling someone something else." He looked at me.

"Which must be," says I, "that she has a British man o' war in sight!"

"Aye aye, sir!" says he and he touched his brow and grinned.

"Make sail to pursue that ship!" says I to Tilling.

"Aye aye, sir!" says he, and the hands rushed to obey even without orders because they'd all been listening. So the helm was put over, the yards were hauled round and the sails trimmed, and *Tromenderon* turned in her massive bulk and beauty. The decks heeled and the topmen did every imaginable thing – again without orders because that's what topmen do when there's a chance of prize money. They did every imaginable thing to get speed out of the ship, and the waisters and idlers cheered them on, and the middies and ship's boys jumped up and down in the fun of a chase, and even the lieutenants were grinning.

But Barker the whaler just shook his head.

"T'aint no good, Cap'n," says he. "We're a fast'un for our size and no mistake, but this ship won't never catch a Michelois Marie which is built for speed before all else."

"I can see that, Captain Barker," says I, "but what we can do is go where she's heading to see who she's talking to and where she's going."

"She's on course for St Michel, sir!" says Tilling.

"Thank you, Mr Tilling," says I, then looked at Pyne, "and since we're pursuing three ships of the line, and might soon be in action …"

"Sir?" says Pyne.

"Send the men to breakfast!" says I. Oh yes, I know that some of you youngsters may laugh at that. 'Send the men to breakfast' indeed! But it's not funny because that's what any sensible officer did. Because if we did go into action, and the tars were to heave and haul at the guns and rigging, then they'd do it all the better with full bellies.

After that we had some hours to be patient. The men gobbled down their food and so did the officers and so did I. When all the eating was done, I gave the order for general quarters and the ship was cleared and ready in record time. All credit to the tars, because they loved a fight and gave their best, and bless their hearts because unlike myself they thought that *Tromenderon* could smash any three that were ever put to sea from France. I know that was their mood because once the ship was cleared and steady on course for St Michel – and the Michelois Marie duly over the horizon having left us behind – I went round the ship, as a captain should to put fire into the men.

I went round with Mr Pyne but I need not have bothered. I got cheers as I walked down the gun decks where the crews were already stripped to the waist, with sweat-bands on their brows, and the powder monkeys standing with reserve cartridges ready in their leather cases. They cheered and yelled and bellowed.

"Jacky Flash! Jacky Flash! Jacky Flash!"
"We'll give it them Frenchy sods!"
"Don't care if it's three or thirty of 'em!"
"God save the King!"
"God bugger Napoleon!"
"And his mother!"

They were all so happy, and all so certain. Even Pyne followed their mood.

"By Heaven, sir," says he, "I can't wait to get alongside Admiral Barzan and show him what real gunnery is!"

"Quite right, Mr Pyne!" says I, because that's what you have to say when the men are listening.

"Steady fire, and mark your targets, my lads," says I in a great shout. And all up and down the gun decks the men cheered.

"Jacky Flash! Jacky Flash!"

So then I went up on the quarterdeck again and stood with my officers around me. The trouble is, as I have said before in these memoirs, that once action is joined – which effectively it was with *Tromenderon* making great speed towards the very place where Barzan's squadron was bound – then there was nothing for a Captain to do. The Master had set the course; the First Lieutenant was conning the ship; the Lieutenants and mids would command the guns and choose targets; the marines would blow the enemy's marines out of their fighting tops, while the Boatswain and his crew would trim the rigging, and the Carpenter and his mates would repair any battle damage.

So, my jolly boys, that left your Uncle Jacob with nothing to do than worry. Thus, by my calculations, the three French ships between them had two hundred and forty heavy guns against our ninety plus ten carronades, and the French Admiral – Barzan – was a gunnery wizard who'd kept his people at life-firing practice for months. So not only were we outnumbered, but the traditional British gunnery advantage was lost.

It was a bad time, believe me, and I was in a rare mood.

"Shut up that bloody noise!" says I when one of the upper deck gun crews started dancing a hornpipe, with the rest clapping and singing. "Mr Pyne? What's bloody wrong with you? I'll have discipline aboard this ship!" But Pyne smiled.

"It's only the hands showing spirit, sir. Fighting spirit!"

Well, I won't tell you what I said in reply to that, since I'm not proud of it. The result was a surly silence and no more hornpipes, and the lieutenants and mids exchanging glances with raised eyebrows when they thought I wasn't looking.

Then it got even worse. For a while we thrashed along and the island of St Michel came up as a smudge on the horizon. We even saw another Michelois Marie at great distance. It wasn't the same one, being rigged different, but it too wore the French flag and it too sent up a rocket.

"See that, Cap'n?" says Barker. "The buggers is out lookin' for us!"

But that wasn't what was worse. What was worse was another shift in the weather. The wind came round to the north, and from the cold of it, it must have come straight from the polar regions. It brought a heavy rolling swell and it brought fog. It brought dense, wet, white fog, and even the lookouts up in the tops could barely see beyond the bowsprit, so we crept along under the least sail that would give steerage way, and we groped like a blind man in a strange house.

"Cap'n, sir?" says Barker, when the fog came down. "Can I have a word, sir?" But I was in such a mood that I ignored him. "It's important, sir," says Barker. "It's a great hazard, sir." I still ignored him. "Mr Pyne? Mr Tilling?" says Barker, turning to them, "it's deadly bad."

"Oh damn you," says I. "What is it?" Barker stamped and saluted. "Best if I shows you on the chart, sir," says he. So I let him. We went into Tilling's day cabin, and looked at the best chart we'd got of St Michel.

"See here, Cap'n," says Barker. "There's few safe approaches to St Michel. Here's the mouth of the bay, here's the rocks, and worst of all is this." He indicated a curved line of crosses on the chart. " 'Cos it stretches out near a dozen miles from just north of the bay in a great horseshoe of a shape. It's currents and rocks and shoals, and it's death to mariners. The Frenchies call it Mashwah Doo Dee-arbler ... The Devil's Jaws!"

[Fletcher detested all foreign languages, especially French, and would not allow me to write down anything other than his ignorant, and phonetic pronunciation of *Mâchoires du Diable*. S.P.]

"The Devil's Jaws?" said Tilling. He smiled and took a little poke at Barker. "Can't even *you* find a way, Captain Barker? You who took us through the Madelaine? Can't even you find a way to go where others don't dare?"

Barker grinned and shook his head. Something tickled at the back of my mind, but I couldn't get hold of it because it bore on something else that I couldn't remember. Meanwhile, the fog was thick and we blundered on at the speed of a plodding cow. Watches changed; night fell; hammocks were slung; and only cold food was eaten with the fires put out since the ship was still at general quarters. We spent two days like that, and then just before noon, the weather shifted again, the sun came out, the wind freshened and the fog blew away.

You have to imagine the change that this brings on the open sea. The shift is colossal. One minute you feel as if the whole world is smothered. You can barely see from the taffrail to the fo'c'sle. You can barely see the topmasts, everything is damp and wet. Your shipmates are grey ghosts, and such sail as can be set is hardly filled. It's like having a wet towel over your face. And then – and in so small a time as you can barely believe – the fog lifts. It blows away. It disappears. In a miraculous instant, you can see the sun and the sky, the vast open wilderness of the horizon, and you are free, and fresh and clean, and you think you can soar like a gull. It's a joyful moment that all mariners know, and you breathe deep with the enjoyment of it.

Or at least you do if you don't find yourself with St Michel island suddenly enormous, and black on your lee, so close that you can see the white waves breaking on the shore. Even that alone stops the heart soaring like a gull, but what sends it sinking like lead is the sudden sight of three French line-of-battle ships, spread out over the ocean in a great triangle with your own ship plumb in the middle of it.

There was a huge groan from *Tromenderon's* people, but the lieutenants and mids went among them and called for three cheers which the tars gave. The marine drummer boys beat a long roll, just to remind us all that we were at quarters. I was up on a carronade slide yet again, putting my glass on the enemy, as was everyone else. It was Barzan's squadron. It was them! It was all three of them! Three of the latest and best that French shipyards could send to sea, and they really did look the part. They were splendid, beautiful, powerful ships. They were some miles off, each was hoisting battle ensigns and coming round to steer towards *Tromenderon*. I do believe I actually heard bugles blowing and drums beating aboard of them. I looked round to yell at Pyne, but he was already yelling.

"Union flag to all mastheads!" says he, and the men cheered again as the colours went up and streamed out in the wind. Then he came over to me where I stood on the carronade and swept off his hat with a flourish. "Your orders, sir?" says he. "Which of the enemy shall we defeat first, before we batter the other two?" Oh God Almighty. Didn't I just envy him in that moment? Didn't I just want to be a simple man like him? No imagination, driven by duty, no dreams outside of the Navy? But his words got yet another cheer from all hands on the quarterdeck because they were just the same as Pyne.

And then ... the wind blew through my mind and the fog cleared just as it had from the sea. I knew what it was that I couldn't remember when I felt that tickle in my mind.

"Mr Pyne, Mr Tilling and Mr Barker!" says I, "I shall need your close attention, and you will oblige me by sending for the Boatswain and the Carpenter, because I shall need special efforts from them besides. I shall also need a dozen or so of midshipmen: but only those that are speedy and bright."

"Aye aye, sir!" says Pyne.

Soon after, *Tromenderon* was close hauled on the larboard tack, under every stitch of sail that she would bear. We were making our uttermost best speed, and straining mightily to go faster. Pyne even had the topmen hauling up buckets of water to wet the sails, in the belief that it would make them draw harder.

We were running away, my jolly boys, we were running away.

Chapter 22

"If Papa had not sent out the Maries, we would otherwise have been trapped in harbour."

(From the journal of Enseigne Antoine Leclerk, aboard *Triomphe du Peuple*, undated.)

Captaine de vaisseau Carbonneau – in command of *Triomphe du Peuple* – was trying to do too many things at once, because *Triomphe du Peuple* was caught in Queen Charlotte's Bay, with the English in sight, and coming on under all sail. Carbonneau was attempting too many things because Barzan was behind him, hopping with anxiety, and yelling comment at every order Carbonneau made, while the Irish-political Donovan – that diamond-loving kisser of Bonaparte's arse – was yelling right along with Papa Barzan, in total ignorance of the sea and everything in it! So it might not have been Carbonneau's fault that he did not – could not – do everything perfectly.

The problem was getting *Triomphe du Peuple* to sea in a great and improper haste when so much activity had been devoted to setting up camp, and getting men and stores and guns ashore. The guns alone were massively heavy and hard to move.

"Leave the God-damn guns!" yelled Papa Barzan.

"Leave them!" cried Donovan.

"Admiral! I *am* leaving them," said Carbonneau, but pointed to the main deck where a team of men on hauling lines were heaving up a 36-pounder that had only just been lowered into a longboat. Thus two and a half tons of iron was swinging under a triple block made fast to the main yard. "I'm leaving all but that one!" he said, "because it's got tackles rigged for lifting and we'll need every gun if it comes to action! There's six of them ashore that I'm leaving behind and that's six too many!"

"Yes, yes," said Barzan, and patted Carbonneau's shoulder. "Do your best, lad. Just do your best." Carbonneau smiled. He loved old Barzan. Everyone did: especially now that he was so old and frail. So Carbonneau did his best for Papa Barzan.

Carbonneau had to bring aboard all hands who were out of the ship, get up *Triomphe's* anchor, and make sail while clearing for action. But that was a matter of detail at which the French excelled. Every man's duty and location at any time was known. In addition, Carbonneau had to bring aboard the Michelois volunteer, who was renowned as the best pilot on St Michel, and who knew every rock, cove, and cliff in the Gulf of St Lawrence. Carbonneau thought that this at least, should be easy: all he had to do was send word ashore to a man so eager to help that he stood constantly at his own door awaiting the summons, and with the crew of a pilot boat standing by.

Also, in addition to being efficient bureaucrats, the French are active and energetic so everything was going well, though with much shouting and discussion. Thus, where Carbonneau stood on his quarterdeck with Barzan and Donovan, everything was activity and movement, with teams of men going at the double before all else, to get the ship to sea. The capstan bars were rigged and the messenger made fast; the men heaved with a will and the cable came aboard, dripping seawater, weed and little fishes. The men at the bars sang merrily, even as the shore-workers came alongside in swift-pulling boats that clustered in shoals around the huge ship, and the men swarmed up and over the side like a boarding party, cheering as they came.

"Good! Good!" said Papa Barzan. "God bless the Michelois! Them and their pretty Maries that kept lookout, and so proud to wear the colours of France! We have to be careful so deep into English Canada. Who knows what ships of theirs might appear?"

"Yes," said Donovan, "but do we know what's coming? We know they spotted an English man o'war. We know that from their rockets. But what is it?"

"Buggered if I know, and buggered if I care," said Barzan. "After all these weeks of practise, all I care about is the chance to put round-shot into an Englishman's belly! I don't care what's coming so long as it's English!"

Then another boatload of men came over the side, and in the rush – and as happens when men are in haste – some of them stumbled, and staggered and fell into the men on the heaving line that was holding up the 36-pounder. The line went loose. It whipped and whirred in the great triple block leading to the gun. Men fell back with skinned palms from trying to hold the line ... and the gun took its chance to plunge down and straight through the bottom of one of the boats alongside *Triomphe du Peuple*.

Men yelled in fear, throwing themselves out of the way as the boat splintered and its broken-back wreckage was hurled into the air. Three oarsmen were killed outright and dragged down with the gun, while another was thrown into the waters of the bay, where he thrashed and throttled, and being unable to swim, he miserably drowned little more than an arm's reach from the men in other boats that tried to save him. So the gun and four men were lost.

But *Triomphe du Peuple* was got out to sea in remarkable time, and that was the main thing as far as Papa Barzan was concerned. He pinched Carbonneau's cheek and grinned as *Triomphe* passed out through the arms of the bay. With the accident of the gun in everybody's mind, nobody noticed that they had failed to bring the pilot aboard: the Michelois seaman who knew every rock, cove, and cliff in the Gulf of St Lawrence. Unfortunately, he'd not been standing at his door after all, and had to be searched for. Time passed, and eventually the oarsmen in the pilot boat could not catch up with *Triomphe du Peuple*, however hard they pulled. They gave up and turned for home, even as the pilot sniffed the weather and looked at the sea.

"Put your backs into it, boys," he said. "There's fog coming."

The pilot was right. The fog smothered the ocean. It smothered everything so that the lookouts of Barzan's squadron couldn't see the shore, the sky, each other or anything beyond their own bowsprits. Barzan and his officers stood wrapped in greatcoats and mufflers on the quarterdeck of *Triomphe du Peuple*. Barzan grinned and nudged Carbonneau.

"See?" he said. "The Good Lord is a republican!" Carbonneau smiled. All his officers smiled. They liked it when Papa Barzan spoke like this, because even though the Great Enlightenment of the Revolution forbade religion, every one of these young men had been raised as a good Catholic. "See?" said Barzan. "The Lord left us just long enough for us to get into formation before he shut down the heavens."

As it turned out, the Lord shut down the heavens for two days, and when finally He lifted the fog, Barzan and all his men looked around in the bright clear light, and they cheered with elation.

"Enemy in sight!" cried the lookouts, and drums rolled and bugles sounded aboard all three ships. Battle ensigns were hoist, and Papa Barzan danced for joy. He threw his arms around even Donovan, and for a moment ceased to detest him.

"Look!" said Barzan. "Look what God has sent us! He put it right in the middle of our squadron! What a beauty! Wait till we blow it mast-less and haul it back to France!" All hands cheered, but Carbonneau – with his glass focussed on the big ship – was unsure.

"She looks French!" he said. "Look at the lines of her! How can she be English? And just one ship as big as that? And all by itself? Have the English Canadians got ships like that?"

"Who cares?" said Barzan, with his own glass on the big ship. "Look at her colours! She's hoist her colours and she's God-damn English! She looks French because those shitty-arse English copy our ships because they can't make anything better!" He turned to Carbonneau. "Monsieur le Capitaine!" he said. "Signal the squadron to engage the enemy! Signal them to pursue with utmost vigour!"

So the three ships of Barzan's squadron came about to close in on the single Englishman. They came round with drums rolling and crews cheering. But then the cheers changed to groans.

"She's running away!" said Barzan.

"Just like that frigate we took!" said Carbonneau.

"That was only proper," said Barzan. "She was just a frigate. But this one's a three-decker!" He shook his head. "I'm almost ashamed for them. I never thought the English were cowards." He paused. "And maybe worse?" Barzan got up into the mizzen shrouds for a better look at the fleeing Englishmen. He climbed awkwardly and with visible effort. He waved away the hands that reached out to help him, even though his strength was failing these days. He clung on, with thin, old hands, and he looked out over the ocean. "That English captain's a God-damn fool," he said. "He's got a fast ship under him; he's set all plain sail, and he's setting still more … and he's heading straight into the Devil's Jaws!"

Chapter 23

At the time I didn't know which of the three French ships was which, but later I learned that *Triomphe du Peuple* – Admiral Barzan's flagship – was a couple of miles astern of *Tromenderon*, while *Bataille du Peuple* was a mile to the north of us, and *Ascendent du Peuple* about half a mile off to the west. Each was a fine, new ship mounting eighty 36-pounders. These beauties had Tromenderon in a three-finger pincer which they squeezed by altering course to bear down *Tromenderon* with '*guns run out and matches burning*' as we said in those days: not that we used matches to fire the guns, because it was all flintlock triggers by then, even in the French service.

Meanwhile, *Tromenderon* was running north, just as hard as she could go and I was in close conference with my senior officers, together with Captain Barker, and the Boatswain and the Carpenter, and a dozen of middies. We were under the break of the quarterdeck with the ship heaving on a heavy swell, while above us every sail was bulging, with constant hailing from the lookouts to keep us informed of the French squadron's movements.

"Enemy fine on the larboard bow, and closing on the port tack!"
"Enemy abaft the beam, and steady on course!"
"Enemy dead astern, and setting stuns'ls!"

But you have to ignore all that, or rather it goes into the part of the mind where it belongs while you get on with what you're saying. It's like keeping your feet when the deck heels. You don't even know you're doing it.

I spoke to the middies first.

"Listen well, you young gentlemen," says I, "for I am about to do something that will need utmost judgement from myself, and instant communication of my orders to the Boatswain and the Carpenter who will be at opposite ends of the ship. So I rely on some of you to be by my side, and others spaced out to carry my orders. Arrange this among yourselves, but do it well. Do you understand?"

"Aye aye, sir!" says they, and the little buggers gaped at me in hero-worship. I was Jacky Flash, you see, and could do no wrong. And so to business.

"Gentlemen!" says I to the rest. "What do you know of clubhauling? Has any of you been aboard a ship that did it?" That made them think, and Pyne was honest enough to be the first to shake his head.

"I know what it is, Cap'n," says he, "we all do. But I've never been in a ship that did it."

"Aye aye!" says most of them. But Owen the Boatswain said nothing, and he was a veteran of forty years' service. He said nothing but looked grim.

"Mr Owen?" says I, "will you not give us your thoughts?" Owen touched his brow and looked at me.

"Well Cap'n," says he. "Years ago I was a hand in the old *Dionama* frigate, under Cap'n Blake, God rest him for a true gentleman."

"And?" says I.

"Well, Cap'n, we was embayed off a lee shore hard by Trabane, in Ireland, and Cap'n Blake – what with there being no room to tack nor wear – he gave the order to clubhaul."

"Go on, Mr Owen," says I.

"Well, Cap'n," says he, "we got the anchor down and ran it out to the stop, with a spring made fast to the anchor ring, but when the strain came on, the spring – the hawser – why, it tore out the timbers between three ports, and heeled the ship something cruel. She rolled right over, and she filled and went down. All hands perished other than me and a few that clung to a spar." He stood straight, touching his brow again. "And that's the God's truth of it, sir!"

I groaned inside. That sort of tale was the last thing I wanted to hear. So I did my best.

"Mr Owen," says I, "we commiserate in your loss."

"Aye aye!" says everyone.

"But you said the 'old' *Dionama*," says I. "Was she an old ship?"

"Aye, Cap'n," says he. "She went down in '81, what was launched in '49." I seized on that because everyone knew that rot killed more ships than shipwreck or the enemy, and all you iron-steamer youngsters should remember that!

"Ah!" says I. "There you are then, her timbers were probably rotten, and ours are not. Ours are prime, seasoned oak!" I smiled and tried to look confident, but Owen had put doubt in their minds, so again I had to do my best. "Gentlemen," says I, "I was aboard the frigate *Phiandra* under Captain Henry Bollington who won the battle of Passage D'Aron and was knighted for it." They nodded: the battle was famous and Bollington was renowned as a gunnery expert and a fine seaman.

"I had the honour to serve in that battle," says I, "and also to be aboard *Phiandra* when Captain Bollington clubhauled off the French coast in a howling gale, and brought the ship and all hands safe out to sea." They nodded again and this time they smiled. You see, it fitted their mythology of Jacky Flash the rollicking boy, God help me. "Yes, gentlemen," says I, "clubhauling is mainly employed as a desperate last resort, when a ship is embayed." I paused. "But it can also do something else."

They listened as I explained, and God help me again because they trusted me. Even Captain Barker, the Newfoundland whaler, smiled when I told him what I wanted from him. He smiled and laughed because he'd got accustomed to standing by me, and being addressed as Captain. He got so saucy that it was in my mind to knock him down for it.

"Ooof!" says he, with all the rest listening, "are you going to trust me with *that* Sir Jacob? Are you going to trust the ship and all hands on *me*?" He looked at the others. "Well I can see how *he* got his knighthood!" says he, pointing at myself. "He got it for bloody bravery!" They all laughed and it lifted the spirits which was good, so he didn't get knocked down after all.

But after that it was all busy work for dozens of men. A hauling line was passed from the lee cathead outside the ship from bow to stern, and brought inboard through the stern-most gun port of the middle deck. Then the line was made fast to the free end of a hawser – a huge rope sixteen inches in diameter, needing a team of men to handle it.

With the hauling line at one end, a measured length of the hawser was made fast to the stern-most strongpoint in the ship, which was the after capstan, then the free end was drawn by the hauling line, and led out through the aftermost gun-port. With much teamwork and careful leaning over the lee rail, the great, stiff hawser was led forward, and secured to the ring of the chosen anchor. In that condition, being fast at one end to a capstan and the other to an anchor, the hawser was now named in sea-talk, as a 'spring'.

Meanwhile, the real heavyweight champion of ropework – a twenty-four inch diameter anchor cable – was led up from the cable tier below and secured to the same anchor ring as the spring. That being done, we were ready for the manoeuvre I had in mind, and which I hoped would give the French a nasty surprise.

Unfortunately, the French were better seamen than I'd hoped. Our course was due north with St Michel on our starboard beam, and straight towards the Devil's Jaws just as fast as *Tromenderon* could go. But one of the French Squadron – *Bataille du Peuple* – was north of us, heeling hard over, and steering to get between us and the Devil's Jaws.

"Enemy coming about to cross our bow!" cries the foremast lookout.

"Sir!" says Pyne, she's aiming to rake us!"

And that was very nasty, my lovely lads, because the worst harm that one ship could do to another was to cross its bow or stern where there are very few guns, and then to deliver an entire broadside down the length of the ship, firing as the guns bear, one after another. Every shot then scours the length of the enemy's deck, smashing and killing and throwing over the guns. If it was done well, then raking by the bow or stern would settle the fight in one stroke.

"Damnation of that!" says I. "Put up the helm, Mr Pyne, and steer to bring us alongside of her. So the wheel was spun, the yards were trimmed and we dashed towards *Bataille du Peuple* with both ships running hard, and racing to get into the best possible position. *Bataille* aimed to cut across our bow, but we planned to deny that and come alongside of her and give our broadside in return. I don't doubt that, since both ships were fast, our combined approach must have been near that of a galloping horse which was something remarkable when, normally, two ships going into action would strike all but tops'ls, in order to keep fewer men aloft and more at the guns. But here we were under all sail and closing at a pace barely believable.

At that point we were at risk of being raked or in collision. And with the ship in the hands of Mr Pyne and Mr Tilling and damnation and buggeration on myself doing nothing, I ran along the gun decks yelling and shouting, clapping the mids and lieutenants on the shoulder, calling out to the gun-captains by name, and saying all the usual things.

"Don't waste your fire! Take your time! Wait for the order to fire! Wait till we're close!" The lieutenants and mids copied me.

"Don't waste your fire!"

"Wait for the order!"

"Wait till we're close!"

From time to time I stooped and looked over a long black barrel and out through a gun port. At first it was only the heaving waves, but then there she was, and what a magnificent sight to see! Pure grace and power under a tower of bulging sail, and charging on at fearful speed with the sea boiling white under her cutwater. What a sight! But it was only quick glances because mostly I wanted to make sure the gun crews did their job. So I was on the lower gun deck when we opened fire, and the French fired seconds after. Christ Almighty, but the noise was awful. You can't imagine how loud a bellow comes out of a 32-pounder, and so much smoke. All hands on a gun deck are deaf and damn near blind at the first salvo. The guns thundered, and bounded back, and were checked by their breechings, and the gun crews followed the drill I'd hammered into them.

As I ran up a companionway to get back to the quarterdeck where duty said I should be, there was hideous blast of sound, and six-foot splinters flew tumbling through the air, and bits of men with them, as a shot came smashing through the side of our ship. The noise and shock of it alone threw me off the stairs, and I grabbed the rail and heaved myself up. I clearly remember stepping on a large piece of a man's hand with a bit of wrist still attached. But you ignore such things in battle. And then I was on the quarterdeck, and the marines were blazing away, and the carronades jumping in their slides, and shot howling through our rigging, and Pyne yelling through a speaking trumpet at someone. Then he saw me.

"Sir! Sir!" said he, "look there! We've got the advantage of them! We're on the lee side of her. She's heeling towards us and rolling heavy, and *they can't open their lower gun-ports!*" I peered through the smoke and, by looking out over the waist of our ship, I could see *Bataille* some ten or twenty yards off, and her upper gun deck blazing and hammering. Then our broadside went off again: Boom! Boom! Boom! Boom! Ripple firing: each crew taking its time and firing after the gun ahead. That blinded us again, because you youngsters must never forget how much smoke comes with a ship's broadside, and how much you are firing blind when close alongside, which is why it's so very easy to miss completely unless you really are close. But then ... yes! Pyne was right. *Bataille* was a beauty, but she was rolling far more deep than *Tromenderon* and that was something the French shipbuilders didn't get right.

That meant that their forty-gun broadside was reduced to twenty guns, since they couldn't open their lower deck ports for fear of the sea coming in. It was their twenty against our forty-five plus five carronades. I was thinking that we must batter her into wreckage, when she fired again, all steady and sure. It was an excellent, well-aimed broadside that sent heavy round-shot straight into our main deck, doing dreadful harm. I even saw a gun blown out of its mounting on our weather side and across the waist and over the lee rail, such as you wouldn't believe possible for such a mass of iron. I saw that and I saw men blown into meat and rags, and others screaming with hideous wounds.

But then our lower decks fired, and all the world vanished in white smoke and colossal noise. When the wind blew the smoke away, we were pulling fast away from *Bataille* because, although we'd been hit bad on the main deck, our sails and masts were intact. Meanwhile, the Frenchman wallowed with her mainmast blown into a stump, a jungle of wreckage over one side and her waist covered in canvas and rigging. But still she rolled, and I saw the damage our guns had done to her *because* of her rolling. She'd taken hit after hit below the waterline.

"Look! Look!" said Pyne. "See where she's holed! It'll be all hands to the pumps aboard of her!"

"Get us back on course, Mr Pyne," says I. With smoke still clinging about the ship, I looked around for Barker and prayed that he'd not been hit by shot or splinter. That was another nasty moment since much depended on him. But there he was, raising his hand in salute.

"Is it up into the foretop, Cap'n?" says he, and you couldn't fault his eagerness, not if you knew what I was asking of him.

"Into the foretop if you please, Captain Barker," says I.

"Aye aye, sir!" says he. He darted up the weather fore-shrouds, hand over hand like a nimble topman, and straight out over the futtock shrouds as a true seaman must, disdaining the lubber's hole, to get up with the fore lookouts. He deserved a cheer for that but the hands were too busy with the meat and wreckage in the waist, heaving overside everything that would go to clear the decks. That, my jolly boys, included the dead and the pieces of dead, for such was the tradition of the Service, but it was shocking to see none the less.

But seamen are seamen, and the mess was cleared, the loose guns made fast, and we had to make do with the guns and men that were left. Again I got up onto a carronade slide, looked ahead, and looked astern, and so did everyone else that had no instant duties. We saw St Michel huge on our lee and we were running hard. There was some sight of white water in a curving line across our course ahead. That was the Devil's Jaws: hard to see, but they were there. It took an expert to know how close we were getting, and when we must steer away from them, especially in a ship going so fast as *Tromenderon*. But Barker was that expert, and this was part of our plan which needed our pursuit to come on at speed. I could only hope that the plan would work, because it was entirely mine.

Looking astern, I saw the other two Frenchmen setting all possible sail, and charging on after us and, by Jove, but they were fine sailing ships. They rolled heavily but they were coming on like mail coaches with the drivers whipping hard. They'd caught up something wonderful while we were exchanging broadsides with *Bataille du Peuple*, and were closing the remaining distance, especially the one that turned out to be *Ascendent*... and puff-puff! Puff-puff! Silent white clouds spouted from the bows of each ship and were blown away. Then thud thud! Thud thud! The sound of their bow-chasers. At first the shot went nowhere. We barely heard the howling of their passage.

"There!" says a little middie, hanging over the side, and pointing to the distant splash of a shot. "They couldn't hit a barn if they were inside of it!"

"Shut your blasted trap!" says I, "or the Boatswain's cane 'll tan the arse off you!" I was under great stress. The key moment must be soon now: very soon, because we were running fair into the Devil's Jaws at such a rate. Much now depended on Barker, and on the teams of men on the lee anchor, the cable, and the hawser. But everything else depended on our French enemies still believing something that was untrue: something that was nonsense. It had all seemed so clever when I had my bright idea, but now I wasn't so sure.

Chapter 24

"Papa Barzan would have saved us. We might even have saved ourselves but for Donovan."

(From the journal of Enseigne Antoine Leclerk, aboard *Triomphe du Peuple, undated*.)

Captain Carbonneau raised hands to head in anguish. He was tormented because, although he deeply respected Papa Barzan, he had been at the battle of the Nile and Papa Barzan had not!

"Admiral!" he said, "I beg you to believe me! It's true!"

"Bah!" said Barzan, but his officers disagreed.

"Yes!" said those of *Triomphe's* officers gathered on the quarterdeck, with many others listening and all saying 'yes'. They said 'yes' because, while few of them had been at the disaster of the Nile, they'd all heard the story, and they knew the Republican Navy's explanation.

"I was there, Admiral," said Carbonneau. "I was aboard *Mercure*. And when our flagship caught fire, we had to cut our cable to get clear before she blew up. The loss of life was horrible. And it was all because the God-damned English knew the ground better than we did!"

"Bollocks!" said Barzan. "The God-damn Rosbifs don't have maps that good. It was all God-damn Nelson taking a risk and getting away with it! If we had that God-damn Michelois pilot with us, he'd have told you we can't get through the Devil's Jaws!"

"Admiral," said Carbonneau pleading. "We can't know that because we never asked him!" Barzan stamped his foot in anger and shouted into Carbonneau's face.

"We never asked him because nobody was so shitty-arsed stupid as to ask such a stupid question! It's seamanship that counts here, not maps and English sextants!" Carbonneau looked away thinking of Papa Barzan's one weakness. He was a fine a seaman, a great seaman, but he was one of the old kind that sailed with his eyes on the sails, his hand on the tiller, and his nose sniffing the wind. He had no mathematics and despised maps and instruments. So Barzan might not understand how good the English were with maps. Then Carbonneau felt ashamed because the thought was disloyal, and anyway who really knew the truth about English maps?

"Papa Barzan," he said, "you know what we think of you ..."

"Then do as you're told!" said Barzan, " and come about, and steer away from those God-damn rocks!" Still Carbonneau dithered; then a lookout hailed the deck.

"*Bataille du Peuple* engaging the enemy!" Carbonneau, Barzan and everyone else turned to look. They stared in fascination as *Bataille* closed with the English monster at great speed and both under a full suit of sails.

"*Bataille's* going to rake her by the bow!" said someone, and there were cheers.

"No!" said Carbonneau. "They'll hit bow-to-bow! Look at the speed of them!"

"Wait!" said Barzan, and everyone gasped as the English ship came about, to run broadside to broadside with *Bataille* and the two ships vanished in smoke, with the heavy detonations of the guns coming seconds later, in a great and repeated pounding. Soon, nothing could be seen, and then a groan rose from *Triomphe's* people as the powder smoke cleared and *Bataille du Peuple* could be seen with her mainmast blown over one side, and the English ship pulling away fast, back on her course.

"There!" said Carbonneau. "She's going through the Devil's Jaws! She's going straight through. It's what I said. The bastards have got better maps than us, just like at the Nile, and they know a way through!" "Captain!" said a signals officer, "*Ascendent du Peuple i*s signalling. She's signalling *Danger ahead.*" Carbonneau and Barzan each raised his glass to look at *Ascendent's* signal flags.

"Good!" said Barzan. "There's one captain at least that knows we're in danger." He glared at Carbonneau. "Signal *Ascendent* to come about. She's further on than us. She'll be on the rocks long before us. Make the signal now!"

"But Admiral," said Carbonneau, "if the English can get through, then so can we! And there's still two of us. If we can catch them and beat them, then it might swing the Americans behind us!"

"If! If! If!" said Barzan. "And what if we lose both ships?" He leapt up on a quarterdeck gun, grabbed at the tarred lines of the mizzen shrouds to steady himself, and turned to address the crew. But he was too old for leaping and grabbing. His fingers slipped and he fell. He fell badly, hitting his head on the gun carriage. There was a gasp from everyone who saw this, and everyone rushed forward to raise Barzan to his feet. But he was totally limp, deeply unconscious, and blood was pouring from a gash that ran from brow to chin.

"Get the surgeon!" cried Carbonneau. "Get him at once!" There was much shouting. The surgeon came running with two of his mates, a dressing was applied, and Barzan was carried below. It was done quickly, and with Barzan gone everyone looked to Carbonneau for a decision. Carbonneau raised his glass. He looked at the wreckage of *Bataille du Peuple;* he looked at the English three-decker, pressing onward at great speed and straight into the Devil's Jaws. He looked at *Ascendent du Peuple* with signal flags still flying, every inch of canvas set, and catching up with the Englishman ... and suddenly Carbonneau was in doubt.

Could the English really be that good with their maps? Had Nelson merely been lucky at the Nile? Carbonneau looked at the men around him, awaiting his decision. He sighed. His instinct as a seaman told him to come about and save *Triomphe* and *Ascendent*, but his pride as a French officer could not let the English ship escape. Not when he might yet take her into Boston as a captive, and show the Americans what France could do. That would be the greatest possible political argument and the greatest possible seafaring argument to persuade America to join France in this world-wide war. But what if he ran *Triomphe* and *Ascendent* onto the rocks under full sail?

Thus, all arguments were equal in Carbonneau's mind and he could have chosen either path if only he could make a decision. Unfortunately, he could make no decision ... but someone else could. Donovan could: Callum Donovan the Bonapartist agent. He had his flaws and plenty of them, but he was just like Bonaparte in being ready to take the great risk, to seize the shining hour! In addition he was just like Bonaparte in being deeply aware of politics, and deeply ignorant of seafaring.

"Follow them!" says Donovan. "If they can do it, so can we!"

Chapter 25

They began to hit us with their bow-chasers. The 9-pound balls came screaming in through the stern windows. Up on the quarterdeck, we heard the smashing of glass and the scouring of shot running the length of the gun decks. We heard that and the screams of men and the resounding clang as a gun was hit. We lost three guns that way, and five men, which was good shooting by the French, and worryingly better than I'd have expected.

But even under fire, every man in our ship was mainly concerned with the speed at which we were running into the Devil's Jaws. It was fast-sailing weather now, with the swell easing and a steady north-westerly filling our sails. But that wasn't good in a seaman's mind when heading straight for the rocks with the two French ships actually overhauling us.

The three of us thrashed onward and the sky was blue, the sea slid past, the wind sang in the rigging, and the spray came over the bows. So wasn't it all pretty and fine, my jolly boys, and a piece of sea-going poetry? Yes, except that everyone could now see white water, black rocks, and grey sandbanks ahead and on either beam. My guts were wringing themselves into knots; my eyes were screwed up tight, staring up at Barker in the foretop, and my mind was praying hard to the God that our Chaplain didn't believe in.

"Almighty Father in Heaven," I thought. "Please let thy faithful servant, Captain Barker, keep a sodding sharp look out. And may it please you, O Lord, that his sodding foot shall not slip, such that he falls out of the sodding foretop." Just then:

"Ah!" A dozen voices as Barker turned to face the quarterdeck and waved his arm. He'd judged that the moment was come.

"Now!" says I, in the greatest, loudest shout that my lungs could deliver. "Put up the helm and bring her into the wind!"

"Aye aye!" cries the helmsman, as he and his mates spun the wheel.

"Let go!" I cried, and the chain of mids carried my order to the Boatswain and his crew at the lee cathead, where one of our best bower anchors was released to plunge in with a measured run of cable, and a measured run of hawser.

At first, *Tromenderon* merely answered the rudder, heeling heavily but not even feeling the anchor go down. But then two things happened together: she came round, head to wind and her fore-sails were thrown flat aback, while the anchor struck bottom and bit. With the cable stopped – secured so it could run out no more – the cable tightened viciously, throwing colossal strain on the anchor bits: the great timbers below the fo'c'sle to which the cable was made fast in the ship.

And then, by God and the Devil, she felt the pull! And by God and the Devil, even the anchor bits groaned and the whole, enormous mass of a three-decked ship – with seven hundred men aboard, and stores and ship's boats, and ship's guns – the whole huge mass was brought up sharp, with the wind forcing her sternwards. Everything aboard that wasn't fastened down, was rolled, sliding or staggering forward. I saw men stumble and even fall. Even hardened seamen. Even I staggered, so violent and sudden was the change in her motion.

And that, my lads, was our first test. Would the anchor hold? Would the cable snap? Would our timbers split under the strain? Which, by shipyard skill, seasoned timbers and good luck, they did not. Then, the wind drove the ship sternwards to swing on the cable like a pendulum fixed to the iron hook below. But that was only half of it. Now came the really tricky part, for this was clubhauling, my jolly boys, and I remind you that clubhauling was a desperate manoeuvre. So now I had to get to the aftermost gun port of the middle gun deck, with mids astern of me, to where another judgement must be made.

That meant running down companionways and along the deck past lines of guns and gun crews, and this time I got no cheers. Instead, the men looked at me in fear, because they'd forgotten *Phiandra's* success and were fixated on *Dionama's* failure. Perhaps they were right because *Tromenderon* was about to feel the pull of the hawser made fast to the anchor beside the cable. But not yet! At the stern-most gun port of the middle deck, the gun and its crew were aside, with the Carpenter and his mates in charge, while the rest of the gun deck – over three hundred men – were looking on, because this was the moment of judgement.

"Out of my way!" says I, to the Carpenter's mates.

"Aye aye!" says everyone. I looked up and down the gun deck, then got my head as far out of the port as I dared, took a good look, then back in again. I closed my eyes and felt the ship's motion. I felt her head coming round and round at the bow.

"Now!" says I. "Slip the cable!"

"Slip the cable!" says the first of my middies, and the word went up the line to the bow.

"Slip the cable!"

"Slip the cable!"

"Slip the cable!"

"SLIP THE CABLE!" cries the Boatswain, and the cable was un-stoppered. It ran out like a monstrous serpent with all hands standing clear, until all the tension came off, because now the hawser was taking the strain. Once again there was a huge groaning of hemp and timber as the ship put its weight into the hawser, which creaked loudly and stretched so tight against the for'ad side of the gun port, as to cut in splintering deep. It convinced me and everyone who saw it that the ships timbers would be split like those of *Dionama*.

But the timbers held and the hawser did what we'd hoped. With the ship going astern, the pull of the hawser on the lee, stern-most side, forced the ship to turn almost within her own length, vastly faster than any ship could otherwise turn, until she was facing exactly back the way she'd come. Up on deck I could rely on Mr Pyne to order the yards swung, such that the wind would fill her sails and get her under way, taking her out of the Devil's Jaws as fast as she'd run in.

There was just one more thing to do, and for the hell of it, for the devilment of it, I did it myself. One of the Carpenter's mates was standing ready with a big axe, because there was no other way when the hawser was under such strain.

"Give me!" says I, and the axe was mine. "Stand clear!" says I, and swung hard. It took two more blows and then the rest of the fibres parted with a sound like gunshots. The entire outboard length of the hawser flew off and away, and was dragged under with the anchor and the cable, which all had to be left and lost. But what was an anchor and rope, compared with a ship and all aboard of her?

Meanwhile, I suppose I really was Jacky Flash. The men thought so, for sure, and they cheered and cheered and there were more cheers when I got up on deck again. But then there was a gasp of amazement and horror, because as we came out of the Devil's Jaws at fine speed, less than a mile on our larboard beam, there was *Ascendent du Peuple* run hard onto undersea rocks, with her foremast over her fo'csle, her mizzen sagging against the mainmast, and the whole ship grinding and heaving as the sails still drew. The ship's people were up in the tops trying to cast loose the sails. It was bad and it was ugly because no seaman ever wishes to see a ship on the rocks. Then there was another gasp from our men as *Ascendent's* fore mainyard came loose and shook off a whole line of topmen into the sea where they would surely drown.

Everything had gone as I'd planned. We'd used clubhauling to reverse our ship's course, and lured that French ship into the Devil's Jaws such that she'd gone onto the rocks. We'd won and were clear and away and should have been happy. But then we *saw* what we'd done. We saw a ship on the rocks and twenty sailormen thrown into the sea.

I saw it. We all saw it. We even heard them cry out, and if I'd been able, then I'd have tried to save them just as hard as if they'd been our own. But I couldn't risk the ship, and we'd never have got there in time. None the less, I knew, in that moment, that any man in the water isn't the enemy but a brother mariner in distress. I've talked this over with many seamen over the years, and everyone who'd been situated as I was that day, agreed that he carried the burden ever after, of not going to the rescue. It's hard, my lads, it's very hard. But the sea life is hard.

Meanwhile, we couldn't dwell on our sorrows, because while we'd been battered by the first Frenchman, and left the second on the rocks, the third was waiting for us all angry, pristine and entire. It's just as well that I didn't know then that the ship was *Triomphe du Peuple,* flagship of the squadron and Admiral Barzan's own ship: Admiral Barzan, who'd trained his gunners as hard as I had. Also, *Triomphe's* guns threw shot of 36 French pounds, which equal 39 English pounds, against our 32s! What's more, we weren't a 90-gun ship any more, because we'd lost fifteen guns: wrecked dismounted or blown overboard.

"*Everyone blamed Donovan. But it was ourselves who listened to him*"

(Journal of Antoine Leclerk)

"Holy Mary, Mother of God!" said Carbonneau, and he didn't care who heard him because the English ship seemed to spin on its keel, and everyone aboard *Triomphe* was staring in disbelief at such seamanship.

"The bastards are clubhauling!" said his first lieutenant. "It's got to be that! What else could it be? They've tricked us! They haven't got a way through. They haven't got better maps. It's a trap!"

"Put up the helm!" cried Carbonneau. "Get us clear while we can!" *Triomphe* at least came round and clear, being way astern of the Englishman and *Ascendent du Peuple*.

"What's happening?" said Donovan, at Carbonneau's elbow. "What's happening?" But everyone ignored him, and Donovan began to worry. Then it got worse: far, far worse.

"Oh Jesus!" said Carbonneau, and crossed himself. "Holy Mary! Holy St Denis!"

"Oh no!" said a dozen voices, and everyone aboard *Triomphe* who saw it, groaned in agony as *Ascendent du Peuple* tried to come about and clear the danger, but ran hard and full onto rocks that smashed her hull and threw her foremast over.

"Oh Jesus and Mary!" said Carbonneau. He could not stop himself from looking up at the signals hoist above: the signals flags still telling *Ascendent* to 'Pursue the enemy'.

"What's happening?" said Donovan, desperate and horrified and knowing that there would be a reckoning in Paris. He shook Carbonneau's arm. "What's happening? This isn't my fault. I'm not a sailor."

"You!" said Carbonneau, looking at Donovan with poisonous hatred. "You ... you ..." Carbonneau had just enough self-control – in front of his officers and men – not to fall into the pit of pouring obscenity and spite on Donovan's head, when he, himself, was to blame for taking Donovan's advice.

"Oh Jesus!" said the First Lieutenant. "Look at *Ascendent*!" Then, "Sir!" he said to Carbonneau, "can I take a boat to go to her aid?" Carbonneau looked all round. He looked at *Ascendent*; he looked at the dangers of the Devil's Jaws and, above all, he looked at the English ship, now coming up fast on his stern. He sighed. He made an appallingly hard judgement.

"No!" he said. "We shall engage the enemy. We shall do what Papa Barzan taught us. We must do that first, and only then we may go to the aid of our comrades." He put a hand on the First Lieutenant's shoulder.

"Bring us about! Lay us alongside of the Rosbifs so that we can do our duty! Our duty to France, our duty to the Republic, and above all, our duty to Papa Barzan!"

Some of the men heard that.

"Barzan! Barzan! Barzan!" they cried, and the chanting spread along the main deck, and down the companionways to the gun decks "Barzan! Barzan! Barzan!" From stem to stern, from keel to topmasts, every man in the ship cried out, as if the ship's heart were beating for him: "Barzan! Barzan! Barzan!"

We saw *Triomphe* steering towards us and I was determined to fight her downwind, on her lee side, having seen *Bataille du Peuple* unable to open her lee gun-ports when heeled over. Perhaps *Triomphe's* captain had seen it too, because he certainly steered hard to avoid that, or maybe he was aiming to rake us by the bow, just as *Bataille* had tried?

In any case, we two ships *Tromenderon* and *Triomphe* closed warily, as I shortened sail down to tops'ls and the French captain did the same, for a steady and controlled approach with time to manoeuvre. I had our 9-pounders going. I ordered the bow-chasers into action at once, and the crews rushed forward, loaded and ran out.

Bang-Bang! They fired together and, by Jove, but the French were only an instant after. There was screaming and howling over both ships, and spars knocked away, and holes punched in sails, but a 9-pounder is only an irritant when aimed at the bows of a big ship.

This time there was no mad gallop, and we two ships slanted into action at little more than walking pace, with myself yelling at the helmsmen to get on the lee of the enemy. I do believe I heard the same coming from them, because we were that close in the end. *Triomphe* was huge, and rolling towards us. I could see the men in the tops, the crews of their bow-chasers plying ram-rods, officers waving swords on their fo'c'sle, and their men cheering.

We turned; they turned. Our marines popped away at their marines with muskets. The gun-captains stood by with lanyards in their hands, waiting for sight of the enemy through the gun-ports. Soon we were only pistol-shot away, with the ships closing bowsprit to bowsprit, and a collision looked certain.

"Shall I call away boarders, sir?" says Pyne, and I wondered. If it came to boarding, then whoever went first had the advantage. But calling away boarders meant less men at the guns. I looked at *Triomphe's* fo'csle, and saw no sign of a boarding party being mustered.

"No!" says I, turning to the helmsmen, "and you bloody well get us under her lee!" I shouldn't have bothered. The helmsmen were already doing their best, and so were the sail trimmers. It was well done by our helmsmen and topmen because, just an instant before the bowsprits touched, even though there was a grinding and snapping of tangled rigging at the bow, the two ships slid clear of each other and ran past at spitting distance. So our broadside thundered and bellowed, and their broadside thundered and bellowed, and you cannot even imagine – you who've never heard it – how appalling a noise is made by a heavy gun when you're in front of it. And you cannot even imagine – you who've never been there – how utterly blinded everyone was aboard both ships with tons of powder exploding in seconds and turning into choking white smoke.

Likewise, you cannot imagine what it was like to be aboard a ship when a heavy shot comes through the side at a thousand miles to the hour, and smashes everything in its path. Even one such hit is dreadful as it penetrates three foot of solid oak, sending jagged splinters in all directions. Oh yes, my jolly boys, even one is dreadful, let alone the dozens that come aboard in a close action, and we were very, very close indeed. In the end it was a straight-up battering match: their gunners against our gunners; their drill against our drill. It was a matter of which ship could throw the most iron when right alongside of each other, such that aiming didn't matter and speed was everything.

"Donovan ran away as soon as the battle commenced."

(Journal of Antoine Leclerk)

Donovan ran below as *Triomphe's* guns opened fire. He had no duties when the ship was in action so nothing was expected of him, and he was very, very afraid. He was afraid because he had good reason to be afraid.

He stumbled as *Triomphe du Peuple* shuddered to the discharge of her guns: one after another in a perfect ripple broadside. The noise was hideous, but it was nothing compared with what followed when the damned bloody English opened fire at a range of less than twenty yards. Donovan choked on the powder smoke; he was deafened by sound; his eyes stared at the long rows of gun crews and massive black guns. He only half saw them through the smoke. They were a pantomime of horror, a study of souls in torment.

But Donovan wasn't afraid of that. He wasn't afraid of gunfire and battle. He was far too preoccupied. What tormented Donovan's soul was the fact that he'd told Captain Carbonneau to follow the English into the Devil's Jaws. He, Donovan had done that, and done it before so many witnesses that he would be unable to deny it: not when everyone else would be straining to save their own lives. And therefore, when the matter was reviewed in Paris – as inevitably it would be – then Bonaparte, who valued only success and wanted only men around him who were lucky, would withdraw all favour from Donovan the clever agent, Donovan the forger, Donovan the maker of cunning arrangements. Instead it would be Donovan who sent three ships to disaster, and then God help Donovan because the guillotine would be calling for him.

He stumbled again as the English shot came in through *Triomphe's* planking throwing iron and splinters in all directions. Donovan got up, pushed past a line of powder-boys bringing cartridges to the guns, and ran down another companionway to be safe below the reach of the English guns. He needed time to think: time to invent something, anything that would shift blame. He got right down to the lower gun deck, where the men and guns were idle for some reason or other. He thought himself safe – at least from the English – when Triomphe gave another broadside from the deck above, and the English replied. Donovan paused and smiled because he'd just thought of something very clever. It really was ingenious. It was the way out. It was all about knowing where the diamond mine could be found! So he didn't have time to realise that he was *not* safe down here, because shot came in so fast that he never even saw the massive splinter – six feet long and a foot thick – that threw him down and ripped him open.

Chapter 26

The Royal Kraal,
North Zulu Land,
In the summer of the 12th Year of the reign of
King Ndaba KunJama,
(1801)

"But still the witch M'thunzi went between Inyathi and Zithulele with evil words."

(From the Saga of Inyathi)

It was night, but fires were burning and all the people were sitting in solemn silence in the assembly ground in the centre of the kraal. The men were massed in military order, while the women and children sat separately, by family and clan. The fires crackled and the light flickered on thousands of solemn faces.

Facing them, the three greatest men of the Kingdom sat with their attendants and some privileged women at the western side of the assembly ground: King Ndaba, Prince Zithulele, and General Inyathi the Buffalo. They sat on stools of ironwood, on raised mounds and with guardsmen behind them.

Thus, the people sat in the night, and were transported into joy by the sound of King Ndaba's Royal Singers: fifty men, chosen for the richness of their voices and trained in the songs of the North Zulu folk. They did no other work than singing, and did not bear arms because they were so precious that they could not be risked in battle.

They sang, and they moved with expressive gestures that enhanced the music. They sang and swayed, and their leader gave the verses of each song in a voice that was powerful, yet smooth and melodic. His singing was repeated and amplified by the rest, in deep and rolling harmonies that shivered the flesh of the listeners. Thus, all believed that the Royal Singers were working a form of magic: one that was noble and kind and splendid.

But there were other forms of magic, and the witch M'thunzi was powerful in all of them. She went hopping to the side of King Ndaba. She went with her followers behind her, and they made a travesty of the lovely singing, by hopping in time with it.

"Royal Majesty, live forever!" said M'thunzi into the King's ear, as his attendants cringed. The King's face was blank and he sat in a puddle of urine, and everyone knew that his soul was lost. But M'thunzi spoke a few words before leaving, and the senile creature twitched as they stirred some fragment of his memory.

Then she hopped towards Prince Zithulele. But Zithulele was fierce and young, and his guardsmen made a pretence of blocking her way with their white shields. She waved them aside. They looked at Prince Zithulele and he nodded. So she had her way, and she poured many words into his ear.

"I greet you, Royal Prince," she said. "He who must be King! We are gathered because tomorrow the regiments will go forth to fight the Arabs. Is that not so?"

"Yes, M'thunzi, the Witch," he said.

"We are gathered, because many of those who go forth with plumes and spears will never return. Is that not so?"

"Yes, M'thunzi, the Witch," he said.

M'thunzi continued with many statements, rhythmically delivered, until Zithulele's attendants gasped to see their prince's eyes roll up and his chin sag. Then M'thunzi came to practical matters and explained to Zithulele that the Arabs were a mere distraction, and that the real enemy was Inyathi. Finally, she warned that Zithulele was about to witness an appalling insult, which must be long remembered.

She snapped her fingers, and roused Zithulele, and she hopped and pranced towards Inyathi the Buffalo. But now the people gasped, and even the Royal Singers stopped in the midst of their music. They gasped because, as M'thunzi approached, General Inyathi raised a hand and his guardsmen stepped forward, planted shields on the ground in front of them, and stamped the ground.

"Ha!" they said, and stood unmoved in M'thunzi's path.

"Stand aside," she cried, "or I shall smell for demons!"

"Stand fast!" said Inyathi. "There are no demons in my regiment!"

"I give final warning!" she cried. "I shall smell out all of you and others besides!" The people gasped again. The men gripped hard on their spears, and the mothers clutched their children. But M'thunzi merely looked back at Zithulele. " Royal Prince?" she said. "This is the great insult that I spoke of. Do you see it?"

"I do!" he cried. M'thunzi nodded, well pleased, then turned to Inyathi.

"So, Prince of Buffalos," she said, "I warn you that ..."

"Get away, old woman!" cried Inyathi with a great shout. "You have no power over me!"

"No?" she said. "When you are about to fight the gunpowder of the Arabs? And the two magic weapons? The two made of gold? Do you think you can win without my blessing?" Many of Inyathi's councillors pondered on that, but Inyathi sneered.

"Go away," he said. "I give this for your magic," and he spat upon the ground. The entire assembly of people was astounded. Some stood. Some ran to their houses. While M'thunzi herself entirely lost her temper. She had hoped to light a fire under Zithulele at the insult of her being denied audience with Inyathi. She had expected that. She had contrived that. But she had not expected outright denial of all that she was, and in that rage she frothed and ranted. Little of it made sense, except repetition of one theme.

"Mine is woman's magic ... men know nothing of it ... woman's magic ... you are nothing ... you are a man!"

Such was her reputation that Inyathi's councillors were wavering. Their fathers and grandfathers had taught them to fear a witch, and a witch's power was woman's power. Even Inyathi regretted what he had said. But someone else did not. Inyathi's wife, Ulwazi, stood forward: Ulwazi who was rescued from the slavers; Ulwazi whom M'thunzi had approached as a possible successor; Ulwazi who was now married to Inyathi and knew him to be a good and noble man.

"Listen to me, witch!" she said, and all the men gaped to see a woman speak, and one so young and so beautiful. "You have no power over the Lord, my husband," she said, "because my husband is followed by so many spears that he has no fear of you, and no fear of gunpowder!"

"Well spoken, O wife of my heart!" said Inyathi, and he stood and embraced Ulwazi and fell in love with her, whom previously he had taken only for beauty.

Then three things happened at once: M'thunzi, the Witch, fell down in a fit; Zithulele's envy of Inyathi became madness, and Inyathi the Buffalo worried about the two magic weapons: those that were drawn on wheels and were made of gold.

"They were like gold, my guns. The bronze all polished. I was so proud of them."
   (From the diary of Auguste Renard, late of Napoleon's Field Artillery)

The guns shone golden yellow in the African sun, and Malmuk the slaver gazed at them as they sat clamped into oaken carriages that each had two big wheels. Each gun tipped slightly forward, such that its long trail was raised up on a second set of wheels that had a shaft and harness for the horses that pulled the guns. Malmuk shook his head in admiration, because any man could see that this was beautiful equipment: ingeniously made and superbly fit for purpose.

Malmuk nodded and beckoned his followers to come and see: his Janissary officers, his Bedouin leaders, and the head-men of the Sudanese spearmen. All these came forward and looked, while the French artilleryman stood with arms folded and with his teams of gunners and drivers behind him. They were under discipline, in quiet rows, even though some of them clearly weren't French but north African, and few were in proper uniforms. They would fight if the money was good. They were mercenaries.

As for the artilleryman himself, his name was Renard, and he did have a uniform, shabby and stained as it was, complete with a blue-white-red sash and a bicorne hat. He hadn't come cheap, even though he was only a sergeant major. Malmuk wondered briefly what had happened to the officers in charge of these guns? But it was wise not to ask such questions and keep to practical matters. Thus, Renard had been late joining the expedition on the long journey to North Zulu Land. He'd had to gallop to catch up: with his guns and men bouncing on the road.

But all was well now. He was here among the rows of tents and tethered animals, and the hundreds of men looking on at the new arrival, and leaning on their spears and muskets. Malmuk consoled himself with the thought that his late arrival was the least problem to be expected from a renegade who'd deserted his own army, taking men and equipment with him.

Meanwhile, Renard smiled and slapped each of the bronze barrels. "There you are, Monsieur," he said to Malmuk. "That's two of Bonaparte's finest: his *lovely girls*, as he calls them. Best field artillery in the world! Everyone knows that: Prussians, Austrians, Englishmen, they all know that." Malmuk nodded. He hated the French, but he knew their military reputation, and he'd learned their language for business need.

Renard continued his lecture. "These are Gribeauval 12-pounders," he said, and pointed. "See there, Monsieur? Screw-thread elevation!" He pointed again. "And these here are levers and drag-lines to train the guns so's they can bear on the enemy, no matter what direction he comes from." He pointed again. "And here's the shafts and harness for the horses. Six horses for each gun to make sure they move fast and easy." Next, he walked away from the gun-carriages to four wagons of strange design. Malmuk and his followers came after him. They stared at the wagons which looked like gun-carriages except that they bore long, coffin-like boxes.

"These is what we call *caissons*, Monsieur," said Renard. "Four horses each to draw them, to keep up with the guns,"

"Caissons," said Malmuk, and Renard threw open one of the long boxes to reveal racks of short, fat cloth sausages. "And these are cartridges," he said, "each one holding a charge of powder and the projectile, all in one go for quick loading, and there's fifty rounds in each caisson." He looked at Malmuk. "And for this job, we've got forty of cannister and ten of round-shot in each caisson."

"Mainly cannister!" said Malmuk. "That's good!"

"That's what you asked for, Monsieur," said Renard, "and my lads can deliver a round a minute. If we give them round-shot from nine hundred metres, and cannister from six hundred … then your Zulus can't even reach us." But the Janissaries and Bedouin frowned, muttering among themselves, and the senior Janissary officer spoke to Malmuk.

"Effendi?" he said. "Does this Frenchman understand the manner of a Zulu attack?" Malmuk turned to Renard.

"You do know that the Zulus charge at the run, don't you?" he said.

"They don't march like your army: they run!" But Renard just smiled and patted the gun barrels.

"We've stopped cavalry with these," he said. "We fire alternately so one's shooting while one's reloading, and that way we deliver a round every *half* minute, which is always cannister at close range when we can't miss. And that stops a cavalry charge, you just believe me. That's cavalry that's *used* to cannon fire, while your Zulus have never even heard of artillery."

Malmuk and the rest were impressed. Renard could see that, and he was pleased because he needed the money from this job, so he hadn't entirely told the truth. Yes indeed he'd seen a cavalry charge broken by 12-pounders: he'd been there. But on that occasion it had been a full, 8-gun battery that stopped the charge, not just two guns.

Chapter 27

Triomphe du Peuple was the finest gunnery ship that I ever fought in all my years at sea. Their drill was fully as good as ours, and they matched us in speed, broadside for broadside. All credit to them for doing that, especially because the *disadvantage* of heavier shot is that they were heaving 39-pound shot into the mouths of the guns at each reloading, while we heaved only 32, and after a while that tells on a man's strength. I learned afterwards that it was their old Admiral that made them fight so hard. They fought for him even though he was down below in the sick bay, having fallen and stunned himself. So it was his drill and his leadership that inspired them.

It all goes to show what the French might have achieved if they'd trained up all their gunners as Barzan did, because the main reason why we always won a fleet action was simply because our gunners fired faster than theirs. So it's a mystery to me – as I've said before in these memoirs – a mystery that Boney never understood this, because the little bugger was an artilleryman by training, so he damn well should have understood. But he didn't, and serve him right.

Meanwhile, and in the end, *Tromenderon* vs *Triomphe* was a battering match in which *Triomphe* was let down by the only flaw in the design of such magnificent ships as the *du Peuple* class: they rolled too much. Whether or not it was my efforts to get under the lee of *Triomphe*, or whether it was just her rolling, the fact was that she never got her lower deck into action because the gun-ports were under water on the downward roll. So it was our full battery against their upper deck, giving us nearly a two-to-one advantage even with fifteen of our guns knocked out.

But even then it was close, and for another reason. The French very often aimed high in a close action, with the aim of dismasting us, so that they could then manoeuvre into a position of advantage such as firing into the stern. So, while we always fired into the hull to hit their guns and their men, the French always aimed aloft. Or rather those did who hadn't been trained by Barzan. That old salt made them fire into the hull just like we did.

The result was that after more than an hour of close action, and firing blind as I've said, *Tromenderon* and *Triomphe* drifted apart because, on both sides, the gun crews were exhausted, having fired away more shot in that time than ever they'd done before: them and any other ship in the world, if you ask me.

On our gun decks the men were flat and gasping beside the guns. They were soaked in sweat, and they lay beside the ruin that each side had inflicted on the other. There were dead men, broken men and pieces of men all round. There were guns thrown over and gaping holes all down the sides of the ship, where light streamed in beside the gun-ports. There were groans and sighs, and men dying and bleeding, and the surgeon's mates doing their best to get the wounded down below. I had all hands helping them – including myself, my officers and mids – all hands who hadn't been exhausted at the guns, and what a business it was in dealing with the dead and the mangled dead.

But we were still under sail and under way, and the smoke cleared when the guns stopped firing. I got up on deck again and looked at *Triomphe*. I looked at her and saw that she was even worse off than we were. We'd taken heavy losses and been savagely battered, but at least our ship was alive, with men going about their duties, even if they staggered and stumbled. *Triomphe* was a dead ship. She never actually struck her colours; they were still flying, but she was finished as a fighting ship.

There was so much to do aboard *Tromenderon* that it wasn't for some hours that we could turn to *Triomphe*. There were shot-holes to plug, wreckage to heave over the side, the chain pump to repair which had been smashed, wrecked guns to be secured for fear that they should go loose across the decks. There was even some damage to the rigging, because shot will go where it will sometimes, and not go where it's aimed. We had to get some food and drink into the men, and of course there was a huge task of attending to the wounded. Finally, with action ceased, and with so many killed, we had to give respect to the dead and prepare them for a decent burial, sewn up in their hammocks.

This was done quickly, since dead bodies don't keep, and it was done with the minimum of words from Dr Goodsby. All hands stood bareheaded as the hammocks – dozens of hammocks – went over the side to the sound of the Boatswain's calls.

With that miserable duty done, and late in the day, I took our longboat – hastily repaired of its shot-holes – and a dozen marines, a couple of officers, and a boat's crew armed with cutlass and pistols, and we pulled the miles that the ships had drifted apart. I went myself because I'd guessed what we might find aboard *Triomphe*, and even though I never wanted to be a Sea Service officer, I was one indeed, and couldn't pretend that I wasn't, and I wasn't going to give this task to someone else. Also, I took the surgeon and his mates even though they were now as exhausted as our gun crews.

So we went aboard … and now, my jolly boys and my jolly girls too, your Uncle Jacob is going to spare you any full description as to the state and condition of *Triomphe* as we found her, and especially the state and condition of her dead and wounded. I shall spare you that because there are some things in life that are best forgotten, and which should not be hauled out from the dark into the light. But so that you should know a little of it, I will give you one example.

As we boarded, the men spread out in case there was any attempt at resistance – which there was not. I saw one of our tars heave up his guts at something, and then wipe his mouth, and take his cutlass and lean over a poor, ruined thing that had been a man. It was opened up and spread out such that you could not believe it could live, and yet it did live, and it clutched at the air and moaned for its mother. So the tar took his cutlass – entirely without anger – and gently put the point to the breastbone, and leaned sharp and swift to bring an end to suffering. But as he did this, one of our lieutenants turned on him. The lieutenant's name was Eaton and he was only seventeen but I'd brought him along because he spoke French.

"You bloody villain!" says Eaton. "You'll hang for that!"

"Hang and be damned," says the seaman, looking at the dead man, "but if ever I'm like him, then please God you'll do the same for me!" Eaton drew breath to shout, then fell into sobs, and don't any of you reading this think that he was weak, because you can't see what was all around him.

"That's all right, lad," says the seaman, and put his arms around Eaton. He was old enough to be his father. "Never mind," says he, and patted Eaton's back.

That's just one example for you and it's quite enough.

And now there was much to do, so we got on with it. First we roused out every fit Frenchman left in the ship, and I kept Mr Eaton busy – which was good for him – translating my orders. So all their small arms went over the side, and the French officers were mustered on the quarterdeck away from the men, though there weren't many of them: only the Captain, whose name was Carbonneau, and just two lieutenants had survived. Eaton gabbled away in French to Carbonneau, who looked more dead than alive, and Carbonneau saw sense, agreeing that if his ship was to be saved, then his people and my people must work together. But first he gave me his sword.

"Monsieur," he says to me, and bowed. The French are like that.

"Captain," says I and we raised hats to each other, because I suppose we're like that too. Then he chattered away in French, looking me in the eye.

"He's asking if we could send a surgeon across," says Eaton. "Their surgeon and all his mates were killed when a shot came into the orlop." Eaton looked round. "But I think our surgeon's gone below already."

"Good," says I, "tell him that."

After that, there was the same grim and tedious work to do aboard *Triomphe* as aboard *Tromenderon*. Having made sure that *Triomphe's* people were not going to fight, and having taken Carbonneau aboard *Tromenderon* to make sure he couldn't change his mind about surrendering, I gave command of *Triomphe* to Mr Pyne as the rightful reward of a first lieutenant after a successful action. Thus, the grim and tedious work was all his. But he didn't mind. He was too dull and serious for that. Of course he did a good job though, and he got *Triomphe* in a state to make sail within two days.

Just one more thing of importance – very great importance – happened before I left *Triomphe* and returned to Tromenderon. One of our men came running up to me and touched his brow.

"Mr Tate's compliments, Cap'n," says he, Mr Tate being our surgeon, "and would you please join him down below, Cap'n." He looked at me with an odd expression. "Mr Tate says it's something wonderful odd, Cap'n." He touched brow and stamped again. "So if you'd follow me, Cap'n, I'll take you down."

I went with him, and once again I'll not go into detail regarding the sights, sounds and smells of a surgeon's operating workshop down on the orlop deck, after a monstrous hot engagement. I'll only say that this one was worse than usual, having taken some heavy hits from our guns. It was below the daylight, lit by lanterns. I had to step between the wounded and crouch down, because the deck-head down here was only five feet high. There was Mr Tate beckoning from a corner. He wore a blood-stained apron, his sleeves were rolled up and he looked very, very tired. God knows how he could do such work as his under such conditions. But he did, and his mates were doing the same all round, with men still untended and waiting, and crying out for help. Perhaps that's why Tate was brutally short in what he told me, because he was constantly looking over my shoulder to choose which patient was next.

"Captain, sir!" says he, and stretched out his hand. "I think you should have this. I think it's real." I reached out, and he dropped into my hand something incredible. It was a diamond, a blue-white diamond bigger than a hen's egg. It twinkled in the lantern light. It bloody near spoke to me. It beckoned to me. It was indeed wonderful. Tate pointed down to a man laid on the deck: a red-haired man, covered in blood-soaked bandages, and mumbling to himself.

"He had it in a pouch round his neck," says Tate. "His name's Donovan and he's Irish. I think he was with the French. He keeps talking about a diamond mine. He was torn open by a splinter, and I can't do any more for him."

"Diamond mine?" says I, but I'd lost Tate's attention, because one of his mates was calling his name and waving.

"Must go, sir," says Tate, and he was off, working on someone else. I looked at the diamond, and looked at Donovan, and he blinked and focussed on me.

"Who the bloody bastard hell are you?" says he.

"What's this?" says I, showing him the diamond.

"Damned if I'll tell you," says he, "because it's mine, you fucking English bastard, and it's going to save me. So I'll tell you nothing!" But then he told me everything, because he was dying and he was raving, and I suppose he was talking to himself really. "It's the Blue Star, you bloody bugger, and it's worth half of France, and Bonaparte'll love it, and bless me for it, and there's plenty more where that came from."

"Where did it come from?" says I.

"Buggered if I'll tell a bloody sod of an Englishman!" says he. "The Zulus have got them. They wear them in their hair. They've got a diamond mine by a river, and never a bloody damned word of it shall you hear from me!" But he said a great deal more, particularly about *Sheba's Breasts*, whatever they were. He went on and on about them. They were the main marker and signpost to the mine. He said enough to make me think that a determined man, with the right ship and some good charts, might be able to find this river, and these Zulus … and the mine …

Then he was gone. He sighed and died, and his eyes closed. I looked at the diamond and it looked back at me. It broke the light into rainbows, and it got inside of me with a fearful hunger for possession. I wondered what it was worth and I looked round, putting it into my pocket. Then I looked around again. Mr Tate seemed to have forgotten about the diamond. He was up to his elbows in blood, shouting for someone to bring him a sponge. He never even looked at me as I squeezed past him on my way back to the quarterdeck, and then back to *Tromenderon* as soon as possible.

As I've said, it took two days to get *Triomphe* fit to make sail, and it was the same for *Tromenderon*. But that didn't mean fit to get back to England, or even fit to reach Boston where it would have been wonderful indeed to show off such a prize as *Triomphe*. The problem was the limitations of what could be done by ships' carpenters while afloat and at sea. So, with both ships heavily damaged below the waterline, the best we could do was head downwind, into the St Lawrence seaway and make for Quebec, in British Canada, for full dockyard repairs.

There was another factor too. *Bataille du Peuple* and *Ascendent du Peuple* had managed to save most of their people, since *Bataille* plugged some of her leaks and got under way with pumps going non-stop. This meant that she could manoeuvre for a while, and as *Tromenderon* and *Triomphe* were firing into one another, *Bataille's* captain was organising the lowering of boats, and the building of rafts. Thus, on the day after the battle, a sad little flotilla of boats and rafts came inching towards *Tromenderon* under a flag of truce. There were many hundreds of men aboard who were deadly afraid, knowing that *Bataille* must soon sink, and that boats and rafts could not reach anything French, and that they were at the mercy of *Tromenderon's* guns.

I put forward Mr Eaton again to speak with the French captain, and since there was no question of our leaving them to sink or starve, we fed and watered them, and took them in tow. But I made sure that it was *Tromenderon* that did the towing. I had no wish to put dangerous ideas into the mind of *Bataille's* captain, such as might have occurred if he were – with hundreds of Frenchmen – within a rope's pull of *Triomphe* where many more Frenchman were under guard of a small British prize crew.

There was just one more thing to do before we set off, with rag, tag and bobtail towing astern. That was to give honours to Admiral Barzan, who never recovered from his fall. He was an old man, at the end of his time, and he died in the sick bay under *Triomphe du Peuple's* fo'csle. All the surviving French officers begged that he be given proper burial. Since all aboard *Tromenderon* were profoundly respectful of what Barzan had taught his gunners, I said yes, and went myself in full dress to stand on *Triomphe's* main deck as a service was given by a Catholic chaplain who was only aboard because Barzan wanted him. Goodsby went too, in his robes, and I saw him snivelling as they brought out Barzan sewn into a hammock with a round-shot at his feet and under their flag, just the way we do it. Then they gave their national hymn, the Marseillaise, and slid him over the side. Perhaps even I snivelled a bit, while the French crew – every man of them – were streaming tears and shaking with grief.

When finally we got under way, with damaged ships, and boats and rafts in tow, and with the constant risk of losing them – especially the rafts – we were over two weeks getting down to Quebec which should have been a few day's sail. But there we were received with rapture and with amazement that we'd managed to overcome three French ships of the line.

Or at least we were received with rapture by the British officials who ran the city and by the redcoats who held it for King George. Because although General Wolfe took Quebec from the French in 1759, most of the city's people still spoke French and thought of themselves as French. So at best they were ambivalent about our war with Napoleon, and at worst they were on Boney's side, like the Michelois and their Marie fishing boats.

So I never liked Quebec even though it was a fine city, and one of the biggest ports in North America. It rose up on the heights to the north of the St Lawrence river, with spires and fine stone buildings. It had its theatres, shops, assembly rooms, and paved streets. But I always had that feeling that the people – the French people – growled under their breath and cursed the British when the British weren't listening. On the other hand, Quebec had a good, deep-water harbour, and it had the skills and materials to make *Tromenderon* fully ready for the long voyage home to England. *Tromenderon* was given priority while *Triomphe* was anchored and left, for the moment, although the dockyard people were all over her with their sketchbooks and rulers 'taking her lines' as they said, to record the beauty of her construction, and these sketches would go home with *Tromenderon* for the Admiralty to see.

While the repairs went on, the French were made prisoners ashore so that we were rid of them, and after that, we had to be patient. During that long wait, we learned that *Bataille du Peuple* eventually sank while *Ascendent* broke up on the rocks, and the cheeky Michelois – being bold and ingenious seamen – made money for years afterwards by salving *Bataille's* guns. I say the cheeky Michelois, because having watched the battle of the Gulf of St Lawrence from their Maries, they instantly got rid of all French flags, denied ever flying them, and the Quebec authorities didn't investigate for fear of trouble among the French majority in their city.

Then, by the time *Tromenderon* was declared fully fit, we were deep into the Canadian winter when no captain would face the North Atlantic. It wasn't until April of 1802 that we sailed for England, and it wasn't until June – June 15th in fact – that we finally dropped anchor in Portsmouth, and found that something amazing had happened.

Chapter 28

"I got on well with the Arab. He liked a drink and was good company. But I'd never trust him."

(From the diary of Auguste Renard)

Renard laughed. He poured some more brandy into Malmuk's cup.

"I thought booze was forbidden to you lot," he said.

"Only if we get found out," said Malmuk and he laughed too. He looked round, and then shuffled a bit closer to Renard. The two of them were sitting by a fire in the night, with the expedition's tents all round them. The rest of the men were round their own fires, while the Janissary sentries paced their beats, and the horses and camels shuffled and snorted in their tethered rows. The animals were anxious because the African night was never quiet. Beasts howled in the distance, and insects buzzed and chirruped constantly. They were a pest.

"So tell me again about stopping a Zulu charge," said Malmuk. "Can you really do it?"

"Yes!" said Renard. He kept quiet about having only two guns rather than eight, because that didn't matter if the enemy was going to be a load of savages. Instead, he concentrated on something else. "Well," he said, "we'd need cover on the flanks in case they try to get round us. We'd need cover, just like we would against cavalry, because nobody's going to be so stupid as to come straight at us. Nobody charges down the muzzle of a gun. They always try to go round the flanks or take us from behind."

"I see," said Malmuk. "So what do you mean by cover?"

"The Janissaries will do very nicely," said Renard. "Get them formed up on our flanks ready with volleys and bayonets. That'd do it."

"Good!" said Malmuk, and Renard held out the bottle, having had quite enough cross questioning on this matter.

"Here," he said, "have a drop more, and tell me about these Zulu girls. Why do they fetch so much money?" Malmuk smiled.

"You've never seen one, have you?" he said.

"No," said Renard.

"If you had, you wouldn't ask."

"That good, eh?"

"Oh yes! And they have spirit. They fight back."

"Fight back?"

"Indeed. And our clients like it." Renard thought about that.

"Hmm," he said. "D'you think I could have one? Just to try out?"

"No," said Malmuk. "They have to be pure – untouched – or they're worthless."

"I'd still like to have a little go," said Renard, but Malmuk wagged his head from side to side.

"Oh no," he said. "You can't do that, 'cos it would set a bad example, and then we'd never take home a single virgin." He smiled. "I can trust the Bedouin, but we have to set an example to the camel drivers because they'd screw their own mothers if they got the chance." He looked straight at Renard. "D'you know what we do if they spoil one of the girls?"

"Go on, tell me," said Renard.

"We get them all together – the camel drivers – so they can all see what's happening, and the Bedouin grab the one that did it; we lift up his skirts, and we cut off his balls and stop the bleeding with a red-hot iron."

"Oooooof!" said Renard. "All right! I'll go without." He laughed and poured some more brandy. "So tell me," he said, "how much do they sell for, these girls? Because that's been puzzling me." He pointed to where his guns stood, together with their caissons. "You've got me and my 12-pounders, together with my twenty men and twenty-five horses, and you know that I don't work cheap."

"You don't!" said Malmuk.

"And then," said Renard, "you've got five hundred Turkish Janissaries; you've got a hundred Bedouin and their mounts; you've all those camels and their drivers. Are you telling me that you can sell Zulu girls for enough money to make a profit on all this?" He waved his hand at the tents and men. "And who's paying, anyway? The Bank of France? The Rothschilds?"

"Well," said Malmuk, and perhaps he'd taken more brandy than he was used to, because a man had to be careful with alcohol. Everyone drank it in Cairo, but everyone had to pretend not to. So everyone was careful not to drink too much. But Malmuk wasn't in Cairo now, and Renard had been generous with his pouring. "Well," said Malmuk, "yes, the girls go for amazing prices, and clients come from as far as Morocco and Persia, so we can sell every one, and at a very great price."

"But?" said Renard, looking at Malmuk's expression. "Go on, tell me. You can tell me." And he poured out some more, which Malmuk drank.

"But actually." Malmuk looked all round to make sure nobody was listening. "Actually, we go after the girls to keep everyone's mind off something else."

"So?" said Renard. "What's the something else?"

"It's the diamonds," said Malmuk.

"Ahhhh!" said Renard. "You mean the diamonds the Zulu girls are supposed to wear in their clothes?"

"Their headbands," said Malmuk. "It's only the senior wives, and some of their leaders too, and they've got to come from somewhere. There has to be a diamond mine. We've had scouts out ahead for months – Bedouin scouts – asking questions of the natives, and frightening them with what's coming." He looked towards the guns. "Especially the French 12-pounders."

"Yes," said Renard, "but who's paying for this expedition? And what do they expect to get back?" He poured more brandy. Malmuk's head was dizzy now and he was indiscreet.

"Who's paying?" said Malmuk. "It's supposed to be Abdel Boutros the merchant, but really it's an alliance of political people. This is a deep, deep secret and never spoken of, but if there's a diamond mine, then they want it." He took a gulp of drink, and some of it ran down his chin. "This expedition is just the first step," he said, "because if we find the diamond mine, we'll come back with a real army and take everything. We'll take North Zulu Land. We'll take it from the Zulus and have it for ourselves."

Chapter 29

It was amazing. We were at peace. Even as we'd been exchanging broadsides with *Triomphe du Peuple,* the politicians had been scheming their way out of a war, because it cost too much money to run one. It would have been nice if we'd known that before we opened fire and killed quite so many of one another. But I suppose it's another example of the fortunes of war, which no man can predict. As the French say, it's *Fortunes de la Guerre.*

[Note that this phrase constitutes the only words of French that Fletcher would ever allow to be properly spelt: a unique oddity of behaviour. S.P.]

In fact, we learned that the war was stopped before we even dropped anchor off Portsmouth, since it was hailed across to us by every vessel we passed. A treaty had been signed at Amiens in France on March 25th, and Britain and France were at peace for the first time since 1793, which is a long time. It was long enough to have shaped my youth and ruin my life, haul me away from my true destiny in trade, and into the bloody Navy to face shot and shell, storm and shipwreck, rupture and ruination.

Meanwhile, the Peace of Amiens bore down hard on what happened next, since no government wants to pay for a navy in peacetime. *Tromenderon* was therefore 'put into ordinary' which means anchored and kept safe, but with yards and topmasts struck and most of the men and stores removed, until such time as she might be needed again. Her people, including myself, were discharged, such that all the officers went onto half pay, though the ship's big three permanent warrant officers: Boatswain, Gunner and Carpenter, stayed with her and lived in her, as was tradition and procedure. They even brought wives and families aboard.

The hands – the hundreds of uniquely skilled men who manned and sailed a ship – were paid off and allowed to scatter into the winds, or into the merchant service if they were lucky. Mostly they were happy enough, having a great pile of gold waiting in back pay, and which I moved mightily to make sure they got. But as seamen do, most of them would blow it away on tarts, drink and trinkets and probably end up begging.

So for one reason or another, there was no great farewell dinner as there had been when *Euphonides* was paid off in '99. Thus, our crew – our community – which once had been over seven hundred strong was dispersed, some to one ship, some to another. I certainly didn't get another portable chronometer, but only a bread basket by the silversmith, Paul Storr, which my officers bought as a farewell.

And it wasn't just government meanness that made us glum aboard *Tromenderon* even though we'd won a victory and stopped the French plan for a sea base in the Gulf of St Lawrence. The trouble was that our fight against *Triomphe* had left too many shipmates sewn up in their hammocks. Also, the east-bound voyage – even in April – had been under wet, grey skies, with foul seas, and ourselves short of lime juice such that there were cases of scurvy aboard, which was supposed to have been obliterated in the Navy. It left the ship unhappy.

The nearest we got to a ceremony took place when I went over the side into the launch to go ashore with my sea chest. Those who were left of the ship's people paraded in their best. I shook hands with my officers and said some words, and then the lieutenants manned the launch with the new Number One – who had replaced Pyne – at the tiller. I will also report a brief conversation I had with Surgeon Tate as I shook his hand, since others have reported it differently.

"God bless you, sir," says he.

"Aye!" says those around us, which was cheerful.

"Will you go to your family in Kent, sir?" says Tate.

"Yes," says I. Then he paused and lowered his voice.

"And the stone, sir?" says he. "Have you got it safe?"

"Oh yes," says I, and moved on.

[This conversation was famously disputed within the Navy. Thus, officers standing by Tate and Fletcher insisted that Fletcher's reply to the question *"Have you got it safe?"* was *"No, Mr Tate, I'm afraid*

I lost it." Later, in London, when challenged in White's Club for the truth of the matter, Tate declared, "*Out of respect for Sir Jacob I decline to speak further.*" Thus the matter was never resolved, but should be considered beside Fletcher's intoxicated desire to possess the jewel. S.P.]

After that I got three cheers. And so to the Port Admiral who, by the further fortunes of war, was Penholme-bloody-Forbes, promoted to a new post! And he still didn't like me one little bit.

"I've read your report," says he waving it in the air and scowling, "and I'll tell you Fletcher that I don't believe more than half of it! Have you sent the same to the Admiralty, sir, because I'm damned if they'll believe it either? French naval bases in Canada? Americans ready to go to war on us? One ship of the line against three? I'll tell you, sir …" He went on and on, and I didn't listen, because it was a waste of time arguing with him. Who cared, because the newspapers believed me, and once the Quebec shipyards got *Triomphe* fit to sail, Pyne brought her into Portsmouth by late 1802, and then everyone and his dog believed me.

Meanwhile, my commission was finished, I too was a half-pay officer, and I was free to go wherever I wished. So I did go to my family in Kent. I went to Hyde House, my sister and brother-in-law's home, and was received with huge dinners, a comfortable bed and smiling faces, but – tragically – still no drink was allowed since Brother-in-Law Josiah was an Eastern Wesleyan, and thought drink was the highway to sin. But it was jolly to see the children: Jacob, John, Sally and Sophia and the two new babies – born since I went to sea – Matthew and Mark who were twins.

As before, I ran them up and down the garden, though this time it wasn't in a wheelbarrow, because their pa had made them a small carriage to be pulled by a pony. I piled them all aboard and got between the shafts. Even young Jacob was with them, who was shooting up tall and putting on muscle to the degree that the kinship between him and me was clear. It was all most pleasing except that he was fixed on the sea life, wanting to be like his uncle, and wouldn't believe me when I told him to stay ashore in his father's business.

I had a few quiet days. Then one evening, with the children in bed and the servants elsewhere, I had a word with Josiah and my sister. I showed them the Blue Star, told them everything, and asked what they thought.

Surgeon Tate was right incidentally. I'd kept it safe: very safe. I'd kept it on my person ever since I first picked it up. So we were sat at the table, and the first thing my sister did – for she was a sharp 'un and no mistake – was take the stone and make the test: she scratched a glass with it and then scratched the hard steel of a carving knife.

"I see," says she and fixed me with her eye. "Jacky, are you going to keep it for yourself?" I said nothing, so she pressed on. "Because it's *Prize*, isn't it, Jacky?" says she, clever woman that she was. "Anything taken from the enemy comes under the Admiralty's Prize regulations, doesn't it, Jacky? So shouldn't you declare it? And have you even any idea what it's worth?" I still said nothing, so she turned to her husband. "Josiah, I think you should take Jacky into Canterbury tomorrow to meet Mr Wolff."

So he did. Wolff was a jeweller with a big shop on Sun Street, between the Guild Hall and the Cathedral. The sign over the shop said:

Samuel Wolff and Son
Jewellers of London, Amsterdam and St Petersburg

I'd never seen so much gold and silver as in his shop windows, and he had two big fellows in livery coats and tricornes at the front door, armed with staves to be used against anybody who felt light-fingered. But these beauties touched hats to Josiah and me. In we went, and we were soon sitting in Mr Wolff's front upstairs show rooms where only the best clients were entertained. Wolff was elderly, skinny, dark-eyed and immaculately neat: excessively neat because he constantly plucked at his cuffs and twitched his cravat to get them perfectly right. He wore small, gold-rimmed spectacles on his nose, and he sent for refreshments as we sat down on Wedgewood chairs by a Wedgewood table.

"Oh!" he said when I put the stone on the table. That's all he said but he stopped plucking and twitching, sitting rock still for a while, just staring. Then he snatched the stone away in his fist, as a servant came in with a silver tray, coffee pot, cups and cakes. When the servant had gone, he put the stone back on the table and looked at me and Josiah. "Please wait," he said and got up and ran out. I didn't like that. But Josiah smiled.

"Don't worry," he said. "I've known Wolff for years." So we waited and heard feet on stairs and voices above, and then Wolff came back with a couple of old men, stooped and ancient, but also immaculately neat, and obviously brothers. They were thin and dark, bald and shrivelled, and they needed help just to walk in and find chairs.

"My father," says Wolff, "and my uncle, Asher."

"Good day, gentlemen!" says I and Josiah, but the three of them ignored us and stared at the stone, which was shining in the middle of the table. The two old men gasped, and sat down like sacks of sand being dropped, never taking their eyes off the diamond. Then they gabbled furiously to one another, interrupting and raising voices, and poking fingers for emphasis. This was all in some guttural language which I think was Yiddish. Wolff stood by and looked at them, nodding and occasionally saying something. Then the two old men sighed. The father spoke to me, and pointed at the stone.

"Give?" says he. "Please give?"

"Papa doesn't speak English well," said Wolff. I could see that. But I gave him the stone, and he lifted it up and gazed in awe. Then there was more speech between the three of them and waving of hands, and the son ran out again and came back with a jeweller's balance and weights. They weighed the stone, and the father smacked his palm against his brow in disbelief. They weighed it three or four times more, shaking their heads, and the father looked at me and chattered away in Yiddish.

"Papa," says the son, "English!"

"Bah!" says the father. "You do English. You tell him!" and he jabbed a thumb in my direction. "You tell him!" The son nodded. He took a breath, picked up the stone and looked at me.

"Do you know what you've got here?" says he. "Do you realise that this is probably the biggest cut diamond in Europe? And possibly the world? The value is beyond counting. Beyond belief. We cannot even begin to put a price on it."

"So is it real then?" says I. He just laughed, and so did his father and uncle. They laughed and laughed, and they pointed at me in derision of my ignorance. Then the father frowned and chattered at me, and spread hands in a questioning gesture.

"My father asks who cut this stone?" says Wolff. "The style is not Dutch nor Russian, nor any style that we know. So who cut and polished this stone? It is the work of expert craftsmen in some great city!" He looked hard at me. "But which city? Where did it come from? Who did this work?"

We got no further because I wasn't going to tell Mr Wolff any more. Not him or his pa or his uncle because they already knew too much. But how else was I to make sure that I really did have a diamond and not a piece of glass? In the carriage going back to Hyde House, Josiah pointed out something that should already have been obvious.

"You say the stone comes from Africa?" says he. "And that the women of this Zulu tribe wear such stones in their headdresses?" I nodded. "Well," says he, "I can imagine that these Zulus might dig diamonds out of a mine. But who does the cutting and polishing? Can the Zulus do that?"

I didn't know, and it was the beginning of not knowing much else, because I didn't know what to do next, and that even included wondering if I wanted to go back into trade! That was even though I now had such an opportunity for trade as never before in my life. I was free of the Navy. I was a wealthy man. I was living with people I could trust absolutely, and they were already in trade. My sister had the same head for business as myself, and she and Josiah would welcome me as a partner. Everything was perfect except for something that was in my mind and wouldn't go away. It wouldn't go away because it came back every time I took that stone out of the pouch – because *yes* I was wearing it round my neck just like that red-haired Irishman. It came back every time I took it out of the pouch and looked at it.

And by Jove, but I looked at it, my jolly boys. I looked at it and gazed at it. I wanted it, and I wanted more. I suppose that's the engine that drives any man of business. You always want more. But this time it was a different kind of *more*. So I moped around for days, and didn't show proper interest in anything and finally my sister spoke to me. She got me alone in the garden, and she spoke to me.

"What's wrong, Jacky?" says she, and knowing me so well, she went straight to the heart of it. "It's the diamond, isn't it?"

"Yes," says I.

"So what are you going to do with it?" says she. I told her what was in my mind.

"Ah, Jacky," says she, "and you think you're not a sailor?" She leaned across and patted my hand. "But you are. So I think you'd better get yourself a ship."

Chapter 30

The Royal Kraal,
North Zulu Land,
In the summer of the 12th Year of the reign of
King Ndaba KunJama,
(1801)

"By witchcraft, the followers of Prince Zithulele were persuaded to perform great wickedness."

(From the Saga of Inyathi)

The elite company of the N'gwenya regiment – the Crocodiles – stood in the darkness just inside the northern wall of the thorn hedge around the kraal. They were the victors of many battles. They were sixty strong. They were tall men in the fullness of their strength. They were formidable men indeed, and all the better for their grey hair because one veteran is worth three youngsters in battle.

Each man bore a broad-blade spear of extreme sharpness and a black shield that would make no show in the night. Equally, there were no plumes, no regalia, no noise, no sound: only intense attention as the men gathered close around their commander, Prince Vumindaba, who was the adopted younger brother of Prince Zithulele. They gathered around Vumindaba, and around a small figure wrapped in monkey skins against the cold of the night.

Even these bold men were uneasy to be so close to M'thunzi, the Witch. They cringed at her ugliness and stood back from her stench. But she had to be there because, while Vumindaba had explained everything, he was only of *adopted* royal blood, and she knew that she must give power to his words.

"Listen, O soldiers of N'gwenya!" she said.

"We listen," they said, in deep and whispering voices.

"You go forth to cleanse the nation!" she said. "I have proved to you that Inyathi the Buffalo plans rebellion, and that he will kill our rightful King and his rightful heir. Do you know that?"

"We know."

"And do you know that all men are cursed for eternity, if they do not fight for their King and his rightful heir?"

"We know!"

"And do you know that your entire regiment is with you?"

"We know!"

"And mustered in the dark beyond the kraal?"

"We know!"

"And that the regiments of the Buffalo know nothing of this?"

"We know!"

There were many more words from the witch to place hatred in minds where once there had been love for Inyathi the Buffalo, and this was most difficult because even a witch must struggle if she seeks to persuade with arguments which are obvious lies. So it was a triumph of witch-work that M'thunzi sent away the elite of the N'gwenya, ready to do murder, and trotting swift and silent behind their commander. She saw them go; then she scuttled off at equal speed to be far away when the killing was done: far away and therefore not involved.

Vumindaba was a good soldier and the attack was well planned. He led his sixty men through the kraal in excellent order and excellent silence. Then, well before they came to the house of Inyathi, or rather the cluster of houses where Inyathi's attendants lived around him, the sixty split into three streams so as to attack the main house – the biggest – from three directions, thereby preventing any possibility of escape. The only criticism that might have been made of the attack was Vumindaba's failure to notice the absence of dogs: the absence of the big, sica hounds that defended a Zulu house at night, and reacted with loud barking when anything approached which was not safe and proper.

Thus, Vumindaba himself was first man in through the entrance to the big house, and was first to put spears into the bodies of those asleep on the bed ... and first to discover that the bodies were bags of grass and not human flesh. So he turned in the gloom.

"Where are they?" he said to those who had followed him in.

Then there was a great noise. First the roaring of the sica dogs that had been held by their masters with hands over their muzzles. The dogs were insane with anger and hurled themselves on the backs of the men standing facing the big house, and who were taken unawares and suffered savage wounds from ferocious teeth. Then there was a great shout. It was the war cry of Inyathi's regiment. Men gave this shout as they poured from Inyathi's houses, fully armed, fully awake and charging shield-to-shield and spear-to-spear against Vumindaba and his men. Inyathi led the charge because, while Vumindaba was a good soldier, Inyathi was a great soldier, and Inyathi had long since guessed that, sooner or later, there would be treachery at night.

Even so, Inyathi's men were outnumbered because only so many could be hidden in the houses. They were outnumbered but fought fiercely and Inyathi fought most fiercely of all. He had already pulled spear from three men when he seized the opportunity to attack Vumindaba.

"He's mine!" he cried, and shoved two of his men aside as they went forward to engage Vumindaba. Then it was a great fight between skilled men. Others stopped fighting and stood back sweating and gasping to watch the artistry of it. They pointed to Inyathi and Vumindaba, and cheered and called, and other men came running from their houses to see what was happening.

Inyathi felt iron four times in the first seconds, but struck deeper in reply. He struck deep and never forgot to draw blade against flesh after a miss.

"Uh! Uh!" said Vumindaba, as the blade sliced. Inyathi hooked his shield round the side of Vumindaba's, pulled it aside, and sunk his spear deep between Vumindaba's ribs. But that was not enough for so practised a spear-man as Inyathi, and the spear was jerked out and driven in again, three times.

"Iklwa! Iklwa! Iklwa!" cried Inyathi, as he thrust and pulled, and his men roared their approval. It was the end of Vumindaba, who fell down choking in his blood. But it was not the end of the elite sixty of the N'gwenya regiment. They took up spears again and fought to the last, and every man fell with all his wounds in the front. They went down because Inyathi's men were also the pick of their regiment. They also were grey at the temples, and even if outnumbered they were swept forward by the victory of their General over Vumindaba, and also by the righteousness of their cause. The N'gwenya men, however, knew in their hearts that a witch's words – while infinitely cunning – were not necessarily virtuous, not necessarily wise, and not necessarily true.

Now Inyathi and his men were surrounded by a growing crowd of people, who ran from all sides of the kraal. Also, his women and children came out from the houses where they had stayed hidden. Ulwazi the lovely, ran to Inyathi and looked him over.

"Good!" she said. "You have taken no serious wound, my husband."

"My lady," he said and embraced her, even with shield and spear in hand, and gasping from deadly combat. "And you?"

"I am unharmed," she said. She looked at the dead and wounded lying in the dark, and one in particular. "Vumindaba!" she said. "So Zithulele did this?"

"Yes," said Inyathi, "Vumindaba always was the little boy who did things for his brother!" He shook his head. "So it was Zithulele. Him and the witch!"

"Look," said Ulwazi. "Vumindaba's still alive. He's saying something." Men and women closed in on the dying Vumindaba, who looked up at Inyathi and sneered.

"You have lost, O Buffalo," he said.

"Huh!" said Inyathi. "It is not me who lies on the ground, O Prince adopted."

"No, but soon it will be," said Vumindaba, "because my regiment is mustered at the gate, and yours is not!"

"Ah," said Inyathi, and made swift judgement. "First," he said "*this* is your reward, O traitor, to do this when our whole nation is threatened by the Arabs!" And he finished Vumindaba with a stab to the throat. Then he spoke to his men. "Now we must run," he said. "We must run to the kraal of my father. From there we can muster our forces, but not here. This kraal is deep in the power of the witch."

"The kraal of your father," said his second in command. "A good place. A safe place!"

"It is much more than that," said Inyathi. "It is close to the caves of M'thunzi, and the caves are the source of her stones. If we hold the caves, we may hold her power."

"As you speak, we obey," said his men. Inyathi looked at Ulwazi.

"Tell the women to fetch what they can. We need food and drink for the journey."

"At once, husband!" she said, and ran to the women, clapping hands and giving orders.

"Now, stand with me," said Inyathi to his men. "We may need to fight our way out, and we cannot leave by the gate because the N'gwenya regiment is there. We must cut through the hedge on the opposite side. Fetch tools and axes. Be quick!"

Chapter 31

Lord Spencer picked up the stone. There was bright, morning light from the big windows in the office and, as ever, the stone turned the light into rainbows that twinkled and flashed most wonderfully. By George, but I loved that stone. Spencer stared at it for a long time. Then he put it down and looked at me.

"You took a risk, Sir Jacob," says he, "in letting this out of your grasp."

"Well, my Lord," says I, "in the first place you're a man with the weight of the Kingdom sitting on you, even when we ain't at war." He nodded at that. "And I wanted to speak to you direct, rather than through some lesser person."

"Huh!" he said. "Such as an admiral perhaps?" I ignored that and pressed on.

"So the stone was my letter of introduction," says I, "and I came a few times to this building, asking if you were in residence. It was only when I knew that you were here that I gave it to the officer in command of the guard to take to you. So it's not as if I put it in the post." Spencer smiled. He was not one of the Penholme-Forbes brigade. I think he actually liked me, though you have to be very careful with such as him. They may like you, but they still *use* you. Anyway, he smiled.

"Yes," says he, "you're a clever man, Sir Jacob, and no mistake. And you're well known too. That officer of marines recognised you instantly and do you know what he said when he gave me your diamond?"

"No," says I.

"He said, '*It's Captain Sir Jacob Fletcher, my Lord: the celebrated midnight runner.*'"

And here I pause to make sure that all you youngsters shall learn from the above words. I pause so that you shall know how unjust the world can be. Because here was your Uncle Jacob returned from a great victory over our ancient enemy. I'd defeated three of the finest ships the French ever made, I'd persuaded the Americans to keep out of the war, and I'd stopped Napoleon from building a naval base in the Gulf of St Lawrence where he could threaten all of Canada. I'd done all that, and yet what did that bloody damn marine remember me for? My bloody damn naked run! And Spencer was just as bad.

"And are you staying again at the Metropole Hotel in Drummond street, Sir Jacob?" says he, with a laugh. Then the laugh stopped and he looked at the stone. "I assume that this is a true diamond," says he, "because otherwise, why would you send it to me?"

"It's real, my Lord," says I. "You can take it all round Hatton Garden and they'll tell you."

"I see," says he. "So where did you get it?"

I thought very carefully about that. We were in Spencer's big office in the Admiralty building on Horse Guard's parade, where he had his official residence. The office was hung with gilt-framed portraits of great men – everyone from Francis Drake to Spencer himself – and it was decorated with maritime instruments, globes of the world and Chinese urns. "Fletcher?" says Spencer, holding the stone forward to me. "Where did you get this?"

I still wondered, and an army band played outside, and the crunch of boots sounded in unison as ruler-straight lines of red coats drilled. I could just about see them through one of the windows: them and the gentlemen and ladies admiring them. Then the band stopped and some sergeant major bellowed the incomprehensible nonsense that sergeant majors bellow.

Then the boots came down in a single stamp, and I made up my mind. I told him everything, taking special care to mention everything that Donovan the dying Irishman had said to me down on *Triomphe du Peuple's* orlop.

"Good," says he, when I was done. "I'm glad you said that, Sir Jacob, because rumours of all kind have been running round the Service regarding a huge diamond that might – or might not – be in your possession."

"Oh?" says I. I didn't know that because I'd not kept company with Sea Service officers recently.

"Oh indeed," said Spencer, "so what are you doing here? You have for years protested that you do not want to be in the King's service, and now you are out of it and can dabble in trade to your heart's content. So why are you here, and why have you shown me this diamond?" He tapped it with a finger. "Which I assume to be of some truly colossal value."

"It is, my Lord," says I.

"And so?" says he. So I told him. I told him all without stopping for a breath.

"I want to go after the source of it because there's a mine somewhere in Africa and I think I can find it. That mine is full of stones just like this one, so give me a ship and I'll go and find it and bring back the stones."

He looked at me and he looked at the diamond, and I could see that he was intrigued. I think the stone was talking to him, just as it had done to me. He turned it over and over, and held it to the light. But then he shook his head and put it down and I was sure he was going to say no. "Sir Jacob," says he, "Fletcher, Fletcher? What am I to do with you? As I have said to you before, you may protest that you wish to be a man of business, but you are a magnificent, fine seaman, a decisive and natural leader, *and a bloody pirate at heart!* So listen well. I can see that the Egyptians of Cairo will want your diamond mine, because their wealth is not based on manufacture. But our wealth *is* based on manufacture. It is based on manufacture, industry and international trade, and so is that of the French! Thus, have you not realised that Napoleon Bonaparte had hold of this." He tapped the stone. "But he used it merely as a persuader, to get Mr Cooper of Boston on his side?"

"Oh," says I.

"So I will tell you what we shall do with this gem," says he, and I held my breath as he pronounced doom. "It will go as a gift, from yourself, myself, and the Sea Service ... to His Majesty the King, for inclusion in the Crown Jewels, or such other use as might please His Majesty."

"Oh bugger," says I, but only to myself. That and much worse, because I thought that all was lost: not only my beautiful diamond, but the plan that had been incessantly in my mind ever since that Irishman told me where to find the mine.

"But," says Spencer, "although you are a rogue, and a villain, and I do not doubt that your intention was always to keep for yourself most – or all – of such diamonds as you might find."

"No, my Lord!" says I. "I would bring them back for England!"

"Oh do be quiet, Fletcher," says he. "Do not take me for a fool." He leaned forward. "But you have the Devil's own luck, because the Astronomer Royal has been pestering me for months to send a ship down the coast of Africa to embark an expedition of *natural philosopher gentlemen*." He sneered slightly at that. "Gentlemen who will observe a total eclipse of the sun, which is predicted to occur in the approximate location of your diamond mine."

"Ah!" says I.

"Yes," says he, "and so, Sir Jacob, because the nation is not ungrateful for your exploits in the Gulf of St Lawrence, and despite your unfortunate reputation with many in the Service ..."

"Yes?" says I.

"I am resolved to give you command of that expedition ship, and then, provided you give every possible assistance to the learned gentlemen, and enable them to make their philosophical observations, then should there be sufficient time, and no risk to the ship ..."

"Yes?" says I.

"Then you may search for your diamond mine, on your faithful promise to bring back half of what you find." He paused. "For England, just exactly as you have said."

"You have my word on it, my Lord," says I, and he laughed.

[It is indicative of Fletcher's character that he applied to Lord Spencer, seeking a ship for his plan of the diamond mine, when he could easily have paid for a ship and crew himself, from his own considerable fortune. He did not do so because, despite his ever-denied love of the Service, he once admitted within my personal hearing, that it was intolerable for him to sail under any flag than that of the Royal Navy.]

Spencer laughed. But he did what he promised, and a few weeks later I was a Sea Service officer once again, on full pay, with my King's Commission document in a tarred canvas bag for me to read out to a ship's crew: the crew of HMS *Enable*.

The sun was shining; the gulls were calling; the air was fresh, and I was in a launch manned by tars, pulling out from Portsmouth Point.

That's the run of sandy beaches on the crooked little peninsula on the eastern side of the mouth of Portsmouth Harbour. It's known to seamen as *Spice Island* for the spicy fun that's to be had there, all lined as it was with strolling trollops, galloping shops, taverns and pawnbrokers. It faces Gosport to the west, with the Isle of Wight south, across the Solent. This sheltered body of water between the mainland and the Isle of Wight is called Spithead, and is where the Royal Navy has anchored since Noah was a lad, and his ark still trees.

There, at anchor, among every kind and condition of ship, was *Enable*: my new command and a fine one too. She was a three-masted, ship-rigged vessel of just four hundred tons, so you youngsters might wonder why I was pleased with so modest a vessel after the beautiful *Euphonides*, and the mighty *Tromenderon*. But *Enable* was just perfectly what I needed, being a twin of Captain Cook's ship *Endeavour*, which Cook declared to be the finest ship ever made for a voyage of exploration. So I hoped and expected that *Enable* would be the same.

Like *Endeavour*, *Enable* had been cat-built for the Newcastle trade which needs exceptional ships: square-sided, deep in hold for cargo, round in the bow to rise with the seas, and purpose-built for the dangerous business of carrying coal down the east coast to London. It's dangerous because of the rocks, shoals and a lee shore, and even more dangerous for a collier because, if she does get holed, her cargo of coal – being dense and heavy – will drag her down, quick as a wink, with all hands lost.

Which is why, my jolly boys, a Newcastle collier was built so well and so strong. As we drew close, I could see that *Enable* was no beauty, but stout and sensible. She was ninety-five feet long and thirty broad. She had ten 9-pounder guns, two carronade 24s, and a dozen swivels. She had two lieutenants, half a dozen mids, four warrant officers, seventy-five seamen, some ship's boys, and twelve marines, besides eight civilian gentlemen – of which philosophical persons I'll say more later. That was a tiny crew compared to *Tromenderon's*, but never in all my time at sea did I have a better one.

And the reason for that, my jolly boys, was that with England at peace, and the Navy throwing its men ashore, then any King's ship that did go to sea found hordes of seamen jostling for a place. There wasn't one pressed man aboard *Enable* and the Navy had already hand-picked her crew even before I arrived, choosing from seasoned seamen, nimble topmen, and a pair of lieutenants: Mr Chivers and Mr Long who were exceptional navigators and map-makers. We even had a surgeon, which ships of that rate didn't normally have. But *Enable* was special because the First Lord smiled upon her. So perhaps he did like me after all.

There was no ship's band though, just a fiddler and a chanty-man. Nor did I take any followers with me except one: the Rev Dr Goodsby. He'd made strenuous efforts to keep in touch, since his Father was pressing him to take seriously his trade as an angel-maker, and this Father had worked influence to get Goodsby into a county cathedral, now that Goodsby was come ashore.

"I'm to be *Deacon-Prebenderite of the Chasuble*," Goodsby wrote, in a letter to me, "that, or some-such title, for I cannot bring myself to study the Anglican hierarchy with enthusiasm. Therefore, Sir Jacob, since you know my true feelings in this matter, if ever you should take command at sea again …" and so on, and so on. But I felt for the poor swab, having all my life been driven likewise into a profession which was not of my choice.

So *Enable* had a chaplain as well as a surgeon and I had a first-class secretary and confidant. Goodsby was so keen to get away from his cathedral that he was already in the ship when I came aboard. As for the crew, they grinned and cheered something wonderful, and had the sauce to shout out Jacky Flash, as they stood on the little main deck – which really did seem small after *Tromenderon*. Since this was a peacetime commission, every one of them was delighted to be aboard, and they clapped hands as the fiddler played the *Lincolnshire Poacher* which was known as my favourite tune.

"Welcome aboard, sir!" says a lieutenant stepping forward and raising his hat. "I'm Chivers, Sir Jacob, and I have the honour to be Number One. Delighted to be under your command, sir!" He was the right sort: tanned face, mature, broad and sound.

"Jacky Flash! Jacky Flash! Jacky Flash!" says the entirety of the crew, in a great shout.

"And I'm Long, Sir Jacob," says the other lieutenant. "Honoured, sir, honoured!" He likewise looked good. Neither he nor Chivers were anything other than seamen. And then a familiar face.

"Sir Jacob!" says Goodsby, beaming, happy and free of the church.

"Dr Goodsby," says I, "most pleased to have you aboard!"

Then it was Jacky Flash, Jacky Flash, and all hands grinning like apes and thinking they were on a pleasure cruise up the Thames, with women aboard and rum flowing. So first I read my commission aloud, and then it was time to educate the ship's people by the *other* ceremony of my coming aboard, and myself happy to have a good justification for the doing of it.

"If you'll be so kind, Doctor?" says I to Goodsby, and I gave him the commission document, together with my hat and coat and sword. Then he got my weskit and shirt to go with them. "So!" says I, looking at the crew, and some of the fun went right out of them. "Which one shall it be?" says I, "because either one of you stands forward, or I'll come among you and take you one at a time."

"Ooooooh!" says they, and they looked at one another.

"Make your choice, my lads!" says I, and swung a few punches into the air, just to get my arms moving. "Make your choice or it's every one of you!"

"Pah!" says one of the biggest, and off came hat, coat and shirt, to the vast relief of the rest. He had muscles and tattoos, and a broken nose. There's always one such aboard ship so it's just a matter of finding him. But by Jove, weren't the rest of them happy!

"Irish Mick! Irish Mick!" says they, all together in a cheer.

"Bloody English cowards the lot of you!" says he. "Can't you see the Cap'n's just playing games, God love him, and I'll be playing games just the same?" If so, it was a dirty game because I've seldom faced a man who fought so dirty, what with kicks between the legs, and fingers in the eyes, and spitting and swearing. I could see why Irish Mick was cock of the lower deck. But it was all done quickly because I had a longer reach than him, and it really isn't fair for any of you little people to fight someone like me. Even the Hoxton Chippy went down in the end, because you must understand that – for me – it's as if it would be for *you* if you were fighting a child.

So Irish Mick ended up with his nose a bit more crooked, and spitting blood not words. But he grinned and touched his brow in the end, and he got double grog – him and his messmates – and do you know, my jolly boys, that was the entire end of the ship's people thinking they were on a pleasure cruise. I repeat what I have said so many times before in these memoirs, that mine is a kindly and gentle method for showing the crew precisely who is in command, and which method avoids flogging, stopped grog or any other such nastiness. But you do have to be something like my size and strength to make it work.

After that, there was the usual gathering in of livestock and of preserved food – biscuit, salt-beef, pickles, split-peas and the rest, and in so doing we took advantage of another of a collier's virtues: its great capacity for cargo. Given this, and with so few men aboard, instead of the usual three to four months of food that a warship could take aboard, we had room in *Enable* for over a year's supplies, which was a great comfort when sailing for parts unknown, for an unknown time, and no safe ports within easy reach. On the other hand, I had to get used to living in a day cabin that would have been no more than a wardrobe aboard *Tromenderon*, and I couldn't even stand up without stooping in the stern cabin, which was the biggest in the ship.

I also had to get used to having a company of *natural philosopher gentlemen* aboard. These were what we call scientists in this modern world, though Spencer used the old words. But by whatever name they were a problem. There were eight of them, and they came aboard with a great mass of equipment packed in cases heavily lined with straw. I must admit that, once taken out and put into use, they were fascinating in the extreme because they gleamed in polished brass, with bright lenses, and meticulously marked out scales of great complexity. They made my expensive Jesse Ramsden sextant look like a schoolboy's ruler.

These scientist gentlemen were a problem – three separate problems in fact – because, first, they were outside of ship's discipline, not being in the King's service or subject to the Articles of War. Second, they were not subject to my own kind of discipline, being very well-connected socially. One was a baronet, two had knighthoods and every one of them had been chosen by a committee including the Astronomer Royal, the President of the Royal Society, and the Archbishop of bloody Canterbury! So I couldn't ask them to put up their fists and be knocked down, could I?

Just so that you shall know who they were, here they come in alphabetical order of surname: Sir John Applemere, Mr William Brentford, Mr Charles Ealey, Sir David Southerland, baronet, Dr Robert Talleyrand, Mr Reginald Vaughan, and Sir Daniel Yorke.

I give them in alphabetical order because the third problem was that they had no discipline even among themselves. Although Baronet Sir David was supposed to be in charge, he was not because they were constantly splitting into factions based on their differing interpretations of the observations that they made, and some of these splits became vicious. Talleyrand

and Vaughan even came to blows once, which was laughable to see since they made such a mess of it, slapping at one another's faces and not even making a fist.

But all this came late in the voyage, because having set sail on August 14th, even in sunny summer we had a bit of a blow in the Bay of Biscay. *Enable* with her round bow, rose and fell to the waves exactly as she was meant to. So for long, hard days our scientific gentlemen were heaving up their guts over the lee rail, or into chamber pots down in their little cabins. I never saw such obeisance to Father Neptune, and the crew thought it hilarious, which in the end was good for ship's discipline because the people decided that they were figures of fun – most of them anyway – and, therefore, that the liberties afforded them were not to be envied.

I must also mention one additional item of human supercargo that came aboard at Portsmouth: Mr Adrian Halfpenny, gifted upon us by the Royal Society for his supposed skills as an elephant hunter, tracker, trekker, bang-up marksman, woodcraftsman and linguist. He was a tall man, all wrinkled by years of sun, and not much more than gristle and bone. He could have been any age from thirty to seventy, and I never did find out which. He was also one of those irritating swabs who try to crunch the bones of your fingers when you shake hands with them on first meeting.

"By Jove, sir," says he when he tried that on with me and I gave it right back. "But you're a man, sir! A man and no mistake, sir!" He said this in a big bold voice that gave the impression of a big bold man. But it was all puff and nonsense, because he was an absolute shirker when it came to anything dangerous. What he was really good at was sinking vast quantities of drink: that and languages, because I'm obliged to admit that he really was good at African languages, and we could have done nothing without him: at least where diamond mines are concerned.

And so, *Enable* sailed south. The weeks passed and it got very hot. We came round the enormous bulge of north-west Africa and down past the Bight of Benin. Then we began searching in earnest, and found something we were not looking for. We found a war: just when we were at peace for the first time in nine years.

Chapter 32

The Plain of the Green Grass,
North Zulu Land,
In the summer of the 12th Year of the reign of
King Ndaba KunJama.

"Prince Zithulele the traitor, led the greatest host he had ever commanded."

(From the Saga of Inyathi)

Prince Zithulele rejoiced in the moment. He stood on a hill with war-shield and spear. He stood splendidly plumed and arrayed, and with the bright stone of his father, the King, bound round his brow. He stood with his most senior commanders, all in equally splendid dress, and armed for war.

But that was nothing compared with the army that was paraded before him in rigid ranks. Thus, the magnificent N'gwenya regiment was drawn up in traditional array: ten great columns of six hundred men, each column divided into ten companies of sixty, and each separate unit dressed in perfect formation. Zithulele gazed at the regiment, swelling with pride that such men were under his command. He gazed at them and slowly raised his spear in salute. His commanders copied him in a poetry of movement. Then Zithulele drew breath and gave a great shout:

"Yoo-petta! Yoo-no! Men-erva!" he cried, and the regiment responded. Every man of the six thousand raised spear, and repeated the sacred words.

"Yoo-petta! Yoo-no! Men-erva!"

Then all six thousand beat spear butts into shields in a deep, resonant pounding. The earth shook. The hills echoed. The ponderous, irresistible sound transported Zithulele into an ecstasy of belief in his cause, and in the wisdom of the witch, M'thunzi.

"Now you must go forth," she had said to him in that night of seeming failure. "Inyathi is not slain, but he has run like a coward and his honour is stained." She reached out a claw of a hand and shook Zithulele by the elbow. "He has run! He has run! That is worse for his cause than if he had died like a man. Do you understand? You have not lost. *You have won!*"

"Yes, Holy Mother," he'd said.

"Now is your time! The N'gwenya regiment is already yours, and others will follow if you achieve a victory!"

"Yes, Holy Mother."

"Our scouts have found the Arabs. Now is the time for you to strike before even they know that you are coming. But you must be swift. You must meet them in their strength, and stamp them out with one blow. And then the Kingdom will be yours!"

Zithulele thought on her words, and in the immensity of his pride he dipped his spear towards the enemy. He dipped, pointed and stabbed.

"Huh!" he cried.

"HUH!" cried six thousand voices, and the N'gwenya regiment went forward in a steady trot, under discipline all the way.

"I saw them come. I'd never seen anything like the speed of them."

(From the diary of Auguste Renard)

Renard stood in front of the guns and looked at the Zulus. It was a shock, a great shock. They were so close that he didn't need his telescope. A whole army of them had appeared in seconds. They'd crept up somehow, using cover and the lie of the land, and they'd come at speed. The 12-pounders weren't even loaded! But that was a blessing because the Zulus were already too close for the round-shot that he would have used first.

"Cannister!" he yelled to his gun crews. "Short range cannister!" He looked at the Janissary officers. Good! They had drums rolling, bugles blowing and the men forming up on either side of the guns. There was just time for that. Five minutes earlier and they wouldn't have had time.

Then the Zulus started beating on shields and the sound got into Renard's belly and wrenched his guts. Renard ran back and past the guns, where his men were ramming home cartridges and priming touch-holes.

But Renard wasn't running away. He had many defects of character but cowardice wasn't one of them. He was running to where the horses were tethered. He drew sword and hacked at the ropes and leathers. Then he smacked a horse hard on its rump. He smacked another. The horses reared and whinnied and staggered.

"What are you doing?" said one of the horse handlers.

"Shut your trap, you whore-shit, or I'll shut it for you!" said Renard, and the man got out of his way. "Don't just run off!" said Renard. "Help me! Get 'em moving!" The horse handlers knew Renard, and knowing how nasty he could be, they helped. They joined him in getting the horses to run away. Then Renard got out of the dip where the horses had been, and he watched them run before rushing back to the guns. The crews had heard the galloping. They looked afraid.

"Where've the horses gone?" said one of the gun-captains.

"Gone!" said Renard. "So now there's no shitty escape and you've got to man your shitty gun! Right?" Renard ran to the Janissary commanding officer, who was stood with his lieutenants, all gripping the hilts of their yataghan swords in their fancy silver scabbards. They were Turks, they were tough, and they looked steady. But Malmuk was among them and he was pissing himself in fright.

"We've got to stand, right?" said Renard, and he pointed at the Zulus. "They'll come at a run, right?"

"Yes," said the officers.

"Have all the horses gone?" said Malmuk.

"All of them," said Renard.

"Will your men stand?" said Renard to the Janissary commander.

"They'll stand," said the Janissary, "because God help them if they don't!" Renard looked at the two lines of Janissary infantrymen: one on either side of the guns. They were in uniform and looked good: red caps, red jackets, voluminous blue britches, and modern English muskets. They were drawn up with front rank kneeling, second rank standing, bayonets fixed. But whatever their officer said, they were looking over their shoulders which was a bad sign, because that's what men did when they were getting ready to run. Renard looked at the Bedouin, mounted and ready, out beyond the infantry. They'd be gone for sure – and never doubt it – on the instant that guns and muskets couldn't hold the Zulus. They'd be gone and they'd take nobody with them.

"Oh shit!" said Renard, knowing that it was all up to the two 12-pounders: just the two of them. Running to the guns, he went among the crews doing what Napoleon did – Renard had seen him do it. Renard acted cheerful. He slapped backs; he pulled noses; he tried to make them smile. But the beating of shields was awful. Then it got worse. The beating stopped. The thousands of Zulus began some sort of chant in their deep, base voices. They came forward at a steady trot and they most definitely were not savages. They came on in ranks and files like Napoleon's Old Guard, except that the Guard didn't move that fast.

"Zithulele saw everything. He saw the results of the plan which he had made."

(From the Saga of Inyathi)

On his hill, Zithulele saw the leading ranks of the N'gwenya go forward exactly as he had ordered, closing in upon each other to form a single dense column aimed at the golden tubes.

This was his very own idea based on M'thunzi's words. He would stamp out the wheeled magic in a single blow!

"Ah!" he said, as the N'gwenya gave their war shout and charged to overwhelm the enemy with their spears.

"I couldn't believe it. If we'd gone on our knees and begged them it couldn't have been better."

(From the diary of Auguste Renard)

"What the fuck are they doing?" thought Renard, looking at the Zulus in amazement. "They're coming right at us!" He looked at the Janissary commander who spread his hands in amazement, while the Janissary lieutenants yelled at their men to aim inward, to concentrate fire on the ground in front of the guns. "*They're charging a battery from the front!*" thought Renard, "Nobody does that! They're mad. They're coming right into the muzzle-blast!"

He couldn't believe it. He couldn't believe his luck. He thought of Napoleon who always said that you had to be lucky, and that you changed plans to suit, if you *were* lucky. So Renard shouted at his gunners.

"Both together!" he yelled, over the noise of the Zulu charge. "Both guns together, *not* one after another. Both guns at once, to knock 'em shitless.

But not before I give the word!" The two gun-captains stood swinging their linstocks to keep the matches bright. They nodded to Renard, while the second captains spun the elevating screws to aim point blank. The dense mass of Zulus came on at a run, and the gunners didn't even have to aim because the Zulus were coming to them! They were charging straight down the muzzles of the guns.

"Couldn't be better, couldn't be better!" Renard judged distance, and raised his sword, and the Zulus bellowed and shouted and came on at fierce speed in a packed mass of shields and spears and faces and running legs. "Wait for it! Wait for it!" cried Renard, then ... "FIRE!"

Chapter 33

By the time we were past the Bight of Benin, we had an established routine aboard *Enable*. Watch succeeded watch; the ship's bell regulated our lives; the decks were holystoned each day; and the guns run out for live firing, as is my eternal dedication. In addition, Halfpenny, the great hunter, was halfway through the gallons of drink he'd brought aboard, while the scientific gentlemen had found their sea-legs. One of them – to the surprise of all hands – proved to be a damn fine shipmate.

That was Mr Ealey, one of the youngest of them: only in his twenties but a fine mathematician, and remarkably sharp-minded. Though I have to admit that the entire shoal of our scientific gentlemen were very clever in a scientific/mathematical sense and, since astronomy was their trade, they came aboard with the essentials of celestial navigation already in their heads. But Ealey stood out as special, because he got on something wonderful with my two lieutenants, Chivers and Long, who weren't much older but were veteran seaman – both had been round Cape Horn more than once – and these two adopted Ealey like sea-daddies.

The result was that, given the approval of our lieutenants, the hands also took to Ealey and treated him as a ship's officer. Ealey was shown the ropes such that soon, he could hand, reef and steer, and run aloft with the mids. Even more remarkable was the fact that he could calculate the ship's position each day, faster than Mr Chivers, Mr Long or our sailing master. So wagers were laid as to who'd be first, and there never was a ship with so many men aboard that could wield a sextant or stand a watch.

But then we came to business, since we were entering the latitudes of the coming eclipse and it was time to run close inshore, looking for the best place to set up our astronomical observation camp. To my mind, this was also the best place to begin the hunt for the diamond mine!

I should make clear, in this regard, that all hands knew the voyage had two purposes because I won't have secrets aboard ship, and on a ship the size of *Enable* everyone soon finds out everyone's business in any case. After all, what else is there to talk about during the long night watches?

> [Note that Fletcher was totally sincere in his detestation of any attempt to keep secrets from a ship's crew: the *people* as he always called them. He believed that men are happiest when told the truth, and he detested his past duties as a secret agent in France under the orders of Lord Spencer and William Pitt, the Prime Minister. S.P.]

One evening, with the ship under easy way and the vast continent of Africa on our larboard beam, I held conference on the quarterdeck, since there was no cabin aboard *Enable* that was big enough for everyone who had to take part. But no matter because, even with the heat of the day gone, it was stuffy down below, while on deck there was a bit of breeze and it was still light. The Boatswain's crew had rigged a table with sailcloth for a cover, and the necessary charts laid out, held down with paperweights.

"Gentlemen!" says I.

"Captain!" says they: the scientific gentlemen, the lieutenants, the Sailing Master, Mr Halfpenny – sober for once – and Dr Goodsby. They were present and so were all the rest of the ship's people who weren't actively sailing the ship. They were standing by and paying attention because, as I've said, I'll have no secrets aboard ship and everyone knew it was time for decisions. So:

"Aye aye, Cap'n," says they.

"Now then!" says I, pointing at the charts, "these are the best that the Admiralty and the Astronomer Royal could provide. We must now choose where to go ashore to set up camp for the observation, and to begin our search inland." After which, everything was surprisingly easy because there was a river within a day's sail – the huge Falso – which was ideally suited to receive the shadow of the eclipse, and which also had something else.

"Here, Captain," says Mr Ealey, with the scientific gents nodding beside him. Ealey put a finger on one of the charts. "We've made a special study of every chart available." He looked at those on the table. "Including some not here."

"Yes," said one of the others. "We even got some from Hereford Cathedral."

"A cathedral?" says I. "Why a cathedral?"

"Hereford Cathedral, Captain," says Ealey. "They have a famous collection of medieval maps, including some from the early days, when the Portuguese first went down the coast of Africa."

"And so?" says I, and everyone nodded.

"See here," says Ealey. "The mouth of the Falso has islands that would be ideal for our observation. We'd be right by the ship; we'd have constant fresh water, and we'd be safe from anything coming out of the interior: natives, wild animals or whatever. And look here," says he. "Look here, by this tributary to the Falso." We all looked. "There's a pair of large hills – two thousand feet high at least – which the Portuguese maps called *Seios de Sheba.*"

"So?" says I.

"That means *Sheba's Breasts*, Captain," says Goodsby.

"Ah!" says I, "the great landmark pointing to the mine."

"That's right," says Ealey. Then Halfpenny pushed forward.

"May I see?' says he in his best manly voice, and we stood back while he looked at the charts.

"Falso?" says he, shaking his head. "No! It's *Haipo* in Swahili, the river Haipo, and it's unknown territory to Europeans. The river and all its tributaries are called *Haipo* in the local languages. *Haipo!* All of them. It's famous among the Bantu people because none of them will go near it. The Kongo, the Kuba, the Lunda: they won't go near it! Even the Bunoro and Bugan won't, and they're warrior tribes. They won't go near it for fear of the Zulu."

So that was it, my jolly boys. That was the river for me, and I took *Enable* into the two-miles wide mouth of the Haipo on October 20th, where we dropped anchor by a nice big island: high and dry, with firm ground for the camp, and plenty of trees for timber. Then we landed stores and supplies and the Boatswain and Carpenter put up huts and platforms. All the beautiful instruments and gear were taken ashore in their packing cases, to be mustered for action.

It was a sight to see, because just as it is with the complexities of steam, I do love to see a piece of mechanism, well turned, well polished and cunningly made for a purpose. While the tars were heaving and the Carpenter's mates were sawing and hammering, I took a little holiday – a half day's worth – and let Ealey and Applemere show me the expedition's instruments.

"Eight inch refractor, Captain," says Ealey, "to throw its image on a screen, because you dare not look at the sun."

"Le Grange barometer with vernier scale, Captain,' says Applemere.

"Bartlett hygrometer with compensation …"

"Large-scale astronomical quadrant by Pierce of London …"

"Maximum/Minimum thermometer …"

It was a jolly holiday, but the diamond mine was nagging. So later on, once the hands had gobbled down their dinners and taken the day's second quantum of grog, I had a word with some of my officers and scientific gentlemen. After that, I brought all hands aboard from the shore camp, because I wanted them all to know what was going forward. Again we assembled on the quarterdeck, as *Enable* rode steady on two anchors and the river Haipo put its arms around us, beckoning me into the vast, dark interior.

"Gentlemen!" says I. "And all aboard of us!"

"Aye aye!" says they. Even the scientific gentlemen said, "aye aye," so merry a crew we had become.

"Tomorrow," says I, "I shall leave the ship under the command of our First Lieutenant Mr Chivers, while the observation camp shall be under Sir David Southerland, upon whose good leadership we can all rely!" Which was rot, of course, because Sir David couldn't lead water downhill. But sometimes you have to say these things even if you don't believe them. None the less, the scientific gentlemen all smiled.

"Hear hear!" says they, and they clapped Sir David on the back so that he blushed. I suppose they were enthusiasts after all.

"Aye aye!" says the crew. They even cheered, so perhaps Sir David and his beauties might do a decent job after all? Not that I cared. I had other plans.

"Meanwhile," says I, "I shall take the longboat, rigged for sail with all the provisions she can bear, to pursue the second aim of this voyage."

"Huzza!" A really big cheer this time, and all smiling faces from the people. I had a reputation for sharing out prize money, and they doubtless thought that this applied to the sacks of diamonds I'd bring back.

"I shall take with me the following men," says I.

"Ah!" says they, all bright-eyed and leaning forward.

"Lieutenant Long will be my second in command," says I, "and Mr Ealey will join us to take observations inland." Sir David nodded. Ealey nodded. They'd particularly asked for this. "I shall also take Mr Halfpenny," says I, "to be our guide among the native peoples." Halfpenny nodded, but he wasn't nearly as happy as Long or Ealey, who grinned at one another like boys on a jaunt. "And finally," says I, "I shall need five marines and five seamen to man the oars, and..."

"Me, sir!"

"Me, Cap'n!"

"Me! Me! Me!"

I was drowned in shouting. They clearly thought that every man of the longboat would soon be stuffing his boots with gemstones so they couldn't hold back. I left it to the Boatswain and the Sergeant of Marines to choose among them, and in the end they drew lots.

We pulled away from the ship next morning after breakfast. Everyone cheered, everyone waved, and the tars and marines put on a good show and pulled hard. The boat was a big 'un for a ship the size of *Enable*, though I'd have chosen it myself if it hadn't already been aboard. It was large, strongly built and roomy. In those days – early in the century – longboats were falling out of favour in the Navy, and the launch was preferred as a slimmer and faster boat. But in my opinion a launch was merely prettier, because Cook's expeditions years ago had shown the value of a longboat on a voyage of exploration, being seaworthy under sail, and a heavy load-carrier. Ours was rigged for a gaff mainsail and a small head sail. But the wind was in our faces that first morning, and we had to pull.

We had all the stores we could carry; we were floating on fresh water; we had a brace of pistols and a cutlass for each seaman, and the marines had their muskets. Besides that, we had a box of trade goods, and finally the longboat came with its own armament: a 12-pounder carronade on a slide in the bow. I stress that it wasn't that we were looking for a fight, because by all accounts the Zulus came in hordes. But if you turn up on foreign shores with just a weak smile and unarmed, then it lays wicked temptation before the locals who might then take liberties with you.

We also had all the scientific instruments Mr Ealey needed. We had extra rum for Mr Halfpenny and finally we had Dr Goodsby as well, because he came to me complaining that he had nothing to do aboard ship or in the observation camp. That's what he said, but I smelt the diamond fever on him. He'd heard all about the Blue Star from me, so I suppose it was my fault and I took him with us.

And there we all were, my jolly boys, pulling against the current till the wind shifted, and then we made sail. Africa slid past on either beam without effort on our part. Everyone yelled aloud at one of the wonders of Africa, as we saw a herd of monstrous great creatures by the shoreline. They were like enormous slimy slugs, and they turned their great mouths towards us with bulging eyes and stuck-up ears. The whole crew of them stared at us and we could even hear the noise they made: a honking, grunting wheezing that made us laugh. They were hippopotamuses.

[In defence of the Queen's English, I explained to Fletcher that the correct plural is 'hippopotami' but I soon regretted doing so, and I should have possessed more wisdom than to speak out. S.P.]

This time it really did feel like a holiday. We lounged on the thwarts in the hot sunshine, all in straw hats, calico britches and shirts, except for myself and Mr Long who wore service coats, as duty required. The boat forged upriver, and the people gave her a name – *Betsy* – and asked me to bless her with a tot of rum over the bow. So I did, and all hands got one besides. Which goes to show how silly men can be when they think they are on the sure and certain path to treasure, and for a while life became even better. Indeed, it became wonderful because we found – in excess – the one thing that sailormen love more than rum.

We were three days upriver where the river banks slim down to about half a mile's width, when we found the tributary river that would lead to Sheba's Breasts. I left the navigation to Long and Ealey because they were enjoying it, spending hours with charts, sextants, boat compass and fob watches. Also, I could see that, while Ealey had learned seamanship from Long, Lieutenant Long had learned astronomy from Ealey! He'd learned it and liked it. They spent hours calculating just when the shadow would fall over us, and precisely where it would fall first. We all grinned at this and thought no more of their eclipse than something for the textbooks, to be read by those who enjoy them.

Which all goes to show how wrong you can be, and all you youngsters should take note that you never know what's coming next, nor what's important and what is not.

Meanwhile, from the second day we could already see the twin, rounded shape of the two mountains that some Portuguese mariner, long ago, had seen and thought of a woman's upperworks. But I don't know where he got the Sheba from: the Queen of Sheba? Who cares. I certainly didn't.

Ealey and Long got us accurately into the lesser river, and then it was hard pulling all the way, with shifting winds that didn't know where to settle. The river soon got narrower too: merely some hundreds of yards. There were trees on either side: not jungle as you might imagine it, but tall trees reaching up to the light, with bushes and scrub between. Then the river banks pinched in, and the current came down stronger, and all hands had to take turns pulling in order to make way. It got so hard that even I had to take an oar to give rest to others, with myself being careful – as always – not to pull too hard for fear of breaking the timberwork: a lifelong problem when you're as strong as me.

So I was facing astern as the boat came to a bend with particularly heavy foliage around us. Mr Long was beside me pulling hard – we were both *without* our blue coats on this occasion – and Mr Ealey was at the tiller. As we came round, I saw Ealey's mouth drop open, and the men taking their rest beside him, likewise dropped jaws. One of them was Goodsby.

"God almighty!" says he, calling on the deity that he didn't believe in.

"Avast pulling!" says Ealey. "Boat your oars!" That was the command to hold oars clear of the water. So we did as he said, and the longboat slid on for a bit, and the water chuckled under our bow. We oarsmen could not help looking over our shoulders. And there, my jolly boys, was a sight to see!

Less than fifty yards off, there was a crowd of the most delectable, creamy-brown female creatures any sailorman ever saw. Some of them were up to the waist in water; others were stepping up onto the banks; others were dipping some sort of gourd-vessels into the river to collect water. Behind them, some way off, there was a native village of round houses inside a dark, tangled fence. The smoke of hearth fires rose over it, bending in the wind, and there were other folk by the hedge, and some herds of cattle. But nobody looked at them. Because as I told you earlier, we were looking at the one thing that sailors love more than rum.

By Jove, they were gorgeous. Apart from some sort of girdle round the waist and a tiny skirt of beads with nothing under it, and apart from headbands and bracelets ... they didn't have a stitch of clothes on! They were all glistening and shining with water, and Sheba's Breasts be damned, who'd look at *them* when there was the real thing in profusion, standing up like melons. Except when their owners moved, and then they bounced. Oh, by George, they did. And you should have seen the looks on their faces. They weren't frightened. They didn't scream and shout and cover themselves. Not them! They stared at us strange beings in our strange craft and our strange clothes, and they looked down their little noses, and sneered as a princess sneers at a beggar. They got out of the water in their own time and stood looking at us, until one of them took command. She clapped hands and said something in their language, and a couple of them set off fast towards the village. All of us goggled at their twinkling buttocks as they ran.

I looked at the woman who was in charge and I couldn't see anything else but her. She was young and she was extremely lovely even by the standards of those around her. She had such grace of movement, such dignity, such a wonderful figure, and it wasn't like being in Europe when you never knew what you'd find under a woman's clothes. No, by Jove, it wasn't. Not when you could see everything for yourself.

So she had all that, and she was obviously used to giving orders. She stepped forward from the rest, and they stood fast behind her, while she stared hard at us — and at me in particular, being so big as I am — never showing a flicker of fear. What a wonderful creature. I was disturbed: profoundly disturbed, and even more so because she had a funny look on her face when she looked back at me. Then:

"Sir!" says one of the tars, "they're coming!" He pointed. He had to say it a few times before I took note. He even put a hand on my arm, and I realised he'd been talking. I'd not been listening because I'd been occupied with the lady. "Look, Cap'n!" says he. I turned and saw a number of men coming out of the village, bearing long shields and spears.

"You in the bows!" says I. "Stand by the carronade! Oarsmen: back starboard, pull larboard! Bring her round so the gun bears! All the rest: look to your firelocks!" The men from the village came on at a steady trot. I frowned. It was odd. They didn't run in a mad clump with some outpacing the others. They came on nice and steady, in ranks and files, led by a man with a headband full of ostrich plumes. The last time I'd seen such feathers was in my sister's hair when I got knighted, but this was very different, my jolly boys, because the future for us in the boat looked short and brutal.

Chapter 34

The Kraal of N'tombela,
By the river Haipo,
In the first months of the War of the Arabs.

"With enemies on all sides, Inyathi was not safe: not even in the kraal of his father."

(From the Saga of Inyathi)

Inyathi, the Buffalo sat with his father, N'tombela. They sat on stools while their attendants sat on the ground in crescent formation around them. N'tombela's stool was the higher of the two, as was natural and proper when a son sat with his father, and N'tombela's guardsmen stood behind their master. They stood tall and grim, because – like him – they had all been great men in their time. But N'tombela had taken severe wounds in past wars, and now even though his mind was strong, his left arm and left leg were weak, especially the arm which he could no longer use.

As well as the leading men of the kraal, a group of high-status men sat together in a place of honour on the right hand of N'tombela. These men wore the leopard skins of officers, and the regalia of other kraals and regiments, and they kept their own thoughts, occasionally whispering among themselves.

In addition, N'tombela's women stood with Inyathi's women on either side of the Guardsmen. They were ready with food and drink, and by discussion among the women, they now looked to Inyathi's wife, Ulwazi, as their freely accepted leader. Even N'tombela's wives accepted this: a proof that Ulwazi was a diplomat as well as a great beauty.

Beyond this assembly of the elite, the people of the kraal were also present in their numbers, watching everything with silent fascination.

Finally, and in fascination of all those gathered, there was a bedraggled company of some fifty men, who stood facing N'tombela and Inyathi. They stood with heads bowed, and without spears or shields, having left these at the gate of the kraal in sign of humble respect. They were led by one who leaned heavily on a stick, and even with a stick, he could not stand without a man on either side, holding his arms to keep him upright. He was bound about the body with thongs that held patches of dried grass woven tight to form wound dressings. These dressings were damp, and blood leaked from them.

Like N'tombela's guardsmen, these sad creatures had once been great men. They had been captains of the N'gwenya regiment. But now they were here to beg forgiveness, and the wounded man who leaned on a stick was Longelo, the senior surviving officer of the N'gwenya.

"So," said N'tombela, "we have heard your words, Longelo, such that you come to me in supplication only because you are shamed!" He turned to Inyathi, "But you must give judgement, my son, because when the N'gwenya still had their pride, they tried to kill you!"

There was a great silence, and all present looked on as Inyathi thought. Then he spoke, and he proved that it was not only his wife who was a diplomat.

"Honoured father," he said, "I say now – even before hearing another word – that the person at fault in all these matters is the witch, M'thunzi!" A great gasp arose at these dangerous words. "I say *that*, even though there are questions to be asked." He faced Longelo. "I now ask, what do you know of the golden fire-tubes? Tell me everything!"

Longelo sighed. He clutched his stick.

"They were like nothing ever seen on the field of battle," he said, and he appealed to those with him. "Do I not speak truth, my brothers?"

"You speak truth!" they said, and Longelo continued.

"When we charged the golden tubes," he said, "there was a thunder that broke our ears, and a flame that blinded our eyes. We were stunned as if struck with clubs. And there was a great smoke, a rain of bullets, and the front ranks of the regiment were torn apart. Even those behind who were not struck down, stumbled over those who were, and so we hesitated, and then the thunder and flame came again! And then again!" He groaned at the memory. "And then the regiment ran away." He sobbed in shame, and tears soaked his face and fell from his chin. "It was magic!" he said, and again he appealed to those behind him. "Tell him, my brothers, tell Inyathi the Buffalo the truth: tell him that it was a great witchcraft and the punishment upon our regiment for following Zithulele and for ..."

"No!" cried Inyathi. "It was not witchcraft, because witchcraft cannot be touched or felt. Witchcraft works only in the dark and in the minds of men." He said this, and stood and went forward, laying a hand gently on one of Longelo's wound dressings. "See!" he cried. "This is blood. It is blood from a wound, and wounds are not inflicted by witchcraft, but by spears!" He paused and looked at his father, and the councillors, and especially at the officers of famous regiments. "Wounds are inflicted by spears," he said, "or by the bullets of the Arabs. So! I say to you that the golden tubes are *not* magic but merely the muskets of the Arabs, in a new and vastly bigger form!"

There was profound silence at this, and the officers of famous regiments looked at one another.

"So the enemy that we face," said Inyathi, "the real enemy, the wicked enemy, is the witch M'thunzi, who caused Zithulele to divide our people by an attack on myself, and who then caused Zithulele to charge in frontal attack, upon a weapon we did not understand!" Inyathi looked round and saw approval of his words. His father nodded; the councillors nodded; and – best of all – the officers of famous regiments nodded. "And, therefore," said Inyathi, taking Longelo's hand and raising it high, "I forgive the N'gwenya, because they were deceived by the lies of the witch, M'thunzi." He turned to the officers of famous regiments. "And I beseech and exhort that all of Zulu Land shall stand together in this time of war against the invaders!"

It was a great speech, and later when the kraal returned to normal life, Inyathi sat with his father outside his father's house, with only a minimum of attendants and Ulwazi standing behind him with food and drink.

"I am proud of you, my son," said N'tombela. "You are not just a soldier, because you use words even better than spears."

"Ah!" said Inyathi, "but who taught me?" He raised a cup to Ulwazi, and she poured beer for her husband and father-in-law, who both drank and thought for a while.

"So,' said N'tombela, "from what the N'gwenya have said, the Arabs are still far away to the east, and could be attacked before they reach us, if we had the means." He looked across the kraal to a cluster of houses that were given over to the officers of famous regiments. "So will they follow you, my son? They came from across Zulu Land, but they came only to listen, and because of your good name."

"And yours, my father!" said Inyathi.

"Perhaps," said N'tombela, "but I still ask if they will follow you? They smile while they are in my kraal, but they are divided among themselves. Most of them would follow Zithulele in battle because he is the true heir to the King, and he is the choice of M'thunzi, the Witch, who…"

"My father!" said Inyathi, "forgive my interruption. I will have no witches in this matter. Zithulele and I have faced each other once on the Plain of the King and the matter was not decided. The tradition of our people is that there must be a great muster of all regiments, when the matter shall be decided. This is work for spears, and not witches or magic."

"No, my son," said N'tombela. "It is a matter for magic too. M'thunzi has great magic, and the regiments will follow the greatest magic. How will even you defeat the golden tubes without magic?"

"I don't know,' said Inyathi, "not yet."

"My husband," said Ulwazi, "and honoured father-in-law. May a woman speak?"

Inyathi looked at his father, and his father looked at Inyathi, and they smiled because neither of them could refuse anything when Ulwazi asked.

"Speak, O impetuous woman!" said N'tombela.

"When I was rescued from the Arabs," said Ulwazi, "I saw muskets fired and I saw that once they have fired it is a long time before they can fire again. In that time, a musket-man may be killed with a spear."

"We know," said Inyathi. "We make use of this fact."

"So," said Ulwazi, "it is merely a matter of finding some similar weakness in the golden tubes." The two men smiled. "Either that," she said, "or we must find golden tubes of our own." The two men laughed and laughed.

"More beer!" said Inyathi.

"More beer!" said N'tombela, and father and son shook their heads in fondness at such foolish words from so lovely a creature, because how could a woman understand warfare?

But some days later, Inyathi was called urgently to the riverside beyond the kraal. He ran through the gates with a company of spearmen, and there – by the river – he saw strange new men and a strange new thing, and he thought of Ulwazi's words.

Chapter 35

It was a very nasty moment. There were just fifteen of us in the boat, with ten muskets and five brace of pistols, together with the carronade. Now you might think that's enough to put fear into tribesmen who don't know firearms – if of course they *didn't* know firearms – but there must have been fifty or sixty of them coming on at the trot, and there was a whole column coming out of the village: many hundreds of them. They were chanting some sort of battle cry as they came. They looked deadly serious, and they looked as if they knew how to use their spears.

"Halfpenny!" says I, and reached out and shook him. He was in the thwart just ahead of me. He was staring at the spears and cringing. "What are they?" says I.

"Zulus!" says he.

"Ah!" says I, and for the first time I took my eyes off the bouncing titties and looked at the headbands on some of the women ... and, by Jove, look what was shining in them! I couldn't believe I'd not noticed that before. It just goes to show how much a man can be blinded by female flesh when he hasn't seen it for a while.

Then the advance company of Zulus was at the riverside and the women were clearing away, with the lovely one clapping hands and shouting. The man with the ostrich feathers was yelling at his men, who lined up behind him like the brigade of guards. It was amazing to see. It really was like the redcoats I'd seen on Horse Guards Parade. You could have measured their lines with a ruler.

"Ha! Ha! *HAH!*" they all says, and stamped feet, and stood stony silent. The man with the feathers looked straight at our boat from fifty yards distance. He had a shield and spear like all the rest, but he made no threatening move. Then the longboat swivelled in the current, with the oars not pulling, not under way, and so she turned more broadside on. The man with the feathers took another step forward and I saw his jaw gape at something.

"Back larboard, pull starboard," says I, to bring the carronade to bear again.

For a short while, we stared at them and they stared at us, and having seen some of their women really did wear gemstones, I was wondering how to get talking to the man with the feathers without a fight, because if it did come to a fight, then – given the numbers of them and the numbers of us – our firearms would keep us alive for about ten seconds before we got comprehensively butchered. That's if we were careful and took good aim.

But then, the man with the feathers said something to the very lovely woman. She bowed and said something back, and all the women moved away. The man with the feathers slowly raised his spear and shield, took a step back and lowered them to the ground. This brought a deep gasp from the men behind him, and they too lowered their weapons, though they didn't put them down. They just stared at him in surprise. Then he surprised me. He cried out something in a loud clear voice. I shook Halfpenny again.

"What's he saying?" says I.

"I'm not sure," says Halfpenny. "It's not quite Swahili. It's not what I'm used to."

"I don't care if you're bloody used to it or not," says I. "Just bloody well tell me what the bugger's saying!" I was under some stress at the time, as you might imagine.

"Err ..." says Halfpenny. "He says his name is Inyathi. Inyathi the cow ... or maybe buffalo? And he wants to have speech ... talk to ... talk to the fat man ... *big* man? That'll be you, Captain." And so, my jolly boys, everyone in the boat looked at your Uncle Jacob, and your Uncle Jacob wondered what to do.

With the current running hard, and a good pull on the oars, we could have been off at galloping speed. Then, since the Zulus had no boats nor bows and arrows, and provided we kept in midstream, we'd have been clean away, and back to the ship in no time. But what about the diamonds? What about the mine? Even as I wondered, I saw the gems gleaming on some of the women.

"Hold her steady," says I. "I'm standing up."

"Aye aye!" says Mr Long, and I stood up as slowly and carefully as I could, because standing up in a boat is a bad thing to do, and none of you youngsters should ever try it. But up I got, to a gasp from the Zulus, and I stood looking at Inyathi the Cow, or Buffalo or whatever he was. I took the pistols out of my belt, put them down, and I raised my hands over my head. Inyathi nodded and raised his hands just the same.

"Now then lads," says I, "get us ashore, smooth as a tart's arse, and don't tip me over." "Aye aye!" says Mr Long. All hands pulled slow and easy, and the boat grounded a few paces from the man with the feathers. He was a precious fine 'un: not near so big as me but straight and upright and handsome. He had some sort of black ring round his head, with his hair cropped – they all had that ring – and he had a leopard skin over his shoulders which I took to be a badge of rank. He had all that and the same damn-your-eyes look on his face as an English Lord at the head of a county regiment. This was not a modest man.

"Now," says I, "let me get out, then pull for midstream and stay there." Mr Long frowned.

"Shouldn't we wait until you're …" says he.

"No!" says I. "Get into midstream!"

"Aye aye!" says he. Out I got, over my knees in water, and reached back and hauled Halfpenny after me. He didn't want to come, so the boat rocked. He whimpered something pitiful, but out he came, splashing into the water, and clinging to me in fright. I hauled him upright and reminded him of his duties. I did this quite forcibly, as you might expect. In case some of you youngsters might still be of gentle years, I won't repeat exactly what I said. But – in essence – I advised Mr Halfpenny, the Great African Hunter, that if he did not jolly well stand up and act like a man, then I might become jolly well cross with him.

So there we stood, just the two of us facing Mr Inyathi the whatever-he-was and all his men – of which there were some hundreds – with the longboat safe out on the river, and the water draining out of our shoes. It was there, under the hot African sun, that your Uncle Jacob began one of the finest business negotiations of his life. I was able to do this because I could see from the first instant that Mr Inyathi was after something just as much as I was. He must have been or he'd never have laid down his weapons to entice me ashore.

Of course, I had to bear in mind that what Mr Inyathi was after might just possibly be myself and Halfpenny roasting over a slow fire. Or maybe the pair of us in a cooking pot? Who knows? That would depend on whether they liked their dinners fried or boiled.

Two things persuaded me to take the risk. First: the fact that Inyathi had stared fixedly at the carronade in the bows of the longboat. He'd gazed at that gun in exactly the same way that we'd gazed at the bums of his women folk. Second: and while I had the sense not to stare, I had another look at the lady in charge of these women folk. I learned later that her name was Ulwazi. Looking at her, I decided that I didn't want to run away just yet.

Of course, there were the diamonds to consider as well. If we did run, then that would be the end of them.

So we had a little word, did Inyathi and I. His proper title was Inyathi, the Buffalo: *General*, *Prince*, Inyathi, the Buffalo if you please! He was a very great man indeed among his people. We stood a few paces from each other, with hundreds of folk looking on, and Halfpenny translating. To give Halfpenny credit, and although he sweated like a pig with the strain of it, he got better as his ear tuned into Inyathi's speech. Also, I found that talking through an interpreter isn't half so hard as it might seem, because when the other man speaks, you can't understand him, but you get a few seconds to judge his expression and manner before your translator comes in with the words.

So it went like this:

"*Gabble-gabble-gabble?*" says Inyathi. Halfpenny frowns and thinks.

"He wants to know who you are and what you're doing here," says Halfpenny.

"I am an officer of King George of England," says I. "Here on a voyage of exploration."

"*Gabble-gabble-gabble!*" says Halfpenny, and Inyathi nods.

That was the style of it, and I'll not deliver any more because it would be tedious. But at the end of an hour or so, each party was comfortable with the other, and Inyathi was ready – for the moment – to accept *my* tale that I was here to pluck the flowers and sketch the landscape, while I was ready – for the moment – to accept *his* tale that he welcomed any subject of a great king.

The result was that my party came ashore and set up a camp, and gifts were exchanged. Inyathi got a Swiss music box, some silver tankards, and a dozen of best Sheffield cook's knives, while we got a nice young bullock for our dinners with some pots of native beer, and some women came along to do the butchering and cooking. One of them was Ulwazi who was in charge.

That was it for the moment, between myself and Inyathi. We'd each taken the measure of the other, and I marked him out as a sharp 'un, to be dealt with very carefully, and not all in one go. So we parted for the moment. He went back inside the village – they called them kraals – with his troops, and I sat down with Goodsby, Long and Ealey, while the hands put up tents and the native girls did their cooking. You will note that Halfpenny wasn't sat down with us. That's because he was up on his feet chattering with the girls in their language, and swaggering round like the big bold fellow that he was not. It made us smile, but talk was all that Halfpenny did, because however friendly was the welcome, Inyathi left a company of armed men nearby to keep an eye on us. In any case, I'd already warned all hands not to touch the native women because that's basic good manners among strangers. After all, how would you like it if a foreigner pinched your sister's tits in your living room?

Which was all very fine, and very sensible of me... except that I could not keep one of the native women out of my mind. It was Ulwazi. I couldn't think of anything else and I stared and stared at her. It was rude and stupid, and the hands noticed. But I couldn't help myself and I'll tell you why. First be warned that I'm not Jane Austen, who I once met in Bath: a tight little creature she was, and not much fun. Now I've not read any of her books, but everyone says they're wonderful. So if Miss Austen were writing this, she'd explain that it can all happen with a single glance. She'd explain, in her pretty little words, that a man and a woman can meet, look at one another, and that's it, in one eyeblink.

Well, my jolly boys – and jolly girls too – before I met Ulwazi, I would have said that such an instant entrancement was nonsense. I'd have said that and more, because I do declare – just in case you haven't noticed – that I don't write romances. But precisely that entrancement happened to me when I saw Ulwazi standing on the bank of the Haipo river, with the wet still shining on her body. Or at least it started by the riverbank. When she came back, in charge of the cooking brigade and, as I saw her on that second occasion, it hit me like a typhoon. She was so lovely that it bloody well hurt to look at her. She was amazing.

I looked and looked. The feelings inside of me filled me up, rolled me over, and sank me.

She was the one for me. She was the one and there could never be another, even though I can't imagine why, because you – who've read these memoirs – must know that she wasn't the first lovely woman that I'd met. Hadn't I so very recently been with Perse? And herself as lovely as a china doll? All round and pink and white? And hadn't there been shoals of them before? By Jove there had. But none of them were like Ulwazi. Not before nor after, not ever. So, if there really is such a creature as the love of a man's life, then she – my jolly boys – was the one for your Uncle Jacob: Princess Ulwazi of the Northern Zulus.

It all came over me at once, and by God and all his angels what a moment that was! My heart was going like the trip-hammer in an iron works and what's more I could see that something was going on inside of her: the look on her face was very odd, but she kept staring back at me. Then I realised someone was whispering in my ear. Well, not really whispering. Just insisting without shouting but insisting very hard. It was Halfpenny.

"Captain, sir?" says he. "*Sir? Sir Jacob?*" I ignored him a while, but then Ulwazi looked away, and the spell eased off a point or two.

"What?" says I to Halfpenny, and I saw that he looked worried.

"Watch out, sir, 'cos she's his wife!" says he.

"Who is?" says I, in my stupidity.

"*She* is," says he, "Ulwazi. She's Inyathi's wife. So you'd best not grab hold of the bits that bounce!" Normally he'd have got my boot up his breech for his cheek, but I just about had the sense not to do that, and anyway I was mainly concerned with wondering what Ulwazi was thinking. I wondered and wondered.

I wondered until the next day when I found out.

"This was the time when temptation fell upon the lovely Ulwazi, wife of Inyathi the Buffalo."

(From the Saga of Inyathi)

Ulwazi left the kraal at dawn, the day after the white men came in their boat. She left by the command of her husband, to supervise the bringing of food and water to the white men in their small houses of cloth and timber. These little houses were most ingenious and had been built at great speed. But this was not surprising because everyone knew that white men made ingenious things.

The women sang as they followed Ulwazi, bearing their loads on the short walk to the riverside, and all of them smiled at the foolish faces of the white men. Because as the women approached, the white men arose and stood with such naked lust in their eyes as no man with decent manners would ever display.

Ulwazi thought they made a poor comparison with the company of Zulu guardsmen encamped separately, who sat by their fires merely nodding in acknowledgement as she passed by, and which was most correct. She looked again at the goggling eyes of the white men and wondered if their mothers had raised them without discipline? Or perhaps this is how all white men behaved in their own land? In that case they would give all power to their women, by revealing that the women had that which men desired! Ulwazi nodded in return to the guardsmen and passed by in dignity.

But dignity was spoiled as a crowd of small children came running out from the kraal. They scampered and leapt and raced, crying out in their high voices, and making a great noise. Ulwazi smiled because the whole kraal had been full of talk of these white men and their boat. They were exotic strangers of such bizarre appearance and behaviour that only one of them could speak properly, and *he* used the wrong sounds and mixed up his words. So the children had come running to see the strangers, and to find out whether they really did have fur like monkeys, spines like porcupines, or any of the other oddities that their parents – in jest – had told them. There was a great cacophony of young voices, as the children gathered in front of the white men's camp and called out and chattered and laughed.

Then something strange happened: something strange and wonderful. The giant came out of one of the cloth houses. Some others were with him, but Ulwazi did not look at them. She had been waiting for the giant. She realised that. She had seen him yesterday and felt the stab as he looked into her eyes. He was huge. He was a bull. He was fair of face, and his hair was black with a thin white streak. All the children gasped and fell back, but he laughed and made no move forward. Then one of the children cried out.

"Indlovu!" he cried: *elephant!*

"Indlovu! Indlovu! Indlovu!" cried all the rest, and they clapped hands in time to the words. The giant laughed, and the children saw something in him that they liked and trusted. Surging forward, they fell upon him, plucking at his clothes and pulling at his hands. He laughed again, and seized up a little girl, throwing her into the air and catching her. All the rest shrieked and closed in, begging to be lifted up. The children adored him. They were joyful in their happiness: joyful in his presence.

Ulwazi felt the stab again. She felt it deeply and tears ran from her eyes. She had never seen a man so wonderful. She was a married woman. Her husband was the finest man in the Kingdom. He was handsome, brave, clever and kind. He had raised her to the greatest height that a Zulu woman could achieve. He acted in every way as a husband should, and beyond even that she knew that he loved her!

Despite all this, she did not love him. Her marriage had been so splendid and dutiful that there had been no need for love. But now she did love someone.

Chapter 36

"The Janissaries finished off the rest of them: all those that weren't dead."

(From the diary of Auguste Renard)

After the Zulus ran and the smoke cleared, Renard leaned on one of the hot gun barrels and wiped the sweat and powder-stains from his face with a piece of rag. Or he tried to. He spat on the rag and tried again.

"Pah!" he said, and turned to one of his gun crew who was standing useless as he stared at the hideous offal in front of the guns. "Oi!" said Renard. "Stop shitting-well standing there and get me some water! *Now!*"

The Gunner brought a bucket of water. It was for wetting the sponge on the back end of a rammer: the sponge that went down barrels to put out sparks before the next cartridge. The water was dirty but it would do. Renard soaked the rag and wiped his face. Then he looked at the other gunners. They were all standing gaping, and one was heaving up his guts. Some weren't veterans and had never seen what cannon fire does to human bodies.

Renard had another look and felt some sympathy for his men. Some of the remains were still moaning. But not for long. The Janissaries were out in long lines, dipping their bayonets. The officers shouted and kept their men moving. They even stabbed a bit with their fancy swords, bending down occasionally to pick up anything worth taking. Renard wondered if he should go out and have a go? He was as keen on loot as any soldier. But no. He was too tired, and what did a load of savages have anyway? It wasn't like Venice or Milan. Renard sighed, remembering those happy days when Napoleon went through Italy like a dose of salts and Renard had filled his knapsack. He shook his head sadly. It had been gold candlesticks, pocket watches and strings of pearls! And all that gone on whores and drink! And cards. But at least he'd enjoyed himself. He smiled at that.

Later, the column and the guns moved off to be clear of the battle debris. They made camp in a nice clean place by a stream, and there was a celebration. They'd done well. Just two guns, a hundred Bedouin and five hundred Janissaries, and they'd seen off thousands of Zulus. It was surely a sign of things to come.

Later still, Renard sat with Malmuk and the Janissary leaders in their smart uniforms. The Bedouin didn't join them because they were full of religion and never dined with infidels. Renard thought *more fool them* because they were missing out. It was all neat and tidy, with camp chairs and a table, and service by the Janissary servants. There were even candles. After a good dinner and plenty of wine, the most senior Janissary nudged one of his juniors, and spoke to him in Turkish. The junior nodded, reached into a pocket and put three jewel stones onto the table. Everyone looked at them and gasped, and the stones flashed in the candlelight. The senior officer spoke. He spoke French for the benefit of Renard and Malmuk.

"These we picked up on the battlefield," he said. "We took them from the brows of leaders among the Zulus." He looked at Malmuk. "Effendi," he said, "I have my sources and I know this great secret of yours." Malmuk frowned and struggled to understand because he'd had plenty to drink and neither he nor the Janissary officer were perfect in French. But Renard understood.

"What secret?" said Renard. But his expression betrayed him, and the Janissary officer laughed.

"Oh!" said the Janissary, "so you know too? That we're really here for the diamonds and not the Zulu girls?"

Malmuk looked at Renard. Renard looked at Malmuk. They shrugged. Malmuk sniffed and pointed to the diamonds.

"Maybe," he said, "so why are you showing me these?"

"Because, Effendi," said the Janissary, "if we can prove there is a diamond mine in Zulu Land, then the leaders of your people will raise a great army to conquer Zulu Land. I would like to be a part of that army." He smiled. "For a share of the mines." Now Renard laughed.

"And you'll need gunners too!" he said. Malmuk thought carefully. It was good to see the stones because they were evidence that the mines existed. But Malmuk had no authority to offer what the Janissary and Renard wanted … except that perhaps … that didn't matter?

"I can't promise anything," he said, "because that's for those above me." The Janissary leader frowned and reached out to take back the diamonds. "But ..." said Malmuk.

"But?" said the Janissary and Renard, together.

"But," said Malmuk, "we have just proved that nothing in Zulu Land can stop us. So there is no need for a great army! We can go where we like, and take what we like. Meanwhile, our friends the Bedouin," he said looking across to their camp fires, "who are now *out* of this discussion." Everyone smiled. "The Bedouin scouts tell us that the main Zulu kraals are away to the west so that is where we shall go." He looked round the table. "To find the mines and take them for ourselves!"

"Ahhhhh!" they said.

"What's more," said Malmuk, "and you, Renard, will like this."

"Oh?" said Renard.

"If we're after diamonds, we needn't be particular about any Zulu girls that we find. So we can *all* try them out: including you!"

Renard liked that very much indeed.

217

Chapter 37

I found out what Ulwazi thought the next day. She came out from the kraal with some women, bringing us food and beer, and a lot of little kiddies came out too. They made such a noise that I went out to look. I'd been in my tent with Long, Ealey and Goodsby, going over our maps to look for the diamond mines, though I did notice that none of them were paying much attention to the maps; they kept looking at Goodsby as if they were waiting for something from him.

I think he was about to speak, when there was such a chatter and yelling that we all went out to see. There they were, and what merry little things: a crowd of children all quite young and tiny, such neat little faces and such smiles. You couldn't help but smile back. One of them said something in their own language and they all shouted it out. I laughed, and then they were all over me. I was happy because I've always liked children and they seem to like me. It was like pulling my nephews and nieces along in their carriage.

Which is all very fine, but then something dangerous happened. In the middle of playing with the children, I saw that Ulwazi was nearby and looking at me, and the typhoon hit me again because I could see that it was hitting her too. I could see by the way she looked at me. So I'm afraid I put down whichever of the children I was holding, started towards Ulwazi, and she started towards me. But someone had the wit to stop me. It was Goodsby. He got himself in front of me, and held out his hands. I could see the concern on his face.

"Captain!" says he. "*Sir!* You can't, sir, you just can't!" He beckoned to Long and Ealey, and they came and stood beside him in support.

"Ware of her!" says Long. "She's a lee shore, and certain death!"

"Yes! Yes!" says Ealey.

I was barely paying attention, but I saw that Ulwazi had stopped and was looking at Goodsby, Long and Ealey, and nodding in approval of them. She called off the children, turned away and busied herself with the women who'd come out with her, bringing food and drink. After a moment, she turned and led them off, except for looking back over her shoulder just once. She looked at me and I could barely support the pain of her walking away.

I stared and stared after her before finally noticing that Goodsby was trying to talk to me. It was him alone, because the other two had left it to him. I also noticed that all our party was up and staring at me, and they all looked worried.

"Sir," says Goodsby. "Sir Jacob! Captain! We've talked this over and I am a deputation, sir, in accordance with the traditions of the Service. So I beg a word, sir." He was frightened that I might knock him flat, but he held his ground and insisted, "I am a deputation, sir, and you must respect a deputation and listen!" Everyone nodded, including Long, Ealey and Halfpenny.

I groaned. I was unhappy: very unhappy because I knew what Goodsby was going to say.

"Go on, you swab," says I. "Let's bloody well hear it!" Which wasn't fair to him at all.

"Can we step aside, sir?" says he, lowering his voice. I sighed and nodded and we walked off until the camp couldn't hear us, but every one of them was looking, and so were the Zulu guards in their camp nearby. Goodsby pointed at them.

"See that, sir?" says he. "They've noticed already, so there can't be any more of it for fear of what her husband might do: Prince Inyathi! Halfpenny says he's got thousands of men behind him, and if he tells them to, they'll snuff us like candles! Halfpenny says these warrior tribes are deadly serious over wives, and adultery gets settled in blood." I just shook my head. I couldn't help it. Goodsby tried harder. "It's the look on your face, sir, and she gives it right back, the same look. We all saw it, sir. We saw it yesterday and just now it was even worse! But it can't be, sir, because it'll get us all killed! Everyone's noticed: *everyone!* She's his God-damn wife, sir!"

He went on some while and finally I nodded, because inside of me I knew that it was impossible between Ulwazi and myself. But, by Jove, it was hard, and I hope none of you youngsters ever get crossed like that when you care so much.

And so:

"Well done, Dr Goodsby," says I, "well spoken." I shook his hand because that's what you do when your friends are doing their best for you, and you know you're in the wrong. It's not like defying your enemies, and you have to give in with good grace.

"Aye aye, sir," says he, and the matter was not mentioned again. It was not mentioned but that didn't stop the pain coming back, and I had to fight hard to deny it.

Later in the morning, Inyathi came out. He came out in full regalia of plumes and robes, with a strong force of guardsmen bringing stools for himself and myself to sit upon, and advisers and wise men to sit behind him. More important, he came with an elderly-looking man who had a withered arm and a limp, and who turned out to be his father N'tombela, who was treated with huge respect by the Zulus. Thus, N'tombela had the highest stool to sit on, and although he left most of the talking to Inyathi, he was another sharp 'un, and Inyathi looked to him constantly.

Also there was a cluster of men who sat separately from Inyathi and N'tombela, but were also men of note. They too wore plumes and regalia; they too sat on stools, and were representatives of Zulu regiments that Inyathi needed on his side.

Ulwazi was there too, in charge of the food and drink and the women. I took care not to look at her and she didn't look at me. It was safer that way. There I sat in my uniform coat and hat, while Halfpenny stood up translating. Long, Ealey and Goodsby sat behind me, with the rest sat behind them, for the honour of Old England. Also, since the Zulus had their spears and shields, we had our muskets and pistols and I wore my sword.

Then off we went, on a long haul of talk which stopped me fretting over Ulwazi because I do love bargaining and there's an extra spice when you're facing someone who's got you in his fist. After all, where's the skill if your opponent is on a powder keg and you have a match? Not much, my lads, but imagine it the other way round! In that case you must keep your nerve, conceal weakness, and search for terms that suit you both. Fortunately, as the Dutch say: *I've sat in front of hotter fires than that!* Because a few years ago in Jamaica, I'd done business with a lunatic preacher named Vernon Hughes: a frothing-mouth, religious maniac surrounded by murderous savages that took his word as law, while glaring at myself with white round eyes, and sharpening their knives in hope of a bloodbath. Compared to Vernon Hughes, General Prince Inyathi and his father were a pair of English gentleman. Also, the pair of them were under a fearful weight of Zulu politics, and had to beware of what others thought, especially in regiments not their own: that's why the plumed men were there, and they had to be kept sweet.

Most of the day was spent talking, apart from breaks for food and drink and to give Halfpenny an occasional respite from the heavy job of translation. On one occasion, he even went down to the river to duck his head because it was aching with effort. He might have been a poseur and a coward but we couldn't have done without him.

It was slow work because neither side wanted to make concessions too quickly, or reveal secrets without careful thought. Inyathi and his father had to break away from time to time to check with the plumed men that they weren't going to lose support by offering me too much. Note well that I mean *military* support, because it leaked out from everything Inyathi said that he was expecting a war against an invading army, and also that he had problems with his own people including a monster-woman called M'thunzi, the Witch. So you wouldn't want to hear every word, especially as everything went through Halfpenny's translations. Also, everything was *not* discussed in neat and tidy order. Here is a flavour of it, but bear in mind that this is only a summary, given as if spoken directly between myself and Inyathi.

"My people face invasion from a force of Arabs," says Inyathi, "who come armed with magic weapons, and I think you have such weapons yourself."

"What sort of weapons?" says I.

"Tell me about the black thing on the front of your boat," says he.

"The carronade?" says I.

"Is it a tube filled with gunpowder, which throws lead bullets?"

"Yes, it is."

"And does it make a great and thundering sound, with much flame?"

"Yes it does," says I, and all the plumed men nudged each other.

"Good," says he, "because I will need that weapon in my service."

"Perhaps," says I, "but it will need a proper carriage."

"What does that mean?" says Inyathi, very suspicious.

"The gun's on a slide-mounting in the boat," says I, "and that's no good for land service. We'll have to take it back downriver for a wheeled carriage to be made aboard my ship." That put a fright up Inyathi for fear that we Englishmen would get into our boat and disappear! So the following was agreed after much discussion and some nervousness among my people.

"I'll stay here then," says I, finally, "while my men take the boat to our ship to be fitted with a land-carriage, and more than that, we'll rig *two* guns for land service to show good faith." That went down well – at least on their side – and later it was my turn.

"My King has sent me to look for diamonds," says I.

"We have such stones," says he, "worn by the elite. They come from deep caves."

"A mine?" says I, trying to keep my excitement in check. "A diamond mine?"

"Call it what you wish," says he. "It is a place where many caves run into the rocks."

"Do you place any value on these diamonds?" says I as casually as possible, and that really did cause heated discussions between Inyathi and his advisers.

"If you enter my service with your fire weapons," says he, "and turn them on the Arab invaders, and if you stand with me at the mustering of the regiments." He paused and checked to make sure he'd carried his own people with him. "Then, when I am victorious, you may take all the diamonds that you want."

Finally, there was one last breaking away from the discussions. Inyathi insisted that we show what the longboat's carronade could do.

"I must know that this black tube can truly breathe thunder and flame," says he, "because it is of different form and colour to the tubes in the hands of the Arabs. I must see with my own eyes, and hear with my own ears." This brought a vigorous agreement from all those around him, and much waving of fly whisks and sticks. Previously, they'd kept quiet as a church when the Parson preaches, but the chance to see the gun speak was too much. Of course I said yes, and off we all went, down to the river where the boat was moored. I had the carronade cleared for action, the trigger-lock screwed in place, and a charge rammed down with a round-shot on top. All the Zulus were gaping on the river banks and talking to each other like the audience before a play starts.

So there I was, in the boat with a gun-crew and men at the oars, to get the carronade pointing safely downriver. Then I took up the firing lanyard.

"Halfpenny?" says I to him, who was standing on the riverbank.

"Captain?" says he.

"Warn them it's going to be loud."

"Aye aye!" says he, and shouted out in the Zulu tongue. Then I jerked the lanyard.

"Snap whoof!" said the trigger-lock.

"BOOOM!" said the gun as it shot back up its slide. The longboat rocked, and out came a jet of flame and a cloud of smoke and, by Jove, but those Zulus loved it. Just for once, all their formidable, manly dignity disappeared in a gleeful shouting, jumping, clapping of hands to ears and laughing. It's fireworks, you see? Everyone loves fireworks and none of these people had ever seen the like before. God knows where the shot went. Nobody even noticed that, but it didn't matter.

It took a few more rounds after that, but those few pounds of powder and iron sealed the agreement. There was much detail, but in principle it was simple: we could have the diamonds if we fought Inyathi's little war. Or was it a big war? I wasn't sure. But the whole of the agreement was later proclaimed by a herald, who stood up beside Inyathi and bellowed for all to hear, with Halfpenny shouting it in English. This procedure – I should point out – was the Zulu equivalent of a legal contract signed in blood, and witnessed by King George, Napoleon Bonaparte, the Czar of all the Russias and His Holiness The Pope. So God help either side if they defaulted.

After that there was a great feast, with cattle slaughtered and beer by the gallon. That night there were bonfires with some of the most wonderful singing by a Zulu choir, and wonderful dancing by their girls. Ulwazi was one of them: she was leading them, and oh dear me but she was graceful. Every movement was like a song inside me. I had to take care to keep some dignity on my face and not let my feelings show. It was bloody hard. I was also tired with the effort of the day as we sat cross-legged in the night around the campfire, with the moon above us and faces shining in the firelight.

But I had to pay attention to Halfpenny who had a lot to say because he'd picked up all sorts of extras, by listening to the men who'd sat behind Inyathi. They'd argued among themselves, and either forgotten that he could understand them or thought he just wouldn't hear. But he did hear and learned a lot of what was going on in Zulu Land that Inyathi hadn't mentioned.

Apparently, M'thunzi, the Witch was a tremendous creature among the Zulus, and could 'sniff out' demons within accursed men, who were instantly killed. Also, it was only M'thunzi who knew the way inside the diamond mines, which were a complex labyrinth: easy to enter but hard to get out of, and which – to our surprise – were somewhere close by! It was also only M'thunzi who chose which of the elite women, or men, would wear a diamond in the headband.

But Inyathi hated M'thunzi because of the 'sniffing out' and therefore – amazingly – he actually hated the diamonds and wanted rid of them! He wanted rid because they were a source of M'thunzi's power and because the Egyptians and Arabs were constantly raiding Zulu Land for the diamonds as well as slave girls. Meanwhile, M'thunzi hated Inyathi and, with the present Zulu King lost in senility, she backed his son Zithulele against Inyathi in the coming fight to settle who would be the next king.

Therefore, my jolly boys, when we 'stood beside' Inyathi at this muster of regiments, we wouldn't be watching a review of the troops on Horse Guards Parade, but taking part in a pitched battle with us in the middle, and probably on the losing side since more regiments followed Zithulele than Inyathi!

Fortunately, there was no doubt now that the diamond mines were real, and that Inyathi would let us take our fill of them if we kept him happy. So I needed to think, and to talk things over with somebody – the obvious choice being Goodsby. I took him aside the next day, after breakfast, and we walked along the riverbank.

Note that the relationship between us was shifted because we weren't aboard ship under discipline. So he spoke as an equal which was good because he was a clever man and I needed advice. I needed his advice even if it was tainted with diamond fever – which it was – but you can't have everything, my jolly boys, not in this wicked world. Therefore, I told him absolutely everything. And then:

"But if we do what Inyathi wants," says I, "we'd be waging war on Egypt and Arabia without permission from the Admiralty."

"Only a little war," says he, "if we're lucky. And it would be against slavers, not an actual nation."

"And of course," says I, "we'd go home with the diamonds."

"Which Lord Spencer *said* we could do," says he.

"Yes," says I, "go on, Goodsby!"

"Well, sir," says he, "all that Inyathi wants is a pair of field guns. It's not as if we'd advance into battle with the infantry. It would be two guns, defended in some safe place by the Zulus, and hurling shot and shell into an enemy that can't hit back!" That almost made me smile, because leaving aside the possibility of counter-battery fire from the enemy's guns, which the good doctor seemed to have forgotten, his words were a fascinating insight into how far the Rev. Goodsby had come from his peaceful role as ship's chaplain. I wondered just what Gentle Jesus might think of Goodsby now? But I didn't say that. Instead:

"Of course," says I, "but we would have to persuade the men to do it." He laughed at that.

"Never worry in that respect," says he. "They'll follow you anywhere, Sir Jacob!" He laughed again, so jolly as he was with the diamond fever. 'Why," says he, "all you sailors are half pirates anyway."

"Perhaps," says I, "but what about the scientific gentlemen? They're not pirates and they might carry the tale home: the wrong tale to the wrong people."

"Not necessarily," says he, and he delivered some more un-Jesus thoughts. "Not if they got their share of the diamonds," says he, "because they're all hard up for funds are scientific gentlemen, and why do they have to know *everything*? Why can't they be left with their astronomical observations while we do our bits of fighting? After that, we can fetch the diamonds and explain any *necessary* details afterwards?"

"What about Ealey?" says I. "He's here with us, and he's a scientific gentleman. D'you think I should talk to him?"

"No, no, no, sir!" says he, "let me do it."

"Why?" says I. "Is he afraid of me?" Goodsby smiled.

"Not at all, sir," says he. "Ealey's taken to the sea life something wonderful, so he's like all the rest now, and he thinks you're Jolly Jack Flash!"

"But?" says I, because I could see it coming.

"But," says Goodsby, "he is not *committed* to the sea life. He is rooted ashore, and so – with your permission – I would offer myself as go-between, to seek out, and bring to your attention, any problems that Ealey might have with our proposals."

So that's what we did, and a damn fine piece of luck that we did so, because it ended up turning your Uncle Jacob into such a wizard as made M'thunzi, the Witch, look like a fairy godmother.

Chapter 38

"Then the most faithful of Ulwazi's women stood forth and gave warning."

(From the Saga of Inyathi)

"Grandmother," said Sizakele, "I must speak with you. I speak for all those of the women who love you and who would stand between you and danger, even if the danger were a lion."

Ulwazi nodded to Sizakele, and motioned that Sizakele should sit, which she did. She sat at Ulwazi's knee while Ulwazi sat on a stool outside the house of her husband, Prince Inyathi, in the kraal of Inyathi's father. Other women stood by and watched. Some were formally dressed and had come with Sizakele. Others were there for the day's work in and around the house. But no work was being done, and there was silence as all the women paid close attention.

"You are gracious in speech, O Sizakele," said Ulwazi, which indeed she was because Sizakele was an old lady, more than three times Ulwazi's age and it was Sizakele who was a grandmother, while Ulwazi still had no children. But it was a great courtesy among the North Zulu folk to address a woman as grandmother. "I ask why you have come to me, O Sizakele," said Ulwazi, "you who truly are a grandmother, and many times over."

"Ahhhhh!" sighed all the women, in appreciation of Ulwazi's good manners.

"I come on a most important matter," said Sizakele, "and one so important that I ask for speech in your ear." Ulwazi nodded.

"You may speak," she said, "and into my ear."

Everyone watched closely, because everyone knew that careful approaches had already been made to Ulwazi by faithful intermediaries. Otherwise, it would have been unthinkable for any woman to approach the wife of a prince and seek speech into her ear. But everyone also knew that in some matters of wrongful behaviour, it was customary to give warning and thereby give opportunity for repentance and correction.

Sizakele stood, and came close to Ulwazi, speaking into her ear such that no other person could hear, although most could have guessed what was said.

"O Princess," said Sizakele, "we all know temptation. We are all frail. We all love you. But there must be no more gazing upon the White Giant. He may look at you and it does not matter, because white men have no manners. But you may not look at him! Not with such love in your eyes. Do you understand?"

"I do, grandmother," said Ulwazi, and indeed she did, and was ashamed.

"There is still time," said Sizakele, "because your husband pretends not to know, and all the men pretend with him. But all the women are speaking of this, and the matter cannot be contained much longer." Sizakele paused. "Do you hear me, O Princess?"

"I hear you," said Ulwazi.

"So listen further, because I speak in kindness," said Sizakele. "Your noble husband is gone to tour the regiments, to seek their help. He travels urgently as time is short before the Arabs fall upon us. But he will be back soon, and this matter must be ended before then. Do you hear me, O Princess? This is most serious and most urgent."

"I hear you, and thank you, O Sizakele," said Ulwazi.

After that, Sizakele sat down, and there was formal speech, and refreshment was offered. Then Sizakele arose and left, with her followers behind her. They left satisfied. All were smiling. All was peaceful. All was settled.

Except that it was not settled. Ulwazi beckoned her most trusted woman. The woman came close and Ulwazi spoke into *her* ear.

"I must see him," said Ulwazi. "My heart is dying."

"I concurred because I could not resist the opportunity to play God."
(From a letter of March 23rd 1804 from
Mr Charles Ealey to his father)

The voyage downriver was an easy one. Long, Ealey and Goodsby were aboard with the tars, with Long in command, who wouldn't have made sail even if the wind had been favourable. With a current so strong and the hands pulling with a will, the journey was done in half the time of going upriver. The sun shone hot; the sky was blue; the hippos were still basking and honking, and all aboard the boat were merry.

"There's the island," said Ealey. "You can already see the observation platform and some of the instruments." He took a telescope and focussed. "Yes," he said, "and they've seen us. They're waving."

"Yes," said Long at the stern with the tiller, and he yelled at the oarsmen as they tried to look ahead. "Keep stroke, you buggers!" he said. "We're pulling straight past, as you bloody well know. I want to be in hailing distance but no closer."

"Aye aye, sir!" they said, and clank clank went the oars in steady rhythm. The longboat went forging past the island, heading for the anchored *Enable* where men were lining the rails and up in the shrouds, and cheering. The nearest the boat came to the island was a pistol-shot from the little pier that the tars had built for the convenience of boats. Men were out from the island's tents, and were on the pier and waving.

"There's Sir David," said Ealey, "and Sir Oliver and the rest." He waved back. "They're shouting but I can't hear."

"That's my plan," said Lieutenant Long. "The Captain said we're not to talk to them, 'cos least said, soonest mended." He drew breath and let out a mast-head roar: "Aaaaall's well!" he cried. "Aaaaall's well!" He turned to Ealey. "And that's all the news they'll get from me!" Ealey laughed.

"Let's get aboard," he said, and soon the longboat was alongside *Enable*, where the cheering stopped as soon as the crew saw that their Captain wasn't in the boat. Instead there were anxious groans.

"Where's the Captain?" cried Lieutenant Chivers, in command of the ship. "He isn't ..." "No!" said Long. "All's well! The Captain is safe with the Zulus, sir, and Halfpenny with him for company." Long smiled at that, and everyone in the boat laughed. They remembered how hard Halfpenny had pleaded not to be left behind. Not when his rum had run out and he was frightened.

"He's with the Zulus?" said Chivers in surprise, "and safe?" The men cheered again. "And what about the diamonds?" he said. "Any sign or sight?"

"Aye!" cried the ship's crew.

"I'll tell you when we're aboard, sir," said Long, "'cos there's a job of work to do for all hands, and especially the Carpenter's crew!" As soon as

Long's people were out of the boat and aboard ship, there was a meeting on the quarterdeck so that Lieutenant Lord and Mr Ealey could tell all to Lieutenant Chivers, and most especially to the Gunner and the Carpenter. There was an intense and technical discussion.

"So we're to build land-service carriages for two carronades?" said the Carpenter, and he shook his head and puffed his cheeks. "That's gonna be a sod of a job that is! That's if it's to be dished wheels, and spokes and hubs? That's skilled work, that is, and takes a seven-year apprenticeship to learn!"

"Just do your best," said Lieutenant Chivers, "with whatever we have aboard."

"Are you sure the Cap'n wants carronades?" said the Gunner.

"Oh yes," said Long, "and he wants the ship's two 24-pounders." The Gunner frowned.

"If it was me," he said, "I'd want long guns if it's for field service. Why don't we mount a couple of our main deck 9-pounders? They only weigh ten hundredweights while the carronades are fourteen and they're for short-distance work, in a sea action. They haven't got the range, you see." Lieutenant Chivers looked to Lieutenant Long.

"It has to be carronades," said Long. "The Zulus saw the boat carronade fired and they loved it, so they're expecting something like it. They might not be happy with anything else. Also, the Captain has some ideas about how to use the carronades, and he's spoken to the Zulus about it. So it has to be carronades."

"What about caissons for the ammunition and shot?" said the Carpenter. "Them'll need wheels an' all, and must be made weatherproof."

"Whatever you think, Mr Carpenter," said Long.

"And does the Cap'n want fixed ammunition?" said the Gunner. "All in one bag so as to go down the bores quicker?"

"Whatever *you* think, Mr Gunner," said Long.

"What about tackles for hauling?" said the Carpenter. "Are there gonna be 'osses or is it down to man-hauling?"

"Man-hauling," said Long. "There are no horses in Zulu Land." The Carpenter and Gunner nodded. All hands set to work under their direction and the job was done inside of two days, which was an achievement. But while the job was in hand, something equally important had happened.

Quietly, and in the stern cabin, Mr Ealey and his friend Lieutenant Long were busy with their maps and calculations concerning astronomical matters. They thereby came to a most interesting conclusion.

"It will mainly be here," said Ealey.

"Will it be complete?" said Long.

"Yes," said Ealey, "it will be intense."

"And are you sure about the date?" said Long. Ealey took a breath and thought.

"Yes," he said, "but only if this map is accurate, and our measurements of latitude and longitude are accurate."

"Hmmm," said Long. "I suppose it's the best we can do."

"It is, and it's a matter of being there in time."

"Precisely. And time is pressing, and we must tell the Captain."

"He's a tremendously cunning man."

"He is! He'll find a way to use this."

"If we're in time."

Finally, and just for the pride of what had been achieved, one of the field-mounted carronades was set up on deck while the other, in collapsed form, was already stowed in the longboat. Lieutenant Chivers and Lieutenant Long stood with Mr Ealey for the show, and the crew gave three cheers.

"Proceed, Mr Gunner and Mr Carpenter!" said Chivers.

"After you, Mr Carpenter," said the Gunner.

"Aye aye!" said the Carpenter. "If you'd look here, gentlemen, the wheels is the big problem. I've neither time nor skill for proper 'uns, so these is plank wheels and is solid, but they's six foot in diameter, to roll easy rough ground, and shod with iron tyres, and the axles is cranked so as to splay them out more at the bottom than the top, for to keep them from wobbling."

"Very ingenious, Mr Carpenter," said Chivers.

"Aye!" said everyone.

"And see here at the stern of her," said the Carpenter, "elevation is by wedge, and the trail is split, and the load balanced so two men can raise her up." He and one of his mates demonstrated. "She can be towed like this, by any number of men."

"And triggers, and flints and fixed-shot and powder horns," said the Gunner, "is all stored in the caisson here, that our Carpenter made, and a credit to him and his mates, because all I did was take things out of store and pack them in."

"Well done, Mr Gunner and Mr Carpenter," said Lieutenant Chivers. "And since time is pressing, we'll dismount this gun for heaving over the side, then issue a tot for all hands. After that, I assume Mr Long that you'll be off upriver?" That was indeed Long's intention, though *Enable's* barge had to go in company with the longboat because two guns, plus carriages and the caisson was too great a load for one boat. Fortunately, there was no shortage of volunteers to man the extra oars, and once again the matter was settled by lot, with those left behind envying those who faced the hard pull upriver.

Long had his men at the oars and roaring out a shanty, even as night fell. They were quieter later on, when the strain told on them, but they rowed all night because time was pressing, and Mr Ealey was still checking his calculations so long as there was light to see by.

Chapter 39

I was alone with her just the once, but I dream about it still. I dream about that little time, which was probably less than an hour, sitting in a shaded place on the banks of the Haipo. It was all sheltered from view, in a little sunken corner with bushes all round, and a little beach with plenty of nice round pebbles. It was the sort of place where David would have got his sling-stone before facing Goliath, and she was there too. Ulwazi was there.

It started when one of her women came into our camp. It was just myself and Halfpenny sitting round the fire because the longboat was gone back to *Enable* to get the carronades. Inyathi was gone too: gone on a tour of the kraals to gather support, but I'd had a word with him before he left.

I liked him, which was a shame, all things considered. I liked him a lot. He seemed a straight man. He and I sat outside his house, with just a few of his advisers. We talked about the carronades, which he was most anxious to do so as to get the best use of them.

"They're fearfully deadly," says I, "and they throw hundreds of bullets, or a heavy shot. But they're best at short range. Can we trick your enemy to coming close, perhaps with the carronades hidden?" Halfpenny put that to Inyathi, who nodded eagerly: him and his advisers too. He gave a quick reply, and Halfpenny looked at me.

"He says *yes,* sir," says Halfpenny, "definitely yes! He says that they're good at hiding themselves. They're good at …" He searched for words, and Inyathi saw that and came in with something to help. "Ah!" says Halfpenny, "he's saying they're good at entrenchments, sir, good at digging in, and covering up with leaves and branches so the enemy can't see them." Inyathi nodded. "They dig and cover," says Halfpenny.

Next day Inyathi was gone with a strong force of men. They were off at a fast trot that would have left a British light infantry company for dead.

I saw them go. After dark, that woman came into our camp. She was young and pretty and Halfpenny leered at her, so I told him not to. She whispered to him at some length, and he leered at me – the rascal – until he saw my expression. Then he corrected himself, and sat up straight.

"Ahem," says he, "this ... er ... lady, sir, she's saying, I think she's saying, that if you follow her tomorrow along the river when all the kraal is busy at some festival or other ..." He looked at her and she nodded and whispered again. "... then that might be good, sir. For you, sir," Then he said something to her in Zulu, and she bowed and ran off into the dark.

The next day I followed her and she led me along the river to a place where a forest began. It was a forest of funny, twisted little trees: miserable things compared to an English oak or beech, but very dense and with paths running through. She picked one and I followed. Soon we were out of sight of anything other than the birds and insects chirping all round. I followed her to the quiet corner beside the river; she bowed to me and motioned me forward, then ran off. I suppose she kept watch after that? She surely must have done.

And there, my jolly boys, in that quiet and private place, Ulwazi was waiting for me. She was sitting on a patch of grass, but stood as I appeared. I gasped at the sheer beauty of her, and it wasn't just the fact that she wore little more than beads, and her body was exquisitely lovely, because I'd seen lovely women before. This one was different. She was infinitely special, and so I gasped at the sight of her ... and by God and all his angels, she gasped right back at me! She did. She did. I'll never forget it as long as I live, because never, ever, was I so delighted, because I could see that she thought the same of me as I did of her.

Now I'll not be false-modest. I know that women like me. They always have, and it's a lucky gift if you've got it. So this wasn't the first time that I'd had the glad smile from a woman. But this was different, because I loved her. I loved Ulwazi and always will.

> "*On sight of the White Giant, the lovely Ulwazi was intoxicated with emotion.*"
>
> (From the Saga of Inyathi)

Ulwazi drew breath in a gasp as he came into the secret place that she and her trusted woman had chosen. She gasped because he was a great and powerful man. He was the bull, the lion and the elephant, and he was wonderfully handsome. She gasped even though she was already married to a great and powerful man who was also wonderfully handsome. But this man was different because she loved him, and she could see that he loved her in return.

Instantly he took a step towards her, and held out his arms. She took a step towards him. But then she remembered her duty to her husband and her people. So she raised a hand palm-outward and fell back. He gave a sigh and he too fell back. She nodded and smiled, and sat down a small distance from him, waving a hand to signal that he too should sit.

After that, she tried to talk to him; she tried to explain that she was here to say goodbye. But it was exceedingly difficult.

She wouldn't touch me. She held up a hand to stop me, and I stopped dead because that's what she wanted. For myself, I'd have swept her up and thrown her in the air like those little kiddies, and caught her and held her forever, damn the diamonds, damn the Navy, and damn everything. My devious, cunning mind – because yes I am devious and cunning – was already charging down that path …

Keep quiet about this!
Don't tell Halfpenny!
Don't do anything yet!
Wait till the longboat's back!
And then grab her and run …

And so on. If you've read this far of my memoirs, you could probably write the rest yourselves. But she said no. Instead, the two of us sat looking at one another, and we smiled, and then she started talking in her language, miming and waving her hands. I didn't know what the hell she was trying to say but it was beautiful to watch, what with her being so graceful in every gesture. Even her voice was beautiful.

After a while she got sad, and finished talking, and looked at me. It was obviously my turn. I had a go at explaining what I had in mind, which of course she didn't understand, so I tried mime, which made her laugh and the laugh tickled my spine most amazingly. I chattered on and waved hands to little effect, and we weren't even there very long because the servant girl turned up and said something urgently. Ulwazi stood and blinked at me. I knew it was time to go, and that we weren't going to see each other ever again. Not like this. Not in private. So I stood and stepped forward, knelt before her, and took her hand and kissed it. She was in tears; I was in tears, and the servant girl was in tears, because that's how it hits you, my jolly boys. At least that's how it hit me, and I thought the hurt was unbearable.

But it was worse later on.

Chapter 40

"I wasn't going to trust the Bedouin. Not once they found out about the diamonds."

(From the diary of Auguste Renard)

Renard was mounted and out with the Bedouin scouts. He was there because he didn't trust them. Renard was, therefore, protecting his only asset in this life: the two 12-pounders and their gunners, because he was worried that if the Bedouin did find a Zulu army in ambush, then they'd be off and gone without bothering to tell anyone else.

Also, Renard would always rather ride than walk, and he fancied himself as a good horseman. Riding was no hardship, and now he was out in front of the column together with Mohammad Al Rahman, the Bedouin leader, and a troupe of riders. They were Al Rahman's best men: his eyes and ears. They were chosen as quick thinkers and they were good scouts. Renard knew that because he'd been a hussar before he was a gunner, and the French hussars were the finest light cavalry in the world according to Renard. He'd have been a hussar for ever if they hadn't thrown him out.

Renard had to admit that Al Rahman's men were good, but Renard still didn't like Al Rahman, with his mouthful of gold teeth in a brown, wrinkled face. Al Rahman was a skinny little bastard who must have been born in the saddle because nobody could ride like him – certainly not Renard, which was an irritation. Thus, the Bedouin were always doing tricks on horseback. Their favourite was leaning out of the saddle at the gallop to pick things off the ground with a sword point. They could all do a turnip, but Al Rahman could pick up a lemon.

Now Renard rode beside Al Rahman, who grinned at him, chattering in Arabic just to annoy Renard, because Renard knew only a few words of Arabic, while Al Rahman spoke fluent French when he had a mind to. They went at a steady canter with the rest mainly spread out ahead, and everyone looking and searching, while a rear-guard of two men came behind, just in case, because they were coming into Zulu Land. They'd already found and burned out a small kraal. But Renard thought the women were a disappointment. They were too old, and none of them wore diamonds. He looked at Al Rahman, who must have guessed what was in Renard's mind, because he spoke French.

"Do you see any diamonds here?" said Al Rahman, waving a hand at the scenery. "Tell me at once if you do!" He laughed and kicked his horse into a gallop.

"Shit-head!" thought Renard, because the Bedouin knew they were only on wages and wouldn't be getting anything that glittered. He kicked his own horse, and caught up with Al Rahman, acknowledging again that Al Rahman knew his job because, once more, he was going forward to make sure his men were alert.

Renard galloped and the dust and wind stung his eyes. He was galloping over an undulating plain that ran to the horizon on all sides. There were some stunted trees with branches like crooked fingers, and grass was everywhere: grass, grass, grass. There were vultures up in the sky, and horned beasts of every kind. Were they deer? Antelope? Something else? Renard didn't know and didn't care. All that mattered was the pair of huge, round-topped mountains ahead. The Bedouin said they were called *Breasts of Sheba*, and they were the signpost into the heart of Zulu Land, so that's where the column would have to go: the rest of the Bedouin, the marching Janissaries, their mounted officers, and Renard's own precious guns in the middle. Then suddenly there was shouting.

"Hi! Hi! Hi!" Some of the riders, way out in front, were yelling and waving swords. They were a long way off and the yelling was faint – Renard could only just hear it – but he could see the swords flashing and it put a fright up him, because the Bedouin did that when they sighted an enemy. It was a jolt and a fright, but it was an accustomed fright, because Renard was a veteran, and any sensible man took a little bit of fright when the enemy appeared without warning.

"After all," he thought, "you might get killed by the enemy," and since he really was a veteran, he laughed. He quickly caught up with Al Rahman who'd reigned in, produced a telescope, and was looking ahead. Renard's horse snorted and stamped in annoyance at being stopped. But Al Rahman's beast stood utterly still while its master used his telescope.

"Clever little shit," thought Renard. "How can he get a horse to do that?" Then Renard spoke aloud. "What is it?"

"Zulus!" said Al Rahman.

"How many?" said Renard. "Are they in force?"

"I can't see," said Al Rahman. "Not properly, but look!" He pointed ahead. "There's a line of hills right in our path. They're big and they're in the way; my men are circling round in front of what looks like a pass through the hills. They're raising dust, but they're not running." He snapped shut the telescope and put it away. "Come on Frenchman, let's go and look!" Off he rode with Renard behind, and the rear-guard behind him, and the riders to the left and right closing in.

"Pop pop!" Gunfire came from ahead as Renard put weight in his stirrups and leaned into the charge, the wind whooshing in his ears. "Pop pop pop!" More gunfire and puffs of smoke over the Bedouin riders, and sword blades going up and down! Renard's fright turned to excitement. He was a good enough horseman to feel for his own sword at the gallop, because the Bedouin advance-guard weren't running away from the Zulus: they were cutting them down! Renard drew his sword: a hussar's curve-bladed sabre. He didn't like the artillery sword because it was straight and no good for hacking, and everyone hacked in a close action. So thought Renard.

With his horse going full tilt, Renard was among the fighting in seconds. Yes, there was a pass between the hills with a stony way through that curved into the distance and there were high-sloping sides. There were Zulus: dozens of them, and they chanted and beat on their shields and out hurled spears ... Holy Jesus! One shot past Renard with a hiss and a gleam just a hand's width from hitting him. His horse whinnied in fright and staggered, as a whole clump of Zulus – hundreds of them – ran down the hillside and into the melee where twenty Bedouin horsemen were beginning to make minced-beef of those few Zulus who were forming a shield-wall to keep the Bedouin from getting into the pass.

The Zulu reinforcements nearly won the day. They got in among the horsemen and the fight was fierce and intense: sword, pistol and musket against leather shields and stabbing spears. Renard was surrounded by rearing horses, fierce faces, agile limbs, slashing blades, men falling, men crying out and Zulus head-kicked to instant death by iron-shod hoofs, with blood spattering in all directions.

Bang! Bang! Nearby a Bedouin fired his pistols, then drew sword and gave a downstroke that cleaved a Zulu skull from crown to jaw. Bang! Bang! Bang! More gunfire, more kicking and biting, and Renard with a Zulu grabbing each leg. The one on the right went down at a single cut, but it was hard reaching over the bucking, twisting horse to cut down to the left. It took five blows to make the Zulu let go. More Zulus poured down the hillsides which was bad for the Bedouin, until Al Rahman showed that he was more than a clever horseman. He raised voice in a great shout from the very middle of the fight, and with Zulus all round him, who were chanting and stabbing.

"Hi! Hi! Hi!" he cried, and his men heard and followed.

"Hi! Hi! Hi!" they cried. They cried out all together and it put heart into them and they laid on all the harder. Even Renard joined in.

"Hi! Hi! Hi!" he cried, and so the horsemen made a great noise. It seemed to turn the fight, because suddenly the Zulus were running. They were running and presenting the Bedouin with a cavalryman's dearest dreams: broken infantry fleeing over open ground.

"Hi! Hi! Hi! Hi!" The Bedouin spurred their horses and gave chase, going at it hammer and tongs. They pursued the Zulus right through the pass – more than two miles – cutting down every Zulu they could find, and then they trotted back and found a few more, and cut them down for good measure. Finally, when they were done, and they and their horses had stopped panting, they wiped their swords, reloaded their firearms, and gathered around Al Rahman in triumph. He spoke to them in Arabic.

"Is there anyone here who's dead?" he said. "Speak up!" They laughed at the ancient joke. "Anyone wounded?" A few said yes: but remarkably few. "Anyone missing?" Three were missing completely, and a horse had come in without its rider. Al Rahman thanked God for His mercy, and was well pleased. "Well done, well done," he said to his men, and gave rapid orders. They nodded, touched brows in salute, and did as he bid. Then Al Rahman explained to Renard in French.

"It looks like three or four dead, and a few wounded – that's not bad."

"How many of *them* did we kill?" said Renard.

"What do you think?" said Al Rahman. "You rode the length of the pass. You saw them lying there."

"A hundred?" said Renard. "More?"

"More, I'd say," said Al Rahman. "I've sent men to check beyond the pass, because we know that the pass itself is secure, and that the column can come through." He looked at the sun which was now low. "But that will be tomorrow," he said. "Best not to do it in the dark."

"Yes," said Renard, and begrudgingly added, "you did well Mohammed Al Rahman. You and your men. You did a good job."

"Thank you, Effendi!" said Al Rahman. "You are too kind. And now you can go back to the column, and tonight – as every night – in your famous book of words where you record your life, you can write of this battle." He smiled. "Do take care, Effendi, to give some small credit to myself!" Renard and Al Rahman both laughed, almost coming close to friendship.

Chapter 41

Everything happened fast after that, which was good because it kept me from thinking about Ulwazi. Also the dates became important once the longboat came back upriver. It came with *Enable's* barge in company. Long, Ealey and Goodsby were aboard and two grinning boat loads of tars who thought they were going to stumble over diamonds the instant they got ashore. Also, the tars who'd been before were nudging their mates and pointing at the Zulu girls, to awestruck rapture from the newcomers.

There was great commotion when they arrived and they were received in friendship by the Zulu guardsmen under the command of Inyathi's father N'tombela, while I ran forward with Halfpenny in tow and shook hands with Long and Ealey and Goodsby.

"Sir!" says Long, "is all well with you?"

"Indeed, Mr Long," says I, "and did you bring the guns?"

"Aye aye, sir! All rigged for shore service, with tackles to heave them out of the boats and mount them."

"But, sir," says Ealey the astronomer, all shiny-eyed and keen, "there's something we have to tell you." He frowned and looked at N'tombela and his men, all standing watching. They were listening too: listening to Halfpenny, who'd got so used to translating that he was doing it even now for their benefit. N'tombela in particular was paying careful attention. Ealey raised his eyebrows and nodded slightly at Halfpenny and N'tombela.

"Ah,' says I, and all quiet and easy I added, "Mr Halfpenny?"

"Sir," says he.

"Would you oblige me by putting a stopper on your jawing tackle? Just for a moment?"

"Aye aye, sir," says he, being enough of a seaman to answer in seaman fashion.

Ealey told me. He told me with great enthusiasm and it made me think: it really did.

"So," says I, "it's Sunday today, isn't it?"

"Oh yes," says Goodsby, looking glum because he'd forgotten that, and was still supposed to be ship's chaplain.

"It's Sunday the thirty-first of October," says Ealey. "So we've got twenty-three days."

"That's if our calculations are correct,' says Long, and they all looked at me: Long, Ealey, Goodsby, Halfpenny and N'tombela who could see that something was going on. I thought a bit more. I already had some ideas, but what worried me was the uncertainty. What if they'd done their sums wrong? What if the maps weren't right? There was no knowing.

"Leave it with me, gentlemen," says I. "We must adapt and extemporise. I'll deal with this it as it comes."

"Aye aye, sir!" says they, so cheerful and trusting that it dropped a load on me because sometimes it's hard to be Jacky Flash: jumping Jack Flash who slays the dragons, walks on water, and never fails. Meanwhile there were things to do.

"Let's get the guns ashore and mounted!" says I, which we did to the glee of all the Zulus who turned out in numbers: men, women and children – Ulwazi among them of course – to see the guns on their wheels and the caisson standing by. After that it was another holiday for the Zulus, with more cattle slaughtered, more fires lit, and more singing.

As a climax, we gave fire from each gun to set the echoes booming and the smoke billowing. I had to do that anyway: a few rounds to made sure that the improvised carriages wouldn't come apart under the shock. They did *not* because our carpenter had made them sound. Also we practised man-hauling, first with our tars in the traces, and then with Zulus, who came forward in numbers for the honour of pulling the guns. They were quick to learn, and soon our gun-captains were riding on the carriages and yelling orders as the guns went up and down. The only trouble was that the Zulus were too enthusiastic and ran so fast that I feared for the plank wheels. So in the end it was our men that did the hauling.

On the third of November, Inyathi came back with his men. They came at their usual fast trot, and singing. It was a grand sight, and there was another feasting on beef and beer, and all sorts of ceremonial greetings from N'tombela and the others. They were such formal people, these Northern Zulus, that I doubt even Queen Victoria in her prime was received with more fuss and bother.

Finally I met Inyathi, his father and their senior men. We sat down together outside N'tombela's round house in the middle of the kraal. I had Long, Ealey and Goodsby with me, and of course Halfpenny to translate. It was another long discussion so I'll give you just a flavour, as before, and without mentioning Halfpenny's translation work.

"My father tells me that your … *carronades*," says Inyathi, speaking the word carefully and in English, at which feat all the Zulus drummed spear butts on the ground in salute. I looked at Halfpenny puzzled, and he explained.

"He said the word properly, sir," says he. "He said 'R'. They can't say it. They don't have it in their language, so he must have worked on that." Meanwhile Inyathi continued.

"My father tells me that they are on their wheels and ready for service," says he.

"They are indeed," says I.

"Good!" says Inyathi, "because the Arabs are now close. Their horses are only a few day's march from the Pass of the Mountains and it is my intention to meet them there and punish them." He looked close at me. "It is therefore time for you to stand with me. You and your men and your … carronades."

"We're ready," says I, "but there are things I must know if I am to stand with you."

"Ask!" says he.

"Then, how far off is this Pass of the Mountains?" says I, "and what is it? What sort of ground must we cover, and what's the strength of these Arabs? And how can you know these things anyway?"

The last question took a while to explain, and I was amazed to learn how organised these Northern Zulus were. They had trained men who could memorise a message, run non-stop night and day, pass it on to the next man, going between a network of camps prepared in advance. They could send a message over a hundred and fifty miles in twenty-four hours, and easily keep watch on a column of horse, foot and guns that was advancing at only twenty to thirty miles in that time! It was very impressive.

So in summary:

"The Pass of the Mountains is the gateway through a mountain range to the east," says Inyathi. "Our enemy must come that way, and it is hard, stony ground, and there is open plain between this kraal and the Pass of the Mountains. As to their strength, there are some hundreds of men with muskets, with fifty on horses, and two of the tubes on wheels which defeated the N'gwenya regiment." He looked at his father and the rest, who all nodded most grimly. "But now," says Inyathi, "we have the carronades, and Captain Fletcher!"

And there it was again: the Jacky Flash problem, because the spear butts were being drummed on the ground for me. So was I as good as they all hoped?

"If we meet the Arabs in this Pass of the Mountains,' says I, "how many men can you bring?" This time Inyathi had a long think, and took advice from his father and others. Eventually, he turned to me.

"I must speak truth, Fletcher," says he. "The other regiments are still with Zithulele and M'thunzi. Her magic has persuaded them that only the *son* of the old King can become the new King, even though tradition says that a king is made by agreement of the regiments, not just by kinship of blood."

"So who is with us and who is not?" says I, and Inyathi sighed.

"My father's regiment is with me," says he, to a great drumming of spear butts, and his father's hand on his shoulder. "And my own regiment is loyal," says he, to even more drumming. "We shall, therefore, face the Arabs with one thousand five hundred men, which is far less than the strength of the N'gwenya when they were defeated by the Arabs."

"I see," says I, trying not to look disappointed, while Ealey leaned forward and tugged my arm, speaking quietly. I nodded to Ealey and spoke to Inyathi. "Is it possible to delay meeting the Arabs? How soon will they be through the Pass of the Mountains?"

"How long a delay do you want?" says Inyathi.

"Twenty days,' says I, and he just smiled.

"By then they would be at the gates of this kraal and beyond," says he. "They have already reached an eastern kraal of our people and killed them all. We cannot allow more of this." His father and the rest growled in agreement. "So there can be no delay," says Inyathi. I turned to Ealey, who'd already heard and had sat down disappointed. His big idea would have to wait.

"Right then," says I, "let's make our battle plan. Let's make best use of our guns and the fact that the enemy has to come through this Pass of the Mountains." When I said that, I could see that there was another problem not yet mentioned, because Inyathi's father shook his head, and everyone on the Zulu side looked serious.

"You should know, Fletcher," says Inyathi, "that there is more than one way through the mountains, and that our enemy may choose any one of them, unless we persuade him to come the way that we want." That was a blow because I had assumed there'd be just one rocky pathway where we could face the blighters. But the Zulus were used to problems like this and were cunning at dealing with them: cunning and cold-bloodedly brave. So I stress that the plan we agreed on was very much a Zulu plan. But I certainly couldn't think of anything better.

Three days later we were digging in on the side of the Pass of the Mountains: by which I mean *one* of the several passes through the mountains, because the mountains were more like a cluster of big hills than a solid wall, and there were all sorts of ways through by winding around the hills.

We'd force-marched with the tars hauling the guns and caisson, making our best speed, while the two Zulu regiments went on ahead, as there was no possibility of our keeping up with them. I don't think any of us could have done that on foot, even without the guns. Only mounted men could have matched their fast trot, and we had no horses. By the time we came up puffing and blowing, with the guns and caisson bumping along and the tars heaving, the two regiments were already encamped, with pickets out on the eastern side of the hills to keep watch.

There were fifteen hundred Zulus encamped, and here's the interesting thing: you'd never have noticed. There was a company of them on the western side of the hills, and they received us with salutes, and told us – via Halfpenny – what was going on. Then they led us down one of the passes, and we couldn't see anybody at all, not until a messenger ran on ahead, and Inyathi came round a curve in the pass at double-march, and with a hundred of his elite bodyguard behind him.

"Captain Fletcher!" says he when we met, and his men stamped to attention and stood rock still.

"Prince Inyathi," said I and Halfpenny nodded in approval because I'd got him to school me into saying *prince* in Zulu. I've long since forgotten the word, but I had it then, because if he could say *carronade*, it seemed only polite. But there was no time to be wasted with the Arab column on its way. I was immediately taken on a tour of the pass with Halfpenny, Ealey and Goodsby, while Long stayed to find some place where our guns could fire at anything coming past.

Note well that finding a suitable place wouldn't be easy because we weren't aboard ship where a gun's recoil was checked by gun-tackles: that's ropes and pulleys connecting the gun carriage to ring-bolts in the ship's side. Our guns would have to run back like field artillery, except that the run back would be especially fierce with carronades, being light in the barrel and heavy in the shot. Thus, a good level ledge would be needed with plenty of room behind the guns. So I left Long to it, together with our men and a team of Zulus who'd put aside their spears and shields. Instead, they had axes, and most singular little pickaxes with one short, stubby arm and one which was flat, wide and spade-like. They were ingenious tools for digging because they could handle both soft earth and hard stones.

Even as we left, Goodsby and Ealey were talking about these odd pickaxes and Goodsby said they reminded him of something but he couldn't remember what.

We came back later, just before dark. Inyathi and his bodyguard were with us. He'd heard from his runners that the Arab column was a day's march from the eastern end of the pass, with their horsemen in front. So it was vital to get everything in order. We walked back to the guns – they were about halfway through the pass – and I could see that things *were* in order, because I could see nothing!

I was sure that we'd reached where the guns must be, but I couldn't see them. I could see only the steep-rising slope of the hills and lots of stunted little bushes. Inyathi was watching for my reaction. He smiled and turned and looked up the steep sides of the pass, then raised his spear over his head, and waved it slowly from side to side. And then stap my vitals, because Lieutenant Long and his men rose up out of nowhere, pulled some sort of cover aside, and there were the bloody carronades! They were glaring down on us, just fifty yards to one side of the path, and up about thirty feet. It was amazing. Long and his men grinned at us in the half light, and Inyathi said something to me which Halfpenny translated.

"He says they're dug in and covered up," says Halfpenny. "He says that he picked this way through the hills because it's got earth that can be dug into and bushes for covering up. It's just as we planned, and the two regiments are hidden the same way." He paused. "That's all except the chosen ones. There's no point in them digging in." I nodded. I knew what that meant, and I knew what would be asked of *the chosen ones*.

"And are they all volunteers?" says I to Inyathi. "Do they know what to do? And will they do it?" Inyathi must have guessed what I said, because he replied before Halfpenny could translate. He looked me in the eye and said something. He was asking me a question, and finally Halfpenny did translate it:

"Wouldn't you do the same? For your father and your mother? For your women and your children and your homeland?" That's what Inyathi said and it made me blush because I'd fought for England the last nine years, but only because I couldn't avoid it. So I absolutely didn't know if I would do what we were expecting of these young men: the chosen ones. Would I do that for someone else? Then I thought of Ulwazi, and I thought of my sister and her family, and I thought of Sammy Bone, my dear old sea daddy all those years ago.

"Ha!" said Inyathi, reading the expression on my face, and he smiled.

After that, fifteen hundred Zulus and a small group of Englishmen spent the night in skilfully dug entrenchments, with no fires, cold food, and wrapped in blankets. It was miserable and I was fretting over so many things that I barely slept. At dawn, Inyathi and his bodyguards took the chosen ones to their station at the eastern mouth of the pass. Inyathi led, while the bodyguards marched to either side of the chosen ones as a mark of honour. In addition, every man in the two regiments stood and raised spears as they passed. They raise spears and chanted in their deep, base voices. It was three words over and over.

"Yoo-petta! Yoo-no! Men-erva!" That's what it sounded like to me, and it was obviously something sacred to them. Some expression of deep respect. So off they went to do their duty: their Zulu duty, because it was a Zulu plan.

And then we had nothing to do for hours. Inyathi disappeared somewhere with the rest of the Zulus. I stayed with the guns in our covered-over entrenchment, and we had a bit of salt pork, and pickles, and a tot of rum at dinner time. But no fires, and nothing warm. Nothing happened until late afternoon, when Ealey spoke.

"Listen!" he said, and there was shouting and yelling coming along the pass from the eastern end. We looked at one another. It was starting! The noise grew louder and we could hear a Zulu battle chant and the sound of spears beating on shields. Then there was gunfire, and we heard hoof beats and the whinny of horses. Men were shouting, but they weren't Zulus. The voices were shrill, not deep.

"Hi! Hi! Hi!" they cried, and there were louder hoof beats. Finally we had a very good view of something very bad, as a rabble of Zulus – the chosen ones – ran past, throwing away their shields to run faster, and with a troupe of cavalry right behind.

The cavalrymen wore dirty-white robes, and were wielding scimitars: they were the Devil on horseback. They were North African Bedouin, and they dipped and swung, cut and slashed, slaughtering every man they caught, mainly taking them from behind as they ran. Some of the Zulus turned and fought, and it was hard not to go down to fight beside them as they were butchered before our eyes. The horses were so well trained that their riders could get them to dance on fallen men, trampling and trampling as the riders yelled in glee.

Hi! Hi! Hi!"

Then the slaughter moved on. It went towards the western end of the pass, leaving only the dead and wounded Zulus behind. Some of them were crying out.

"Can we go and help 'em, Cap'n?" says one of my men.

"No!" says I.

"But some o' them lads is still alive, Cap'n!"

"Shut your trap!" says I. "Those lads are doing what they were told to do. Their orders were to make enough of a fight to lead the buggers on, and then run for it."

"But they're getting killed, Cap'n!"

"That's what they volunteered for," says I, "so shut your bloody trap or I'll shut it for you." The pursuit went out of sight round a bend and all was quiet for a while, except that Goodsby had a question.

"Captain?" says he. "Do those men really have to die? Was there no other way?"

"We've got to lure them in," says I. "The Arabs and their mates. They've got to come this way where we're waiting, and they've got to come all merry and bright and thinking there's no danger because they've already dealt with it. It's Inyathi's idea and he's a good soldier."

"I suppose so," says he. I supposed so too, and I only hoped it would work.

Soon after, the riders came back, taking their time and laughing, and never neglecting to lean from the saddle to slice at every Zulu they passed, living or dead. It was worse than the first time. A whole group of them got into a clump taking turns to slice at some poor devil who wouldn't lie down to die. In doing that, they got themselves right in front of our guns.

"Please, Cap'n," says the tar who'd spoken before. "Just one round, Cap'n, 'cos the bastards is right in the line of fire." He pleaded hard and I listened to him. "Please, Cap'n," says he, "just the one round?" I weakened. I couldn't help it. The Bedouin were doing precisely what any cavalrymen did when infantry ran away, but it's an ugly thing to see, and I was with the Zulus. They were Ulwazi's people. I reached for the trigger lanyard to do the thing myself.

But I didn't. If I'd fired it would for sure have ruined the ambush, and maybe let the Arabs get through, and then God knows what.

So we sat quiet and waited again. We let the Zulu dead lie where they fell, and there were a lot of them. In fact, we waited all night, another cold night, and I for one thought that the plan had failed and the Arabs had gone some other way. But early next morning we heard horses again, and the tramp of infantry. We crouched down and looked along the path where they must soon appear from round a bend. We stared and stared and hardly dared breathe as we heard their approach: first the clip-clopping of horses and then we saw Bedouin in their robes.

Inyathi's plan had worked. They were coming our way. They were cheerful as could be and even had a poke with a sword point at any of the Zulus they thought weren't quite entirely dead. How they laughed: ha-ha-ha! Soon the Bedouin were gone and a group of mounted officers went past. They were Turks and they were smart. They were followed by about two hundred men with muskets and fixed bayonets behind standards: not flags but clusters of bright, metal things hanging from cross-bars on a pole with a big crescent moon on the top. They had red jackets and baggy trousers and they marched five abreast.

Then our hearts really started to bump because we heard more horses and the rumble of wheels, and there it came: our target as agreed with Inyathi, the battle-winning French 12-pounders with their limbers and caissons, and crews. The guns were brass, and highly polished, and there were six horses to the guns, four horses to each of two caissons, and the gunners riding on the carriages and limber. They were an assorted mixture: some clearly African, all in untidy clothes and a variety of hats, while one man rode ahead of the guns. He wore a blue uniform coat with gold frogging on the front, and a bicorn hat worn athwartships. He looked like a French artilleryman, and he looked pleased with himself. Behind him and his guns, the rest of the Turkish infantry came on in good step.

They came on, all merry and bright, and I didn't need to speak to my men because I'd told them in advance. There was just the slightest creak and squeak, and a few stones rolling down the hillside as one of the gun-crews shifted their gun's pointing, such that our right-hand gun could bear on the first 12-pounder, and the left-hand gun on the second. Then everything was ready, with locks primed, flints sharp and double cannister loaded. That's forty-eight pounds of musket balls in each gun, rammed home over three pounds of King George's best black powder: say eight hundred balls per gun, and sixteen hundred in total.

The gun-captains took up their lanyards and looked at me. The anticipation was so intense that I wanted to piss my britches and – odd as it seems – I thought of my nephews and nieces hiding in corners of their house, waiting for each other to pass by and be caught with a shout of *Boo!* The delighted, wicked mischief on their little faces was exactly what was fizzing inside myself and my men in that moment because, by Jove, we'd got those murdering bastards. We'd got them something fierce. So I judged the moment ... took another look to be sure ... and gave the word:

"*Fire!*"

Chapter 42

The Royal Kraal,
North Zulu Land,
Late in the 12th Year of the reign of
King Ndaba KunJama,
(1802)

"M'thunzi, the Witch, led Zithulele like a calf to the knife."

(From the Saga of Inyathi)

"You did right to let Inyathi face the Arabs alone," said the witch, M'thunzi.

"But grandmother, holy and reverend grandmother," said Zithulele, "what if he does not stop the Arabs? What if they break through the Pass of the Mountains and enter the heart of Zulu Land?"

Zithulele's councillors and guardsmen noted the extreme of honorific language used by their prince to the witch. They heard, and they awaited the answer to his question because it was a powerful question. They stood behind Zithulele: a dozen councillors and fifty guardsmen, as he faced the witch woman and her tribe crones: most of them mad, all of them hideous, all of them itching and scratching and muttering and picking at sores. They were like an anthill disturbed: a mass of constant movement.

The councillors and guardsmen stood in their manly pride, but in their hearts they were afraid of M'thunzi, and who could blame them? Not when she could sniff out any one of them, such that his comrades must instantly kill him. But still they wondered if they should have stood with Inyathi against the invaders? When all of Zulu Land was threatened? So the councillors looked at one another and whispered.

"The matter is mixed,' said one.

"Entangled," said another.

"Do we face the Arabs?"

"Or follow our prince, who is the true heir?"

Meanwhile, all of Zulu Land knew that General Prince Inyathi had indeed failed to rally the regiments behind him, even under threat of the Arabs and their magic tubes. They knew this, and knew that it was only the power of M'thunzi that had held back the regiments: only M'thunzi's insistence that the regiments must follow Zithulele – in which matter the councillors were in agreement with the witch. But like any reasonable men, they needed reassurance that M'thunzi's council – backed by the threat of sniffing out – was indeed the best council.

"Listen, O Prince of the Blood, who must surely be King," said M'thunzi.

"Ahhh!" said his followers in approval of these words.

"Listen, and learn," she said. "If Inyathi faces the Arabs, perhaps he will win, and perhaps he will fail. In either case you will have all the regiments behind you to face either Inyathi or the Arabs, and in either case you will have such strength in numbers that you will surely win."

"Even if we face the magic tubes that broke the N'gwenya?" said Zithulele, and the councillors and guardsmen looked at each other, shuffling their feet.

"Even so," said M'thunzi, and uttered a great and monstrous lie. "I know that you will win," she said. "I know it as surely as the sun rises in the morning."

"Ahhh!" said the guardsmen, and they nodded to each other, because none of them knew that M'thunzi was so blinded with hatred for Inyathi, that her hope was that – before else – the Arabs would oblige her by killing Inyathi.

Thus, the guardsmen were deceived, but the councillors were not. They were clever men. They lived and breathed politics: the deadly, clan-based politics of Zulu Land, where disputes were settled at the point of the spear. Because of this, they were practised in the art of studying faces. They saw the untruth on M'thunzi's face. Then, looking at one another, they pushed forward the eldest of them to whisper in the ear of Zithulele.

The witch frowned horribly, but Zithulele listened. He licked his lips and gathered his courage.

"Most reverend and holy grandmother," he said, "you know that I stand in your shadow, and follow the truth of your words." M'thunzi clenched fists and waited.

"And so?" she said.

"There are men who say," said Zithulele, "that you curse Inyathi only because he would stop the sniffing out, and because he would send away the shining jewels that ..." M'thunzi immediately shrieked and spat and stamped, stabbing a finger at Zithulele, and all her women did the same, such that the stench arising from them was appalling.

"Listen, son of the old bull!" she screamed, frothing at the mouth in a rage beyond bearing, because she could tolerate no criticism at all, let alone criticism that was accurate and true. "Listen to me if you really do hope to become the new bull! Listen well because I have spies: spies everywhere, and they tell me of a great weakness of your enemy. Inyathi has a beautiful wife, and he has fallen in love with her, but she has fallen in love with a white man that Inyathi has taken into his bosom. Inyathi is a fool and should be left to fight the Arabs. After that, let there be such a mustering of the regiments as was never seen before. Then either the regiments united will kill the Arabs and leave you king, or they will kill Inyathi and leave you king! Do you understand, or must I sniff out a hundred men to prove my power?" She looked at the councillors with poisonous hatred. "And if so, which men shall it be?"

"No, reverend grandmother," said Zithulele, whose courage was gone, as was the courage of his councillors. "I hear your words. Let Inyathi fight alone, and then there shall be a great mustering."

"Good!" said M'thunzi, "and as for the shining stones, rather than see them sent away, I would go into the place of the stones and work magic, such magic as will cause the caves to fall, which I can easily do. I have only to touch the right places."

Chapter 43

Our right-hand gun didn't hit the target. It jumped too much because, as I said, the recoil of a carronade is great. The charge of cannister went high and spattered into the hill across the path, throwing up shoals of dust, clods and stones while the gun deafened the world with its thundering discharge, and blasted flame that singed everything within twenty yards. The charge, therefore, flew over the first 12-pounder. I saw the man on the horse in front – the man in the bicorn hat – cringe in terror with the shock of the discharge, but then dig in his spurs and urge his terrified horse into a gallop.

Our left-hand gun did better, though I had to wait for the smoke to clear to see. Thus, where the second 12-pounder had been, there wasn't one any more: not as a gun on a carriage with its crew and horses. Instead there was ploughed up wreckage, the brass barrel thrown out of its wrecked woodwork, with boots, hats, human limbs and scraps of flesh all around. There wasn't one man alive. They'd all gone down under the blast, and some of the horses had gone down with them, while other poor beasts were kicking and screaming which ain't a pretty sight, my jolly boys, not when horses are hit. You just believe your Uncle Jacob.

Then my tars were heaving the guns forward and loading and pointing. I kept clear because nobody could do a better job than them. They soon shattered our ears with two more rounds, even though they weren't nearly so fast to load and fire as they'd have been aboard ship. The right-hand gun fired first, and both bore down square on the first 12-pounder, where the gun crew were sitting stunned, with ears bleeding from the shock wave of our first fire. They were there one second, and annihilated the next: annihilated, smashed and splattered and the gun was on its back with one wheel blown off and the other slowly going round.

After that we had to hold fire, being totally blinded with smoke, and unable to do any more. I think I heard the Zulu war cries and them beating shields but I'm not certain, because four 24-pounder discharges leave you deaf a good while. When the smoke finally cleared, we could do nothing more at all because battle was fairly joined. There was no clear shot for us into the enemy because the Zulus were up and out of their entrenchments, pouring down the hillsides to fight the Turks hand to hand.

Those who know the Turks say that they make good friends and bad enemies, and from what I saw that day I can believe it. They were taken by surprise – our gunfire must have shocked them – and they were facing a shower of spears thrown by Zulu regiments attacking from both sides. But they fought as a team, and they fought back-to-back with officers yelling and waving swords. They gave volleys so long as they could: volleys that threw down the charging Zulus in heaps. But once the Zulus were on them, there was no chance to reload and it was butt and bayonet against spear and shield. It was ferocious and savage, and I was gripped in fascination as both sides fought like tigers. The fight could easily have gone either way, because it isn't only Turks that make bad enemies, but Zulus too.

What swung the day for the Zulus – just about – was their discipline. Yes, they charged, and yes, very many of them went down under musket fire. But they didn't charge at a mad run. Once they'd thrown their long spears, they went forward shoulder to shoulder, dressing their lines as they went, and closing up as men fell. They hit the Turks in a solid wall, such that the long reach of musket and bayonet was not advantage but encumbrance, with the shields pressing forward and the Zulus stabbing underarm with their close-combat spears that had stubby shafts and long blades, and weren't so much spears as short swords.

It all ended in maybe ten minutes of fighting. That or something like it, and then the surviving Zulus were going up and down to finish off the enemy wounded, because there's no such thing as prisoners in Zulu warfare, and no surrender either. So my advice to those who don't like that sort of behaviour is to leave the Zulus alone.

And now you may ask, what about the Bedouin? What about them indeed! There were a few of them dead in the pass, and a few horses cantering about, wondering where their riders had gone. But most of the Bedouin had run for it as soon as our guns fired and the Zulus appeared. They were last seen going hell-for-leather to escape down the eastern end of the Pass of the Mountains, and back wherever they'd come from. Conversely, none of the mounted Turkish officers ran away, but fought and died with their men, because that's what Turkish officers do. But I think the French artillery officer – if that's what he was – escaped on his horse, because afterwards, none of the Zulus recalled seeing him killed. I certainly didn't see a blue coat among the dead. Not that I looked very hard.

After the battle I was happy to greet Inyathi who'd come through without a scratch, though the Zulu dead and wounded were in the hundreds. In fact it had been *'a very nice thing'* as the Duke of Wellington said of the battle of Waterloo, using the old meaning of *nice*, which meant pretty damn close. But Inyathi was generous with his praise when he and I met just before dusk that day. He came up to our gun position with what was left of his bodyguard, and a lot of them were wounded. Embracing me, he took one of his ostrich plumes from his headband and gave it to me. His men gasped at that, so I suppose it was a great compliment. I've still got the feather. It's in my silver cabinet with the plate and other treasured items. Then he spoke in a loud voice for all to hear.

"The musket men fought hard," says he via Halfpenny, "and I do not think that we would have won without your carronades." For myself I wasn't so sure of that, given the Zulus' cunning at entrenchments and ambush. Also, all we'd actually done was fire twice and hit the 12-pounders that would never have been brought into action anyway. But if someone tells you you've done a damn fine thing, then you don't tell him you haven't. At least I don't, and I advise you youngsters to do the same, and accept the praise. I said something in return about how bravely Inyathi's men had fought, and for a little while we became great friends. That is until personal matters got between us. But that's life, my jolly boys.

Later, there was the business that comes after any battle: tending the wounded of course, which the Zulus did according to their own traditions of wound-healing. Meanwhile, the dead were gathered in and laid out in a mass grave, dug with those funny little picks with the shovel ends. When this was done, Inyathi gave a speech over the mass grave, with his men stood in ranks all round. Then they raised spears and gave that shout again:

"Yoo-petta! Yoo-no! Men-erva!"

It was solemn as a burial at sea, and I can't give more respect than that. Later, and as a matter of respect, the Zulus buried the fallen Turks as well, because they admired them. If you're surprised by that, my jolly boys, then ponder on this, because it wasn't only the Turkish dead that were buried, but all their gear including muskets. Beyond even that, Inyathi had the remains of the 12-pounders buried! A deep pit was dug and in they went, complete with caissons, harness, rammers and all associated gear. It sounds like heavy work, and it was. But when you've got hundreds of men working together, it's amazing how much earth you can shift, especially with the neat little shovel-picks.

Inyathi's reason for this was simple:

"I will have my people live by our traditions," he says to me. "We will live our way, and fight our way, and not become dependent upon devices that we cannot make for ourselves."

All in all, and with the heavy digging, it was two days before we set off back to Inyathi's father's kraal. Meanwhile, I had Mr Ealey pestering non-stop.

"Sir," says he, when finally we got going, "there's fifteen days to go. Do you know that, sir?"

"Is there?" says I, because I hadn't kept count.

"It can still be done, sir," says he, "if we're quick."

"I'll try," says I, but there was something else to do first, and something that would keep Ealey happy, because I was determined to go along with Inyathi and his men on the march, leaving the guns to follow behind, hauled by the tars. It had to be man-hauling again because there weren't enough draft-horses left from the 12-pounders, and tars are not carters so they'd rather pull than drive.

Thus, I was determined to go with the two Zulu regiments, of which there were under a thousand fit to fight, with so many dead and others left behind with the wounded who couldn't be moved. Those who were fit would go at their usual fast pace, but now we could go along because we'd got riding horses and saddles: either Bedouin or Turkish. There were enough for me, Long, Ealey, Goodsby and Halfpenny. The only trouble for me – and this was the something else I had to do first – was to get myself aboard a horse and stay there, because I'm no sort of horseman and detest riding. It wasn't that I'd never ridden before, because I have. But I don't like riding and never will, and neither will the unfortunate nag beneath me, considering my size and weight.

In that case, all credit to Ealey and Halfpenny, both of whom were adept horsemen. They knew the ways of horses and how to keep horses happy on the march, which is an art in itself what with them needing to forage, and be watered and rubbed down. Finally, we went in the middle of the Zulu formation, with Inyathi's regiment in front, and his father's behind. I think Long and Goodsby suffered as much as me on that ride, but how would I know because you don't show your arse to your companions at the end of the day.

What I did do, at the end of the first day, was talk to Ealey, Long, Goodsby and Halfpenny to work out how best to use Ealey's idea. Halfpenny proved very useful with his knowledge of how Zulu politics worked – especially as regards to choosing their king. So when I put it to Inyathi later, it went like this.

We were sat by a campfire at night, the Zulus wrapped in blankets as was their custom. Inyathi and I were on stools and the rest cross-legged, with Halfpenny in the middle as ever, and if you think that the following words from your Uncle Jacob sound solemn and formal, then that's because you end up speaking like that to the Zulus: they're so solemn and formal among themselves that you can't help falling in step.

"Prince Inyathi," says I, "we have fought the Arabs and Turks together, and beaten them which is good."

"It is good," says he.

"So that was the first part of our bargain," says I.

"It was," says he, "and you are halfway to taking your fill of the shining stones." I nodded. I liked that, and I kept going.

"And now there is the muster to consider," says I, "when all the regiments are assembled to choose who shall be the next king of Zulu Land, and I must stand by you with my men."

"Your men and your carronades," says he.

"Yes," says I, "I could do that, or I could do something vastly more powerful. I could work a great magic. It will be a magic that will defeat the magic of the witch, M'thunzi, as surely as your spears and my carronades defeated the Arabs and Turks." There was a gasp from all the Zulus at the mention of M'thunzi, and it was a warning of just how powerful she was. But Inyathi just nodded slowly and asked the important question.

"What shall be this magic?" says he, "and how can you have the power to work it?"

So I told him. It took a lot of words, not all of which were entirely true because, however clever the Zulus were, they weren't experts in spherical trigonometry or any other mathematics. But I had goodwill on my side, so Inyathi trusted me and believed me. Also, he was a man of his own people, and his people saw magic everywhere. I suspect that he thought my carronades were magic, and that I had a bit of magic within me. So it came down to this.

"The magic must be done on a certain day," says I, looking to Ealey just to check.

"Eleven!" says he.

"Eleven days from dawn tomorrow," says I to Inyathi, "so can the great muster be called in time?" Inyathi turned to some of his men and they spoke rapidly to each other with some waving of hands and discussion. Then Inyathi turned back to me.

"Perhaps," says he, "if we send out the summons at once, and if the regiments believe the summons to be urgent." He wasn't sure, not one bit: I could see it so I took a jump in the dark. It was a risk but I couldn't think of any better way to shove a red-hot poker up the stern ends of the regiments.

"Tell them that it is my intention – *our* intention Prince Inyathi – to bring an end to the magic of M'thunzi, the Witch, and that if she and the regiments are not assembled in time, then we shall do it without her!" That brought a huge response from the Zulus. They were up on their feet, shouting and pointing at me and waving hands at Inyathi. That had stirred them up and no mistake. They were terrified and excited all in the same instant. We British think of a witch as a mad old woman muttering spells. But from the behaviour of Inyathi's men that night, it was obvious that the Zulus thought M'thunzi was a cross between the Devil and the Virgin Mary, and that's some combination.

I sat on my stool wondering if I'd made a mistake by going after their blasted witch-queen? If they were all bred up from childhood to believe in her – which they were – was she so deep in their minds that she couldn't be got out? But Inyathi stayed calm and finally he stood, raising a hand for silence. When it was quiet, he indicated that I should also stand.

"Fletcher," says he, "we shall take an oath, this night. We shall swear to bring an end to M'thunzi, the Witch, and her sniffing out, and her tribe of hags, and her cave of jewels. We shall send word to the regiments – exactly as you say – warning that we shall do this on the day that you name." He reached for my hand and I reached for his. "Swear!" says he.

"I swear," says I.

"And I swear," says he.

By Jove, that was a moment. Everyone around us stood gaping in the firelight with eyes as round as pennies, and that wasn't just the Zulus but Ealey, Long, Goodsby and Halfpenny too. To show how serious we were in this plan, Inyathi sent out runners immediately to go ahead of the regiments, bringing word of the victory to the kraal of his father, and ordering more runners to go from the kraal to warn the regiments exactly what was bearing down on the good ship M'thunzi if they didn't turn out on the appointed day.

Next day at dawn we were on the march at Zulu pace, reaching the kraal of Inyathi's father the day after that, which left ten days. On our arrival, a great crowd came out to greet us, all dressed in their best. There was much joyful ceremony, with beating on shields, and singing and laughing, and a feast to follow. The people were led by Inyathi's father, N'tombela, who was too infirm to take the field any more, and was in command of the few fighting men left to guard the kraal. All the old men were with him, and the married women behind them led by Ulwazi. It was joyful to see her, and I'd been longing to see her, but it turned out bad.

She was in charge of the women's traditional greeting of a victorious regiment. She came forward with the choicest maidens of the kraal bearing food and drink, and very lovely they were too with their beads, their coloured wraps and their smiles. None of them were as lovely as Ulwazi though. The food they brought was only water and beans, and it was purely ceremonial. But Ulwazi herself had to hold out the gourd of water, and then the bowl of food, and present them to the leaders of the battle against the Arabs. I was second only to Inyathi in that ranking, and at his own orders too. I remember him smiling as he pushed me forward. I also remember that it was the last time he ever smiled at me.

Which was because he saw the look on my face as Ulwazi offered me the gourd to drink, and he saw the look on her face. I couldn't help it, and she couldn't help it. I was in over my head with love for that girl. I couldn't see anything but her, and she felt the same about me. She had tears in her eyes and she just stared at me … and Inyathi looked and saw, and that was the end of any friendship between him and me. Worse still, from the scowl on Inyathi's face, it looked like the end of the plan that Ealey and I had worked out and persuaded Inyathi to accept, and if we didn't follow it, then the consequences would be appalling. Of course, it had always been about getting hold of the diamonds, but now there was something more: very much more, because Halfpenny had explained what would happen if things went bad for Inyathi at the great muster and M'thunzi was left in power. If that happened, then she would turn really viciously spiteful and take revenge by ordering a slaughter, not only of Inyathi and his thousand men, but also everyone in his father's kraal – and that included Ulwazi.

I ended up thinking that I had made the most terrible mistake in getting Inyathi to challenge M'thunzi. Couldn't I have thought of something else? I didn't know, and I didn't know what would happen next.

Chapter 44

We were left alone for three days. We were left in our camp by the river Haipo, and nobody came near us. No more women came out with food; no children came to play. There was just a strong force of men between us and the kraal. They stood with their shields and spears, and kept watch night and day. Every few hours, others took their place like the changing of the guard. I moped about full of guilt and damning all the world. Finally, the tars turned up with the carronades in tow, and were told what was going on. They sat in little groups looking at me and talking among themselves.

Ealey fretted something dreadful, and he and Long kept checking all their calculations. I'm sure that he wanted to remind me how many days were left as he kept looking at me, but he didn't come near me for the foul mood that I was in. There was a great deal of whispering among the hands. Finally, it was Halfpenny who came forward, which he didn't not do out of courage but for a great desire to cut and run while we still could.

"Captain?" says he, holding his hat in his hands, and giving a little bow as everyone looked on.

"What?" says I.

"Captain," says he, "if you'd listen, sir?"

"Bugger off," says I.

"Captain, sir," says he. "He might change his mind any minute – Inyathi – and order us killed, sir, and we've still got the boats and we could be off, and safe, and gone." I'll spare you most of my reply to that, but I ended with saying:

" ... and if you want to make yourself useful, go and talk to them!" I pointed at the Zulus on duty between us and the kraal. "Go and ask them what's going forward!" So he did, and was talking some while with the officer in charge, and then: God bless us every one! Because he brought back good news.

"We're all going, sir," says he.

"Where?" says I.

"To the great muster, sir," says he. "It's on the day you wanted, sir, and Prince Inyathi is looking to you for your magic. He's doing it because there's nothing else he can do, and because it's already too late."

"What do you mean 'too late'?" says I.

"Well, sir, *he* says ..." Halfpenny pointed at the guard commander. "*He* says that it was too late once the runners had gone out with the challenge, because M'thunzi would already know Inyathi's after her, and she'd tell Prince Zithulele, and he'd tell the regiments."

"Oh," says I, because there it was. Whether or not Inyathi liked me, I was now his only hope. He was outnumbered beyond count by the total of the regiments; M'thunzi would already be planning her revenge, and that left just me and my magic: if it worked.

I talked that over with Ealey on the march, which began that very day. We were on our damned horses again, in between Inyathi's regiment and N'tombela's, who was carried on a litter at the front of the column. I was riding with Ealey, Long, Goodsby and Halfpenny, but I left the tars behind with orders to take to the boats if things turned nasty.

"Is this going to work, Mr Ealey,' says I, "because God help us if it doesn't." Ealey looked at Long, who nodded with just the slightest hesitation.

"Would you like to see our calculations, sir?" says Ealey. "Perhaps tonight, sir? When we're camped? Because it'll take a while?"

"Yes," says I, because all our lives depended on it: our lives and everyone else's.

That night they took me through their workings, with papers spread over our knees and us peering at them in the firelight. I couldn't see anything wrong, except that everything depended on precise timing and on our maps being accurate. Ealey showed me his pocket watch, which was a good one, but I wished I'd had my Harrison H8 which was lost to bloody Ordroyd. Although even that wouldn't have corrected our maps if anything was wrong with them. We just didn't know.

"Well you've certainly done your best,' says I.

"Thank you, sir," says Ealey, "and we've got this, sir." He picked up a small square wooden box which was one foot in all directions and neat and smooth. "The Carpenter made it, sir," says he. I took it and looked closely. At one end there was a tiny hole right in the middle; at the other, there was no wood but a sheet of white paper fixed in place, tight as a drum. Ealey explained what it was for and I was impressed.

"I don't see as anyone could have done more," says I, and gave the box back to Ealey. "I shall look to your findings, Mr Ealey," says I.

Next day we were on the march again with Inyathi ignoring me and not even looking my way. But you can't blame him for that. The column pressed on, and soon we were on a great rolling plain with smooth hills and kraals inside their thorn hedges. Other regiments were on the march, going our way. I should point out that Zulu regiments don't march in silence, even going at the trot. They sing and hum, and occasionally beat time on their shields. For an occasion such as the great muster, they don't go in their usual battle dress – which is basically a state of nakedness – but all arrayed in feathers and plumes and other decorations. They make a fine sight, and a fine sound too, with their deep voices and measured step.

We were heading for what the Zulus call the Plain of the King, which was close by the Royal Kraal, where King N'daba KunJama lived, his son, Prince Zithulele, and her Satanic Majesty the Lady, M'thunzi. Halfpenny knew a lot about them from talking to the Zulus, so I already knew that the old King was lost in dotage, and Zithulele was effectively ruling. I also knew a lot about M'thunzi, though not enough to prepare me for the sight of her.

Our column reached the plain early on the day before the muster, as was Zulu tradition because all the other regiments arrived on that day. So I got the chance to ride round a bit, on my sore bum, to see what was there, with Halfpenny beside me. It was vast, rolling countryside, and the Royal Kraal was on a hillside above the plain. The Zulus had long since raised mounds on the meeting place so that important men and their entourages could be above the common herd, and these men were a sight to behold when they turned up.

You have to imagine the magnificent sight of a Zulu regiment coming forward in its parade dress: coming forward in thousands behind their huge, man-high shields and every regiment marked out by the patterns on the shield fronts, and the number of white bars on the shields as battle honours. Each regiment arrived singing or chanting its own songs, and thousands of feet beat the ground in unison.

"Look, sir," says Halfpenny, "see how they all go to their places? They've been doing this for generations, and they all know where to go." He was right. Even the Prussian guards couldn't have done it better, and I lost count of the numbers. There were thousands and thousands of them, and if they were all followers of Zithulele, then we were well and truly lost if it came to a fight.

But that was only the day before's performance. Just after dawn on the appointed day – the big day, Ealey's day – and when all the thousands had been fed and watered, the regiments lined up in their places. Once lined up, they advanced towards the mounds that I mentioned, and then, by Jove, you should have seen what came out of the middle of the dense-packed ranks, to chanting and yelling and beating of shields, as each regiment outdid the others in pride.

It was the officers, the leaders – Colonels I suppose we'd call them – who commanded each regiment. Each one bore a plain white shield and was covered in plumes, robes, kilts of fur, arm bands, leg bands and necklaces with coloured feathers attached, and most of them had a large jewel front and centre in his headband. Some of these men were quite old, and leaned on sticks, but most were men in their prime. Each was followed by a dozen or so senior officers dressed only slightly less splendidly than him. All these men took their places, seated on stools on the mounds raised for their regiment.

And if you think that was impressive, that's because you haven't heard what came next. A huge procession came out of the Royal Kraal and down to the highest mound. That was King N'daba and his son Zithulele with their royal guardsmen, who were all decorated entirely in white. No colours of any kind, and shields even bigger than any others. They came down the hill with a choir of men in front giving the most wonderful music, and every other man on the plain fell silent to hear. Both N'daba and Zithulele were on litters carried by twenty men each, and the litters were decorated all over in white flowers. When they got close, anyone could see that the King was gone in his mind because his face was slack and his tongue drooped out of his mouth. I was amazed that the Zulus would tolerate such a king, until I remembered that our own King George was a loony.

By contrast, Zithulele was young, very big, and very ugly. He was near as big as me. He looked round and glared at everything, and the regiments raised spears in salute as he passed.

So indeed I looked at the King and Zithulele, and I was impressed. But I couldn't help looking at what went in front of them, and in front of their men and their choir. I couldn't help looking and I didn't need anyone to tell me who it was, though Halfpenny tried.

"That's her, Captain," says he.

"I can see that," says I, because it couldn't be anything other than M'thunzi. There she was, and Holy Jesus, Holy God and Holy Ghost but she was ugly! She was ugly and filthy. She was sun-wrinkled, crooked, nearly bald, and dressed in mere coverings: they certainly weren't garments of any kind, just scraps and bits, and she had a cluster of nasty who-knows-whats dangling from a strap round her waist. She hopped along like a broken-leg spider, and what followed behind her was even worse if anything. It was a company of old women, half-dressed, half-undressed in bits of dead animal, who gibbered and chattered and fell down and got up again as if they'd had a bottle of gin each one. They too were ugly, but in a fiercely fought competition, M'thunzi was the ugliest by far.

She was indeed, and maybe I've had some fun in describing her because I've grown used to the fun of writing. So in case I've given the wrong impression, and left you thinking that M'thunzi was merely a figure of fun, then let me pause a while and add this. M'thunzi reeked of power. She reeked of fear and menace. It's a thing I've seen in others in my lifetime – just a few, a very few – and it's a fearful thing when you meet it, because you don't know how it works or why it works. But it does work and it's hard to resist. I suspect that Bonaparte had it. He had that or something like it. So all you youngsters take my advice: if ever you meet someone like M'thunzi, then mind what you say, watch your back, and get away as soon as you can.

So that was M'thunzi. She led the way to the biggest mound, the one in the middle. She danced all round it, her chorus of beauties with her, and she yelled and screeched, and all the Zulus shuddered. She went round the mound three times like that, and Halfpenny explained.

"She's driving off anything that's evil," says he. "The Zulus think they're everywhere if you're not careful." Personally, I'd rather have had the evil things than M'thunzi, but it wasn't my choice. After that, the King and his son took their places with courtiers and guardsmen all round, and sat on the biggest stools on the plain. M'thunzi sat at the front of the mound, looking out at the regiments with her women beside her. A lot more ceremony followed, with regimental commanders coming forward, kneeling and bowing to M'thunzi and pledging loyalty to the King. Halfpenny started translating, but I told him not to bother. I was more interested in Ealey sat next to me, who had his box raised up and was looking at the paper end.

"Anything yet" says I.

"No, sir," says he.

The ceremonials dragged on until Zithulele stood up and said something to M'thunzi. He pointed with his spear, sweeping it round to cover all regiments, and a great groan went up from assembled thousands. M'thunzi leapt up, making a horrid little dance on the spot, and all her women howled. Zithulele spoke again, and a company of his guardsmen with their big, white shields ran down and stood behind M'thunzi. I counted ten of them with an officer in front. They raised spears and saluted the witch, and then the most appalling ceremony took place. It was the *sniffing out* that I'd heard so much of.

M'thunzi led her women and the guardsmen up and down the lines of the regiments, occasionally kneeling at the feet of some man or other, looking up at him as he trembled in fear. Then, once in a while, she'd point at the man ... and the guardsmen would kill him on the spot! They drove in their spears to another huge groan from the regiments. I couldn't believe it. The victims didn't fight back; their comrades didn't intervene; they just stood and died and fell down. It went on a long time. There were maybe twenty or thirty men dead on the field, and they weren't just other ranks, they were officers. Once again Halfpenny explained.

"Look at him!" says he, "Zithulele?" I looked and saw the delight on his face every time a man was killed. "That's how it works, sir," says Halfpenny. "Anyone he thinks is dangerous, anyone who might start a rebellion, or anyone he doesn't like? He tells the old cow and the poor sod gets it."

It went on a long time until finally M'thunzi and her women and the guardsmen went back to the big mound. She nodded to Zithulele and pointed at us – that's Inyathi, N'tombela, and me and my men. She pointed at us, and you could see then who really ruled over Zulu Land, because Zithulele nodded and stood up. He looked our way, to where we were standing in front of our two regiments. We were easily the smallest fighting force on the plain. I looked at Inyathi and N'tombela, but they still ignored me. They hadn't given me so much as a look all day, and right now they were looking at Zithulele, who was working up a fearful tantrum.

"He's cursing us," says Halfpenny. "He's damning us to their hell, us and Inyathi and all his people. He's saying that M'thunzi is the witch of all power, and the reverend mother …" It went on and on and Halfpenny was sweating with effort, because most of it was poetic and stylised. It went on and on until Zithulele ended up ordering Inyathi and N'tombela to come forward, bringing me and my men with them.

"Zithulele wants you too, sir," says Halfpenny. "He's saying bring the great white ape and all his monkeys." I turned to Ealey.

"Can you see anything yet?"

"No, sir," says he.

"Shouldn't it be about now?" says I.

"Yes, sir," says he.

"Well it had better be bloody soon," says I, "or it might as well not bother." That was a fact, because all the regiments were looking in on us now, waving spears all together in rhythmic waves, and uttering a deep murmur that rolled over the field. They were working up a charge and no mistake. Zithulele yelled again, stamped his foot and waved his spear over his head, then pointed at Inyathi, and yelled some more.

"It's just insults, sir," says Halfpenny, "against Inyathi. He's saying: son of a cleft-palate mother! Son of a eunuch father! Son of a bed-pisser!" Zithulele went on and on. He had quite a vocabulary and in the middle of all that, even as he was still raving, Inyathi looked at me.

"Come," says he. "It is time for your magic." He was desperate. He didn't like me but he needed me. I swallowed hard and looked at Ealey with his box. But he just shook his head.

So off we went, Inyathi and his father with a couple of men to keep him upright, then myself with Halfpenny close by, followed by Lord, Goodsby and Ealey. Off we went on our own with all the spears of Zulu Land threatening, and M'thunzi on her feet glaring at us like a poison snake, and Zithulele still spitting curses. The pair of them got uglier and uglier the closer you got. It was a very, very long and lonely march, and the noise of the regiments' murmurs grew louder and deeper all the while. You could see them straining to be off. We stopped at the base of the big mound and got a sniff of M'thunzi and her girls, which was atrocious. It would've put a public bog-house to shame. It was foul. But Inyathi ignored it and raised a hand, standing firm, with his father beside him.

He got them quiet, which was some achievement all things considered. I suppose they were all curious, but he did have a great reputation among them, and he was a fine-looking man who'd just won a great battle. So maybe it was that. Anyway, he got them quiet. Zithulele left off ranting and sat down, and Inyathi began a speech. He spoke in a great loud voice that carried well. All the regimental leaders will have heard him, if not every man on the plain, and Halfpenny translated.

"I have summoned the regiments today," says he, "because great matters must be settled. We must choose the next king, and we must cut out the rot of witchcraft that has poisoned our people for so many years, and must not …" That's as far as he got before M'thunzi was on her feet, shrieking and screaming. Halfpenny gasped as he listened.

"Oh Christ," says he, "we're done for!"

Chapter 45

I didn't need a translator to tell me that M'thunzi was pronouncing a death sentence. She screamed fury into our very faces, running towards us and pointing, and the closer she got the uglier she looked. But she took good care not to come within a spear's reach. She stopped and turned back and shrieked at Zithulele, who ordered his guardsmen forward. To this day, I remember the sight of a whole clump of them coming down the mound towards us, in a wall of white shields with spears held at the ready, and chanting and stamping and glaring. Since I was wearing my sword, I took hold of it. But I knew it was all over, and I thought how strange it was to have survived shot and shell from the French, these many years, only to end up stabbed by a spear in Africa.

Stamp, stamp, stamp! The white shields came forward, and I actually drew my sword thinking to take one or two of them with me. I saw Inyathi stand in front of his father, and crouch forward behind his shield, ready to do the same.

"Sir!" says a voice at my side. It was Ealey with his box, and an expression of wonder on his face. "It's starting, sir! Look!" The box was a camera obscura: a device for looking into the sun without getting your eyes burned out. The pinhole at one end let in light that gave an image of the sun on the paper at the back, if you held the box up to the sun. In that moment, with the guardsmen nearly on us, I can't pretend that I looked at the box, but I heard what Ealey said: "The moon's in the way. It's the eclipse!"

"Thank God!" says I, and shouted at the top of my voice. "Inyathi! This is the moment. It's what I promised. Tell them that I'm going to kill the sun!" He gasped.

"Yoo-petta! Yoo-no! Men-erva!" says he. He raised his spear and gave a great shout, and pointed at the sun. Everyone looked up, and they shuddered in dread as Inyathi spoke. I played my part, standing firm and pointing my sword up at the sun.

"Listen O people!" says Inyathi. "Because at my command, the White Giant will extinguish the sun. He will turn day into night until the people turn from M'thunzi and listen to me." He said a lot more but I don't think most of them were listening after the first few words, because it was getting dark. There was a great big bite taken out of the sun, and anyone could see it and as far as they were concerned – to quote Psalm 23 – they were walking through the valley of the shadow of death.

The result was panic and terror. Some ran looking for somewhere to hide, but all of them must have thought the end of the world was coming, and mostly they crouched down and held shields over their heads as if to hide the truth from their own eyes. All the regiments did that, including our two. It was weird, it really was. All the birds stopped singing and it grew darker and darker, as daylight really did turn into night. Everything would have been silent except that M'thunzi was hopping about yelling at Zithulele. She was furious with him. She ran up the mound and screamed at him where he hid under his shield.

"What's she saying?" says I to Halfpenny. He listened a bit, then told me.

"She says it'll pass, sir. She says she's seen this before and it'll pass."

"But she can't have," says Ealey. "The last eclipse here was ninety-three years ago."

"Then how old is she?" says I.

We never found out, because it didn't matter. Zithulele wasn't listening. Nobody was listening. They all thought they were going to hell. Finally, M'thunzi sat down in the middle of her ghastly women and they all hugged one another in a stinking heap. Nothing happened. Everything was silent and still and nobody moved.

"How long will it last?" says I to Ealey.

"Total darkness isn't long, sir,' says he. "About ten minutes and I'm timing it. I'll give warning before it passes."

"Well," says I, "we might as well sit down. If we were aboard ship, I'd pipe up spirits for all hands because we've won a battle!" We all looked round, and Inyathi had the grace to look at me and nod in approval. His father did too, and they were the only Zulus still on their feet. They were two very brave men. But they sat down when we did, and Mr Long – true seaman that he was – had a silver flask of rum with him, and we all took a swig. I offered it to Inyathi first, but he shook his head.

So there we sat, in the middle of thousands of terrified men, all hiding away from the dark. It was the strangest thing I ever saw in all my life, and I've seen rock and tempest, fire and flood, earthquake and revolution, and ships blown up with powder-mines. Of course Ealey kept looking at his watch, which he could just about make out, since it wasn't pitch dark, more of a very dim twilight, and if you looked at the horizon you could see a bit of light.

Eventually, some of the Zulus were stirring. They were starting to look out from under their shields. So it was just as well that Ealey judged that the eclipse would soon be over.

"Sir?" says he. "We could give them the second half now."

"Thank you, Mr Ealey," says I, and turned to Halfpenny. "Mr Halfpenny?"

"Sir?" says he.

"Be so good as to inform Prince Inyathi that it's time for him to say what we agreed, and to bring back the sun."

"Aye aye, sir!" says he, and he went over to Inyathi and his father, and spoke all respectful. Inyathi got up, helped his father to do the same, and then nodded at me. No smile, note you, but a polite nod. Then he lifted up his voice for all to hear, which was easy because nobody else was making noise, and everyone stuck his head out from under his shield to listen. At first that's all they did, but they got bolder as he spoke and began to stand up again. According to Halfpenny, this is what he said.

"O people, you have seen the power of my servant, the White Giant. Now I will show you my own power by bringing back the sun. Watch me, O people, and know that I am the true heir to the King, and that my magic is greater than that of the witch, M'thunzi. Note well that just as I bring back the sun, I can make it go away at any time that I choose." After those words, he looked up and pointed his spear at the black sun, and the moment was well chosen – well done Mr Ealey – because the light was just peeping out from one side, and all present gasped in wonderment as the sun came back to life. By Jove, it was a piece of theatre, it really was, and I felt the emotion of it. Even Ealey did, because it really did seem that Inyathi had saved the world from darkness.

As the light came back, Inyathi gave that chant again,

"Yoo-petta! Yoo-no! Men-erva!" He said it several times, and the regiments picked it up: just a few of them at first, but then they were booming it out in their thousands.

"Yoo-petta! Yoo-no! Men-erva!" It shivered the spine to hear them. It was like a great organ giving 'Rock of Ages' in Westminster Abbey. The chant was deeply spiritual and sacred to these people and they gave it together. More than that, when they'd done, and the sun was bright and the regiments in their proper ranks, the leaders of the regiments, in all their finery, came down from their mounds and approached Inyathi. They raised spears and beat on shields. They were acclaiming him as king.

But even then that damned witch didn't give up. She was up on her feet and running from one of the regimental leaders to another, tugging at arms, pulling at their feathers, and shouting. Eventually she gave up with them, ran up the great mound and took hold of Zithulele, pulling him down towards Inyathi. It was grotesque to see her twisted little figure dragging a man who was six foot of solid muscle. But drag him she did. She then spat at Inyathi's feet, screeched in his face, waved to all the regimental leaders, and pushed Zithulele at Inyathi.

Halfpenny was translating, but I didn't need him. Anyone could see what she was at. She wouldn't accept the choice of the regiments. She wanted single combat between her man and Inyathi. It was her last chance, I suppose, and she damn well took it. Not that Inyathi or Zithulele were unhappy with it! Far from it, because they hated each other, and were used to settling matters with spears. All the Zulus felt the same, and in case you youngsters are surprised at this, I point out that not everybody in every land thinks that governments should be chosen by the people voting, because in most places they're chosen by the same process as in Zulu Land. It might be by muskets not spears, but it's the same thing.

Zithulele certainly thought so, because he instantly went for Inyathi without waiting for the referee to make them shake hands. But of course there was no referee, and no rules except *get in there and win!* He went for Inyathi with shield leading and spear held low, trying to knock him down and kill him at a stroke. But all the thousands looking on gave a great shout as Inyathi swerved away, tripped Zithulele with one foot and sent him tumbling over. Zithulele bounced up again and the two men faced each other with spear and shield and edged round, taking care, and looking for their chance. The bellowing and roaring of the regiments was deafening, and the excitement was tremendous with waving hands, stamping feet and chanting.

Stab! Inyathi went forward, and Zithulele got his shield in the way. Stab! Zithulele tried and Inyathi blocked with his spear. I'd never seen single combat between men with spear and shield, but it was just like boxing in that it wasn't a matter of brute force. It couldn't be that or Zithulele would have won because he was by far the bigger and heavier man, and had tremendous reach. They made a fine comparison: Zithulele built like a stone fort, Inyathi graceful and artful. He moved like a dancer, spinning on his heel, and cunning in attack.

It was a long fight with no rounds or breaks, and eventually both men were bleeding from stabs that didn't quite go home. In the end, stamina won because Zithulele tried another bull-charge. Inyathi swerved again, and this time Zithulele was a fraction slow in blocking Inyathi's return thrust. Chunk! Inyathi's blade ran into Zithulele's belly. He staggered and slowed, and tried to come back for another charge, but Inyathi just kept out of his way, and when Zithulele's arms tired, and his shield lowered, Inyathi came in and delivered three stabs – chunk-chunk-chunk – fast as eye blinks and straight into Zithulele's chest, killing him outright.

This brought a huge roar of delight from the regiments. Inyathi was the next king and Zithulele was dead, and that was that. No more argument! The regiment leaders hoisted up Inyathi and carried him round the field to universal acclaim. Then they brought him back, took him to the top of the big mound and sat him on the stool next to the old king, who didn't know whether it was Monday or Sunday but who cared? Instead, everyone listened as Inyathi stood up and made a great speech. Before he spoke, he did make a point of beckoning myself and my men to come up and stand near him, and that was a great relief – or was it – because who could tell what he'd do with us now he was in power? Ponder on that one, my jolly boys, because I certainly did.

He made a great speech and a long one, and I'll do as before and give you just the essence. But note that much of it was delivered more like poetry than ordinary speech because Inyathi was using the speech-making conventions of his people. This included him pausing from time to time and saying the Zulu word meaning '*indeed*' or '*indeed that is wise*'. He gave these words with a rise in his voice, as a question, and the thousands in front of him repeated it in a deep and rumbling chorus. By George, it was impressive.

"*Ngempela?*"

"*NGEMPELA!*"

So here's what he said:

"Men of Zulu Land, and with the approval of our Lord the King." He made pretence of seeking a nod from the poor, old, drivelling creature next to him. "Thank you, O king," says he, and then he was off. "My first command is that the practice of sniffing out shall end forever." He looked round. "Does any man disagree?" Whatever they may have thought, none dared to speak. But there was more. He pointed to M'thunzi where she was crouched among her creatures at the foot of the mound. "Come forward, M'thunzi, the Witch!" She got up and walked through the regimental leaders, and they cringed back in fear of her: they who were the greatest men in the land with thousands of armed men behind them.

I tell you, my jolly boys, if it'd been me and not Inyathi that was in charge, I'd have run her through with the sharpest spear in Zulu Land. I'd have done it there and then, because she was a snake that still had its fangs and its venom. But I wasn't in charge, and Inyathi was, and he made her come forward and stand in front of him.

"So, M'thunzi, the Witch," says he, "you have heard that no *man* disagrees that the sniffing out shall end. I now ask if any *woman* disagrees?" There was a loud gasp because the question was a great one, and also because no man had ever asked a woman to speak at a muster of regiments. Everyone looked at M'thunzi and waited for her reply. Since I was close, I had a good chance to look at her face, and I saw the cunning of it. I saw her think, and consider what was best for herself in that particular moment.

There was a long wait in utter silence but then she laid down flat, in front of Inyathi, and stretched out her black fingernail claws. Taking one of his feet, she planted it on her head, and spoke in a whining voice.

"She's swearing allegiance, sir," says Halfpenny. "She says the sniffing out will end, and that all the trouble was Zithulele's doing. She says that the old king always did want Inyathi to follow after him, and that she never did wish Inyathi any harm." He looked at me. "What a bucket of shite!" says he. I agreed, though Inyathi seemed to accept what she said. But it was politics because he had to consider the many men who were still awestruck by their great witch. He nodded and raised up M'thunzi, though not all the way. He left her kneeling because he was good at politics. Then he spoke on.

"Good!" says he. "I now command that all those who lie slain on this field shall be taken up and buried with honour: each and every one of them!" There was another great gasp and I looked at Halfpenny.

"That's generous," says Halfpenny. "He's hated Zithulele since they were children, and those that got sniffed out were always left for the vultures!"

"I see," says I and Inyathi continued.

"Now, M'thunzi, the old woman," says he, "you will have food and shelter for the rest of your life, but you will make no more witchcraft on pain of being thrown out to starve. Do you understand?" She touched her brow to the ground and mumbled.

"She says yes, Captain," says Halfpenny.

"And I give you this command," says Inyathi, and what a wonderful command it was and a relief to me and my men! "You will lead the White Giant to the caves of the stones where he will take away as many of the stones as he pleases. Do you understand?" There was yet another great gasp and M'thunzi beat her brow on the ground and mumbled.

"Yes," says Halfpenny.

"Good!" says Inyathi, and looked at me. "This will be my half of our bargain," says he. "Once you have taken your fill of jewel stones, you will leave Zulu Land forever. I give you my promise of safety until the moment that you leave, but you must not expect to be safe if you return." Then he bowed, and never spoke to me again. Not one word. It was a great pity because I liked him and admired him, and would have made a friend of him if I could. But that's what happens when two men love one woman: especially when one of them thinks she's already *his* but finds out that she's not. So it was a great pity. But it was nothing compared with what happened in the caves of the stones. That wasn't a pity: that was a bloody tragedy.

Chapter 46

M'thunzi was still dangerous and we didn't realise how dangerous. First she became ill, then she became very ill and couldn't walk and could hardly eat. A great fuss was made of her because Inyathi had given his word that she'd take me into the caves of the stones, and she had to be fit to do it. She had to, because nobody else could find their way round the caves, or get out once they'd gone in! Halfpenny learned that from the Zulus: that and the fact that most of them wouldn't even go near the caves, let alone inside.

"There's all sorts of things in there," says he. "At least that's what they say. There's pitfalls and traps, and there's ghosts and demons. All sorts."

We heard that when we were back in N'tombela's kraal by the river Haipo, where our tars were waiting with our guns and our boats. We went there because it was the nearest kraal to the caves of the stones. We were back within days of the great muster and everyone was delighted to see us. Ulwazi was doing the greeting ceremony again, though she never dared look at me and that was bloody agony.

We were all made welcome by the people of the kraal: that's all of us except the passenger we brought with us on a litter: M'thunzi. She had to be carried because she couldn't ride a horse and she'd never have kept up with a regiment on the march. So she came with us, and was big trouble all the way. Inyathi put only his best men to carry her, and even they were changed every day in case she started working magic on them. But she didn't, or perhaps she did, because she fell ill – claimed to fall ill – on the journey. When we arrived at the kraal, it got worse. Inyathi set aside a big roundhouse for her with only the best of care, and Ulwazi was in charge of the care, because she was the leading woman of the kraal.

That put a fright up me, for what the old bitch might do to Ulwazi, so I suppose Inyathi felt the same. But it had to be Ulwazi as a matter of honour, to prove that Inyathi was doing everything possible to keep his word to me. That's the Zulus for you.

During that time, I was stuck with my men in our camp by the river, and food and drink was brought out each day by the women – though not Ulwazi. The guards were on duty again and we weren't allowed into the kraal. After a few days, when the guard changed at dawn, the officer in charge came up and spoke to me. He came with his men behind him, all in rows, and I stood up as he approached with my men lined up behind me. As I said, the Zulus are so formal that you get like that yourself. But this time it was plain speech, and Halfpenny translated easily.

"He says the old woman's recovered – that's M'thunzi," says he. "She's up on her feet and walking about with the Princess Ulwazi supporting her."

"Ulwazi!" says the officer. "M'thunzi!" and he gave a mime of one person with an arm around another. He spoke on.

"He says she's going to take us to the caves," says Halfpenny.

"Ah!" says I.

"She's taking us tomorrow. Inyathi will be with us, and a bodyguard, and the Princess Ulwazi too, because M'thunzi can't walk without her. So she'll be there: Ulwazi." Halfpenny looked at me. "That's what he says, sir."

"Ulwazi!" says the officer, and nodded.

We left next day just after dawn, and we took a piece of special kit with us. It was Goodsby's idea. He'd come to me with it, even on the ride back from the muster.

"I read Classics at Oxford, sir," says he, bobbing along beside me. "I read Classics before I was ordained and took my doctorate."

"Did you" says I.

"Latin and Greek, sir," says he.

"How nice for you," says I.

"I loved the classical mythology, especially."

"And so?"

"Well, we're going into a labyrinth."

"And?"

"We should do what Theseus did when he entered the labyrinth, in order to be able to find his way out."

"And what might that be?"

"Take a great ball of string, sir, and reel it out as we go in, so we can follow it to get out!" By Jove, I was impressed by that.

"Well sink and burn me," says I, "that's a damn fine idea: a ball of string? I'll set the men to making one." Which I did as soon as we got back to the camp. Fortunately, tars are good at things like that. They unpicked a lot of rope, then worked it all into a long thread on a reel. It was a great comfort, because otherwise we'd have been reliant on M'thunzi to get us out alive.

When we left the kraal, it was some days' journey to reach the caves. It was a journey along the river, so it would have been far easier to go by boat, only there were too many of us, with Inyathi's bodyguard, and others carrying food for the journey, and M'thunzi on her litter again. So mark well that the river was close by the caves, and the river navigable by large boats, or even ships.

On the last night before the caves, there was a moment after dark, with fires lit, when I saw Ulwazi looking at me. There was nobody else looking. Everyone was asleep except a few guards on watch and I was looking for the chance to see her, and see her I did. She was about thirty yards off, and she looked this way and that, and then stretched her arms out towards me. I haven't the words to say how lovely she was and how miserable I felt. So I stretched my arms out, and that was it. Nothing else happened because anything else would have been the death of us.

So if that's romantic love, my jolly boys, you can stuff it where the sun don't shine, because it bloody well hurt. I did love her though. I really did. Dear me. Dear me.

[Fletcher was most profoundly moved by his memories of this African princess. When dictating his memories of her, he became choked with emotion, and had to pause so often to recover himself that I found courage to express my sympathy which - to my very great surprise - he graciously accepted. S.P.]

Next day at about noon, we were at the mouth of the caves and ready to go in. The caves were in one of the Breasts of Sheba: a mountain which rose up by the river. It was all covered with grass and shrubs except at the base on the river-facing side, where there was a whole series of cave entrances in split, jagged rock. They were a line of inky-black holes that looked all the darker for the bright sunlight outside. Inyathi stood with about fifty of his men. I had Halfpenny, Goodsby, Long and Ealey, and

Ulwazi was standing by Inyathi with that ghastly old woman hanging on to her. M'thunzi was stroking Ulwazi's arm, and trying to be nice. She was even more ugly when she tried to smile. But at least she was properly dressed in some decent robes, and they'd combed her hair and washed her, so she didn't stink so much. That was Ulwazi's work I don't doubt.

Also, it wasn't only our reel of string that had been brought along special. Inyathi's men had bundles of torches: wooden shafts topped with twigs cut short, bound round tight and soaked in fat. So here we were at last. Here were the fabulous diamond caves which really existed, and there really was a hoard of diamonds inside. I was excited, even as miserable as I was over Ulwazi, while Halfpenny and the rest were hopping up and down with it. Then Inyathi gave the orders of the day, and all without looking at me.

"He says he will go first with M'thunzi and Ulwazi," says Halfpenny, "and the White Giant and his men will come after. Following them will be twelve volunteers to carry the torches, while the rest of his men guard the entrance." Halfpenny turned to me. "That's 'cos they're shit scared, sir," says he. "Look at 'em! They don't want to go in. Not one of them." Then he pointed to M'thunzi. "But she does. You'd think it was her God-damned birthday!" He was right. The old bitch was grinning without a tooth in her mouth. She was happy as could be. I didn't like that.

The torches were lit and in we went, and this was the manner of it. M'thunzi led the way hanging on to Ulwazi, with Inyathi right behind. Just for once he'd laid aside the big shield that he carried everywhere like an English gent's pocket watch. He kept his spear though. He'd have been naked without that, and we'd all have been blind without the men to carry the lighted torches, and bring up bundles of reserves. These poor devils were shaking in fright, but they did their duty.

I came on after Inyathi with my men, and with Mr Long in charge of the string, and almost at once we found something truly wonderful. It was amazing beyond belief, and I don't mean the jewels. We'd hardly gone a dozen steps into the dark, with the torchlight flickering on the walls and rock, when Goodsby cried out.

"Good Lord!" says he. "Look at this! Just look! Everyone! Look-look-look!" He was mad with excitement. "Look here!" he says, and we all looked at an inscription cut deep into the rock. Someone had first levelled the rock flat, then cut letters into it. It was writing: proper writing, neat and sharp, and done with mallet and chisel. It was this:

CIX CX
LXL1
SPQR

"Skin my precious arse!" says Goodsby – nice words for a clergyman. It's the lost cohorts! Cohorts nine and ten of the Forty-first Legion! It's Quintus Alba's lost cohorts! And look: SPQR! Senatus Populusque Romanus! For the Senate and People of Rome! It's Roman! It must be eighteen hundred years old! No, nearly *nineteen* hundred!"

"What are you talking about?" says I, but Ealey was as excited as Goodsby.

"Bloody hellfire," says he, coming close. "Alba's lost cohorts? I read about them when I was at Eton. It was in the civil war, wasn't it?"

"Yes," says Goodsby, "Antony's civil war after Caesar was murdered. Two cohorts of the Forty-First sailed off down the coast of Africa and disappeared!"

"With the greatest treasure in Roman history!" Goodsby was shrieking now.

"The loot from Carthage, with all the jewels!" says Ealey, and they both looked at me.

"That's what's here!" says Goodsby. "It's not a mine. It's buried treasure!"

They gabbled on like that, with Halfpenny, Long and myself trying to catch up, and all three of us wondering if it could be true. But there were the letters, cut in stone, and they looked just like what you see on Roman monuments, and it certainly wasn't African. Then up came yet another wonder.

Inyathi came to see, with Ulwazi and M'thunzi. They stood beside me in the torchlight, and Halfpenny explained what we'd found in Zulu. Then the most creepy thing happened. M'thunzi reached out and gripped my arm. She let go of Ulwazi and spoke.

"Fletcher," she said, and pointed at the inscription. "This everywhere." She waved a hand. "Everywhere. Great magic. Very old." It was English. She could speak English! It was odd. It was like the speech of a senile old yokel and it was very slow. But it was English. Who knows when she'd learned and how, but she'd learned it. There was something else, too. When she looked at me directly, I felt the power of her and I could see why men were afraid of her. I felt the fright myself, even though she was half my height, a fraction of my weight, and I could have picked her up and snapped her. But when she looked you in the eye, it was like seeing a hideous spider creeping up your arm. It wasn't nice, my jolly boys. It wasn't nice at all.

Then she played another trick out of her repertoire. She looked at Ulwazi, then Inyathi, then me, and pointed to each of us and laughed in our faces. She knew what was going on between us and was mocking us. Inyathi lost his temper. He shouted at her and threatened with his spear and she didn't even cringe, just carried on laughing. So he shouted some more.

"He's telling her to get on with it," says Halfpenny. "Get on with it and show us the diamonds."

"Come," says she, to me. "Come. I show." She grabbed hold of Ulwazi again, and off we went with torches flaring. We went past more and more turnings, all of them marked with Roman inscriptions, and with Long reeling out our string, which was just as well because every turning looked like every other. Then yet another surprise.

"Ah!" says M'thunzi. "See! See here! One of many! Many others." She laughed. She was having the time of her life, wasn't she, because she'd found something nasty. Something in a little alcove. It was halfway between a skeleton and a dried-up corpse. It was laid on one side with the knees almost under its chin and arms around the knees. M'thunzi pointed at it. "This one Isisa, daughter of Langa. Very old."

"What happened to her?" says I.

"Lost in dark," says M'thunzi. "I bring girl for wedding stone. Girl afraid. Run away. No find way out." And she laughed and moved on. We passed several more like that, and M'thunzi named every one. She even spoke to them, inviting them to get up, and when she did that it wasn't only the Zulus who were afraid. Deep in the mountain and in the dark, with M'thunzi giving her best performance, even I thought that one of those shrivelled corpses might twitch. But Inyathi yelled at M'thunzi again, telling her to stop it and get on. She grinned at him and led us in deeper, and deeper. I just hoped that Long had enough thread on his line.

Eventually she stopped. "Listen?" says she, so we did, and a bloody weird moment that was too, standing there in the torchlight with shadows jumping, and even Inyathi showing fright, let alone the poor buggers with the torches. We Englishmen weren't too happy either, because the caves were grumbling at us. That's what it sounded like anyway. There was the most almighty unsettling rumble of movement in the deep of the mountain, as the rock was shifting. M'thunzi raised a finger. "Listen well," says she looking straight at me. "The risen dead. The ancestors. Perhaps they find us?" She said the same thing in Zulu, and all the torch-bearers looked back the way we'd come. They were ready to bolt, but Inyathi shouted at them, telling them to stand fast. I didn't need Halfpenny to translate that. Then Ulwazi spoke, and I did need Halfpenny.

"She says she heard this sound before," says Halfpenny. "She heard it when M'thunzi brought her here to receive her wedding stone. She says she heard it, and no ancestors came. So if they didn't come then, they won't come now!" That's what she said. Those were her words. But you should have seen the way she said them. She stood upright, looking M'thunzi in the eye and stamping her foot in emphasis. By George, she was wonderful. Inyathi thought so too. I could see it in his face. And he spoke.

"He says: hear the words of this woman!" says Halfpenny. "Hear the words of a woman, and if a woman is brave, how can a man show fear?" I saw the way Inyathi looked at her, and I knew that – for him – she wasn't just a wife that was his by custom and law. I could see that I wasn't the only one who loved her. Then he told M'thunzi to get on with it, which she did, having looked at Ulwazi with pure hatred.

Off we went again, down a winding tunnel with another Roman inscription over it, and something else happened that was alarming.

"Sir?" says Long, "the line's running out. Can you find out how far we still have to go?"

"Mr Halfpenny?" says I. "Ask the old cow."

"Aye aye, sir,' says he, and rattled off something in Zulu. M'thunzi just laughed but Inyathi was getting fed up with her, and gave her a prod with his spear. Not enough to wound, but a severe warning. She jumped at that, and spoke.

"Fletcher?" she said. She let go of Ulwazi and grabbed my arm, looking up at me. "You want stones?" She had little black eyes, sunk in pits of wrinkles, and she stared and stared as if getting inside me. "Blue stone is finest. Biggest and finest. Arabs took it from me. Took it long, long ago." Then she jabbered in some language I didn't understand. But Halfpenny did.

"That's Arabic," says he. "She knows that, as well."

"What's she saying?" says I.

"Don't know," says he. "I only know a few words."

Then she went back to English, and perhaps I don't remember right, but I'm fairly sure this is what she said.

"Everyone wants blue stone. You *want* blue stone. You *had* blue stone. You *lost* blue stone." If that's really what she said, then I'm damned if I know how she knew it. But there wasn't time to wonder.

"Get on!" says I pointing to Inyathi and his spear, "or he'll kill you!"

"Huh!" says Inyathi, and waved the spear under her nose.

"Sir?" says Long. "How far, sir? Remember, we haven't much line left!"

"Ask her again," says I to Halfpenny, and he spoke, and M'thunzi looked at me.

"A small way," says she. "Very close."

I didn't trust her. Not at all.

"Halfpenny," says I. "Ask Prince Inyathi if we could leave a chain of torch-bearers behind when the line runs out: each one stopping when he can still see a bit of light from the last one. That way, we can work back from one to another and find the thread." Halfpenny translated that, and Inyathi nodded, speaking to his men. It shook them badly, with some of them actually on their knees begging not to be left alone. But he stamped and yelled, and that was it. So that's what we did when the last inches of string were laid on the ground with the reel. It's just as well that we did too, and just as well that there were enough torch-bearers.

But there were enough, because in fact we didn't have much further to go. We came round a corner and the torchlight showed us a high cavern with rocks large and small all over the ground, but also with a collection of short, square, stone columns, and some statues and chests. There were a lot of these, and some were broken open and some were still sound even after nineteen hundred years. We sighed in wonder. We stood with our mouths open and our jaws dropped. We'd found it! We'd found the treasure!

We'd found the treasure and very much more.

Chapter 47

We ran into the cavern, skidding on a slippery floor of fine sand over solid rock. It was treacherous and you had to mind your step. But even the torch-bearers went forward: the two of them still with us. With just the two we never did have enough light in those caverns and there was constant calling out for it, as discovery after discovery was made. But first – yes indeed – this was what we'd come to find. There was a great number of wood and iron chests, and the chests were full of such a collection of treasure as all pirates of the world would dream of. The open chests had chains and ornaments, lockets, badges, cups, vases and goblets in solid gold. There were precious stones everywhere, and we chattered like boys in the sweet shop.

"God save us, we're rich!" says Halfpenny.

"Emeralds!" says Goodsby. "Look at the size of them!"

"And look at the quality of the stones," says Ealey. "They're all cut and shaped."

"That's 'cos they're Carthaginian," says Goodsby. "They were a great civilisation, maybe even in advance of the Romans."

"Sir!" says Long, "look here. There's tools and weapons, and armour!" That was interesting. So interesting that I left off my busy fingering of the jewels and went to see.

"Bring a light here!" says I, calling to one of the torch-men. He came forward, and there was indeed a heap of metal-ware. It was right in front of one of the square columns, which was about five feet high and covered in writing. I knelt down among the helmets and bits of plate armour, and picked up something familiar.

"It's one of those funny picks that the Zulus use," says I. "There's even a bit of the shaft left."

"God damn my eyes!" says Goodsby. "I knew I'd seen them before. That's a Roman entrenching tool. Every legionary carried one. I saw one in a museum. The Zulus must have copied it."

"And look at this!" says Goodsby, nearly swallowing his tongue in amazement. "Look here!" He pointed at the square column. "Look! Remember that chant that the Zulus give." He looked at the rest of us. "The one they give for anything really solemn?"

"Yoo-petta, yoo-no, men-erva?" says I.

"Yes," says Goodsby, "Now see here, because this column is an altar."

"Yes!" says Ealey.

"And it's dedicated to the Roman trinity," says Goodsby.

"Trinity?" says I. "Isn't that Christian? The Trinity?"

"Yes," says Goodsby. "But the Romans had one too, the trinity of their three most powerful gods: Jupiter, Juno and Minerva!" I looked at Ulwazi, Inyathi and the torch-men.

"So are these people Romans?" says I.

"Well," says Goodsby, "maybe descended from them."

"From the lost cohorts of the Forty-First Legion," says Ealey, "them and local women." Then M'thunzi came over to me. I stood up and looked down at her.

"Old things?" says she. "You like old things? Many more old things ... there."

She pointed and I looked round. The moment is clear in my memory. Ulwazi and Inyathi hadn't understood any of what we'd said. They were looking at us Englishmen and wondering, while Halfpenny was fumbling in the chests and gawping. M'thunzi was pulling my arm and pointing to one end of the cavern. She said something to one of the torch-men and he gave her his torch. She let go of me and went forward with the light, beckoning the one other torch-man to follow. She stopped and pointed, and there was another big cavern! This one was full of things I couldn't make out: stacks and piles and heaps, and here came Ealey and Goodsby actually running to get past me and be first man into the cavern. Ealey snatched the torch from the man holding it, and they were inside and yelling to one another. Long was in there with them, all happy and laughing.

"It's documents," says Ealey, "and records!"

"And cohort standards!" says Goodsby.

"There's heaps of wax-tablet books, and all pristine!"

"And this is a box of scrolls!"

"There's never been such a find!"

"There's years of study here, for every scholar in England!"

"Look! This one says 'History of the Conquest of Carthage'."

I was completely absorbed with all this, so I never looked behind me and I shall regret that until the day that I die. I shall regret it with bitter sorrow. I never saw the stroke delivered. I just heard it: a thump and a gasp, and I turned round to see M'thunzi pulling a knife out of Ulwazi's back and raising her hand to strike again. Inyathi was also taken by surprise. He'd been staring into the second chamber just as I had. He turned on M'thunzi and would have killed her for sure, but he slipped on the sand. M'thunzi delivered more blows, and ran for it as Inyathi went over and hit his head on the ground, and was stunned.

M'thunzi moved fast. She scuttled like the spider that she was, straight to the entrance to the first cave, kicking with all her might at something near the floor while shrieking in Zulu and English.

"All die!" says she. "Stone will kill. But I kill Ulwazi with my hand. Good! Good! I kill with hate for *you*, and *you!*" She pointed to Inyathi and then me, and there came an almighty rumble as a great block of stone began to make its way from above to seal off the caverns. It was sliding down a slot in the stonework. M'thunzi had set off some sort of trigger. It was Roman engineering, something they'd built long ago: the Romans who built the aqueducts and the Colosseum. As the slab came down, it set off rumbling in the rock. I don't think those caves were ever safe, and the lost cohorts must have only chosen them because they were close to a river where their ships could anchor.

So the roof was coming in, and the way out was closing. Normally I'm too big to move fast but Long, Goodsby and Ealey were in the second cave, Inyathi was on the ground, and the two torch-men were too scared to move. I charged forward with all my heart, soul, mind and strength. I fell heavily a couple of times on that blasted slippery floor, but quickly got up again. And then I had to stop, and do a knees-bend, stretching my arms around the biggest rock that I could lift. The big slab was still rumbling down: lower and lower. Bits of rock, stone and dust were falling around me, and I couldn't shift the first rock because it was too heavy, even for me. But it had to be a big 'un, so I tried two more. The thundering rumbling of the mountain got worse, and my third damn rock slipped free. I grabbed it again. I staggered forward with the rock in my arms, and only a narrow slot left of the way out. Finally I fell flat and heaved the rock forward, and just – only just – got it under the slab and stopped it. But everything was creaking and groaning, and my rock was beginning to crack, only just holding open a slot less than two feet wide, and great chunks raining down.

"Out! Out! Out!" I bloody near bust my lungs shouting, and everyone rushed forward for their very lives. I ran back because Inyathi was just recovering and getting up, and Ulwazi was sinking to the ground. Heaving her up, I ran back and was about to shove her through the slot when I saw M'thunzi glaring at me from the other side, knife in hand, ready to stab anyone coming through. Goodsby dashed up, saw M'thunzi, and saw myself afraid to push Ulwazi through. He paused a second, nodded to me, and then bless the brave heart of him for what he did next.

"Leave it to me!" says he. "I'll go." He wriggled under, even though he couldn't defend himself with the old bitch shrieking and stabbing down. But he got up and grappled with her, and then Inyathi also crawled through. He turned and reached out, and I passed Ulwazi to him. Next, the two torch-men were through, and then Long and Halfpenny. I looked back quickly to check nobody was left, and started through myself, but I was too big and got stuck.

I was under the slab even as my rock shattered and splintered and the whole damn cavern fell in with a thundering crash and a cloud of dust. Immediately, the huge slab began moving again, and myself in an absolute horror of being squashed. I wriggled and heaved, and tore my clothes and bust my belt; the block came down with a thump that shook the caves and took the heel of my left shoe. But I got out: just!

I stood up gasping with the effort, my back and arms cracking with the struggle of heaving rocks. There I saw Inyathi stabbing with his spear. He went on and on. He went on in such a fury that, when he was done, there wasn't a body in all those caves that was more dead than M'thunzi, the Witch. So that was a bloody end to her, and good riddance, and damn her to hell, because she'd done for poor Goodsby as well; he was dying with Long and Ealey holding his hands. What a terrible shame that was. What a loss of a gentleman, a scholar and a shipmate. What a damned shame. I don't care what he did or didn't think about God, because – as for me – I have no doubt that such a man as him would be well received on the other side, wherever it may be, and whatever that might be.

But those thoughts came later, and you'll forgive your Uncle Jacob if his attention was elsewhere for a moment, because I was looking only at Ulwazi who held out her hand to me. I took her in my arms again, and I suppose there were a lot of tears. Indeed, I know that there were, as she looked at me and I said all the clumsy things that a man says who isn't used to giving soft endearments. She said a lot of things to me too, and Halfpenny told me later what they were, but you'll forgive me if I keep those words in privacy inside of me, because they are so very precious.

At that moment we all had to run because it wasn't only the caverns that were falling in, but the tunnels started shaking as well. I carried Ulwazi; Long and Ealey carried Goodsby, and we ran, leaving M'thunzi where she lay. We escaped the caves following the torchlight and the string and stood panting and gasping in the light, with Inyathi's bodyguard staring at us.

Then Inyathi was beside me with Ulwazi dead in my arms, and he came as near to forgiving me as was possible for so proud a man. He looked at me and looked at her. Throwing aside his spear, he stood straight and bowed to me. Then he spoke, though not to me. He spoke to Halfpenny.

"He says to tell you, Captain Fletcher," says Halfpenny. "That the bargain made between you is now completed, and his beloved lady is dead because of it. He says: I know your feelings for her and I know that you cannot help them, because any man might love so wonderful a woman. But she is my wife, and I must be the one who carries her home." Inyathi turned to me, bowed again, and reached for her.

So I gave her to him.

What else could I do?

It was over.

Now I had to get my people home to England.

Chapter 48

The Zulus buried their dead much as we do. They do it with great ceremony, with weeping by the women, and singing by the men: beautiful singing. They have a tradition of choral singing that would put the choir of St Paul's to shame. Also, in their hot climate, their tradition is to get the thing done fast. So we stayed the few days to see Ulwazi laid to rest, and Goodsby too in a separate place. They were decent enough to raise a mound for him, and I had the tars make a cross, whatever Goodsby thought. I said a few words over him, with all hands present and hats off.

Ulwazi's funeral was vastly more elaborate, as you might expect. But it pains me something cruel to remember it so I'll just say that it was impressive and dignified.

After that we weren't welcome any more, and a very senior officer of Inyathi's regiment came out to make sure that we got into our boats and went downriver. He told us that the caves of the stones were now forbidden to all men and women. Not that it mattered, because the treasure caverns were buried forever. He also told us that all the gemstones from the headdresses of Zulu Land would be buried in a secret place by order of General Prince Inyathi, and that there would never again be witchcraft in the Kingdom. Well done to him for that, but it was a pity about the stones. There's a fortune there somewhere if anybody dares to go and look.

Then it was all hands into the boats, taking our tackles and gear, our two carronades, and what was left of our supplies. It wasn't a merry journey, but we were more cheerful when we reached the ship and the astronomical gentlemen on their little island. They were absolutely delighted with their observations, and promised to take back such thanks to myself as would make my reputation in scientific circles.

"You will be famous, Sir Jacob!" says Sir David Southerland, when we first met with much shaking of hands.

"Indeed, sir!" says all the rest, beaming happy in their suntanned faces.

"We are resolved that this island shall be named …"

"Fletcher's Island!" says all the rest.

"And that this expedition shall be named …"

"The Fletcher Expedition!" It was all very nice. All very jolly. But I wasn't really paying attention, as you might imagine.

We were a few days getting everything aboard ship, and everybody settled aboard. Then, apart from filling our casks with fresh water, there was nothing more to do, as the ship was so heavily provisioned, even from when first she left England. In fact, we upped anchor on December 12th. After that it was a long and tedious voyage home, with the weather getting steadily worse the further north we went.

Meanwhile, as I've said before in these pages, there are no secrets aboard ship. So here's a little something that we all shared, and that brought a smile on the faces of the ship's people: even the scientific gentlemen. I chose a day when we'd not reached frozen latitudes; the ship was running steady under all plain sail, and not rolling heavy. Then I had all hands to the mainmast, and a table rigged with a large pewter dish in the middle of it.

"Gentlemen," says I, "and shipmates one and all."

"Aye aye, sir!" says everyone and, by Jove, they smiled because they already knew what was coming.

"You've all heard about the treasure caves," says I, "and what went on within them."

"Aye aye!"

"So here's my pickings," says I, pulling a couple of handfuls of choice diamonds from out of my pockets and putting them onto the plate. Everyone gasped as they twinkled and glittered. Then I turned to the one man present who was not merry. "Mr Halfpenny?" says I, and the expression on his face made all hands laugh. But he stepped forward and produced a bread bag, emptying it onto the dish, and everyone gasped twice over, because he had far more than me. You see, when we went into the caves, we didn't go equipped to carry away, because we thought it was just the first visit and we'd be back again. But since it has always been a principle with me to seize opportunity, I'd grabbed what I could get, picking only the biggest stones, and put them in my pockets. But Halfpenny had gone prepared. He had a bread bag hidden inside his britches, and was ready to take his own private share to be kept for his own private self. What a cheeky rogue he was! Though to be entirely honest, perhaps even I hadn't picked up stones for sharing: not at first.

Indeed it was that very possibility that made me wonder what others were doing when nobody was looking? Goodsby was lost, poor devil, and I didn't think Long and Ealey would help themselves but I was sure that Halfpenny would. So I had a little word with him and I soon found out what he'd done. Then I explained what would happen to him if he didn't share. So he did. But, by Jove, he was glum.

When all the stones were on the plate for all to see, Mr Chivers, the First Lieutenant, called for three cheers for myself. I ordered spirits piped up and what a happy crew we were, aside from my own sorrows over Ulwazi.

After that we were some months at sea and the weather got increasingly foul. By the time we sighted England there were icicles in the rigging, all hands were in thick coats and fur hats, but the good old ship was heaving over the waves, just as her builders had intended.

I mention here that Mr Ealey was now recognised as a ship's officer by all hands. He stood watches; he was a superb navigator; he was becoming a fine seaman and we were none of us surprised when he declared his intention to enter into the Sea Service, in which I promised him every assistance within my power. I never wanted to go to sea, as you youngsters well know, but he did.

We reached Portsmouth on March 13th of 1803 when England was still at peace with France. We were well received by the Admiralty, the Royal Society, and by the newspapers. Our hoard of stones was – of course – condemned as prize, with the Admiralty taking half as per my agreement with Lord Spencer. But what was left for us aboard *Enable* came to an astonishing sum of money, and all hands got their shares. There was some legal argument over shares for the scientific gentlemen, what with them not being in the Service, but they were far too well-connected to be balked by King's Regulations. So they got their shares and I got an island and an expedition named after me, for all that I cared.

I was even summoned up to London to meet Spencer, who smiled upon me like the sun, because while astronomical observations counted little with me, they counted a lot with him. They did so because his life was all politics, and the machinations to get that damned expedition going had been political.

He'd scored heavily in getting it done. You have to remember that Sir David Southerland – leading light of the scientific gents aboard *Enable* – was known to take tea with the Archbishop of Canterbury and Her Majesty the Queen. So it counted heavy with Spencer to keep Sir David happy.

I myself took tea in grand company. I took tea with Spencer and his wife, Lady Lavinia, in their London house, which was the size of a palace and full of liveried servants. That was a vast step up socially for me. I wore full dress, and it was all very polite; the silverware was ancestral, and the teacups Chinese porcelain. All very nice and I particularly remember one thing that he said.

"You did handsomely well, Sir Jacob," says he, "in the stones you brought back."

"Thank you, my Lord," says I, and Lady Lavinia smiled.

"But of course," says he, "the Blue Star alone is worth more than all these stones put together!" He laughed merrily. Lady Lavinia laughed too. How happy they were, and how annoying that became, because I'd been thinking about the Blue Star. I'd been thinking and longing, because I'd suffered a most tremendous loss and thought that the world owed me something in return: something to ease the pain.

"Has the Blue Star gone to His Majesty?" says I, "as you intended, my Lord?"

"Oh no," says he, "I was waiting to see if you might return with an even bigger stone." How he laughed. How Lady Lavinia laughed. How I laughed. "It will go to Windsor Castle on the 10th of the month," says he.

"Of *next* month, my Lord," says Lady Lavinia, correcting his lapse.

"Of course!" says he. "The 10th of May, my Lady. By mail coach from the Tower of London, with an escort of cavalry."

I went to my family in Kent after that, and I was very happy among them. The children had grown something amazing. They were great comfort in my sadness at losing my girl. But even so, I began to think of having a house of my own. I couldn't always live with them, and I was determined this time that I was ashore for good. Except that I had visitors while I was in Kent: Mr Long and Mr Ealey came to see me. They came to dinner and stayed overnight which was exceedingly pleasant because, once a commission is over, you can greet your shipmates as friends. My brother-in-law was away on business so after dinner, my sister left us three men to talk over our brandy: perhaps a little too much brandy, because what they said was unguarded and loose.

"You know I am resolved to go to sea?" says Ealey.

"Indeed," says I. He looked at Long, and Long nodded.

"Go on," says Long.

[When dictating the following passage Fletcher displayed a marked reticence and modesty. I have, therefore, transcribed a fair copy of his actual words, which were stumbling and hesitant because of his embarrassment at such praise. S.P.]

"Well," says Ealey to me. "It's just this, Sir Jacob. We owe you our lives, do Long and myself."

"We do!" says Long.

"We'd all be buried in that damn cave, but for you," says Ealey. "And so we'd be honoured to serve under you in any capacity or in any expedition that you choose to lead. Anything at all, sir."

"And it's not just us," says Long. "All hands aboard *Enable* say the same."

"All hands together, sir," says Ealey. "Where you lead, we follow!"

"In face of any threat or danger, sir," says Long.

"Anything you choose, sir," says Ealey.

I thought about that very hard. I thought about it for days and it occupied my mind entirely as I wondered what to do next. At one stage I thought that I really was done with the Service because Lord Spencer took against me something ferocious shortly after that, and he was the ruler of the Navy. So I will leave you youngsters with an example of the behaviour of those who rule over *him*, and the entire nation which owns the Navy: those who sit in parliament and make the laws we are supposed to obey.

The Peace of Amiens between us and the French lasted just over a year: from March 27th 1802, until May 18th 1803. But note this well: on May 13th, entirely without warning and with a legal peace still in force, King George's Royal Navy seized every French merchantman in British Ports, or sailing peaceably off-shore. It took ships and cargo to the value of wealth incredible: that and thousands of poor bloody seamen.

And that was illegal, my jolly boys. It was against the law. But it shows that when a government wants something, then a government takes it and damn the consequences, which is a fine example to all the rest of us, as I'm sure you will agree.

Appendix

(Leading article of May 11th 1803 in 'The London Hermes' newspaper)

Horrid and Appalling Theft of

The Priceless beyond Price

Blue Star Diamond

The shocking attack of yesterday morning, upon a mail coach taken into His Majesty's Service by the First Lord of the Admiralty, is yet another proof of the necessity for the need – the urgent need, the dire need, the supreme and overwhelming need – for

the Prime Minster and Cabinet to take in hand such measures as shall ensure that honest citizens might go about their business in the streets of London, in broad daylight, without fear of banditry and atrocity. Full details of the assault are given within this special edition, but we draw attention here to the fact that the bandits were led by

a huge masked man whom we assume to be responsible for the bold and detailed planning of the outrage, which while criminal and despicable, left injured none of the coach guards, or the escort of dragoons.

We are now left wondering, as all the world wonders: *where is the Blue Star and who has it in his possession?*

CPSIA information can be obtained
at www.ICGtesting.com
Printed in the USA
LVHW100904191121
703743LV00002B/2